"COME ON, BABY."

He smiled his most persuasive smile, raised a challenging brow. "You were in the middle of thanking me. Just keep on doing it."

Lily hesitated, but only for a moment. Then she knelt beside him on the bed and moved until she was straddling his hips. She settled herself carefully on his thighs and reached up, unfastening the hooks of her corset, letting the garment fall to the floor. She leaned down, brushing his lips with hers.

"Tell me if I'm hurting you," she whispered, and he nodded in response, too full of the sight and smell of her to speak, to do anything but reach for her.

Fall From Grace

⋈ MEGAN CHANCE ⋈

HarperPaperbacks
A Division of HarperCollinsPublishers

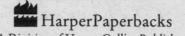
HarperPaperbacks
A Division of HarperCollinsPublishers
10 East 53rd Street, New York, N.Y. 10022-5299

This is a work of fiction. The characters, incidents, and
dialogues are products of the author's imagination and are not to
be construed as real. Any resemblance to actual events or
persons, living or dead, is entirely coincidental.

ISBN 0-06-108489-1

Cover and stepback illustrations by Jim Griffin

First printing: February 1997

Printed in the United States of America

Visit HarperPaperbacks on the World Wide Web at
http://www.harpercollins.com/paperbacks

❖ 10 9 8 7 6 5 4 3 2 1

For Kristin,
who knows all the reasons why.

Through many dangers, toils and snares
We have already come.
'Twas grace that brought us safe thus far
And grace will lead us home.

—*Amazing Grace*
Traditional

Prologue

1864, Outside of Houston, Texas

Twelve-year-old Lily Tremaine cowered in the corner of the stagecoach, curling into the safety of her mother's arms, pressing back into satin skirts that muffled the explosion of gunfire.

"Don't worry, darling." Sarah Tremaine's normally smooth voice was thin and shaking as she murmured against Lily's hair. "Your father will take care of everything. Don't worry. Don't worry."

But Lily smelled her mother's fear in the sharp, sweaty edge of tea rose perfume. She pressed her hands against her ears, pressed her cheek into the leather seat of the coach, trying not to hear the noise outside, the wild stamping of hooves, the shouting. Her father's loud voice was impossible to ignore.

"You have no right! In the name of the Union Army, I demand—"

"Shut the hell up," a voice cracked, "before I do what my partner wants and shoot you where you stand."

"Who the hell do you think you are? This is a peaceful passenger coach!"

"I told you to shut up!"

"I won't have this, I tell you! Don't you know who—"

A shot rang out. Her father screamed, a hoarse, guttural sound. Something thudded against the coach, hard enough so it shook.

"Oh, my God!" her mother shrieked. She lunged toward the door and wrenched it open. "Martin!"

It was the last thing she ever said. The bullets hit her in the chest and in the stomach, flinging her back against the seat. Her scream ended in a gasp.

"Mama!" Lily scrambled over the seat, nearly falling on top of her mother, seeing the blood spread over the pale pink bodice. "Mama, no . . . No!"

She pressed her hand over her mother's wound, but blood flowed through her fingers, warm and sticky. Desperately, she pressed as hard as she could. Her mother's breathing grew shallower; her life seeped between Lily's fingers.

"Lily," Sarah whispered.

"Mama." Lily leaned close. "Mama, you can't die."

"Lis-listen." Her mother swallowed. Lily saw the pinkness of spittle gathering in the corner of her mouth. "Lily, whatever you do . . . stay alive. Survive . . . this . . . bloody war. . . ."

"Mama, please . . . Please," Lily chanted the words as if they were a prayer, but the blood kept flowing. It wouldn't stop; she couldn't make it stop. She whispered against her mother's ear, "Mama, don't die. Don't die. We're almost to San Antonio. It's not far now. It's not—"

Lily felt the life quit her mother's body, a final, gurgling breath, then the horrible absence of sound. She pulled away, staring at Mama's face, at her open eyes and slack mouth.

"No." Lily cupped her mother's face, gripping her

hard, trying to will life back into her. "Mama, no. Don't leave me. Please don't leave me." She stroked her mother's cheek, her bloody fingers leaving stripes like garish war paint. So bright. Lily had never seen blood so bright. Not even her brother Billy's had been that color, and there had been so much more of it; his chest had been gaping open, obliterated by a Union bullet.

"Oh, Jesus. Teddy Lee, look at this."

The voice came from the open door of the coach. Lily turned. The tears in her eyes blurred the stranger's face, but she saw the sunlight glinting off his gun, off his light-colored hair.

Lily looked down at her shaking, bloody hands. She held them out for the outlaw to see. "Look," she said, and her voice sounded strange, thin and reedy and far away, as if it were coming from a tunnel. "She's dead. You killed her."

"Not me," he said. He stepped toward her, but it was as if he were moving through a fog, one that was growing darker and darker.

"Oh, Mama," she whimpered.

The world went black.

"She's a child. We can't just leave her here."

The voice was soft and far away. Lily struggled with the darkness still filling her head, and then it came to her, the images stark, the sounds too loud, too real. Her father's scream, her mother falling against the seats in a balloon of skirts, the blood on her face.

Oh, Mama. Mama. The tears filled Lily's eyes, running over her cheeks, gathering in the hair at her temples. She wanted this to all be a nightmare. She wanted to be in the stage, sleeping on the bumpy road to San Antonio, her mother sitting beside her, her father's bent knees bumping gently against hers. She squeezed her eyes shut, praying to every saint her mother had taught her. *Let this be a dream. Please, let this be a dream.*

"There'll be another stage along."

"For Christ's sake, Texas."

Any hope was shattered by those voices. They were ones Lily recognized, and with them came the hard punch of grief, the press of fear. Mama was dead. Papa was dead. These men had shot them both.

"Someone will take pity on her and take her in."

"Damn, you're a heartless bastard. Just like your pa."

"That's enough, Teddy Lee." It was a third voice. A little tougher, a little meaner, a little older. "Texas is right. Hank'll have your head if we bring her back. What the hell are we goin' to do with a kid?"

"We killed her *parents,* for Christ's sake."

"You mean you killed them." It was that first voice again, the one named Texas. "I told you to watch that trigger finger of yours."

"The woman startled me."

"A mouse could startle you."

"Boys," said the older voice, impatient now.

Lily slitted her eyes open. She was on the ground. She saw them silhouetted against the sun, the glare of the harsh light creating halos around them in the dust. Three men, standing a short distance from where the driver of the coach lay dead near the wheel. Beyond them was her father, his body sprawled awkwardly, the buttons on his blue coat sparkling in the sun. Above him, the coach door swung back and forth in the wind, its leather hinges creaking.

"I don't give a damn what you all say," the voice called Teddy Lee said. "I'm taking her back. She's an orphan now, all because of me."

"For Christ's sake, Teddy."

"She's awake." The voice was soft. It came from the man she'd seen in the coach, Texas, but, as he approached her now, Lily saw he wasn't a man yet, not really. He wasn't much older than she was, but there was a set to his face that brought fear into the empty spot in her stomach and made her squeeze her eyes shut again. She lay as still as she could, though her heart beat so loudly she was sure he must hear it.

She heard him stop beside her. Then she heard the creak of leather and the brush of movement and realized he was squatting there, blocking the sunlight from her face. She held her breath, nearly jumping when he touched her arm.

"Hey there," he said, and there was a gentleness in his voice that belied the fierce look she'd seen on his face just moments before. "Hey, I know you're awake."

She kept her eyes shut.

He shook her shoulder slightly. "Come on now. I won't hurt you. I promise."

Her throat tightened. His words were so tender. But she'd seen the gun in his hand, and in her mind her mother was falling again, collapsing onto the seats while the blood just kept coming and coming.

"Look, I'm sorry about your folks," he said. "Teddy Lee's a little quick on the draw. But we warned your pa, and your ma, well, she surprised us."

Lily felt the tears trickling past her eyelids, squeezing from her eyelashes, and she couldn't help the sob that shook her chest, that had her gulping for air.

"Ah, baby, come on now," he said, and then, before she knew it, he was gathering her in his arms, and she was turning her face into his shirt, wrapping her hands around his bony shoulders, sobbing like a baby in the warmth of his chest while he stroked her hair and murmured words she couldn't understand.

He held her that way for what seemed like hours, until the sobs subsided and became hiccups that came from deep in her chest. Then, gently, he pulled away and helped her to her feet. He reached into his pocket and offered her a bandanna, and Lily wiped away her tears and looked at him through bleary eyes. Right then, there was nothing in his face to be afraid of. He was just a boy.

Near the stagecoach, the other man, Teddy Lee, sighed and shoved back his hat. "Goddamn," he said, looking at the ground. "I can't stand to see a little girl cry."

At Teddy Lee's words, the boy's face hardened. His jaw set, and his blue eyes became chips of ice. Lily stepped back, startled by the change, and the sudden fear that came with it. He was not just a boy after all. He was a boy with a gun.

An outlaw.

Lily caught her breath. Without thinking, she spun away from him, turning on her heel, running as fast as she could over the stubbly prairie. The horizon stretched in front of her, and she ran into it. Somewhere there had to be a town, there had to be . . . something. If she could just run fast enough. If she could get there.

She heard his footsteps behind her, pounding on the dirt, and she ran faster. But she had no strength; her whole body was shaking, and the sobs were coming again, torn from her chest, from her throat. She gasped for air, and then she felt him beside her. She tried to lunge away, but he was on her in a stride, grabbing her arm, swinging her around to face him, pulling her to a stop.

It wasn't Texas at all. It was Teddy Lee. Texas stood where she left him, staring after her, his body so still he looked carved from stone.

"Don't run off," Teddy Lee said. "Look, honey, I'm

sorry. Just as sorry as I can be. But I'm gonna make it up to you. I promise. Just don't run away."

His grip on her wrist was hard and tight, impossible to break, and, when Lily looked into his face, the sincerity in his hazel eyes made her pause.

"Stop playin' around, Teddy Lee!" The older man shouted. "Bring her on back and let's get the hell out of here. Someone's goin' to be lookin' for that soldier."

"Come on," Teddy Lee said. He pulled her into his side, holding her so close she stumbled against him when he walked her back to the stagecoach. Texas had joined the older man, and they were waiting, both faces sober as she and Teddy Lee approached. The boy's hand was on his gun, a light grip, and his body was tense and wary. She wondered where his gentleness had gone, and then told herself it didn't matter. She was a prisoner. Even more so because no one would come searching for her. Her brother was dead and there was no one else. She had no choice but to go where these men took her. Mama's last words came wavering back: *Stay alive. Survive this bloody war.* It was the only thing her mother had asked of her, and Lily would do it. Whatever it took.

"Blindfold her," said the older man with a curt nod. "We can't take her to the cabin like this."

Teddy Lee nodded. His expression was regretful as he took a bandanna and wrapped it over her eyes, knotting it at the back of her head. After that, there was only darkness. Someone—Teddy Lee, she thought—led her to a horse and mounted, pulling her up after. Then she was leaning against his back and holding on as they started off.

There was no talk, nothing but movement and the relentless press of the wind. She started to cry again, and her tears wet the blindfold and coursed down her face. All she could think about was her parents, dead in the heat of the Texas prairie.

It seemed like hours before they stopped riding, and by then Lily was exhausted from crying. Her legs ached and her mouth was dry and full of dust, and she had long since given up hope of anything. She was limp when Teddy Lee dismounted; she nearly fell into his arms when he helped her from the horse.

The blindfold kept her from seeing, but she heard the latch of a door opening and the slow, heavy thud of footsteps ringing hollowly across a porch. Teddy Lee stiffened. In the near silence, Lily felt his fear. It sent prickles over her own skin, and the anticipation of waiting was a cold fire in her blood.

"Well, well," an unfamiliar voice said. "The prodigal sons. What sacred calf have you brought me today?"

"We got two hundred dollars," said Texas. Something, a bag, thudded to the ground. "Union greenbacks."

"Greenbacks? Not gold?"

"We were misinformed," the older man said. "Not only no gold, but there was a Union officer on board."

"We didn't know until he decided to be a hero." It was the boy again, bitterness riding his voice. "He had his family with him."

Silence. Then, "I'm assuming *she* is part of that family?"

"Teddy Lee shot her ma."

"And the officer?"

"Yeah."

"And you decided to bring her here?"

Silence again. The tension grew so taut Lily felt cold sweat starting between her shoulder blades.

"I decided," Teddy Lee said finally, his voice ringing with false defiance. "And I don't care what you say, Hank. I'm keepin' her. I owe it to her."

His fingers tightened on Lily's arm; she felt his trembling. It seemed to go clear into her bones, and she stiffened in the quiet, waiting for a gunshot, fear a sharp, bitter taste in her mouth.

Then she heard the footsteps, slow and steady, coming toward her. Teddy Lee's hand loosened, and he pulled away so quickly she staggered.

"Here now." It was Hank's voice. She felt pressure at the back of her head and the blindfold fell away, leaving her blinking and blind in the sudden sunlight.

It took her a moment to see him, but then her eyes cleared and she found herself staring up into a gaunt and weathered face with chipped ice for eyes. He studied her like she was a bug in a jar.

"What's your name?" he asked her.

"Lily," she said. Her voice broke on the word. "L-Lily Tremaine."

"Tremaine," he murmured. He glanced at the boy. "The officer. That's who he was? Martin Tremaine?"

"Yeah."

"You're sure he's dead?"

Texas paused. His eyes caught hers, and Lily thought she saw that gentleness there again. "Yeah."

"Any witnesses?"

"Just her."

Hank looked back at her. He stepped forward until he was only inches away from her, and then his hand slid to the hilt of the gun in his holster. Lily's mouth went dry as he took it from his belt and weighed it in his hand.

"Jesus, Hank," Teddy Lee protested. "She's just a kid."

Hank ignored him. He lifted the gun. The mouth of it caressed her throat, her jaw, traced over her cheekbone. Lily froze, her heart pounding, her limbs dead-ened. The steel was warm on her skin; she felt the mouth like an open kiss on her temple, closed her eyes against the wickedness of Hank's smile. Lily swallowed hard and tried to pray to her mother's saints, but they had gone, and all that was left in her head was an old hymn, a broken melody.

Rock of Ages, cleft for me. Let me hide myself in thee. The song came to her, a river of strength, a tune that stole her fear and gave her faith instead. Her lips moved to the melody, and suddenly she was singing it, her voice wavering and thin, dropping words into darkness.

"Rock of Ages, cleft for me. Let me hide myself in thee." She opened her eyes and stared up into Hank's face, lifting her chin.

He frowned. Beyond him, she saw the older man and the boy, watching her in surprise. The boy smiled and looked down at the ground, and his silent support only lent power to her voice, until it seemed it was coursing through the sparse and stunted trees.

"Christ." The gun dropped from her temple. Hank stepped back. His frown was gone; in its place was a smile.

Lily fell silent.

The sudden lack of sound was startling. It took a moment before she even heard the birds again. Hank's smile widened. He holstered the gun and stepped forward again, and this time the hand that touched her face was strangely gentle.

"Lily-loo," he said. And then, "How old are you?"

"Twelve," she said quietly. "Thirteen in . . . July."

"You're pretty for thirteen," he said. "Anyone ever tell you that before?"

She shook her head. She didn't like his touch, but it was better than the gun's caress, and she was willing to tolerate anything if it meant he wouldn't kill her.

He leaned closer. She smelled the witch hazel on his skin. "Can you cook, Lily-loo?"

Stay alive. Survive. Lily licked her lips. "I-I could learn."

"Could you now?" His voice was intimate and caressing. It made her uncomfortable, but she didn't know why. "Are you a good learner, little girl?"

She nodded. "I can learn anything," she said. "I'll learn anything you want. Just don't—just don't kill me."

"Anything I want," Hank repeated slowly, thoughtfully. "My, my."

The words made her feel dirty somehow, but Lily kept her head up and held his gaze. *Survive,* Mama had told her, and she would. As long as they kept her alive, she would do anything. One day, she would be strong enough to escape them. One day, she would take her life back again. Until then, she could bear it all.

"Well now, I think we'll get along just fine." Hank smiled a long, slow smile and held out his hand. "Welcome to the family, Lily-loo."

One day, Lily told herself. She put her hand in his.

1

September 1876, Denison, Texas

He rode into town at half past four on a hot and vicious Texas day. Sweat soaked the brim of his hat and gathered at his temples. It crept between his shoulder blades and wet the bandages still wrapped tightly around his ribs.

The discomfort meant little to him; it was nothing compared to the constant ache in his lung and his hip, nothing compared to his need to find her. He could even ignore the limp that had grown stronger in the hour it took him to find someone who recognized her description. The bartender at the saloon had never seen her, nor had the livery man. The storekeeper had only shaken his head and turned away. It was finally, ludicrously, the milliner who pointed out the boarding-house where she was staying.

"Right there, at the end of the street. The one by the tree," the woman had twittered, pointing out the shop window. "So you're her husband then? How wonderful that you've returned! She bought two hats from me yesterday. There was a darling little straw poke with cherries on it. Oh, I do hope you'll let her keep them! She looks so dear with those ribbons at her chin—"

He had nodded and smiled, and walked out the door while she was still talking.

Once outside, he stood in the hot sun, staring at the three-story wooden building at the end of the dusty street and the huge live oak shading it, hearing the bustle and noise of the railhead nearby, smelling the smoke. The pain in his lung was growing fiercer now. It was hard to breathe, and his hip ached enough that the thought of getting back on his horse made him wince. He wondered for a moment if she was really in that boardinghouse. Perhaps the milliner was wrong. Perhaps it was someone else instead, some other woman with red-brown hair and brown eyes.

But he knew it wasn't. He'd tracked her all the way from Lampasas, and the fact that it had been so easy told him she wasn't trying to hide. Perhaps she was even waiting for him. Again, as he had every mile of this trip, he felt a surge of relief at the thought, along with a now-familiar desperation. He wanted to believe she would be happy to see him. He'd staked everything on believing it. If he was wrong . . .

He didn't want to think about if he was wrong. She'd only been gone three weeks and already he couldn't keep his thoughts straight, already that mean-edged recklessness was taking hold of him. His humanity was slipping away; he could feel it disappearing, piece by piece, along with any trace of compassion he'd ever had, and the thought of using the big Frontier Colt in his holster came too easy and too often.

Even the nightmares had stopped coming.

His gut knotted, and the sweat between his shoulder blades turned icy cold. He squinted against the sun, trying to spot movement in the boardinghouse windows,

but he saw nothing, and there was no point in waiting.
He'd waited too long already.

He limped over to his horse and unhitched the reins,
leading the animal down the street, ignoring curious looks
as he forced steps out of his tired hip. The smell of town,
horse dung and heat, dust and refuse, filled his nostrils. It
seemed forever before he stopped in front of the roughly
painted sign that read "Rooms to Let." He pushed back
his hat from his forehead and looped the reins around the
hitching post. Then he hoisted his saddlebags over his
shoulder and made his way toward the door.

A squat, slovenly woman answered his knock. She
checked him over with too-large, protuberant eyes, and
then smiled and held out her hand. "Lookin' for a
room, honey?" she asked. "I got the best one in the
house jest for you. Down at the end of the hall. Noise
from the saloon won't bother you none there."

He shook his head and smiled. "No, thank you,
ma'am. I'm not looking for a room. Just a boarder."

"A boarder?" She hesitated. Her eyes narrowed.
"You ain't one of those bounty hunters, are you?"

He laughed. "No, ma'am."

"'Cause I got no business with them."

"I can see that."

"They're always makin' trouble. Not that I'm boardin'
anyone hidin' from the law, no, I'm not. Not at all."

"I'm sure you're not, Miss . . ."

"*Mrs.* Walston," she corrected emphatically. "Though
I'm a widow now."

He nodded patiently and tried to peer past her into
the house. "Well, Mrs. Walston, I was told my wife was
staying here."

"Your wife?" The too-large eyes widened in surprise.
She crossed her pudgy arms over her gingham-covered
breasts, pulling the fabric taut. "Well, I—"

"Red hair, brown eyes? About so high?"

She looked doubtful. "I got no call to be breakin' up families, you understand, mister. But if you don't mind my askin', how come your wife ain't with you?"

He gave her his most charming sheepish smile. "Well, now, Mrs. Walston, I have to admit," he leaned close to her, whispering, "I came home drunk, and we had a bit of a fight. I'm afraid she's stewing about it."

She clicked her tongue at him. "Can't say as I blame her. My mister had a time with that devil liquor himself."

"I've come to apologize."

"Ah. Well, then." She visibly softened. "Third floor, first door on the left. But no trouble, you hear me? I won't abide trouble." She jerked her head toward the end of the hall. Then, as he came inside and started toward the stairs, she said, "Hope you brought a present, mister. Presents always help."

He patted his saddlebags and grinned back at her. "Oh yes, ma'am. I've got plenty of presents."

The hallway was close and dark, the stairs narrow and cracked. The saddlebags weighed on his shoulder; he heard the harshness of his own breath as he climbed painfully to the first landing. The smell of oil and dirty wicks permeated the hall even though the lamps were out, and on the second floor the stench of unwashed bodies was so strong he nearly gagged.

The third floor, when he finally reached it, was no different from the others, except it was hotter. He thought the smells had faded as well, or maybe it was simply that he had grown used to them. The thought that in a few moments he would see her—it shouldn't make his heart beat so rapidly, it shouldn't raise that longing deep inside him.

But it did. God help him, it did. His father's words rang in his mind: *"She betrayed us, goddammit. Why can't you get that through your head? It was her."* His mouth went dry. It could not be her. It wasn't her. The words were like a song in his head.

He closed his eyes, focusing on the pain in his lung, in his hip, focusing on the heaviness of the saddlebags and the sweat dampening his hair, delaying the moment. It reminded him of the game he'd played with himself when he was just sixteen and lovestruck at the sight of her. The game it shamed him to think about now. Whirling the cylinder of the revolver, asking himself the questions. *She loves me, she loves me not. She loves me . . .*

He swallowed and opened his eyes again, feeling as weakened by the thought of her as he'd always been. He braced himself on the wall next to the door and let his hand rest against the rough wood for a second before he knocked. The door bowed beneath the force of his knuckles.

He heard nothing. Not at first. Then it was there, the quiet squeak of a bed frame, the sigh, the sleepy, muffled step.

Then her voice at the door. A rough whisper.

"Hello? Who's there?"

His voice felt coarse and gravelly in his throat. He forced out the words. "Hey, Kittycat," he whispered in return.

A pause. It seemed to last forever.

"Texas?"

He listened for some inflection in her voice. Fear or longing or disbelief, but he heard none of those things. Her voice was as flat as the high plains of the Llano, the voice he'd taught her. It was a skill she'd learned well, that hiding of emotion. *Never let them know what you're thinking.* Ah yes, she'd learned it very well.

His exhaustion overtook him at that moment. He leaned his forehead against the door. Everything depended on now, on this second. Everything. The knowledge weakened him so much he could barely stand. "Let me in, Lily," he said. "Let me in before I collapse on the floor."

The door swung wide so quickly he nearly did fall. He caught himself on the frame and looked down into the face he'd thought about, dreamed about, for the past three weeks. Lying in Schofield's sister's house, writhing beneath the unsteady, probing hands of the doctor, he'd thought about nothing but Lily, and now he drank in the sight of her. She looked fresh and innocent standing before him, her coppery hair loose down her shoulders and back, her face flushed with sleep. She was clutching a thin, worn wrapper around her corset and drawers, but at the sight of his unsteadiness she let go of it and reached for him.

"Oh my God, it *is* you! Texas!" The flatness left her voice, leaving real joy in its wake, a joy he saw reflected in her eyes.

He nearly collapsed with relief. He'd been right; the knowledge washed away his despair, his fear. He didn't know enough ways to thank God for it, and so he let himself sag into her arms, too wearied by relief to do more than offer up vague tributes.

Her hands were cool and firm, her body strong as he leaned against her for balance. The scent of her, a scent he didn't recognize—roses?—seemed to envelop him as she helped him to the bed. He slumped on the mattress, letting the saddlebags slide to the floor. She lifted the hat from his head and laid it aside, and the touch of her fingers in his hair was cool and tender and invigorating.

Across the room, he saw the hats the milliner had sold her. A straw poke bonnet with cherries and red ribbons to tie beneath her chin. Another, smaller one of dark green velvet, adorned with black ribbons and an enormous black feather. He gestured to them weakly. "Pretty hats," he said.

She smiled a small, vulnerable smile. "You're alive," she said breathlessly. "I can't believe you're alive."

He leaned back on the headboard. The carved wooden posts banged against the wall; the whole bed shook. "We're all alive."

She looked startled for a moment. "All of you? But I saw Hank—"

"Pa's fine. But they got him. Him and Bobby. They're in the jail at Lampasas."

"And Schofield?"

"He's waiting back at his sister's."

"I can't believe it. All of you." Her words were hushed, her lips trembled when she smiled. "Thank God. What happened? Tell me everything. I thought—I thought you were dead."

She looked so young, so innocent. Clad in her underwear, with her hair falling free, she looked as innocent as a woman could. The only thing that marred the illusion was the thick scar that glared at him, ruddy and ugly, from her throat, a scar that creased her jaw, that marred the skin behind her ear. It was difficult to look at it without knowing what it was and what had caused it. A hanging scar. It was impossible to see it and not know exactly who she was, a woman on the run from the law. A woman known as "Lily the Cat" in three states.

The sight of the scar brought his guilt back so hard it lodged in his throat and made him hurt. But it reassured him, too. The hats had unnerved him somehow. He had seen them and thought she would be different in some fundamental way. But she was just the same. Still his Lily. Still his.

"We should have been dead," he said again, closing

his eyes, remembering. "Petry and his men came from nowhere."

She leaned over him. He heard her movement, felt the brush of her hair against his cheek. "I saw them," she said. "It was almost as if they knew we were coming."

He opened his eyes reluctantly. "Pa and some of the others think someone told them," he said slowly.

She frowned and sat back on her heels. "But who?"

He shrugged. The movement sent pain racing into his chest, and he turned away from her and stared at the tattered, limp curtains lying motionless in the window. "I don't know."

He felt her touch on his shoulder, light but strong, forcing him to look at her.

"Maybe you don't," she said, "but Hank has an idea, doesn't he? He suspects someone from the gang."

He remembered his father's face behind prison bars, shadowed by moonlight and darkness, remembered his words.

"It's me, isn't it?" she whispered. "He thinks I told Petry we were hitting the bank that day."

"You weren't at the copse afterwards," he said reluctantly. "You didn't meet us."

"Oh, Texas," she said, leaning forward. That long, soft hair came over her shoulders, covering her breasts, partially hiding the scar, and there was such frank honesty in her eyes it astonished him. "I thought there was no one to meet. I thought you were dead. And Petry and his men . . . If you were dead, they would come after me. I was afraid, that's why I ran. Without you, I had nothing, don't you see?"

He did see, all too well, and her impassioned words made him feel unabashedly glad that he'd defended her to his father and the others. That honesty in her eyes made him feel strong enough to defend her from the world.

"Yeah," he said softly. "I see."

"Then you believe me?"

He grinned. "Ah baby, I'd believe you if you told me you were God."

She laughed and touched his cheek. "I wish convincing Hank could be that easy."

"It will be," he assured her. "I'll make him believe it."

"If you can," she said.

"I can."

He saw the amusement in her eyes, the soft affection, but she didn't disagree with him again. "So we are going back?"

"We have to." He took a strand of her hair, rubbed it between his fingers, brought it to his nose. Again, that scent. Roses. He looked up at her. "Like I said, Schofield's waiting for us at his sister's. If he can, he'll try to break Pa and Bobby out of jail before we get there, but it would be easier with our help."

"We're breaking them out, then?"

"Well, we're not going to let them hang."

She shuddered. Her hand went convulsively to her throat, and her face paled. Texas swallowed. He reached up and took her hand, pulling it gently away from the scar, and then he touched it with his own fingers. "Don't worry," he said. "We won't let it happen to them. I'm sorry you even know what it feels like, baby. I can't tell you how sorry—"

She shook her head quickly, as if ridding herself of the thought and his apology. "It doesn't matter," she said, starting to move away. "You should be worrying about them, not me. We should go. Now. Tonight."

He sighed and cupped his hand around her bare shoulder—such soft skin—stopping her. "We've got time," he said. "There's no sign of vigilantes, and if the judge comes into town, Schofield'll take care of him."

"You don't want to leave right away?"

"I think tomorrow's soon enough."

She looked at him for a long moment, and then she smiled and he let that smile appease him. His guilt disappeared, melted clean away. He saw the humor that came slow and easy into her eyes. "I haven't thanked you," she said softly.

"For what?"

"For coming back for me." She leaned close. Her breath was hot and teasing. "For believing I had nothing to do with Petry."

"It was easy to believe," he managed.

"Was it?" Her voice was a caress of sound, a murmured hush. She smiled and kissed him, softly at first, and then hungrily, with lips and tongue and hands.

Her hands were in his hair and then at his shoulders, pushing aside his duster, tugging at his shirt. There was almost a desperation in her movements, an urgency he had not felt from her in a long time, maybe ever. He felt himself responding. He grabbed at her, reaching for her shoulders, pulling her close. Her hands pressed at his chest.

Pain stabbed through him.

"Ah!" He jerked away violently, dizzy, pushing at her, trying desperately to breathe. He fell against the headboard, jamming his back into the posts, grabbing at his chest.

"What is it? What's wrong, Texas?"

Her voice was muffled by the ceaseless beat of his heart, the buzz of pain.

"Texas."

He held up his hand, signaling for silence, gritting

his teeth and closing his eyes, waiting for the agony to cease, for it to fade to a dim ache. It did. In only a moment, he could breathe again, and the assuagement of pain was an infinitely sweet relief. In its wake, the constant ache faded in importance and intensity.

He opened his eyes and smiled weakly at her. "Sorry," he said. "I'm not at my best, I'm afraid."

The concern on her face was heartwarming. She frowned. "You were wounded," she said. "I saw you . . . fall."

"Just a scratch," he joked lamely.

A tiny smile tugged at her lips. "Let me see," she said, reaching for his shirt. He let her unfasten it, feeling soothed and reassured by the simple act of caretaking, the evidence of concern. When she saw the stained, dirty bandages wrapping his chest, she stopped. She looked down at them for a moment, an unreadable expression on her face, and then she looked at him. "How bad?" she asked.

"A bullet in my lung and one in my hip," he said.

"In your lung?"

"The ball's still there," he told her. "They couldn't get to it."

Her brown eyes were melting. "Does it hurt?"

He made a feeble attempt at a grin. "Only when I breathe."

She didn't smile back. She moved away and climbed off the bed, shaking back her hair. "I'm sorry," she said. "I didn't know."

He reached out and grabbed her wrist, pulling her back beside him, clutching her thinly clad hip with his other hand, holding her close.

"Come on, baby," he whispered, hearing how hoarse his voice sounded, how desperate he was. He smiled his most persuasive smile and raised a challenging brow.

"You were in the middle of thanking me. Just keep on doing it."

She hesitated, but only for a moment. Then she knelt beside him on the bed and moved until she was straddling his hips. She settled herself carefully on his thighs and reached up, unfastening the hooks of her corset until her breasts were free, letting the garment fall to the floor. She leaned down, brushing his lips with hers.

"Tell me if I'm hurting you," she whispered, and he nodded in response, too full of the sight and smell of her to speak, to do anything but reach for her.

And though she did hurt him, though the ache in his hip spidered through him and his lung burned with the effort of making love to her, with her breasts filling his hands and her soft moans filling his ears, he didn't care. He didn't care about anything at all, except that Lily was back.

Lily was back.

Everything else could wait for tomorrow.

2

He woke to the smell of coffee and roses. For a brief, sleepy moment, he thought it was still part of the dream he couldn't remember, but then he opened his eyes and saw her standing at the side of the bed, a welcoming expression on her face and a cup of coffee in her hand.

"I bribed Mrs. Walston for it," she said, sitting on the edge of the mattress and holding it out to him. "I thought you might need it."

He struggled to his elbows. After the long ride yesterday and the exertion of seeing Lily again, his muscles shrieked with pain. He tried not to show it, but he must have, because she immediately set the coffee aside and helped him lean back against the lumpy pillows.

"Are you sure you'll be able to ride today?" she asked.

He nodded. "I'm sure."

Her brow furrowed with concern. She reached for the coffee again, and he took it from her. It tasted good—hot and bitter—and, along with her presence, made him feel complete as nothing had in a long time. He sighed and leaned his head back against the headboard, reveling in it, feeling the dawn-cool breeze from the open window against his chest, smelling the reedy green scent of the Red River. He felt safe here. Safe as he hadn't been since she'd left, and the thought filled him with contentment and a cocky conceit. He'd been right when he told his father she would never have betrayed them. The gang was her family. He was her husband.

"Texas? Are you all right?"

He grinned at her over the rim of his cup. "Oh yeah. I'm just fine."

The worry left her face and she smiled back at him. "I've missed you," she said quietly.

He cupped her chin in his free hand, pulling her close, brushing her lips with his. He'd dreamed of hearing those words. For nights and nights, it was all he'd thought about. "I've missed you, too," he whispered. The words seemed inadequate in the light of his feelings. "I can hardly wait to take you home."

"Yes," she said. "Home." She drew away from him and got up from the bed, her manner suddenly brisk and businesslike. "You should probably hurry. The day will be gone before we know it."

He laughed. "You're in such a rush to go?"

"Aren't you? Who knows what could have happened in the time it took you to find me? God knows I'd hate to keep Hank waiting."

He took a sip of coffee and put the cup aside. "Well, the thing is, Kittycat, we aren't going straight back to Lampasas."

She frowned. "We aren't?"

"Pa wants us to pick up something on the way back."

The confusion on her face deepened. "He wants us to— Hell, we can't go into Dallas, if that's what he wants."

"We don't need to go into Dallas. We're making a little detour. To Fort Griffin."

"Fort Griffin? But he-he never wanted me there before. What about Ann?"

The thought of his stepmother sobered Texas for a moment and he flexed his hand, feeling the strain in his chest and a little twinge of pain. "Annie died about two weeks ago," he said slowly. "Just . . . gave out. Old Sam said the wind made her crazy."

He looked up at Lily. She was staring at him as if she didn't know what to say, and he knew she probably didn't. He looked down at his hand again.

"Jocelyn's at the farm alone except for Sam," he continued. "We need to pick her up and take her home."

"She's joining the gang?"

"No." He chuckled and shook his head. "No. Pa's planning to send her to San Antonio, where she'll be safe."

She frowned.

"What is it, baby?" he asked softly. "Look, Josie's not—"

"I'm not worried about your sister," she said abruptly. "It's, it's Hank, that's all. Can't Old Sam take care of Jocelyn a little longer? I'd feel better if we went to Lampasas first. Let's break out Hank and Bobby, and then we can all ride to Fort Griffin."

It amazed him that his father had ever thought her capable of betrayal, that Texas had even for a moment wondered himself. He pushed back the threadbare blankets and eased himself off the mattress, ignoring the stiffness in his hip as he crossed over to her.

He pulled her back against him and ran his hands up and down her arms. She relaxed against him, leaning her head back against his shoulder, and he rested his chin on her soft, satiny hair. The scent of roses wafted up to him again, along with the slightly stale tang of sweat. He grasped her arms more tightly, leaned down to whisper in her ear.

"It's all right, Kittycat," he said. "Pa wants it this way."

"He's not thinking," she said stubbornly.

He eased his hold slightly and glanced out the window at the town streets that were just now beginning to wake. "Do you want to tell him that?" he asked dryly.

She hesitated and then laughed shortly. "No. I guess not."

"If we don't show up with Josie, he'll have my head." Texas forced a lightness into his words he didn't feel. "And yours, too, probably."

"He'll probably have mine anyway," she said. "If he believes I was the one who told Petry—"

His voice felt tight. "Don't worry about that," he said slowly. "I'll take care of that."

She turned in his arms, quickly, unexpectedly, pressing against his chest, looking up at him with wide brown eyes dark with worry. Her hands went to the back of his neck, teased his long hair. "You can't promise me that, Texas," she said quietly. "With Hank, there's no telling."

"I'll make him change his mind," he said, and, in that moment, looking at her, feeling her against him, he believed he could. Hell, right now, with Lily in his arms again, he had the strength to believe in everything, even his own salvation. "You're my wife, Lily."

"Your wife," she whispered, and then she laughed, a shy sound. "Yeah. I guess I am that."

"Don't worry," he said, though she would and he knew it. "Don't worry. I love you." And when she melted into his kiss, when she pressed willingly into him and moaned into his mouth, he knew he would do anything to keep his promise. Anything at all.

They were nearly packed by noon. The room was sweltering. The early morning breeze had given way to a stifling, oppressive humidity that seemed to press in all around him. He wanted to be out of it, wanted to be back on the rolling hills, wanted to be moving, always moving.

Lily had paid Mrs. Walston the balance of the rent and sent a boy to retrieve her horse from a neighboring farm. By the time the kid returned with the roan Texas had rustled for her a few years ago, they were ready to go.

She looked familiar to him now, dressed as she was in men's pants and shirt, the heavy gun belt around her hips, her hair braided and tucked up under her hat. No more petticoats, no more corset. He had not even seen the dresses she'd bought to wear with those things. She was shrugging into her coat and grabbing her saddlebags when he noticed the hats, still sitting on the table near the wall, pristine and unworn.

"Aren't you taking those?" he asked.

She glanced over at them and shook her head disdainfully. "No."

"Why not?"

She slung her saddlebags over her shoulder and made for the door. "I was thinking I might try being respectable," she said. "But now you're here"—she sent him a smile—"I don't need them anymore."

She strode out the door, and Texas found himself staring after her. Respectable. Corsets and petticoats and rose toilet water. Unexpectedly, the images came into his mind: Lily in a cherry straw poke and red-and-white gingham. Lily smiling and curtseying to strangers on the street. The thoughts were strangely disturbing; he felt again the discomfort he'd felt when the milliner first told him about the hats, that inexplicable fear that Lily was different and he just couldn't see it. Lily, respectable. It made him think of an old dream. A dream he hadn't thought about in a long time, where the two of them walked down a street together, dressed like normal people, respectable people.

"Texas, are you coming?" Her voice drifted back up the stairs.

"Yeah," he answered distractedly. "I'll be right there."

But he didn't follow her, not right away. Instead, he went to the poke bonnet and picked it up carefully in his hands, letting the red satin ribbons swirl around his wrists, watching the silk cherries shimmer in the sunlight. *"I do hope you let her keep them."* The milliner's words came back to him, her wistful plea. *"She looks so dear with those ribbons at her chin."*

And then, before he knew what he was doing, before he thought about it at all, he opened his saddlebags and carefully stuffed the bonnet inside, tenderly filling the crown with a shirt to protect its shape, covering it with what remained of his clothing. *Someday,* he thought. *Maybe someday.*

He buckled the bag closed and went down the stairs.

She was waiting for him by the horses, looking impatient, squinting beneath the brim of her hat. Her duster was drawn back and the hilt of her gun glinted in the sunlight.

"I wish you'd get another gun," he said when he drew closer. "That old Army's too heavy for you."

She shook her head. "I like it that way."

"Half the time you can't even hold it straight."

She smiled a cold-edged smile that took him aback until he remembered how often he'd seen it, before every bank they'd ever held up, every train they'd ever robbed. "I don't need to shoot straight, lover," she said, and the softness that had been in her eyes since he'd arrived last night disappeared, replaced by that strange, icy danger that had always worried him, the danger that had been lurking there for years, since he'd first taught her how to load and shoot a gun. "As long as I hit a man, it doesn't matter whether I was aiming at his head or his heart."

It sent a chill through him, a vague discomfort. He went to his horse and threw on his saddlebags. "Do me a favor and don't talk like that in front of Josie."

She looked at him in surprise. "Why?"

"Because she's not like us," he said.

She gave him a wry look. "Not like us? She's the daughter of Hank Sharpe."

"Josie's different."

"Different how?"

"Just different."

Just different. He didn't know how else to explain Jocelyn. His half sister had been brought up as ignorant of the gang's activities as his stepmother could make her. The last time he'd seen her she'd been seventeen or eighteen and the belle of Fort Griffin. Pretty, vivacious, and sheltered, Josie had only the vaguest idea of the reality of the gang's life. Pa had gone to the farm outside Fort Griffin whenever they'd finished a job, and he'd worked hard to make it a safe refuge, to be the perfect father to his daughter. The town aided in the deception. Fort Griffin held Hank Sharpe in a kind of reverent awe. He was an outlaw, yes, but he was their outlaw, and the Army or the law never even came close to him when he was in town.

Josie had grown up listening to stories of her father's exploits, and Texas imagined she'd heard her share of tales about his, too, but they were grandiose legends by the time she heard them, more myth than reality, and Annie had always been good about keeping the worst of them from her daughter's tender ears.

He wondered what Jocelyn was like now. She'd be, oh, twenty-three or so, nearly Lily's age. He stole a glance at Lily and saw a world of difference between the two women. Lily was nothing like Jocelyn, and, looking at her now, he didn't know how she could ever be. In the dirty, canvaslike *charro* trousers she wore, with the edge of the hanging scar peeking from her collar, she looked as far from respectable as anyone he'd ever seen.

Suddenly, the impulse that had driven him to bring along that hat seemed absurd, the image he'd had of her wrapped in cherry-gingham seemed as far away and insubstantial as a dream. It embarrassed him to think about it.

"Let's go," he said. He mounted his horse, clenching his jaw against the pain of his hip. He was grateful for the moment it took her to get on the roan; it gave him a chance to steady his breathing. He waited for her to draw her duster more closely about her to hide the gun, and then they were off.

The streets of Denison were crowded, and the sun was growing hotter, and by the time they left town and started on the road, the stifling, too-close feeling he'd had in the boardinghouse was back with a vengeance.

At the first opportunity, he left the road, motioning for Lily to follow him onto the prairie, and, once the road and the city were behind him, he felt good, really good, for the first time in days. Even the pain of his wounds seemed to fade away. During the ride from Lampasas, he'd been too driven with the need to find her to gain peace, but now that she was beside him, riding the open plains with him, the pain in his body seemed to ease, and he let the prairie call to him the way it always had, heard its song in the hot wind.

He loved Texas. He loved the sight of it and the smell, he loved the aridness of the high plains and the scent of burning dust and the endless, endless sky. When he was young and just joining his father's gang, he'd spent hours standing in the twilight, listening to the wind, savoring the seared-grass smell of the air. It was so different from the bayous where he'd spent his first years, so different from the stagnant marshes and the malaise in the air and the deep, reedy stench of rotting vegetation. His love for the freedom of the plains was so strong it had earned him his nickname.

"Jesus Christ, you'd think you were Texas . . ." Teddy Lee's words. So long ago now. Texas remembered that night vividly, remembered the scent of mesquite smoke and the taste of buffalo steak and the anticipation of going into town to buy one of the willing, open-legged whores of San Antonio. He remembered how Teddy Lee had pushed him into the arms of one, saying, "He's only thirteen, but he's as big as all of Texas. Hell, that's even what we call 'im, girls. This here's Texas Sharpe, and you'd better be nice to 'im, or you'll be dealin' with his daddy."

Texas shook his head, dismissing the memory. It was a long time ago. Teddy Lee was gone now. Texas had killed him himself more than ten years ago, but the nickname had stuck, and Texas supposed it was apt enough. The love of this country had never left him. Never, except for the last three weeks, the terrible weeks without Lily.

He looked over at her again, feeling an overwhelming sense of peace when she met his smile with one of her own.

"What are you thinking about?" she asked.

He shook his head. "Nothing," he said. "You."

Her smile widened. He thought it was the most beautiful thing. It added light to her eyes and squared her jaw and added a sweetly innocent curve to her full lips.

"You shouldn't be so obvious," she teased. "You've

told me that often enough. Be careful what you let people see."

"There's no one around."

"No, I suppose not."

"And you're beautiful."

She chuckled and glanced up at him from beneath her lashes, giving him a coquettish look, one he rarely saw. "You're too honest for your own good."

He shrugged. "I call 'em like I see 'em."

She laughed. It was a clear, full-bodied sound, like fresh water after a drought or rain in the dust. The sound of it made his heart swell. How long had it been since he'd heard her laugh like that? Not for months, ah, not for months and months. He loved the sound of it. It filled his mind and his soul the way the Texas prairies did, like sunlight and grass and the fresh, clean smell of dawn. It made him feel real, as if he'd been in some strange, alien place and was finally home again.

"You turn me inside out, baby," he said hoarsely, and then wished he was close enough to grab her when she laughed again.

"Then try and catch me!" she challenged, pressing her heels into the roan's sides, urging the horse into a full gallop through the short, burnt waves of grama grass, toward the trees in the distance.

The dare was impossible to resist, even if he'd wanted to. Texas took a deep breath, clenched his teeth against the pain, and followed her.

They camped that night at the edge of a grove of blackjack oak and tangled mesquite. Earlier, he'd heard the twilight song of a mockingbird, but once the fire had started, the bird had quieted, and now the only sounds were the crackling of the flames and the low hum of chiggers.

Lily was quiet. He'd shot a hare for dinner and settled silently back against a tree as she'd skinned it and put it to roast over the fire. She was aimlessly peeling the bark from a tiny green branch, looking up only when a bit of fat dripped from the rabbit to sizzle in the fire.

The rich, gamy scent of it made his mouth water. He was starving, and the day's ride had left him exhausted and in pain. All he wanted to do was eat and go to sleep. But he felt the sharp pull of the bandages across his ribs, along with a harsher nagging pain, and he knew he had to check his wound before he did anything else. Impatiently, he limped over to his horse and grabbed his canteen. He felt her eyes on him as he moved back toward the fire. His hip was burning, and he sat down carefully, unable to mask his groan as he eased his weight from one hip to the other.

"Texas, you look pale. Are you all right?" she asked.

He glanced up at her and tried to smile. "As good as gold," he said, though his hand shook slightly when he uncorked the canteen and poured some of the brackish water into a cup. He set the tin near the outer coals of the fire and put the canteen aside. Then he shrugged out of his duster and vest and attacked the buttons of his shirt.

"What are you doing?"

The pain was worse today than it had been yesterday. *Probably the result of finding Lily again*, he thought wryly. He looked up from his shirt, from his clumsy attempts to unfasten it.

"Thought I'd take a look before it got too dark," he said, shaking back his hair.

"Does it hurt?"

The concern in her voice made him smile. "Not much," he lied.

He pulled his shirt loose from his pants and shrugged

out of it, and the motion made him wince; it felt as if the muscles in his chest were tearing. His hands were trembling so much when he unbuttoned his long underwear that he cursed beneath his breath and clenched his jaw.

She was beside him in an instant, squatting until she was even with him, taking off her hat so she could see. "Let me help," she said, and he closed his eyes with relief when she pushed aside his hands and began peeling back his underwear, easing it over his shoulders until he felt the chill of the Texas night on his skin.

Her hands were cool and gentle. She bent close to him, the top of her head so close to his chin that if he moved half an inch he would feel the silken touch of her hair. The scent of roses was fading now, and he was glad. That perfume belonged to a stranger. Not to Lily. Not his Lily.

Her fingers jerked at the bandages, and he gasped at the pain of it. She glanced up at him. "Relax," she said. "You've got these wrapped so damn tight I can't undo the knot."

"You can blame Schofield's sister for that," he breathed.

"I will, next time I see her." She worked the knot, her brow knitted in concentration. "There," she said finally, loosening it. "Now, this might hurt just a bit."

It hurt more than a bit. He closed his eyes, focusing on the steady sound of her breathing as she unwound the bandages. The wound felt hot; the strip of linen stuck to it slightly as she pulled it away.

"Good God."

Her words were a breath of sound, hot against his chest. She leaned closer. He felt her fingers probing the edges of the wound, a tender, careful touch that still hurt him.

"It's a nasty wound," she said. "It's a little pink

around the edges." She looked up at him, her eyes large and worried. "You've been overdoing it, Texas. Did the doctor tell you it was all right to ride all this way?"

"That doc's a fool."

"So he did tell you not to ride."

He pushed back his hair. "He didn't tell me shit."

"Texas."

"What does it matter, Lily?" he asked impatiently. "What was I supposed to do, just lie in bed? I had things to do."

"You could have come after me later."

He caught her gaze and held it. "It couldn't wait."

She laughed, a small, breathless sound, and smoothed back a strand of his hair, kissed him lightly on the cheek. Then she sat back on her heels. "Well, you've done it now," she said, her tone quick and businesslike again. "It looks as if it might be festering a bit."

"Nothing a little cleaning won't cure," he said. He nodded toward the fire. "There's some hot water."

She eased her shirtsleeve over her hand and grabbed the cup of water from the fire. He watched as she dipped a handkerchief into it. She glanced up and gave him a small smile before she bent to her work, and her careful, gentle ministrations relaxed him even though they hurt.

It was quiet, just the sound of her breathing and the fire and the chiggers. Finally, she put aside the handkerchief and the cup and settled down beside him.

"How long do you figure it'll be before the judge comes into Lampasas?" she asked.

"When I left, he wasn't due for another two weeks," Texas said.

"And you think there won't be a lynch mob?"

"I doubt it." He shook his head, remembering how easily they'd been trapped, how quiet the town had been after Pa and Bobby had been thrown in jail. There weren't even guards watching outside the building the night Texas had sneaked up to talk to his father and Bobby through the barred windows. "They're just as likely to eulogize Pa as hang him. They hated old Peterson and his bank. He was just another carpetbagger out to screw 'em. We probably wouldn't even have had a posse come after us if Petry hadn't been there."

She was staring into the fire. "So how do you figure he knew?"

"Word gets around," he said. "It could have been anybody."

She was quiet for a long time. So long that the hiss of the fire seemed to grow louder and louder in his ears. So long that the sky took on the fierce blues and golds of sunset. He was just reaching for the stick that held the roasted rabbit when she spoke again.

"You're too trusting sometimes," she said softly.

He snorted. "Oh, yeah, I'm trusting all right. That's why half the state of Texas is after my head."

"Just half the state?" she teased. Then, more seriously, she said, "Maybe Hank is right about what happened."

He gave her a sharp look. "Pa thinks *you* were the one who told Petry."

She waved his words away. "I don't mean about me. But maybe he's right to think it was someone in the gang. Schofield, for instance. Have you ever thought of that? Or maybe it was his sister. Fanny was there the whole time we were discussing the plan."

The thought horrified him. "For Christ's sake, Lily. Fanny wouldn't turn in her own brother."

She shrugged and caught his gaze. "Be honest, Texas. You weren't sure I hadn't done it. I could tell. Yesterday you didn't know who to believe, me or Hank."

Her words pierced through him, more painful because she was right, because, as much as he'd wanted to believe her, there had been that niggling uncertainty, that horrible fear that his father might be right. That same uncertainty that had him riding from Lampasas in a fury to find her.

He reached out, curling a loose strand of her hair around his finger, yanking gently until she leaned close. He kissed her hard. "Ah, baby," he whispered against her mouth. "I believe you now."

She drew away and smiled, running a finger over his jaw before she let her hand drop and turned to look back into the flames. "That's good," she said. "That's good to know."

He pulled the rabbit off the fire and reached for his knife. With easy precision, he cut a piece from the hindquarter and handed it to her. "Have some dinner," he said. "And then let's go to bed. I'm beat."

It was later, much later, that he heard the sound. It cut through his dreams, violent and too loud, the cocking of a revolver. He was awake immediately; his eyes snapped open to stare into the barrel of a gun. An old Army Colt. Standing at the end of it, her finger at the ready, was Lily.

"I told you you were too trusting, lover," she said.

And then she pulled the trigger.

3

He rolled. The bullet drilled into the ground near where his head had been, a steady whine, the hiss of dust.

"Dammit!" Her curse was low and passionate. The hammer cocked again.

He scrambled to his feet, tripping over the bedroll, betting on dark and shadows and speed to save him. But his hip was stiff, and he was too slow, and he knew how damned quick she was. The gun fired again, the crack of it loud and close, a flash of light in the darkness. He heard the ball boring into a tree. It was his only chance. He lunged at her shadow.

He crashed into her, taking her off balance, sending them both falling. They hit the ground hard; his gasp of pain mingled with hers. He grabbed her wrist, feeling a grim sense of satisfaction when she yelped. His grip was tight; he knew she couldn't hold on to the gun for long. Still, his relief was overwhelming when she dropped the Colt, not too far from his fingers, close enough to grab. Clenching his jaw against the pain, he reached for the gun, curling his fingers around the hilt and dragging it into his hand.

"Damn you, Texas," she said, struggling beneath him, pushing at him. She pounded her fist into his chest so hard it took his breath. Christ, it hurt. *Christ.* Except for the pain, he would have believed this was all a terrible dream. But her words were too real, too angry. "Damn you."

"Shut up." He pressed the barrel into her jaw, felt her freeze beneath him.

"Let me go," she hissed. "You won't shoot me anyway. Stop with the goddamned charade and let me up."

"Shut up," he said again, trying desperately to think, needing to think. His palm was sweating around the hilt of her damned gun. "Just shut the hell up."

"If you—"

"Shut up!" He shouted the words, and she quieted instantly. *Think,* he told himself. *Think.* But thinking was beyond him. This had to be a dream. Even the feel of her beneath him was wrong. She was stiff and unyielding, frozen beneath the gun. Not the Lily he knew. Not his Lily.

He grimaced, forcing the thoughts away, forcing himself to act. He yanked up the leg of her trousers, jerking away the knife she hid in a scabbard at her calf. He shoved the weapon into his belt and felt inside her vest for the derringer. It was there, hung on a thong around her neck, nestled between her breasts.

"Damn you," she said.

He tucked the gun away in his own pocket and then eased the barrel of the Colt away from her jaw and rolled off her slowly. He motioned with the gun. "Sit up," he said hoarsely. "Slow and easy, Kittycat. That's the way."

The faint light from the quarter moon shifted over her skin, leaving her in shadow.

"Listen, Texas," she began breathlessly. "It's not what you think—"

"I was a fool once," he said tightly. "Don't think you can make me one again."

"You don't understand."

He clenched his jaw and tried to shut out the sound of her voice and the slow, desperate humiliation deadening his heart. "Against that tree," he said, jerking his head toward a nearby oak. "Get over to it."

To her credit, she didn't say a word. The sound of her boots grating on the dirt, her scraping crawl, was loud and horrible in his ears. He willed himself to concentrate, reached into his back pocket for a bandanna, and tried not to think that this was his wife. *His wife,* who had just tried to kill him.

He reached her in only a few steps. Deliberately, he didn't look at her face. He backed her against the tree and jerked her arms behind her, around the trunk, ignoring her gasp of pain, and, with a few skillful ties, he knotted the bandanna around her wrists, binding her hands closely together. The same hands that had stroked his jaw and tended his wound only hours before.

The same hands that had just fired a gun at his head.

Funny how slowly the truth dawned, how languid and easy, in little bits and pieces, gestures and words that took on deeper meaning in retrospect. Everything was fitting neatly into place, but it was too much for him to grasp right now; he couldn't allow himself to grasp it. Hell, if he did, he'd crumple in front of her.

"Pa was right, wasn't he?" he said, and, though his voice was raw, he made no attempt to soothe it. "You betrayed us. You told Petry."

She didn't even wince. She leaned her head back against the trunk and looked up at the sky. The moonlight glanced across her cheekbones, shadowing her eyes. "I had to," she said, and though he thought he would hear regret in her voice, there was none. "They recognized me in town. They said they'd hang me."

"You didn't think we'd protect you?"

She stared at him. Her eyes were so damn cold. "I've already hung once waiting for your *protection*," she said.

In spite of everything, his guilt overwhelmed him. The image from six months ago flashed before his eyes, Lily unconscious and limp, her feet dragging on the ground. Men scattering from his gunfire. "We didn't expect vigilantes," he reminded her in a rough voice. "You know that. We were on the way."

"You were too late," she said harshly. "The rope was too long, Texas, *that's* the only reason I'm alive. You were too late. It was the rope, not you."

She had not been angry with him then, and she'd never accused him since. "It doesn't matter," she'd said only last night, and now he was startled to see just how much it did matter. She was angry and bitter, and that bitterness stopped him like a fist in the gut. With a shock, he understood, really understood, what she was telling him. She had betrayed him. She had told Petry they were hitting the bank and then she'd stood there and watched while the marshal's bullets slammed into his body. And when that hadn't worked, when he hadn't died, she'd tried to kill him herself.

He wondered why that knowledge didn't have more power, why it didn't tear him apart inside, and then he realized it already had, that it was tearing him apart right now, this very moment, and it was why he couldn't feel anything, why there was only numbness when he looked at her, why the pain in his chest and his hip had faded away.

She wanted him dead.

Ah, what a fool he'd been. What a stupid, lovesick fool.

He'd ridden from Lampasas to find her, had made love to her and kissed her and told her he loved her, and all the time she'd been laughing at him. All the time she'd been planning how best to kill him. He could almost imagine her train of logic: *Not in the boarding-house; too many questions. But if I get him to trust me, to believe me, I can surprise him tonight. On the prairies, he'll be just another body for the wolves to find.*

And he had played so easily into her hands. He had wanted so badly to believe her that he had ignored the things his eyes told him, the things his instinct told him. She was a chameleon, why hadn't he remembered it? She was a liar. He knew she was because he'd taught her himself. He had taught her all those lessons, the lessons in lying and shooting and killing, and she had learned them well. Hell, she was better at them than he was. The only reason he was alive now was that the damned Army Colt was too heavy for her to aim properly.

He looked down at the gun, weighed it in his palm, tried to figure out what to do next, as if he had a choice. His father believed Lily had betrayed them all, and now Texas knew for a fact that she had. To belong to the Sharpe gang required only one thing: loyalty.

Betrayal had only one price.

He squeezed his eyes shut, forcing himself to face the truth. Lily had tried to kill him, and she would try again and again until she succeeded. She wanted him dead. Christ, it was so hard to believe that. But he had to believe it. Because he knew the truth about the bank robbery. Because Lily had ridden with them for thirteen years and she understood the rules. She knew this betrayal would cost her life, and she knew he had no choice but to bring her home. He was bound to the gang by loyalty, by love, by blood. It was his whole life, the only family he knew. He'd thought she felt the same.

He opened his eyes and stared up at the sky, at the slivered moon and the darkened clouds streaking it, at the thousands of stars. There was something else she must have realized, as well. He had promised to convince Pa of her innocence, but the truth was he'd never been able to talk his father out of anything. If Pa decided she was to blame for Lampasas, then no one could change Lily's fate. No wonder she'd tried to kill him. Texas had given her no other choice.

Taking her back would be her death sentence.

But letting her go would be his.

Texas looked over at her. She was glaring at him, her chin raised, her whole bearing stubborn and angry. "What are you going to do, Texas?" she taunted him. "Shoot me?"

He aimed the gun carefully, narrowing his eyes to focus on the shimmering triangle of flesh at the open collar of her shirt, taking no satisfaction at all in the way she faced him down, in the wild and bitter glint in her eyes.

He lowered the barrel. "I'm not going to shoot you," he said quietly. "At least not if you keep your damned mouth shut."

"Oh?" She raised a brow. "Don't tell me you're letting me go."

"No." He matched her sarcastic smile with one of his own. "I think maybe I'll just take you to Lampasas the way we planned."

He was gratified to see the smile drop from her face, the stiffening of her expression.

"You're crazy," she whispered. "You're crazy if you think I'm going with you."

"Then I must be crazy," he answered lightly. "Because in the morning, I'm putting you on that horse and leading you all the way there."

"Then untie me," she said. "I'm a sitting target this way. You know I am."

"You should've thought of that before you tried to shoot me."

She jerked ineffectually at the binds. "Texas."

"No."

"Damn you."

He didn't bother to answer her. He was already damned; her curses hardly mattered. Slowly, he got to his feet, limping to the bedroll he'd abandoned what seemed like hours before.

"Want a blanket?" he asked, picking up hers. He didn't wait for an answer, even if she'd been inclined to give one. He tossed it to her. It landed at her knees; he heard her struggle to pull it up with her feet, felt exhausted by the steady murmur of her soft curses. He tried to ignore her as he sank down against a tree and pulled his own blankets around him. He opened the Army Colt, rotating the cylinder to an empty chamber for safety and slipping it back into place, easing the hammer down. Then, shoving the gun into his belt, he grabbed his own Colt from its holster and put it on the ground beside him, resting his hand on top of it. *Fool me once, Lily,* he thought, looking across the banked fire at her. *But not twice. Never twice.*

He leaned back against the tree and closed his eyes, listening to the night sounds and the deeper whisper of her cursing, keeping his dreams at bay for as long as he could. But he could not stay awake forever. It was

nearly dawn when she quieted. It was all he was waiting
for. He let sleep take him.

In his dreams, he relived it. In his visions he felt again
the subtle horror of entering the too-silent bank, the
keen edge of apprehension piercing his excitement. He
saw the empty counter in strange, shadowed color,
caught the scent of fear and sweat. Then his father's
shout, the harsh crack of gunfire, and suddenly the
world was blood and smoke and sound, and he was
running for his life, running with his duster curling
about his legs and the steel of a .45 cold in his hand.

And, in his dreams, over and over, he saw her face as
he reached his horse. Steady-eyed, watchful. He called
her name just before the bullets took him, and it echoed
again and again in his ears, its rhythms winding
through his pain, through his shock. *Lily. Lily, Lily,
Lily.*

Texas jerked awake, panic racing hot and angry
through his veins, sweating with the force of the dream
and the burn in his chest. For a moment, he didn't
remember where he was. Then he saw her, staring at
him from the tree where he'd left her tied, bringing it all
back in a rage of memory. *Damn. Ah, damn.*

She did not say a word to him. She sat quietly while
he untied her arms from around the tree and didn't
move when he tied her wrists again in front of her. She
stood when he told her to and went into the bushes to
relieve herself when he told her to. She barely touched
the food he put in front of her, but she did drink the
bitter coffee.

Her silence bothered him, but it was her accusing
stare that tormented him more. Accusing, as if he had
done something to her, as if she hadn't tried to blow

him to hell in the middle of the night. With that single look, she had him feeling defensive and guilty, and he hated both the feeling and the way it made him mean.

He did his best to ignore her stare as he tied up their bedrolls and loaded the horses, but he could feel it by degrees, growing hotter and colder, hotter when he yanked the Winchester rifle from her saddle and tied it to his, colder when he hooked her bedroll in its place.

When he finished packing, he stood back from the roan and turned to look at her. Lily stared at him, her mouth set in a mulish line, her fingers flexing and unflexing beneath the confining bandanna.

"Get on," he said, jerking his head toward the horse.

She smiled a sly, cruel smile. "I don't think I can."

He let out an exasperated breath. "Get the hell on, Lily."

She sauntered toward him and stopped just beyond his reach, at the side of the roan. She reached up, grabbing the saddle horn with her bound hands, and looked at him over her shoulder. "I need some help, lover."

The endearment grated on him. He stiffened and moved closer to her, reaching down to hoist her up. He saw her movement from the corner of his eye the instant before she hit him. Her two fists slammed into his chest, sending sharp, agonizing pain rocketing through him, stealing his breath.

He staggered back, choking. She dove for his gun and he jerked forward, grabbing her hands before she got there, twisting her wrists.

She gasped. Tears came to her eyes.

He leaned close, forcing himself to breathe, to ignore the pain. "Get on the goddamn horse," he said through clenched teeth.

Her eyes met his, a brief moment, a glance and then a shifting away, and then she did as he said. Awkwardly she hoisted herself into the saddle, and once she was there, he took a leather thong and tied her hands to the horn for good measure. Then he tied the lead rein to his horse and mounted.

He was relieved to leave the oak grove behind, to ride back again onto the rolling hills. But his joy in the land had disappeared; the colors had faded to a dull, summer-burned brown. The blackbirds circling a nearby grove of blackjack were graceless and loud and greedy. His body hurt, and his mind . . . his mind was ugly.

It was strange how a single moment could define a life, how just one second could change a man. A look, a smile, the heavy, reassuring weight of a gun. It occurred to him that all of those moments in his life had something to do with Lily. There had been his fifteenth birthday, when Teddy Lee first brought her into camp, a sobbing orphan. There was the day Texas had married her. And now, today . . .

The truth was so damned relentless. The vision of her holding that gun on him wouldn't go away. It just kept eating at him, reminding him, tormenting him. He felt as if the last of his innocence had gone, as if Lily, or his foolish image of her, had been the only thing anchoring it in place, the one pure thing in a world he was far too cynical about. But even she was an illusion, as deceptive as everything else in his life. Today had shown him that he didn't really know her at all. He didn't know what she was thinking now, or even what she wanted.

He wondered if he ever had.

He felt that hard disillusionment sidle its way into his heart, its nasty little prick, and, in that one moment, he knew himself as the outlaw he was trained to be, the outlaw the stories made him. An outlaw like his father.

"Texas Sharpe don't care about nothin' or nobody." "I seen him kill a man once while he was eatin' a plate o' beans, casual as you please. Didn't even look up from his plate, and asked for dessert after." "Oh, he's charming enough, you understand. Just don't get him mad at you. He can turn into a devil in nothing flat."

The stories were true enough; they had always been true. Before last night, the recklessness in his soul had been tempered, softened. Before last night, the mere thought of Lily was enough to simmer him down.

Now all it did was make him feel stupid and angry and mean.

"He don't care about nothin' or nobody." Well, now he supposed it was true.

And he knew himself well enough to know that was trouble.

4

She hated looking at him. Just the sight of his back taunted her with her failure, and a glance at his face, at that smug, controlled expression, lodged that failure so tightly in her throat she could barely breathe.

If only she had taken more time last night. The moonlight had made it hard to see, and she knew to take that into account, but he moved in his sleep, and then he was staring into her eyes, and she had taken her chance instead of cutting her losses and coming up with a good lie. She could have fooled him, too, if she'd tried. She was good at lying; hell, she'd made him believe the last twenty-four hours. She could make him believe anything.

Damn, what a fool she was. She had underestimated him. She'd forgotten how quick he was, how mean anger made him. Now, instead of riding back to Denison, she was a prisoner, and if she didn't find some way to get out of these ropes, she would be a corpse the moment they rode into Lampasas.

Panic made her heart race, and even the knowledge

that this was her own fault didn't ease it. If she'd taken the time to make sure they were all dead after that robbery, she wouldn't be here now. She should have been sure. But instead she'd ridden off, afraid that Petry would turn on her, as well, eager to taste the freedom she'd dreamt about for so long. She'd been too impatient, and now she was paying for it with her life, unless she could find some way to fool Texas again.

If she could just get him to loosen her from the saddle horn, even for a moment.

She coughed. When he didn't turn around, she coughed again. "I need some water," she croaked.

He looked over his shoulder. He looked worn out; fine dust covered his face, and his cheek was red where he'd batted at some stinging fly. But he looked anything but worn down when he met her eyes. She saw the hard calculation in his gaze, the wariness.

"I don't suppose you want me to die before we get to Lampasas, now do you?" she asked.

"Not really," he said with a sigh. "It'd slow me down to have to bury you out here."

She bit back a reply, watching him carefully as he dismounted, seeing his bitten-off moan and his wince as he untied the canteen from his saddle and limped toward her.

He stopped just out of range of her foot and grabbed the halter on the roan. Then, he uncorked the canteen with his teeth and handed it to her.

"You'll have to untie me," she said, lifting the canteen as far as she could. He had her bound so tightly to the saddle horn the give was only a few inches. "I can't reach it this way."

He grabbed the canteen out of her hands. "I don't think I'll take that chance, if you don't mind," he said. "Bend down."

She glared at him, knowing her frustration was horribly, furiously transparent. He was not going to untie her, and he was not going to come close enough for her to put a solid kick into his chest, and she hated him for that. She wanted to turn away, to refuse the canteen, but the smell of the water was tantalizing in the heat, and she hadn't had a sip all day.

She bent down until he could hold the canteen to her lips. He tilted it for her, and she gulped greedily at the warm, metallic water, so greedily that some ran down her chin into her collar and pooled dirty and wet on the fabric of her shirt.

She leaned away and, for a moment, the taste and the renewing strength of water was enough to make her forget everything. She closed her eyes, enjoying it, and then she opened them again to find Texas staring at her strangely.

He grabbed a handkerchief from his pocket and motioned to her. "Bend down," he ordered again, pouring water onto the cloth.

Warily, she did. To her surprise, he wiped her face with the dampened cloth, cleaning away the dust, the grime, pushing back the tendrils of hair she'd long forgotten about, the ones sticking to her cheeks, her throat.

Then, as if it were the most natural thing in the world to have done, he stepped away and recorked the canteen.

"We're almost there," he said. "Another few hours." He shoved the handkerchief back into his pocket and turned around, limping back to his horse without waiting for her to answer, without looking back.

Her face tingled from the water and the roughness of cotton against her sunburned skin. She had not realized she was even uncomfortable until he'd ministered to her, and now she felt much better. Much, much better. It was the kind of thing he'd always done when they were riding together, one of the small kindnesses she always forgot and he never did.

The familiarness of his gesture surprised her; she felt vaguely uneasy.

Damn, she wished he had never found her.

They rode into the yard of the farm late that afternoon. It looked as shabby and beaten down as every other farm in this part of Texas, but there was one thing different about it: Jocelyn Sharpe.

Forever after, Lily was to remember that when she first saw Texas's sister, Josie was polishing silver. It was a huge, beautifully wrought teapot, and it seemed as out of place in this dog run of a house as Jocelyn Sharpe did on the Texas prairies. She was like the bluebonnets that bloomed in the spring on the plains, surprising and unexpected, yet fitting in so perfectly it was hard to imagine that the plains could ever be barren again.

Lily's soul did not normally lean toward poetry, but, then again, she rarely saw women as bone-deep beautiful as Jocelyn Sharpe. And that was the only way to describe her. The moment Texas had hustled Lily through the door, tired and sore and dirty from the long ride, she thought it. The sight of his sister was renewing somehow; the surprise of her melted away Lily's exhaustion.

Jocelyn's profile was pure and classic enough. She had Texas's high forehead and the square line of his jaw, but when she turned to face them, an expression of happiness and greeting on her face, all of those features became feminized and graceful in a way Lily had never seen before.

"You're here!" Jocelyn set aside the silver and the rag she was polishing it with and hurried forward, wiping her hands on the apron tied around her mulberry-colored dress, swiping at the loosened strands of her dark hair. She nearly threw herself into Texas's arms, so hard he staggered back wincing before he smiled and enveloped his sister in his arms.

"Pa wrote and told me you would come, but I wasn't sure when." Jocelyn spoke into his shoulder, then drew back and smiled and hugged him again. "I was beginning to lose hope!"

Texas grinned and held her out at arm's length. "Well, we're here," he said in a slow, easy drawl. "Josie, you haven't changed a bit."

"I certainly hope I have! I was little more than a child the last time I saw you!" All of Jocelyn's words ended on an upswing, a perpetual bubble of excitement. "It's been five years!"

Five years. Since they got married, Lily thought.

"A long time," Texas agreed. He glanced up and, when his eye caught Lily's, he stiffened as if he'd forgotten she was there. He motioned toward her. "I've brought someone for you to meet," he said. "Josie, this is my wife, Lily."

Lily didn't miss the edge of derision beneath the words. Just to spite him, she smiled and stepped forward. "How lovely it is to meet you," she said with exaggerated courtesy. She held out her bound wrists. "Forgive me if I don't shake your hand."

Jocelyn's warm smile of greeting died on her face. She stared at Lily's hands, her hazel eyes wide and almost green against the darkness of her gown. "Your . . . your hands are tied," she said. Her gaze rose to Lily's face and then moved quickly to Texas. "But why?"

"Because I like her that way," Texas said negligently. He strode farther into the room. "It looks about the same," he said, gesturing to the well-made, plain furniture, the whatnot in the corner that held odds and ends of silver and porcelain. "Except that chair. That chair must be new."

Jocelyn didn't answer him. She had a worried, uncertain look on her face. Her hands nervously smoothed her apron. Again, Lily thought how much Texas's half sister looked like him. Jocelyn was much more feminine, of course, and her hair was deep brown instead of Texas's dark blond, but there was something about her face, about her gestures, even about her voice, that made her a Sharpe through and through.

And Lily could have left it at that, if not for Jocelyn's eyes. Because Jocelyn's eyes were not Sharpe eyes. They had to be Annie's one legacy, and they haunted Lily now. In them she saw innocence and confusion and naiveté. And she could not remember ever seeing those things in a Sharpe before.

Never in Hank. Not even in Texas.

That innocence sharpened Lily's instincts. The desperation she had felt since Texas had first knocked on her boarding room door came back with a vengeance; her mouth watered at the unexpected opportunity. Her chance for escape was standing before her. Jocelyn Sharpe was malleable as pure gold. If she could somehow get her to untie these ropes . . .

Lily stepped forward, pasting on her best smile. "He's just teasing you," she said in an undertone. "It's nothing really. A game we play, that's all."

"I see," Jocelyn said, though it was clear from her expression that she didn't see at all. It didn't matter; Lily didn't give a damn what Jocelyn Sharpe saw or what she understood. There was a rifle in the corner, an old Sharps Carbine from the War, and Lily wanted it in her hands.

She smiled and glanced at her husband, who was studying the books in a messily loaded bookcase against the far wall. She held out her hands to Jocelyn.

"If you don't mind," she said in a low voice.

Not low enough. Texas spun on his heel. "Don't touch her," he ordered.

Jocelyn jumped. "But Christian—"

He winced.

"Christian?" Lily snorted in disbelief. "Don't tell me that's your name. *Christian?*"

"Of course it's his name," Jocelyn said. "Haven't you ever—"

"Be quiet, Josie," Texas said slowly.

"Christian," Lily said thoughtfully, rolling the name on her tongue, looking him steadily in the eyes. "Now what do you suppose your mama was thinking when she named you that? Was it a wish?"—she smiled challengingly—"Or a prayer?"

He was quiet. He held her eyes for what seemed like a long time, and then he turned away. She'd hurt him, she realized, and the thought made her feel satisfied in a mean, senseless sort of way.

"I don't understand," Jocelyn said slowly. "What's going on here? Christian?"

Texas had turned toward the window, bracing his hands on the windowsill to gaze outside. The battens were open, but there was no breeze moving his hair. He looked like a statue standing there, solid and implacable and dangerous with that gun riding his hip.

Dangerous, damn him. Fear made Lily's chest so tight she could barely breathe. It was so sharp she could taste it. He was her executioner—unless she could get out of these damn ropes.

"Where's Old Sam?" he asked.

"He's in the barn," Jocelyn said distractedly. "Christian, will you answer me, please? What is this all about?"

"It's better if you don't know," he said shortly.

Jocelyn frowned. "That's ridiculous. I insist that you tell me what's going on. I'm not a child. She's your wife, for goodness sake! Your *wife*. You can't just tie her up like a wild pig."

Texas turned from the window. His blue eyes were hard and cold, and he didn't take his gaze from Lily's face even though he directed his words to his sister. "You want the truth, Josie? All right, here it is: My beautiful wife there is a cold-blooded killer. She tried to shoot me yesterday, and she'll shoot you today without a second thought if you let her near a gun. Don't smile at her, don't look at her, don't talk to her. You're too damned naive. She'll wrap you around her little finger."

Lily raised a sarcastic brow. "You're so flattering, lover."

He glared at her.

Jocelyn frowned. "I can't believe that."

"Ask her," he offered tightly. "Go on."

Jocelyn hesitated, and then Lily felt those big hazel eyes focused on her. "That can't be true," Jocelyn said softly. "I don't understand why you would do such a thing. He's your husband."

Lily met her eyes and shrugged, deliberately nonchalant. "You've never been married, have you?"

From the window, Texas made a sound of disgust. "Look, Josie, just don't talk to her unless I'm around, all right?"

Jocelyn hesitated, and then she nodded slowly. "Yes. All right."

Lily leaned back, banging her shoulder too hard on

the rough-hewn wall, saying nothing as Jocelyn walked away. It didn't matter what Texas said, there was curiosity in Jocelyn Sharpe's beautiful eyes, and Lily could see it even if he couldn't. That knowledge brought with it a sense of relief. Depending on how fast Jocelyn could ride, and how long it would take her to get packed and ready, there was about a week between here and Lampasas. Plenty of time to win Josie's trust. Plenty of time to escape.

Escape. The word filled Lily's mouth with bitterness. For years, it had been the only thing on her mind. The lynching six months ago had only made her long for it more. The chance to keep the promise she'd made to herself twelve years ago, to leave behind the gang and the violence and the constant threat of death, to return to the life that had once been hers, the life her parents had given her.

She'd thought she had, too. She'd thought Denison would be a new place to start, a place where she wouldn't be "Lily the Cat," a place where sheriffs and marshals and men who wanted the notoriety of shooting a woman outlaw didn't exist.

But that, too, had been an illusion, as much of one as the last twelve years she'd spent with the gang. *Her family,* she thought derisively. What kind of family was it where love was only bought with violence? Where everyone was expendable except for Hank? Darling, wonderful, manipulative, selfish Hank.

She looked over at the man who had been her lover for the last five years, the man who had been manipulated into marrying her out of a misguided, foolish sense of love, and felt again the contempt she'd felt since his botched rescue. That contempt hadn't died in the last three weeks, and neither had her burning impatience, her desperation.

She had liked him once, she knew. Once, maybe, she had even loved him. There had been days, before the bank robbery, when her fear and bitterness hadn't pushed everything else away, when his reckless charm and those laughing blue eyes and that too-long hair still captivated her. But those times had grown fewer and farther between in the last months, and, in the light of Petry's threats, they had seemed so inconsequential, such a stupid reason to die.

She looked at him now, leaning against the windowsill, talking carelessly with his sister, and she hoped the feelings she'd had for him never returned. She felt a resentment and anger toward him that burned the way the ropes around her wrists burned, the way the hanging scar had branded her skin.

At least there was no point in pretending anymore. That was a relief, if nothing else. Texas wouldn't expect her in his bed, and she wouldn't have to make love to him and smile and talk as if she cared.

All that mattered now was getting Jocelyn to help her, and that would be easy enough. As beautiful as she was, Texas's sister was just an innocent farm girl. A few kind words, a pretend confidence or two would be all it took. Easy enough.

If she could just get Texas the hell out of the room.

She was just getting ready to join them when the door beside her opened, blasting the harsh Texas sunlight into the darkened cabin, along with a goodly amount of dust. A bent, old black man came into the room wrestling with a crate, a rifle slung over his back and a broad, floppy hat covering his face. Both Texas and Jocelyn looked up, and a smile plastered across Texas's face.

"Old Sam!" he said, coming forward. He took the crate easily from the old man and set it aside, then enveloped him in a hard hug. "Damn, it's good to see you."

When he pulled away, the man he called Old Sam was smiling. "Why, Mister Christian, I didn't know you was here already."

"Just rode up ten minutes ago."

"Well, look at you." The old man's dark eyes softened as he looked at Texas. "Miss Annie would be proud to see you, that's for sure."

"I'm sorry I didn't get the chance to see her again," Texas said gently. "I shouldn't have stayed away so long."

Lily couldn't stand it. Not the maudlin, sorrowful words nor their implication. Neither Old Sam nor Texas had even glanced her way, and she supposed she was hidden enough in the shadows to keep it that way, but something contrary inside her made her step forward.

"Don't cry, Christian," she taunted. "After all, you had a wife to consider. And I don't suppose Annie would have welcomed me." She held out her bound hands to Old Sam. "Hello there. I'm Lily."

She had not expected a welcome from Sam and she didn't get it. His eyes darkened; she saw contempt and dismissal when he looked at her. He'd been Hank's freedman forever, at least since she'd joined the gang. No doubt he already knew all about her. And he was that strange anomaly on the Texas prairies, a loyal servant who idolized his mistress.

But, though he ignored her outstretched hands, he nodded briefly to her, and his words were stiffly polite. "Nice to meet you, ma'am. Any wife of Mister Christian's is welcome here."

She lifted a brow. "How kind you are, Sam." She gave Texas a thin smile. "Why, he adores me already."

Texas frowned. "Go sit down, Lily. And shut the hell up."

She sauntered over to a well-padded, frayed chair, her boot steps sounding too loud on the packed mud floor, and sank into it. Then she threw him a challenging smile.

"Here I am, lover. I suppose you want to tie me to this, too?"

"Don't tempt me," he said quietly, turning back to Sam.

Immediately, Jocelyn was beside her, wringing her hands in her skirt, glancing at Texas as if she expected him to admonish her at any second, which he probably would, Lily figured.

"Would you like something to drink?" she asked. "It was a long ride, I know."

Lily didn't want to accept anything, but the thought of a drink of cool water reminded her of how parched she was, how miserable that ride from Denison had been. Her mouth suddenly seemed full of dust, her skin gritty and rough. She looked at Jocelyn's porcelain skin and felt immediately dirty and coarse.

The feeling was so overwhelming she couldn't bring herself to say anything, but it seemed she didn't need to. Jocelyn hurried off to fetch the water, and she was back in moments, holding a large, dripping metal cup. She stopped short in front of Lily, and the hesitation on her flawless face was almost painful to watch.

"Do you . . . need help?" she asked.

Lily shook her head and reached out. Water splashed over the side of the cup when she took it, spotting her boots, puddling on the floor. She held it tightly between her fingers, and the first cool taste of the water on her tongue had her gasping for more; she gulped it so fast it pooled, cold and uncomfortable, in her stomach.

She finished the last of it, took a great, gasping breath, and handed the cup back to Jocelyn.

"More?"

Lily shook her head. "Thanks."

Jocelyn stood there holding the cup in her hands, looking vaguely uncomfortable. Her eyes kept darting to Texas and Sam, whose conversation was a low murmur punctuated by laughter.

"Don't be so nervous," Lily said dryly. "I won't bite."

Jocelyn smiled weakly. "I'm sorry," she said softly. She leaned forward a little, and her tone took on the whispery murmur of secretiveness. "It's just that . . . I've never met a lady outlaw before. And I've heard so much about you. Did you really try to . . . shoot . . . Christian?"

Lily gave her a laconic look. "If he says I did, I must have."

Jocelyn straightened and took a step back. "You're quite dangerous, aren't you?"

Lily laughed shortly. "Not as dangerous as your pa, but I'm sure you know that."

"Is he really?" Jocelyn smiled, a considering look in her eyes. "I've heard that, but the only Pa I've ever known is a very kind and gentle man."

Lily nearly choked. "You mean Hank?"

Jocelyn's smile widened. "I suppose he might be different with me."

"I suppose so."

"But I think he hides things from me." Jocelyn leaned forward again, and her eyes sparkled with something that looked strangely like excitement. "Mama used to say his was no life for a lady, but I always thought it would be wonderful to go with Pa. To ride the prairies, to face danger every day. How exciting it must be! And for a woman, too! Don't you find it so?"

Lily stared at her, momentarily surprised by the realization that beautiful, poised Jocelyn Sharpe had a hankering for excitement, for adventure.

How interesting it was. How very interesting.

She wondered what Texas would say if he knew his sister longed to live the life of an outlaw. She thought about how appreciative Jocelyn would be if Lily taught her how.

The thought made her smile. She motioned to the cup in Jocelyn's hands. "Why don't you get me a little more water, Josie?" she said softly. "And I'll tell you all about it."

5

Dinner was ham hocks and beans and corn bread, a simple enough meal, but apparently another of Jocelyn's talents was cooking, because Lily hadn't tasted such ambrosia since . . . oh, hell, for a long, long time.

She ate at the table with the rest of them. Texas rarely let her out from under his eye, and he refused to untie her to eat despite his sister's protests.

"Get it through your head, Josie. She's dangerous. Got it?"

Josie nodded, but her sideways glance to Lily was uncertain, and she smiled when Lily caught her gaze.

Lily looked down at her bound wrists, felt the sting of the red, raw skin beneath the twisted bandanna, and told herself to be patient, to wait. Everything would happen soon enough. Soon enough.

She sat across the table from Old Sam, who pointedly ignored her despite her attempts to taunt him. It was as if she weren't there, she thought, and, in the darkness of the cabin, she felt invisible, felt as if she were disappearing in shadow. The lit oil lamp in the middle of the table only accentuated the feeling, and as dinner went on she began to feel suffocated by the dimness and the heavy smells of food, imprisoned by magazine pictures pinned to mud-chinked walls and roughly made, doily-covered tables tilting beside worn, overstuffed chairs.

She wasn't used to a home like this. Hell, not used to *any* home. The abandoned cabin where she and Texas stayed between jobs was nearly empty except for a bed and a few chairs and table and a stove. No one who came upon it would ever know anything about who lived there, and she preferred that to this house, where personality lived in every corner and every breath of air, too easy to trace, to find, to capture.

She grasped her fork between her bound hands and managed to angle it between her fingers, wishing she could eat on the broad porch in front, out in the open air, among the harnesses and tools and saddles gathered there against the cabin.

"It may take me a day or two to finish packing," Jocelyn said, splitting a piece of corn bread and spreading sorghum syrup onto it. "Sam says we can hitch the mule to that old cart out back and get most everything."

"Some of it, Miss Jocelyn," Sam amended quickly. "I don't know how kindly your pa would take to us bringin' a whole load of furniture."

Texas looked up. "We may have to send someone for the furniture."

"But I think I can—"

"Just a few things, Josie," he said quietly. "If it were just you and Old Sam, well, that'd be one thing. But you're riding with Lily and me, and that's something else."

Jocelyn frowned. "I don't understand."

"It's just another part of all that excitement I was telling you about," Lily interjected. She took her cup in her hands and lifted it in a salute to Texas before she took a sip. "We call it dodging the sheriff before he nails your butt to the wall."

She saw Texas's face tighten, saw him struggling to rein in his temper. He looked at Josie. "She was telling you things?" he asked, his voice deadly quiet. "I thought I told you not to talk to her."

"You said not to if you weren't around," Jocelyn pointed out delicately. "But you were standing right there, Christian. And it was nothing anyway. Lily was just telling me some stories."

He glanced at Lily, and, if she hadn't known him better, she would have been chilled to the bone by his cold stare. "That's all?"

She shrugged. "That's all, lover."

"Stories about what?"

"About your famous exploits, of course," she said. "Though, off the top of my head, I could only come up with two. Come to think of it, only one was really an exploit."

His fingers tightened around his fork. She saw the whitening of his knuckles and the quick stiffening of his jaw.

At the end of the table, Jocelyn laughed. "Oh, Christian, we were just joking. What happened to your sense of humor? Lily was only answering some of my questions about you and Pa. Mama never told me anything. And your life, why, it sounds so exciting!" She put down her fork and leaned forward, her face shining. "I declare, it makes me want to rob a stage myself."

Texas threw a quick look at Lily, one she couldn't interpret, and then he said, "It's not that romantic, Josie."

"I think you're just trying to dissuade me," Jocelyn said. "I read the paper every month or so, and Mama

had a whole drawer of clippings about you and Pa.
When you robbed the Overland Mail, they just went
on and on about what heroes you were, stealing from
those carpetbaggers, fighting the government and
all."

The hero worship in Jocelyn's eyes would have been
uncomfortable if not for the opportunity that lay there,
as well. Lily tried to think about that, about how easy it
was going to be to use her, and not about the Southern
Overland Mail robbery. Not about the capture that had
almost cost her life.

Texas laughed shortly, and Lily knew by the bitterness in his tone that he was remembering it, too. "Yeah,
we were heroes, all right."

"Well, *I* think you were," Jocelyn said. "And there are
other people in town who think the same thing." She got
up from the table, collecting empty plates, setting them
on a shelf by the washtub in the corner. "In fact,
Christian, I was thinking perhaps you wouldn't mind
going into Fort Griffin with me and meeting a few people before we go. Everyone's heard so much about you,
and it's been forever since you've—"

"No."

Josie turned, surprise on her face. "No?"

Texas didn't look up. He was staring down into his
coffee, his blond hair falling forward, hiding his expression. "I don't think it'd be a good idea, Josie."

"Why not? It would only take an hour or so. Surely
we've got time."

"Maybe Mister Christian just don't want to go," Sam
put in quietly.

Lily cocked a brow. "Maybe," she needled softly,
"he's a coward."

He shook back his hair and looked up. "Lily," he
said slowly. "Shut the hell up before I gag you."

"Please, Christian!"

"Hell." The curse was an explosion of sound. He scraped his chair back so hard and so quickly it tipped on its legs and clattered against a small table loaded with porcelain dishes. He barely gave it a look. He was on his feet in seconds, out the door so fast it screeched on its hinges and thudded shut behind him.

Lily watched him go. "Temper, temper," she murmured wryly.

Jocelyn sat down again at the table, her cheeks flushed, her hands playing nervously with a fork. "He and Pa used to have these awful fights, and he'd take off and ride, oh, for hours sometimes."

"Yeah," Lily said. "He still does that. Though it's not just horses he tortures these days."

Jocelyn looked up quickly. "What do you mean?"

From across the table, Old Sam sighed loudly. "Peggy still needs milkin', Miss Jocelyn," he said. "She's overdue."

Lily glanced up at him. He was watching her with a strange glance, but she caught the warning within it, and the silent threat. She smiled mockingly back at him, unabashed. She'd been threatened by the best. No old servant was going to tell her what to do or what to say.

But before she could turn back to Josie, Texas's sister rose. "Of course, you're right, Sam," she said. "Maybe I can find Christian out there and calm him down."

Lily snorted. "Good luck."

"You do that," Old Sam said. "I'll watch her."

There was no mistaking who he meant by *her*. The word was so heavy with contempt it nearly sank through the floor. Jocelyn didn't seem to hear it, though. She grabbed the metal pail by the door and nodded.

"All right then. I'll be back."

The room seemed to grow even darker when she was gone. Lily rested her elbows on the table and leaned forward.

"You don't like me much, do you, Sam?"

His deep brown eyes bored into hers. "I don't like you at all."

She laughed shortly. "Now, why is that, I wonder? I never met you before, I'm sure of that. I never hurt you to my recollection. Never killed a black man, or woman, so I don't suppose you're missing any relatives on account of me."

He didn't say anything for a moment. He took up his coffee cup, but he didn't drink from it, and he never took his gaze from her face.

"Miz Annie."

It was all he said, just those two words, but those words were deep and quiet and full of dignity. And they filled her with sudden hot anger. *Miz Annie. Miz Annie.* How often had she heard those words, said just that way?

Too often. Too damned often.

Lily scooted back the bench violently, unable to keep her cool or control herself, furious that this simple man had got the best of her so easily. If she'd had a gun she would have threatened him with it, but, as it was, her throat was tight and her fingers felt numb and she wanted to get as far away from him as she could. Him and that damn dark gaze.

"You can't run from it, Miss Lily the Cat," Sam said quietly, her nickname singsong and insulting. "You can't go far enough."

No, not far enough. Not today. But for now the window was here, and beyond it the darkening prairie, and the scent of the dusty, hot Texas air cooling into the balm of evening.

For now. But she dreamed of later, when she was far away and free, when there was nothing left to fear. Then, she'd take her revenge on the little stooped man sitting at the table.

And put this whole damned life behind her for good.

His temper was forgotten by the time Texas came back inside; the anger that had driven him to walk to the back of the barn and stay there had left him. It wouldn't have taken so long to calm down if he'd been able to ride, or even to walk, but his hip was burning and he ached all over, and sitting on the empty keg behind the lean-to was about the most he could do. And it was soothing enough, sitting with the chickens scratching at his feet, listening to the evening sounds and Josie's quiet humming as she milked the cow, the clank of the bucket and the slosh of milk.

In the quiet, he'd even forgotten Lily.

There'd been a moment when he'd cursed himself for leaving her with Josie in the cabin, before he heard his half sister's unmistakable step in the barn. Then he'd realized Old Sam was with Lily, and Sam would guard her as well as Texas could. For the moment, it was a relief to trust her to someone else, to relax and not worry about a knife in his ribs or her equally sharp words.

He paused outside the front door of the cabin, taking one last, deep breath, nearly choking when his lung protested, and wished they were on the road again. He felt tightly strung. The pain in his soul was pricking, itching beneath his skin, making his fingers twitch. He wanted to move on, into the mindless nothingness of the ride. He wanted things taken care of so he could get back to Lampasas and the rest of the gang. Back to where things were always the same, where he could count on Schofield's foul mouth and Bobby's brow-wrinkling worry and his father's ceaseless spouting of Shakespeare.

But even the thought of the gang wasn't comforting, and Texas wondered if maybe he should ride into the Flat to try his hand at a game of faro. The Beehive was down there. He remembered his father telling him about the saloon, remembered him reciting the rhyme scrawled on the sign outside. What was it again? Ah, yes. "Within the hive, we are alive; Good whiskey makes us funny; Get your horse tied, come inside; And taste the flavor of our honey."

Texas smiled and glanced beyond the yard, back toward the road that didn't become a road until much closer to Fort Griffin. Whiskey sounded good, too, so good his mouth watered at the thought of it.

But then he heard Josie's voice inside, and Sam's low-pitched answer, and Texas turned back to the cabin. He was too edgy to go to the Flat tonight. He didn't have the patience for cards, and he knew from experience that whiskey wouldn't dull the edge; it would only make him meaner.

No, it was better to go inside and talk and laugh with Josie and Sam, to ignore Lily as much as he could, to find some measure of peace in innocent company.

He ran a hand through his hair and opened the door.

The noises of the nightly routine were somehow soothing. Jocelyn was at the washtub, scrubbing dishes, her steady hum a mindless, constant rhythm punctuated by the clicks of the rifle Sam cleaned at the table.

Only Lily was unoccupied. She leaned against the windowsill, her bound hands dangling in front of her, her face turned so he could see her profile as she stared outside. It reminded him for a moment of the boardinghouse where he'd found her, the way she'd stood watching at that window, too, just that way.

He barely had time to register the thought before she turned to look him full in the face, a bitter smile curving her lips.

"Back from wandering the earth, cowboy?"

He ignored her. Deliberately, he turned away and sank into the nearest chair, leaning into its padded depths and balancing his booted foot on the crooked footstool beside it. It rocked beneath his weight.

"Pa make this?" he asked.

Josie looked over her shoulder. "Why, yes. How did you know?"

He kicked at the stool with his boot. "I can tell. Pa's never known shit about carpentry. There's not a straight edge in this place."

At the table, Sam chuckled. "Ain't that the truth."

"Mama never seemed to mind," Josie said. She pulled her hands from the soapy water and shook them for a moment before she dried them on her apron. "I think she was just happy to keep him around the house, whatever it took."

"I imagine so," Texas said. He stole a glance at Lily, but she was expressionless, still staring out the window as if she hadn't heard a word. Such toughness, such pure ice. Not an emotion in place, nothing in her eyes. But he knew she had to be feeling something.

She was so damn good it scared him.

He turned away quickly, before he could forget that he didn't give a damn what she thought or felt, and glanced up to find Old Sam watching him carefully. Suddenly, a game of cards didn't seem like such a bad idea.

Texas forced a grin. "Got any cards?" he asked.

Old Sam *tsked* in mock dismay. "Have we got cards? Of course we got cards."

"How about you and me wrap ourselves around a game of poker?"

Josie stacked the last of the dishes. "Just you two? That's not fair." She swooped to the table and sat down, spreading her skirts and tossing her head like the best female dealers in Dodge City. "I think you should ask us ladies if we'd like to play. I know I would."

"You know how to play poker?"

She gave him an arch look. "I have many talents, brother. And yes, I can play. Pa taught me a few years ago."

Texas eased from the chair and strode over to the table. "All right, then. Far be it for me to bar a pretty lady from the game."

"You're only saying that because you think I'll lose."

He leaned close and grinned. "Honey, I'm betting you'll lose."

Jocelyn flushed and reached for a jar full of spare buttons. "We can play with these," she said steadily. "And Sam, you tell him I can play with the best! I've even beat Pa a time or two."

"She's mighty good," Sam agreed. "You'd best prepare yourself for a battle, Mister Christian."

"We'll see about that." Texas sat down and leaned back in the chair at the head of the table, forcing himself to relax, to enjoy his sister's company. "Where're those cards?"

Old Sam put the rifle aside and got to his feet, heading for the wooden desk that sat in the cramped corner at the back of the room. He rummaged around for a few moments and then came back with a well-worn deck.

"Those marked?" Texas teased.

Josie looked past him, toward the window. "Lily! Lily, come on over and join us, won't you?"

Sam set the deck in front of him. Texas took it into his hands, thumbing through the softened cards. "Leave her be," he said quietly, his good humor, or the pretense of it, anyway, melting away. "She's fine where she is."

Josie ignored him. "Lily," she insisted. "Come over here. Don't tell me you don't know how to play poker."

"I know how," Lily said. Her voice was quiet, steady.

"Then join us, please. I'd like you to."

He had never before realized how relentless his half sister could be. It had to be Pa's legacy; God knew it wasn't Annie's. His father's second wife had been as malleable and acquiescent as clay.

He didn't have to hear Lily's steps to know she was coming over to the table. He felt her long before he heard her, felt the chill spreading over his shoulders and down his back, felt it sharpening its blade on his heart.

She pulled out the rough bench with her boot and sat down, her hands on her lap, her brown eyes icy and challenging, her lips set.

"So, here I am," she said. "Deal the cards."

His pleasure in the game evaporated, though Texas kept the smile on his face. Josie's excited expression was enough to justify the pretense. He shuffled through the cards one last time and shoved them over to Old Sam to cut, and then Texas dealt them with a practiced flick of his wrist. "Eights and aces wild."

He tried not to look at her, but he found himself glancing at Lily despite himself, watching the awkward way she grabbed at the cards, sliding them facedown to the edge of the table and gathering them clumsily into her bound hands. She turned the cards toward her, kept them tightly hidden against his eyes.

She looked up, catching his gaze. "Why don't you just ask to see my cards, Texas?"

He grinned evilly back at her. "If I wanted to see your cards, baby, I'd take them from you."

At the other end of the table, Josie sighed loudly. "Please, Christian, stop tormenting Lily."

He frowned at his sister. "Why the hell do you always take her side?"

"What am I supposed to do? She's obviously your prisoner." Josie's hazel eyes flashed. "You've got her practically hog-tied."

"She tried to kill me."

"So you say."

Texas laughed shortly and sat back in his chair. "You don't believe me?"

Josie gave him a disgusted look. "Well, really, Christian, don't you think you could be exaggerating just a little? Why, she's just a woman. She hardly looks big enough to kill you."

Lily chuckled. "She has a point, lover."

"Shut up."

"You could keep her still with one hand," Josie went on. Idly, she shifted a card from one spot to another. "Seems to me it'd be easy enough to—"

"Josie, you don't know what the fuck you're talking about."

"Christian!"

He threw down his cards. "Jesus."

"I think we should untie her." Josie smiled.

Texas felt a headache starting behind his eyes. "I'm not going to untie her," he said tightly. "And I better not catch you trying, either."

"But it just seems so unfair."

"You'd best watch it, Miss Josie." Old Sam's voice boomed through the room, though he hadn't raised it at all. "You listen to Mister Christian on this one."

Texas squeezed his eyes shut for a moment in relief.

Josie frowned. She threw an apologetic look at Lily, who shrugged nonchalantly and looked down at her cards. Jocelyn sighed and focused her attention on her own hand.

Texas caught Old Sam's gaze and nodded tersely. At least Old Sam knew how dangerous Lily was, and Jocelyn listened to him. He hoped it was enough.

He looked at his wife. She was scrutinizing her cards as if she saw the future there. Hair had escaped from her braid to dangle around her face, her brow was prettily furrowed in concentration, and the fine bones of her cheeks, of her jaw, were accentuated by the shadows. In this light, she seemed everything Josie thought she was. A mere woman. Slender and delicate. Easily overcome. Once, perhaps, she had been those things. Certainly once she had been innocent. But between his father and himself, they'd changed that. They'd created a woman as relentless as the weather, as accommodating as a whore. As dangerous as a rattlesnake.

For a moment, a brief, yearning second, he wanted his illusions again. He wished he could look at her and see only the innocent girl who had idolized him.

Too late, the voice inside him taunted. *Too damn late.*

"I'll take two," Josie said, pushing her discards toward him.

His fingers tightened. He forced his gaze away from Lily, smiled at his sister, and dealt her two cards in return.

"I'm good," Lily said, fanning her cards.

He nearly laughed at the irony of her words.

It was late when they finally got to bed. Sam customarily slept in the lean-to, so Texas and Lily ended up in the covered dog run. It had been a long time since the roof was mended—another one of Pa's nontalents—and the moonlight shone through the cracks in the shingles, cold and blue. The chill night wind whistled from one open end of the porch to the other.

Texas pushed at the saddlebags cushioning his head and tried to get comfortable. It was an impossible task. He was restless from a night of pretending to be companionable, of laughing at his sister's jokes and trying to ignore the woman who was now curled at his side. He wished now he had gone down to the Flat. Maybe bought a whore. A bordello's bed, with its stale smells of perfume and sweat, would have been preferable to this hell. Preferable to feeling Lily beside him and knowing that two days ago they'd made love and wishing despite himself that they could do it again. He didn't know how he could still want her body, as disappointed as he was in her soul, but then he decided maybe it wasn't that so much as it was that she was pressed into him, warm and soft and acquiescent in sleep, and this way she reminded him of the girl she'd been.

He closed his eyes, breathing deeply of the Texas night, of air that was clean of dust and smelled of grass and dirt and woman. In her sleep, Lily murmured and eased away, and his side was cold where she'd been.

The chill moved through him, into his blood and his heart. It seemed to seep into his very soul. He remembered a girl, a laughing, teasing girl, a girl with a ready smile and a readier wit. He remembered curling his arms around her, helping her steady a gun, whispering in her ear, *"Breathe in, that's it. All the way into your lungs. Now, let it out when you pull the trigger. Slow. That's the way, baby. Take it slow."*

He turned and looked at her. Her braid trailed over

the edge of the bedroll, her breathing was steady and rhythmic, a lullaby of sound. The murmur of it carried deep into his soul, a part of himself he could not deny, as much as he wanted to. Hell, he'd loved her since she was twelve years old. He'd thought they would be together forever.

He fell onto his back again and stared up at the crack in the roof, at the pale moonlight and the diamond chips of stars. In the distance, he heard a coyote, an answering howl. He heard the rustling of the straw mattress in the lean-to and smelled the smoke trembling from the chimney. Life was everywhere tonight. In the skies, in the ground, in the little house.

Too bad there was none inside of him.

6

The next morning, Lily sat with Josie on the broad porch and watched Texas and Old Sam fasten down the farm. Sam was readying the cow and penning the chickens to take to a nearby farm until Hank could send someone for them. The pigs they would just let run wild—they did mostly anyway—and hope they'd be able to catch one or two when someone came back.

Jocelyn was shelling beans, and they looked to be poor ones, too, their pods withered and striated with webbed cracks. But Josie kept on, twisting at the hardened shells until the beans clattered into the old metal pie tin she held on her lap.

"Not a good year for farming," she murmured, shaking her head slowly.

Lily studied a centipede crawling between the roughened boards at her feet. "Yeah?"

"What the grasshoppers didn't get, the drought did. I'll be lucky if I end up with a bushel of sweet potatoes."

"Good thing you're on your way to San Antonio then."

Josie sighed. Her hands stilled and her gaze went to Texas, who squatted at the far end of the porch mending a crate for the chickens. "I suppose so," she said. She looked abruptly at Lily. "Have you ever been there?"

"San Antonio?" Lily shrugged. "Once or twice, I guess."

"What's it like?"

Lily tried to remember San Antonio, but the only things she could recall were the banks and the town square and the churches. "They have some nice churches. A lot of churches."

"Oh." Jocelyn smiled gently. "No wonder Pa wants to send me there. He's got too much religion for his own good."

Lily nearly fell off her chair. "Hank?"

"When I was a little girl, he used to read to me from the Bible every night. And he never let Mama do a bit of work on the Sabbath. Not once."

Lily just stared. Hank Sharpe a God-fearing man? The thought left her speechless; she couldn't begin to imagine it.

"I'm afraid I disappointed him," Jocelyn went on. "I was never as close to God as he wanted me to be. I used to beg him to tell me about his adventures instead." She smiled a small, sad smile. "I suppose he's locking me up in San Antonio to make sure I learn my lesson."

"Yeah, well, Hank's good at teaching lessons, that's for sure," Lily said.

"I don't mind it, really I don't. I know he thinks it's best for me. It's just that . . . " Jocelyn sighed again. "I'll practically be a prisoner there, you know. I'll never have the chance to really live. Not the way you do."

Lily snorted and held out her hands. "This is living, all right."

"Oh, Lily, you know what I mean. I would love to be a part of the gang. Just once. I know Pa wanted to protect me, but sometimes it's—well, it's stifling, if you must know."

"Stifling." Lily stared off into the prairie, into the sky that stretched cloudless to the horizon. It seemed a perfect life to her, one full of safety and peace. The kind of life she dreamed about. She closed her eyes for a moment, forgetting Jocelyn's silly romanticism, and listened to the unfamiliar sounds of the men working nearby. "I don't know, Josie. Seems like a pretty good life to me."

Josie laughed disbelievingly. "You mean this? Feeding chickens and milking cows? Working every day until you could almost die for a change?"

"It's better than some things."

"Maybe. But you can't tell me *you'd* trade what you have for it. Riding the prairies, camping beneath the stars, gambling in some old saloon."

"Gambling?" Lily asked.

Josie took a pod between her slender, work-roughened fingers and twisted. "Pa used to go into the Flat every now and then to play faro. I always thought it seemed like such fun."

"It's not what you think."

"No?" Josie leaned forward, her eyes shining. "You mean you know? You've gone into gambling saloons yourself?"

"Sure." Lily leaned back in her chair and wondered how the hell she was going to get Jocelyn Sharpe to shut up and untie the ropes around her wrists.

Jocelyn paused. "But you're a woman."

"So?"

Another pause. Then, "Christian!"

Lily looked over to see Texas twist around as if he'd

been shot, throwing aside the cage and half rising to his feet in one fluid motion, his hand going reflexively to his gun, his gaze ricocheting to her. Lily saw the half second it took him to note that she was still bound, saw the swift calculation in his face before he relaxed. His hand eased off the hilt of the Colt, but his gaze remained wary.

"Jesus," he said, inhaling deeply. He took off his hat and ran a hand through his sun-streaked hair. "What is it, Josie?"

"Could you come here a moment? I'd like to ask you something."

Slowly, he limped over to them, thinly veiled impatience in his eyes.

"What is it?"

"Lily and I were just talking."

His glance shifted to Lily. "More stories?"

She smiled her most saccharine smile. "Just trying to make you look good, lover."

Jocelyn sighed loudly. "And I've decided I'd like to go into the Flat and play faro."

Texas's face tightened. His eyes narrowed as he looked at Lily. "Dammit, Lily,"

"I had nothing to do with this one."

"Now, why don't I believe you?"

"Maybe because you're a suspicious son of a bitch."

"It was my idea, Christian," Josie put in quickly.

He turned on his heel. "The Flat's no place for a lady."

"But Lily says she's been to saloons before."

He didn't bother to turn around. "Like I said."

"Christian."

He stopped, swiveling slowly back again to face Jocelyn. His hat brim shaded his face. Lily couldn't read his eyes.

"Please," Josie pleaded prettily. "You know what Pa'll do once we get to San Antonio. He'll lock me up like a nun in a convent. I just want to see a little of life before that happens. Just a game of faro, brother. Why, it would only be for an hour or so. And, if you go with me, I'll be perfectly safe."

His hesitation was almost amusing, especially because Lily knew what his decision would be. Josie was a lady, as he'd said, and he wouldn't be able to see beyond that. He wouldn't be able to accept the thought of his sister in a seedy, dirty saloon, much less the reality.

Lily thought of the gambling halls she'd been into in her life. Places filled with overly perfumed whores and men who hadn't bathed in weeks, rotgut whiskey and straw-and-mud-covered floors. There was nothing romantic about them unless you'd been on the road for three weeks without eating a hot meal or feeling the sting of liquor in your throat. Then, she supposed, they were romantic enough. If nothing else, they were full of talk and people and . . . freedom.

Lily stared down at her wrists, feeling a rush of adrenaline that made her palms sweat. The Flat. It might be Josie's gambling paradise, but it could be Lily's chance for escape. There were men there who would do whatever she asked. A simpering smile, the promise of a grope behind closed doors, hell, there were a hundred ways to get what she wanted. And all it took was one man. One stupid, drunken fool, and she'd be free.

"No, Josie," Texas said finally, grinding Lily's momentary fancies to dust. There was a strict finality in his tone as he made his way painfully back across the porch, an echoing resonance in the hollow, erratic thud of his footsteps. He walked by the chicken cage, picking it up without stopping, and kept going out to what was left of a split-rail fence. It was the farthest from Lily he'd been the whole morning.

Lily's jaw tightened. She knew that voice. He was not going to change his mind, at least not any time soon. She glanced at Texas's sister, whose whole bearing seemed to slump at her brother's refusal, and thought of how easy it would be to win her confidence now, in the light of her disappointment.

"He's not going to change his mind, is he?" Josie asked.

Lily shook her head. "No."

"He didn't used to be such a . . . such a—"

"Stick-in-the-mud?" Lily provided.

Josie laughed breathlessly. "Yes. Yes, that's it exactly."

"I've been thinking the same thing."

"I remember once, when he and Pa were in town, and Christian helped me sneak off to this dance in Fort Griffin. We danced all night, until dawn. He was flirting with the girls, and I had my pick of soldiers." Josie closed her eyes, obviously lost in the memory. "Pa threatened to whip us both something fierce, of course. But Christian just laughed in his face and rode away." She opened her eyes again, staring off into the distance as if she were seeing the scene again before her. "I wish he was still like that."

There was something sad about the words. Sad and, hell, so innocent. How easily Josie let things show. Such bare emotions she had. It made Lily uncomfortable. It was too easy, taking advantage of her. Josie was so damned trusting. Like some little kid. Lily looked away, shading her eyes the best she could with her bound hands, squinting against the sun and the gritty wind, liking the harshness better than talk or questions, wishing for just the sound of the prairie, for quiet to last another minute, another hour.

"You know, Pa didn't come to the funeral."

Josie's voice was so soft, so wistful, it seemed to come from the far side of a dream. Lily lowered her hands. Texas's sister was staring into the distance, her fingers curled around a bean.

"What?"

Josie blinked and turned to look at her. "I thought, well, I imagined Pa would come for Mama's funeral, but he didn't show up, and then he sent you and Christian alone, and I wondered, was he so busy—"

"Texas didn't tell you?"

"Tell me what?"

Lily looked back at the field, at Texas, who was silhouetted against the sun. She didn't know why he hadn't told his sister that their father was in jail, or why Hank hadn't bothered to mention it in his letter, and it suddenly made her angry. Angry that they protected the girl so much. Angry that Josie didn't know enough to be wary of her, to be wary of anyone. She was everything Lily wasn't: trusting and generous, friendly and open. She was a woman who would fall headlong into any trap Lily laid for her, a woman so innocent she was asking to be hurt by the world.

Hank had created her as much as he'd created Lily. His perfect innocent. He'd given Jocelyn a warm home, a loving family, a safe refuge—all the things he'd deliberately kept from Lily. Everything he'd taken away from her.

Lily had the sudden, fierce urge to shatter Josie's illusions, to see the starkness of horror in those big hazel eyes, to be the devil to Josie's angel. Lily leaned forward, resting her hands between her canvas-covered legs. "Hank's in jail," she said deliberately.

Josie gasped, paling. "What?"

"You heard me." Lily heard the meanness in her voice and didn't care. "He's in jail."

"But—but I don't understand."

"What's to understand? Jail is jail."

"But why?"

"You mean to tell me you didn't read it in the newspapers? We must be losing our touch." She felt a small surge of satisfaction when she saw the way Josie faltered.

"I didn't read anything," she said in a hushed voice.

"We robbed the Lampasas bank," Lily told her. "Hank and Bobby were caught."

"My God." Josie's voice was a hush of sound. She dropped the bean, her fingers whitening on the rim of the pie tin. "How long—how long has he been there?"

Lily shrugged. "About three weeks, give or take a day."

"Three weeks? Oh, Lord." Josie paled and grabbed Lily's arm, fingers squeezing tight. "Will they hang him? Is he in danger? Tell me he's not in danger."

"Is who in danger?" It was Texas's voice. Lily started. She swung around to see him standing by the porch, his booted foot resting on the edge. He wiped the back of his forearm across his face.

Damn, he was quiet. And fast. Moments ago, he'd been clear out by that old fence, seemingly oblivious to them. Seemingly, Lily reminded herself. She saw the scrutiny in his eyes now and realized he'd been aware of them the entire time, had been watching her.

She narrowed her eyes. "We were just talking about your illustrious pa," she said, not even attempting to keep the bitterness from her voice. "Poor Josie didn't know he was in jail. She thought he'd missed her mama's funeral on purpose."

He stiffened. Lily saw the quick flare of anger in his eyes. Then he looked at his sister. "He wouldn't have missed it, Josie," he said quietly. "He was just . . . detained."

"Lily said he was in jail."

"That's just a temporary thing."

Josie stiffened. "What do you mean, temporary? They've let him go?"

Texas paused. "Not exactly."

"Not exactly?" Jocelyn's voice rose slightly. She put down the tin so roughly beans clattered over the side. "We have to go. Now." She rose abruptly to her feet. "Perhaps I can talk to the judge. Maybe I can—"

Texas stepped forward. He grabbed Josie's shoulder, quieting her with just a touch. "He'll be fine, Josie," he said.

Wildly, she looked at Lily. "Is that the truth?"

Lily shrugged. "They won't hang him," she said. "Not for a while anyway."

Josie's breath expelled in a gush of sound. She jerked from Texas's hold. "I don't understand you two," she said. "We should be there, helping him. You're acting like it doesn't matter, like you don't even care."

"Josie." Texas reached out.

She spun away. "Don't you placate me," she said. "Don't you dare. I've already lost my mother; I won't lose my father, too."

Before either of them could say a word, she ran into the house. The door cracked shut behind her, vibrating against the walls, knocking loose clods of chinked mud to scatter across the porch.

Texas glared at Lily. His fingers curled around the gun, an impatient caress, and he leaned close, so close she felt the heat of his breath against her face. "Do something like that again, Lily, and I'll make sure you regret it," he said. His voice was dangerously soft.

"You keep promising that," she goaded. "When are you going to live up to it?"

"Don't tempt me." He backed away, straightening. He looked at the closed door of the house, his breath escaping in a heavy sigh. "Christ. What the hell am I going to say to her now?"

"Try promising her something."

"Like what?"

"Like the Flat." She smiled at him, feeling a sharp sense of satisfaction when he frowned. "She wants to gamble, Christian. Let the girl gamble."

After the bright daylight, the inside of the cabin seemed painfully dark, the air close and heavy. He stood there for a moment, shutting the door slowly behind him, letting his eyes become accustomed to the dimness, cooling his impatience. He hated this kind of thing, soothing when he was too angry to soothe, reassuring when there was nothing comforting to say. It was one of those things that Pa was good at and Texas had never got right. He was used to charming his way out of scrapes, a pretty smile, a teasing word, but as far as comfort went, hell, he could comfort cattle during a long night, but that was the extent of it. And he knew instinctively that Jocelyn wouldn't be that easy.

Damn Lily anyway.

He searched the shadows for his sister and found her slamming around the stove, her back toward him, her shoulders stiff. Texas rubbed his jaw, pushed back his hat, and stepped farther into the room.

"Josie," he began.

She didn't answer.

"Josie, please."

She swung around then, clutching a frying pan in her hands, holding it as if she meant to use it as a weapon.

"Don't you dare try to charm your way out of this one," she said, her voice trembling.

He held up his hands. "All right, all right, Josie. Just calm down."

"You didn't tell me Pa was in jail. Even he didn't tell me."

"There was no reason for you to know."

"I'm his daughter!"

"Ah, hell, Josie." Texas sighed. "There was nothing to tell. We've been caught a dozen times. Pa's been in jail before."

She frowned. The frying pan lowered slightly. "He has?"

"Yeah. Four times, maybe five. It's never meant shi— anything."

Her frown deepened.

"If I know Pa, he's already out. Schofield was talking about springing him three weeks ago."

"Springing him?"

"Helping him escape," Texas explained impatiently. "Pa's escaped the law too many times. No jail in Lampasas is going to hold him long."

"You're not lying to me?"

"Do you think I would be here if I thought he was in real trouble?"

The frying pan lowered. She set it on the edge of the stove and crossed her arms over her breasts. "How did he let it happen? Getting captured, I mean. Lily said it was . . . a bank robbery."

The words made his insides twist. "Yeah," he said. "It was a bank robbery."

"But something went wrong?"

"You could say that." He moved to the table, the only thing between them, and leaned against it to support his aching hip.

"Is that how you were wounded?"

He looked at her in surprise. "Did Lily tell you that?"

She shook her head. "You've been limping since you arrived. It's hard not to notice. I thought maybe—"

"I was shot," he said briefly. "In the hip and the chest."

She made an involuntary move toward him, one he stopped with a raised palm.

"It's all right. I've had enough of nurses. Thanks just the same."

"Are you in pain?"

His jaw tightened. "Not anymore."

She didn't believe him, he knew, and he didn't care. He watched as she came to the table, as she leaned into it, her palms flat against the wood.

"I'm sorry for what I said out there," she said quietly. "I was wrong, I know. It's just that I was . . . upset."

He nodded.

She looked up at him. "I feel so isolated here sometimes, Christian. Especially since Mama died." She turned away briefly, and when she looked back at him her hazel eyes were wide and full of pain. "But even before that, I used to wonder what you all were doing. I used to steal the newspaper from Mama whenever she wasn't looking in the hopes that I might see something about you and Pa and Lily. And if there wasn't anything, I'd make up stories instead." She laughed slightly. "It was silly, I know. But it was what I did."

"You don't have to explain."

"But I do. I do. Because I want you to understand. Pa wants me to go to San Antonio and get married and have a family, and I'm happy enough to do that. I *am*." She leaned forward, and there was an avariciousness in her expression, an urgency he found startling and strangely compelling. "But I want to live first. I want to know if the stories are true."

"Josie—"

"Don't protect me, Christian. Just for a day, let me see what life with you and Lily is like. Just once, and I'll be happy. I promise."

His voice felt tight, forced from his throat. "You'll see too much of it anyway."

Her fingers clutched the edge of the table. "Please, Christian."

He tried to reach inside himself, to pull up an engaging smile, to tease her out of it. But he had no reserves left; the last few days had stolen them from him. He felt as if he were drowning, as if things were crowding up against him too fast, waters covering his head, and he had the odd sense that it was all due to Lily, even though it was his sister staring at him with that pleading look on her face, his sister begging him, and there was nothing about her that was like Lily. Nothing at all.

His lung was aching. Every breath felt too shallow.

"Josie," he tried. "I don't think it would be a good idea."

She smiled at him. "Just a game of faro, Christian," she said. "What could it hurt?"

What could it hurt?

He didn't want to think about the answer to that question, and so he gave in. Crumbled like gypsum beneath a heavy heel.

"All right then," he said heavily. "All right."

7

They rode for Fort Griffin late the next afternoon. The morning had been spent taking the animals to another farm and packing Josie's things. They shoved the porcelain into crates to store in the lean-to, but they took most of the silver with them. Josie clucked anxiously over it as she stowed it in her saddlebags, and Texas had watched her impatiently.

All he really wanted was for her to hurry. He wanted to get moving again. He needed to get moving. By the time they finally started out, leaving the cabin unlocked for wanderers who might need shelter, Texas's muscles were so tight they shrieked with pain when he got on his horse.

When the house was just a speck in the distance, he inhaled deeply, pulling the burned-grass smell of the prairies fully into his lungs, ignoring the nagging sharpness of pain. Yesterday's apprehension had turned into an urgent need for the smoky haze of a saloon and the rough heat of whiskey.

His fingers clenched spasmodically on the reins. Tension stiffened his spine. Though it was only a few hours, it seemed an eternity before the walls of Fort

Griffin came into view. Over the last miles, the road had grown more and more crowded, heavy with cavalrymen and buffalo hunters and wagons laden with dour-faced men and drawn women. The hunters he ignored, the women he grinned at, and the soldiers . . . the soldiers he looked away from, wondering if any of them recognized him from his days as a Confederate guerilla, wondering if they remembered Sharpe's Raiders at all or if they hated him as much as he'd once hated the Union.

"Should we get a room, Mr. Christian?" Old Sam asked from behind.

Slowly, Texas turned in the saddle to look at him. "Yeah," he said. He glanced at Lily. "We'll need one."

She met his gaze, squinting at him from beneath the shadow of her hat brim. "Planning to tie me to the bed while you're looking for a good time?" she asked.

"And deprive myself of your charming company?" He turned away. "I don't think so."

Just the sound of her voice sharpened the edge on his mood. He pressed his horse to a faster pace, not slowing until they reached the narrow, dust-filled streets of the makeshift boomtown shadowed by the walls of Fort Griffin. The Flat.

He looked over his shoulder, watching Lily's deceptively casual gaze, her expressionless face, and he wished he could just tie to her to the bed, as she'd suggested. Tie her and leave her and go off by himself to gamble and drink until the moon was falling again in the sky and his emotions weren't so damned raw. But privacy was a luxury in these places. Most of the hotels around here consisted of common rooms, one for the men and one for the women, and an instruction to "Lay where you can."

Lily would stay a prisoner for maybe fifteen minutes in a place like that, about as long as it would take her to enlist the sympathy of some poor, misguided woman.

She'd be out the window and gunning for him in no time at all. No, it was better to keep her close by, where he could at least make sure she wasn't trying to beguile some idiot into untying her wrists.

Old Sam stopped. "Mr. Sharpe used to talk about this place," he said, gesturing to the building they had almost ridden by.

Texas drew back on the reins and looked over. The sign hanging from the splitting green lumber of the narrow balcony should have read "Ella's Hotel," but the "T" in "hotel" was so punctured with bullet holes it said "Ella's Ho el" instead.

Texas eyed it skeptically. Four of the five windows on the lower floor had panes that were broken or gone completely, and there was a mangy dog sacked out in front of a door that hung too crooked to close all the way.

"Pa used to stay here?"

Old Sam gave him a sorrowful look. "It's the best one in town, he used to say."

Behind him, Lily snorted. "I've stayed in worse."

So had he. Texas glanced at his sister. A little scowl creased Jocelyn's face, creating tiny, worried furrows between her eyebrows. One hand possessively clutched the saddlebags holding her silver. But when she caught his gaze, she straightened, bringing her hand back to her reins. The frown on her face disappeared.

Lily laughed derisively. "You'd better sleep on that silver tonight," she said, "or it might not be there in the morning."

Slowly, painfully, Texas dismounted, pulling his rifle with him. He handed the reins of Lily's horse to Sam. "Watch her," he directed, and then he stepped onto the porch of "Ella's Ho el." The dog barely opened his eyes when Texas approached. It didn't budge when he stepped over it and pushed open the door.

The hotel was no better inside than out. The smell of greasy fried pork and unwashed bodies was strong, and those odors mingled with the ones coming off the street, manure and dust and the sweet blood scent of rot. The lobby held one or two pieces of filthy, threadbare furniture, most of it now harboring men busy snoring off their hangovers. Behind the front desk was a tall older woman dressed in black, her face so thin and pinched he thought it might break if she tried a smile.

Texas walked over and leaned against the counter. "You Ella?" he asked.

She gave him a disdainful look. "There ain't no Ella."

"This is a hotel, though."

"Look around you, mister. Do we look like a general store?"

He smiled thinly. "You got any room for two men and two women?"

She slapped open a thin leather-bound ledger and glanced quickly over the lines. "I can squeeze you in if you don't want food, too."

"What's for supper tonight?"

"Salt pork and bread."

Texas pushed back his hat. "I reckon we can go without then."

"That'll be two bits per person, and I need that money in advance."

He reached into the inside pocket of his duster and pulled out a small buckskin bag of twenty-dollar gold pieces, all that was left from a stage they'd robbed outside of Waco a few months before. He handed her one, and she looked at it suspiciously, frowning as she opened a lockbox and made change. But she didn't give the silver to him. Instead, she stacked it beside her on the counter, far enough away that he would have to lunge to reach it.

"What's your name?" She took up a pen and dipped it in ink. Big blotches dripped onto the counter; she swiped them with the sleeve of her rusty black dress.

"Tom Short."

She lifted her eyes. They were very small, and as black as her dress. Her voice lowered. "You Hank's boy?"

He glanced at the door. "Who's Hank?"

She snorted and leaned over the book, scrawling his name. "Who else with you?"

"My wife, Lena, and my sister, Jenny. We've got an old servant with us, too. You need his name?"

She scrawled *+1* in the margin and shoved the book aside.

"Third floor," she said. "Men on the left and women on the right, though I suppose you can take your wife with you if she don't mind the company."

He tipped his hat to her. "Much obliged."

Her eyes slipped to his hip, and then to the rifle swinging from his hand. "And keep your trigger finger in your pocket. We ain't even supposed to have guns inside."

Texas smiled thinly. "I'm privileged."

"You certainly are," she said. Then, deliberately, she reached into his pile of change and picked up a single silver coin. She held it out to him, her expression carefully blank.

He stared at it, at the coin clutched between her thin, bony fingers, and then he touched the brim of his hat and nodded. "You keep that," he said.

She palmed it with the rest, a smooth, practiced movement. "Much obliged."

He turned on his heel and walked awkwardly back toward the door, feeling the sharpness of her gaze between his shoulder blades, cursing himself for using the family alias. It had just cost him a twenty-dollar piece, and God knew he had few enough of those left. Texas stepped through the door and over the still-sleeping dog.

"We've got a room," he said in answer to Jocelyn's curious look. "And your name is Jenny Short. Don't forget it."

"Jenny." Jocelyn frowned, and then she smiled. "Oh, how wonderfully dramatic."

Lily gave her a laconic look and settled back in the saddle. "Where to next, cowboy?" she asked. She nodded toward the street. "Any of these places take your fancy?"

He glanced at the buildings lining the street, most of them built of undressed lumber, with one or two canvas tents scattered between them. Freighter wagons rumbled through the dirt streets, raising clouds of dust that obscured the signs.

"Where's the Beehive?" he asked Old Sam.

Sam gestured to the far side of the street, and Texas followed the motion with his gaze. There it was. He could barely make out the sign on the front of the building. A painted beehive, and below it the box letters of the rhyme his father had told him.

"That's where we'll go," he said. He tied his horse to the hitching rack in front of the hotel and then tied Lily's. Josie was already dismounted, looping the reins of her gelding beside his.

"I think I'll stay here, if you don't mind," Old Sam said. He climbed from his horse and squinted at the street. "Don't believe I'll be too welcome there, if you catch my meaning. And it's best if I just keep a watch."

"Why, that's ridiculous," Jocelyn said. "You should be having a good time with the rest of us."

"Leave him be," Texas said. "He's right. It's best if he stays."

"But—"

"He's a Negro," Lily said bluntly. "They'd as soon shoot him as deal him a hand."

"I guess you understand that better than anyone, Miss Lily," Sam said, his voice bland as milk.

Texas stiffened, but, to his surprise, Lily only smiled.

"Why, Sam. And here I was thinking you didn't have a sense of humor."

"Shut up, Lily," Texas warned. He slung his rifle over his shoulder and unknotted her hands from the saddle horn, then stood back as she dismounted awkwardly.

"Josie," he said. "Do me a favor and don't cause any trouble in this place. Just do what I say, when I say it."

Jocelyn nodded. "Of course. I understand."

"I'm going to have my hands full enough." He glanced at Lily, who was watching him with an annoyingly unreadable smile.

"That means you, too," he said. "Just shut the hell up and don't make me shoot you."

"Of course, lover."

"Call me that again and I'll put a bullet through your brain just for the sheer pleasure of it."

Jocelyn gasped. "Christian!"

He didn't bother to look at her. Impatience heated his blood, and that smile of Lily's, hell, it fed that emptiness deep inside him, made him want to walk away and keep on walking.

With effort, he ignored it. He looked at Josie. "My name is Tom," he said. "Tom Short. She's your sister-in-law Lena. Think you can remember that?"

Jocelyn nodded warily. "Yes."

"Good." He handed his rifle to Sam and grabbed Lily's arm so tightly she winced. "Then let's go."

The Beehive was just as his father had drawn it, a small place with a rhyme on the door and enough smoke and stench to choke a chimney. In spite of that, or maybe because of it, the room was full; so much so that he and Josie and Lily barely elicited a glance when they shoved their way through the door.

That was fine, he thought. More than fine. He glanced back at Lily, who was looking around with an uninterested gaze, and then at Jocelyn. His sister had never looked more Lily's opposite, and it was more than just her height and her dark coloring that made it seem so. Where Lily was bored, Josie was fascinated; her eyes were wide and excited, and there were high points of color on her cheeks.

But, then again, Lily had been in these places a hundred times before and, like him, she knew they were all the same. There would be the same sharp dealer at the faro table and the same painting of a Bengal tiger on the wall behind. There would be a drunk falling over his cards and a gambler who cheated and watched everyone else to make sure they didn't.

Always the same. There had been times when that very thought made him tired, but not today. Today, he felt a sense of wicked, ironic belonging.

"Oh, no wonder Pa spent so much time here!" Josie's voice was loud over the clink of glasses and talk. "Why, it fairly shivers with excitement, don't you think?"

Lily shrugged. "Where's the bar?"

He didn't release his hold on her arm. He saw the bartender just beyond, smelled the sweet scent of bourbon and the thin and bitter hop of beer. "Right this way," he said, pulling her with him. He glanced back at Jocelyn. "Follow me."

He felt his sister's hand on his arm, felt her stumbling behind him through the crowd, but he didn't slow or ease back. He wanted to reach that bar, and then after that the faro table. Josie had begged him to show her this life; well, she'd see it just the way it was.

He pushed his way toward the bar, dragging Lily up beside him, and ordered three whiskeys. He downed his in one gulp and Lily drank hers awkwardly in two, and Josie took little, ladylike sips while he ordered a couple more.

The whiskey was raw, but it tasted sweet and good. He handed the other glass to Lily, watching her grip it clumsily in her bound hands, and then he ordered a third and pulled his sister and Lily toward the faro table.

It was the most crowded table in the house, and as Texas drew closer, it was easy to see why. Presiding over it was a woman. Not the kind of woman he would have expected to see in Abilene or Dodge City. This woman stood back from the table coolly, a charming but unapproachable smile on her face, her bearing stinking of aristocratic southern lady. The only thing that marred the effect was the bright red hair piled on her head.

The hair of a whore, he thought. But this woman was no prostitute, it was clear. She dealt from the spring-loaded box with the agility of a longtime gambler, and her eyes were clear and assessing. She rarely even looked at the abacuslike casekeeper that kept track of the cards, but she didn't miss a trick, he'd bet on it.

She was the dealer he wanted.

"Here," he said, moving forward, angling his shoulder through the others. There was a small table off to the side, close enough that he could watch Lily while he played, and he steered them there first. He shoved Lily into a chair so hard the whiskey she held spilled over her hands.

She glared up at him. "I take it I'm not playing."

"Not today, Kittycat," he taunted. "You just sit there like a good little wife."

Josie hung back. She looked at Texas uncertainly. "What about me?"

He gave her an impatient smile. "Do what you want, Josie. I'm going to play. If you want to watch, then come and watch."

She hesitated. She looked at Lily, and then back to him, and Texas sighed and walked the few feet to the redheaded dealer who beckoned him like some cold and haunting siren.

He felt a wave of relief when he got to the faro table and looked down at the oilcloth cover bearing the painted likenesses of the thirteen spades. He reached into his pocket for the little bag of coins and drew it out, weighing it in his hand.

It was as if the scent of money drew her. The woman dealer looked up, her eyes suddenly sharp, and gave him an artfully practiced smile. "Care to make a bet, mister?"

He grinned at her, pushing back his hat and inclining his head slightly. "Ma'am, it feels like I've been waiting forever to play at your table," he said.

"Oh?" She raised a slender brow. "You know me, then?"

"No, ma'am." He shook his head, winking audaciously. "But before the night is over, you'll know me. I'll be the one collecting all the money."

The men around him hooted. The woman laughed. "You're a big talker, mister."

"I never lie."

"There isn't a man alive who hasn't said that," she said. Her well-manicured hands came to a rest on the dealer's box. She nodded toward the bag in his hand. "But I'll tell you somethin', sugar, Lottie Deno listens a lot better when there's money on the table."

Texas's smile widened. He drew out a gold piece and

set it down, pushing it slowly to rest on the layout, on the ace of spades. Lottie gave him a long, lingering look and drew a card from the slot in the dealer's box.

"Loser's the Jack of Diamonds," she said. The man who stood beside her, the lookout, gathered money from the table so fast his hands were nearly a blur. Lottie glanced around the table. Her gaze came to a stop on Texas. "You haven't lost yet, cowboy. Any other bets?"

The challenge was like honey, too sweet to resist. Texas flung another coin on the table, negligently shoving it beside the first. It glinted in the light of the oil lamp.

"You must be feelin' lucky," Lottie said.

Beside him, a man whistled long and low. Texas winked. "I'm always lucky."

"We'll see about that," she said. She drew another card and laid it faceup on the table. The Ace of Spades. "Well now, mister, looks like you're right. At least your luck's holdin' for now."

The lookout doled out the chips, and Texas laughed and slid them to a different space, another card. "The tiger's on my side, Miss Lottie," he said. "You'd best be prepared to lose a little money."

She smiled enigmatically and dealt again.

He glanced up to Lily's table. She was sitting there, leaning negligently back in her chair, Josie talking beside her. Still there. Still his prisoner. He smiled and grabbed another whiskey from a passing barmaid. He *did* feel lucky tonight, as if nothing could go wrong, and it seemed as if fate was lending a hand because he kept winning and the whiskey kept coming, and soon the cards and the oil lamps and the smoke seemed to blur and grind in front of his eyes like a giant kaleidoscope, colors and images and bits and pieces like refracted glass.

The whiskey and the smoke were burning his throat and, though he felt the pain in his lung and the ache in his hip, those pains seemed to come from someplace deep inside him, a place too deep to feel. The world compressed into three things: Lily sitting at that table, Lottie Deno dealing the cards, and his growing pile of chips. As the minutes went on, he stopped caring about his sister and his wife. He glanced up at Lily now and then to make sure she was there, but mostly he gave in to that tingling in his fingers, to the lure of fate that pooled warm as whiskey in his gut.

He felt someone lean against him, the soft press of hair against his cheek, a slender hand gripping his shoulder. It was Jocelyn. She leaned over him, smiling in that beguiling way she had, her eyes alight with pleasure.

He thought he heard her say something. Something like "This is wonderful," but he wasn't sure and he didn't care. He wrapped his arm around her waist and held her close and breathed deeply of her skin, catching the subtle scent of roses. Roses to match her, the way they hadn't matched—

Texas glanced past her to Lily's table.

It was empty.

"Goddammit!" He jerked away roughly. "Where the hell is Lily?"

Josie frowned. "Why, she's just where I left her." She twisted slightly. "At the table, or, well, she *was* just there. Oh heavens, where did she go?"

He lunged away from the table and pushed his way through the crowd. Damn Josie for distracting him, damn himself for being distracted. It had only been a moment, a second, but it was all Lily needed. He knew that. Goddammit, he *knew* it.

"Runnin' for your life, Sharpe?"

The voice brought him up short. It was low and deep, touched with challenge. The kind of voice he'd heard a hundred times before. The kind of voice he was good at walking away from.

He stopped and turned, looking into the face of a tall man wearing a challenging expression and a custom-tooled silver Frontier Colt.

"You talking to me, mister?" he asked softly.

The man snorted. "See any other killers in this room?"

"I suppose that depends on who the hell you are."

"Who I am?" The man smiled a broad, missing-tooth smile, and his hand rested on the gleaming Colt in his holster. "Why, I'm the man who sent Texas Sharpe straight to hell."

The crowd went dead quiet. Texas's hand went to the hilt of his gun. He heard a woman gasp. Josie. Heard the murmur of his name through the crowd. "Texas Sharpe. Good God, that's Texas Sharpe!"

The stranger was no threat, Texas knew. The man could be disarmed with a few words. But it suddenly seemed like such a hard thing to do. So hard to think of the right words, to care about dying when there was nothing about living he cared about.

He looked into the man's face, and all his pain seemed to coalesce on one center, to pool in the darkness of the stranger's eyes. "I'm already in hell, mister," he said, and then he stepped back and smiled and let his hand fall from his gun. "You think you can save me?"

8

She was halfway to the door when she heard the silence. It was quick and deadly and far too familiar. Lily spun around. With the unerring accuracy of habit, her gaze went straight to Texas. Not playing faro now, but standing in the middle of the saloon, facing down another stranger.

In a moment, she took it all in: Josie white-faced at the faro table, a hand pressed to her mouth, the slack-jawed attention of the crowd, and the tall, dark-eyed stranger who smiled as he issued his challenge. Lily had seen it before, in every town, in every backwater trading post with a saloon and an ambitious man with dreams of glory. Killing any member of the Sharpe gang would bring instant notoriety, and there were men who searched the countryside for that very opportunity.

The man challenging Texas now was just that kind. She saw that ambition gleaming in his eyes, that slight nervousness in the way he stood, holding back a little, always holding back. It was their biggest mistake, always had been, because Texas had a sixth sense that way. He could sense even the slightest nervousness, he knew how to charm and beguile his way around it. In the last three years, she'd only known him to draw his gun twice in a situation like this, and that was with rash young boys too determined to walk away from. This man was nothing like that. It would take Texas five minutes to talk his way out of it.

She didn't even have to run. Texas was too involved to notice her. Lily laughed softly to herself and started again toward the door.

But then something stopped her, a flash of movement, a sound, and Lily turned just in time to see the challenger lift his gun, heard the agony of Josie's screamed, "No!" as the man pulled the trigger. The shot cracked through the air, missing Texas by inches. The mirror behind the bar exploded, sending a rainfall scatter of breaking glass onto the floor.

Texas had not even touched his gun.

"No! Don't hurt him! Please don't hurt him!" Jocelyn cried out.

The stranger angled his head toward her. "Why don't you tell your lady friend to shut the hell up?"

"Jenny," Texas said, not taking his eyes from the other man. "Stay out of this."

"Oh, please . . ." Josie's voice broke on a sob.

The stranger fingered the trigger, swaggering with confidence. "Well now, Texas Sharpe, I figure you ain't so tough after all. I heard you was a fast gun, but maybe that was just a lie. Maybe you're just another yellow coward."

Texas just looked at him, but it was a look Lily had never seen before, a look . . . Damn, it was empty. World-weary, ancient, remote. He smiled, but there was a barrenness to that smile, a lifelessness that made Lily go still.

She waited for him to back away, to smile a charming smile, to cast his easy glance over the crowd and coax everyone back to a nervous, noisy normality, the scene she'd watched played out a dozen times before.

But he didn't move, and she knew suddenly that he wasn't going to shoot. He wasn't going to talk. He was just going to stand there and let that man kill him. He was just going to die.

"Oh my God!" Josie's voice was a harsh squeak. "Lily, do something!"

Texas laughed. The sound was without amusement. "Come on, mister," he urged, taunting, mocking, goading. "Show me you can aim."

"Lily!"

Lily stood frozen, escape forgotten, everything forgotten. Texas's expression was so blank it etched his face into sharp shadow planes, cheekbones and square jaw and nose, and his full lips were stretched so tight it seemed impossible to believe he had ever smiled.

She had never seen him like this. It was as if . . . as if he welcomed death. As if he *wanted* it.

The stranger aimed and smiled.

"Prepare to die, Texas Sharpe." He cocked the hammer. The click of it reverberated through the smoky room.

"Not so fast, Johnny." The voice was loud and steely. Lily looked toward it. The faro dealer, the woman Lily had dismissed as a sharp-eyed flirt, came from behind the table, a derringer in her hand, her expression determined.

The man called Johnny glanced at her, but he didn't ease his finger from the trigger. "Stay out of this, Lottie."

"I don't think so, sugar," Lottie said. "You've already shot up one mirror, you don't get to try at two. Give me the gun."

It seemed as if the entire saloon held its breath except for Texas, who simply stood there watching while the woman walked past him to Johnny.

"Hand it over, boy," she said, holding out her free

hand. "Or I'll send Sarah for the sheriff. And I know for a fact you wouldn't like that." When he hesitated, she grabbed the gun from his hand. With a quick, one-handed motion, she opened the chamber, spilling the cartridges onto the floor, kicking them aside to roll beneath the tables, a loud clatter and spin over the planks. She looked at Texas.

"I don't know if you're really who he says you are," she said steadily. "But you'd best get the hell out of here."

Texas nodded, glancing over to the faro table, and Lily followed his gaze to where Jocelyn leaned limply against the wall. The oil lamp flickered, sending its play of light and shadow over Josie's pale face, making it seem as if the painted tiger on the wall was dancing above her head, tangling his claws in her hair.

"Come on, Jenny," Texas said. "Let's go." He turned to the faro dealer, tipping his hat. "My pardon, Miss Deno," he said quietly. "You just keep that money on the table, for your trouble."

The dealer nodded. "Much obliged, mister."

Lily watched as Josie stumbled toward him, tripping on the hem of her dress. Her breath came in little sobs, audible in the strained silence. Josie clutched his arm as if the motion could keep her from falling over, and her face was so pale—Lily didn't know a face could be that white.

They came toward her, and Lily heard the men all around gradually going back to their conversations, heard their quiet undertones, their mutterings. "He's crazy as a loon." "Jesus, did you see the way he just stood there?"

Woodenly, she waited. Escape was gone, a fleeting thought, a long-ago dream. In its place was a shock she could not quite shake, a strange and deadly fear. She could not lose the image of Texas's empty eyes, and she could not silence the voice inside that taunted:

This is your fault. All yours. You made him want to die.

He glanced over at her, but there was no interest in his eyes, none in his voice when he said, "Still here, Lily?" He looked away and shoved the door open with his shoulder, and Lily followed them out, blinking in the harsh sunlight. The hiccup of Josie's shocked sobs filled her ears, a sound so loud it blocked the pass of the freighters, the shouts of men, and Lily stood on that porch and listened to that sound and thought the town should have changed somehow. But the streets were still dusty, and the wagons were still careening through, and men were still laughing and talking and going about their business as if the sound of gunfire in the Beehive saloon was so commonplace it was hardly worth mentioning. Probably it was.

"I-I don't understand what you did," Josie said. She pulled away from Texas. Her teeth were chattering. She wrapped her arms around herself and squeezed tightly, her sobs making her words jerky, nearly incoherent. "My God, Christian, you—"

He glared at her and Josie choked back the rest. He stepped off the porch and began to walk quickly, leaving them to follow.

Josie stumbled after him. "I don't understand," she said again in a small, small voice. "I don't understand."

Lily took her arm. "Come on."

"But—

"Shut up, Josie," Lily advised her. "And walk."

It was just after sundown when they stopped riding. The sky was a deep, rich blue with only one or two stars for decoration, and the horizon still glowed with a sliver of pink-gold light. The shadows were dusky on

their faces, expressions hard to read. They didn't build
a fire; it was too easy to trace smoke on these plains,
and they couldn't take the chance that someone had
decided to follow them from Fort Griffin. Dinner was
cold beans and dry, crumbly corn bread, and silence
came too easily.

Lily sat at the far side of the camp. Texas was cleaning his gun in the darkness; she heard the soft click of
metal against metal, the whisk of the bore brush.

She glanced at Josie. Texas's sister huddled near the
horses, close to Old Sam, her legs drawn up under her
skirt, cradling her head on her knees. She had been
quiet since they left the Flat, her face tight with unasked
questions, her expression haunted.

That, at least, was something Lily understood.

She looked at Texas, just a shadow in the darkness, and
she thought of the way his eyes had looked inside that bar,
how empty they'd been. His whole body had seemed hollow as he stood there goading that man, waiting for a bullet that never came, and in her mind that image blended
with her memory of the night she'd tried to shoot him.
That was when everything had gone out of him, she knew,
as if whatever it was that kept him living, that made him
Texas, had just been sucked away, leaving him as dry and
busted as wheat stalks in a drought, and she had not been
able to drop the odd and uncomfortable feeling that he'd
been that way since and she just hadn't seen it.

She shivered and leaned back against her saddlebags,
huddling into her duster, drawing it closer against the
cold and the memory of Texas's expressionless face,
telling herself not to care. She couldn't help it if Texas
loved her too much, she couldn't be responsible. She was
just as she'd always been. Nothing had changed, not her
need for escape nor the wish for a different life nor the
fear that had driven her to betray the gang in Lampasas.

She felt again the bite of the rope against her throat, felt its burning, rasping slide to her jaw, and she focused on it, drew it around her like the duster, settled into it until it blocked the memory of Texas's face and she was shivering and anxious in the cold night. She let herself remember the night they put the noose around her neck, the smell of burning oil and the sweat of fear. She let herself remember how she'd stared into the darkness, waiting for him to come. She hated the memories, but they were better than feeling she was to blame for the change in Texas. Better than seeing that look on his face and contrasting it with his joy and relief at finding her in Denison. It was better than caring. She could not afford to care.

In the darkness, she heard movement. She glanced up. Jocelyn came toward her, a swish of skirt, a hushed footstep.

Josie motioned to the ground beside her. "Do you mind if I sit by you a while?" she asked in a quiet, tearstained voice.

Lily wanted to say no, but, before she could, Josie sat down and drew her knees up, wrapping her arms around them, huddling in the same way she had near the horses. For a minute, maybe two, she was quiet. All Lily heard was the soft cadence of her breathing. Then Josie sighed.

"I should never have insisted we go," she said quietly.

"You wanted adventure."

Josie's silence was as eloquent as a sound. Lily exhaled softly, deeply. She leaned her head back and looked up at the stars spangling across the sky.

"He wanted to die," Jocelyn said. "He was going to let that man shoot him."

"Yeah."

"But why?" Josie's voice was a whisper. "I don't understand why. What happened to him?"

Lily kept her eyes on the sky. She watched a star slide through the darkness and felt that same falling inside of her, that same sense of inevitability, of fate. Texas had loved her too much, and she had not loved him at all. *She* was what happened to him, it was that simple, and yet it was much more complicated than that. Because Texas had made her the woman she was today. He had taught her how to be ruthless, how to be smart. He had taught her that caring for someone could mean death, that trusting was forbidden.

She had not forgotten those lessons. She wondered why he had expected her to. The fact that he had made her nervous and wary, and, dammit, afraid. She had always known exactly how to handle Texas, how to manipulate him, but now she felt out of her depth, now she wasn't sure what he was thinking or what she should do about it.

Josie sighed again. "I guess—I guess I don't really know him that well. Does he always tempt death that way?"

"He's an outlaw. There's a lot of money in killing him, you know. Must be a three-thousand-dollar bounty on Texas's head now."

She hadn't answered the question, Lily knew, but it was the most she could offer Jocelyn, an answer far simpler, and much easier to accept, than the truth.

She felt Josie's stare in the darkness, felt the silent start of her question, then felt the words fall, unasked, into the cold.

"I see," Josie said, though it was clear she didn't understand at all. "So when we went into the Flat, he knew he might be challenged?"

"There's always the chance."

"Does he fight many duels?"

"Duels?" Lily laughed harshly. "I wouldn't call them

duels. There's nothing romantic about them. It's not like the newspapers say."

Josie was quiet for such a long time Lily began to feel uncomfortable. She was ready to gather up her bags and grab her bedroll when Josie spoke again.

"Have you ever . . . killed anyone?"

"They don't hang people just for smiling at someone the wrong way."

"I guess not." Jocelyn sounded thoughtful. "How does it feel?"

"To hang?"

"To kill someone."

"I don't know," Lily said slowly. "Like nothing, I guess."

"Like nothing?"

Lily heard the dull surprise in Josie's voice, and she had the odd, unsettling notion that she'd disappointed her. But what was even more surprising was the way that realization rattled around inside her, the way it made her feel uncomfortable and strange, the same way Texas had made her feel today, when she'd seen such emptiness in his eyes, when he'd cocked his brow and taunted Johnny to *"Show me you can aim."*

She huddled further inside her duster. "Yeah," she said, hearing the defensiveness in her own voice. "Like nothing. Now leave me alone."

She said the words and she meant them, but when Josie got up in a rustle of skirts and a swish of movement and walked away without a word, Lily felt curiously alone. The night was suddenly very dark around her.

9

He watched them talk as he cleaned the Colt, as he separated the cylinder and eased the bore brush into each chamber, as he oiled the metal with a greasy rag. He heard the whisper of their conversation like a dream in the night, quiet and faraway as the barks of coyotes, a language he could not understand.

He didn't want to know what they talked about, or even what they thought. When Lily lifted her face to the skies and the moonlight limned her fine features, he though how pretty she was, so pretty it hurt. But it was a prettiness that only sat on her skin; it didn't go any deeper, and, though he thought he should care about that, he didn't.

Texas saw the scene in the Beehive again, crawling before his eyes. He smelled the smoke and the bourbon and the fear, and he wondered when loving Lily had become so important that everything else faded to nothing in its power. He knew who she was—hell, he'd made her what she was—but in his mind "Lily the Cat" had always been separate from the Lily he loved.

He hated what he'd made her, what they'd both

become. He hated seeing the scar on her throat and knowing he was responsible for that, too, that she blamed him. And he wished, suddenly and completely, that he'd let her run, that she was halfway to Mexico by now, hiding in some little *ranchería*, sitting in the sun and smoking corn-husk cigarillos and watching the days pass by.

Except she wouldn't be doing that, he reminded himself. She would be hunting down his father, hunting him. If he let her go, the bullet he wanted would come someday, and though he could accept that—it was fitting somehow—he could not accept his father's fate so easily.

Texas sighed and put aside the brush and the rag, feeling his way around the pieces of the gun, putting it back together. He'd done it so often he knew the fittings by touch, knew exactly how one piece lay against the other. Like him and Lily. There had been a time when he knew the feel of her body as well as his own, when he could look at her and know what she was thinking just by the set of her face.

But maybe that had just been an illusion, too.

He shoved the gun into his holster and looked up at the cold and empty Texas sky and wished he were someplace else. Anyplace but here.

Lampasas, Texas

There was nothing like a Comanche moon.

Hank stared out between the heavy metal bars of the window at the streets of Lampasas. The big full moon lit them like daylight; they were empty and quiet. No guards, no damned sheriff. No one. It was the perfect night for an Indian raid, or a jailbreak.

He smiled, easing away from the wall, and looked

over at Bobby, who sat on the edge of the thin, thread-bare mattress, shoulders hunched forward, hands buried in his shaggy, coal-black hair.

"They'll be here soon," Hank said.

Bobby glanced worriedly past the bars and into the main room of the Lampasas jail. There was a desk scattered with papers and an oil lamp burning away, but, other than that, it was as quiet as the streets outside.

"They'd better hurry." Bobby sat up, his expression so furrowed and bleak that his large nose looked even bigger on his face. "Hansen only went to take a piss, and—"

"We can take Hansen." Hank brushed away Bobby's worries with a wave of his hand. "Good Christ, you'd think you were afraid of a little gunfire."

"I'd feel better if Texas were here."

Hank laughed shortly. "He'll be here soon enough."

"Yeah," Bobby said in a low voice. The wooden frame of the bed creaked as he got up and leaned against the bars, staring morosely out at the jail office. "I'm afraid of that, too."

Hank laughed again. "Poor Bobby," he taunted. "You're a regular Hamlet. Give me the soliloquy, why don't you? 'To be or not to be . . . '"

"Shut up, Hank."

Hank stepped toward him. He leaned close, felt the sharp touch of satisfaction as Bobby stiffened at his proximity. Ten years Bobby had been riding with him. Ten years, and he still jumped when Hank wanted him to.

"What's wrong, Bobby?" he whispered. "Is your poor heart bleeding again?"

"No." Bobby shook his head and swallowed. "No."

Hank poked his finger at the bandage covering Bobby's upper arm. "She wanted you dead, my friend. She wanted us all dead. 'Hell hath no fury . . . '"

"How do you know Texas will bring her back?" Bobby asked quietly. "Maybe he won't find her."

"Oh, he'll find her." Hank thought of his son, of the last time he'd seen him, the way Texas had stared off into the distance, heartsick, heartworn. Christ, the yearning for her had been so starkly written on his face Hank would have to be blind not to see it.

It sickened him, just as it always had, but, then again, Hank knew that yearning was what kept his son from riding off for good.

Texas had his faults—he felt too quickly and too much—but, in spite of it, Hank wanted his son beside him. He wanted to be able to trust him, wanted to believe Texas was completely loyal.

Hank rubbed his jaw thoughtfully. There had been times lately when he hadn't been sure, and that pained him. His own damn son, and yet he hadn't missed that evasion in Texas's eyes, the growing discontent. If Bobby or Schofield had shown it even once, they would be dead.

And as for Lily, sweet Lily . . . She had been trouble for a long time now, but Hank had allowed himself to overlook it, knowing how Texas felt about her. Too, he had to admit he found a special irony in the fact that Lily, a woman who had never given her loyalty to anyone or anything, was the only person who could inspire it in his son.

It was an irony that used to amuse him and didn't any longer. Now he had every intention of making her pay for landing them in this hellhole of a Texas prison. Before he made her pay for the gunshots that weakened his son and the strife that had existed between himself and Texas since Tommy Lee had brought her into their camp all those years ago.

Thinking of her made Hank restless. He drew away

from Bobby and paced back to the tiny jail window. The night was falling away from him, that big Comanche moon growing smaller and smaller as the hours went on. Anxiously, he grabbed the bars, scanning the streets. Nothing. Dammit, where the hell were they? Just past midnight, Schofield had said. Just past—

Then Hank saw them. Two horses, walking slowly and carefully, clinging to the shadows. Schofield and that idiot shopkeeper he'd talked into helping. The moonlight glinted off their faces, on the guns at their hips. Hank's restlessness disappeared, replaced by an anticipation that made his mouth water. It was time.

He heard the rasp of the front hinge, the scrape of the door against the gritty, mud-packed floor.

"Here comes Hansen," Bobby whispered.

"Perfect," Hank murmured. He left the window and sat on the bed, leaning against the cold adobe wall. "Sit down, Bobby," he instructed quietly. "Sit down. 'Good things come to those who wait.'"

Near Fort Griffin, Texas

The sun started out hot and stayed that way. Texas lowered his hat over his eyes, shading them from the dancing heat waves that wavered before him, turning the dusty gold hills into dream landscapes, molten images. He heard the slow *clop clop* of Lily's horse behind him and the easy rhythms of Josie's and Old Sam's mounts, a lulling, mesmerizing sound. He was tired and his body ached, and the lullaby of the horses' hooves made him want to close his eyes and go to sleep.

But in sleep there were dreams, and he was tired of those, too, so he kept his eyes open and stared at the horizon before him as though it held something to anticipate.

That was the biggest irony of all, of course. Moving forward only meant Lampasas, and Lampasas meant Pa, and since they'd left Fort Griffin, dread had settled around Texas like a vulture waiting for something to die. He tried not to think about it. He tried not to remember that his father would want Lily to pay for her betrayal. But it was always there, in the back of his mind, trapping him. He wished he'd never found her, never known the truth. He wished hope was still inside him. Hope instead of terrible, aching despair. What a relief it would have been to spend the rest of his life looking for her in every town, in the face of every barmaid. What peace to believe that one day they would meet again, and she would throw her arms around him and be happy he was alive.

"Do you suppose we might rest soon?" Josie rode up beside him. With a limp hand, she brushed hair back from her face, leaving a streak of dust across her skin. "I think I might die if we don't stop."

"You won't die," he said tersely.

"Surely there's a water hole around here somewhere. Or a river."

"Maybe."

"We could rest then. Just long enough to get off this horse. I swear she's put a permanent kink in my backside."

"There's a lot of riding still to do, Josie. You'd better get used to it."

She was quiet. Quiet, though he felt her scrutiny as she rode beside him. Texas stared straight ahead, too tired to care if he upset her, too tired to answer any of her ceaseless questions. Finally, as he knew she would, she asked the question he'd been waiting for.

"What's wrong with you, Christian? You—you've changed. It's like you're some stranger."

"You've never known me that well."

"That's a lie and you know it," she said. "You're my brother."

"A brother who came and went," Texas said bitterly. "When was the last time you saw me, Josie? Five years ago? Six?"

"Maybe it was. But I remember who you were then. You were brave and honorable. Like Robin Hood."

There was such pure belief in her voice, such conviction. There was a time when he would have laughed it off, when he would have changed the subject with a joke and a ready smile. But he didn't feel like smiling now, and he wished Jocelyn weren't here, that he didn't have to deal with her naiveté and her romanticized notions. Texas Sharpe, hero for the people, enemy of the Reconstruction. She looked at him as if he held the world in his hands.

"Robin Hood is a fairy tale," he said harshly.

She flinched. "That's what you were to me," she insisted. "You and Pa robbing those stagecoaches, showing those filthy carpetbaggers they couldn't just come in here and steal."

He turned to her angrily. "It wasn't about heroism, for Christ's sake. It was about money. *Money.* That's always been what it's about. We needed it. They had it."

"No," she said stubbornly. "I won't believe that."

"Believe it."

"Then what about yesterday? Are you telling me you've always been like that, too? That you've always just stood there and let men shoot at you? What's that about, Christian? Stupidity? Or cowardice?"

Her face grew pinched and tight when she said the words, and her eyes were dark with a disappointment and pain that made him feel sick. Texas turned away, suddenly unable to meet her gaze, to answer her accusation. His hands tightened on the reins so hard he felt the strain in his wrists, his shoulders.

"I'm sorry," she whispered. "I shouldn't have said that. I didn't mean it."

"It's all right."

"No." She shook her head. "No, it isn't. It's just that . . . I don't understand you anymore, Christian, and I wish I did. I wish I knew what made you hate life so much. It used to be . . ." Her voice trailed off and then picked up again, a sharpness in the constant murmur of the hot wind. "I was remembering the last time you visited. That time you woke me up in the middle of the night to go riding. D'you remember that?"

"Yeah. I remember."

"It was so dark, and I was scared to death we were going to fall into a prairie dog hole or a ravine or something. But you just laughed and kept riding, just as fast as you could. It was all I could do to keep up with you."

The memory was sharp in his mind. It was all there, stored deep in his soul, the mindless joy of that night, of the cool air against his skin and the smell of darkness and moist earth and damp grass, the exhilaration of his horse's hoofbeats vibrating into his body. He heard Jocelyn behind him, heard her breathless laughter, her call to *"Wait! Let me catch up!"*

"You were so alive then," Josie mused. "I was always so jealous of that, you know. Of the way you just seemed to know how to live."

Her words brought a sadness he didn't want to look at, didn't want to feel. "It was a long time ago."

"I don't want to believe you've lost that," she said. "You were so happy then. You were just getting ready to marry Lily, I remember." She sighed. "I asked Pa if I could go to the wedding, but he wouldn't let me. I

was always sorry about that. It must have been wonderful."

The innocence of her statement would have made
him laugh if the truth hadn't been so painful. His wedding had consisted of a judge in San Antonio and a hot
summer day with flies and dust and the smell of dung
and tortillas hanging in the air. They had just ridden
back from robbing some stage out of Houston, and he
and Lily were both sweating and hot and dirty. They
had celebrated with a ten-cent bath and a stringy steak
and a hotel room where the rest of the gang had sat
around playing poker until two A.M., his father
included, and they'd all got so drunk that Texas had
taken her against a wall without even undressing when
they were finally alone.

Pretty damn romantic.

"It was nothing like you're thinking, Josie," he said.
"Just a judge in a bar in San Antonio. It was hot."

She gave him a strange look; it reminded him of a little bird cocking its head. "Is that all you can say about it
now? That it was hot?"

Those subtle accusations again, that insinuation that
he should be more than he was, that he should be the
man who had pulled his sister awake in the middle of
the night to go for a moonlight ride. But he was not that
man any longer. Except for memories, nothing inside
him showed he'd ever been that man.

He didn't answer Josie, and she didn't ask him any
more questions, and, before long, he had forgotten that
she ever had.

10

The water was muddy and warm, but it felt good just the same. Lily splashed it over her face, sluicing off the dirt clinging to her skin, letting it run down her arms to sting the raw welts of her wrists.

She was grateful they had stopped finally, even if it was only at the edge of this nearly dry buffalo wallow. She was tired of riding, tired of plodding along in the cloud of Texas's dust, of the heat and wind and the constant glare of the sun. But, mostly, she was tired of her fear. It grew with every hour, with every step that brought her closer and closer to Lampasas and Hank, until now all she could think about was escaping.

But she'd used up the best of her plans, and it'd got her nowhere. Unless something changed tonight, tomorrow would bring Lampasas and sure death. And, for the life of her, she couldn't think of a way out.

She frowned, glancing back at Texas. He stood on the gently sloping bank of the wallow, staring beyond her into the shallow, muddy pool of water. His whole body seemed limp and lifeless. His shoulders slumped. He looked as lonely as Lily had ever seen him. She felt the rise of guilt again, pushing through her fear, and she swallowed it and tried not to think about the part she'd played in making him that way. He seemed so vulnerable now, and, though one part of her hated that about him, and hated the shame she felt over it, there was another part that welcomed it. If he wasn't exactly the Texas she knew, at least that vulnerability was more like the compassion she remembered. At least there was something about him that reminded her of the friend he'd once been. Perhaps she could appeal to that. Perhaps she could—

Tell him how you feel. Tell him the truth.

The thought came out of nowhere, odd and startling, and Lily swallowed. The truth. She wondered if she even knew how to do that anymore. It seemed such a simple thing; hell, other people did it every day. But she'd spent too many years living the lessons Texas had taught her. *"Never let anyone know what you feel," "Never tell anyone anything you don't have to."* The words were engraved in her mind, so much a part of her that the thought of going against them now made her feel sick.

She would never be able to do it. Not in ten years, not in a hundred. Just the thought of going up to him and asking for help made her mouth dry and her palms clammy. And the thought of telling him how afraid she was of Hank . . .

Lily squeezed her eyes shut, dug her nails into her palms. There were no other choices. It was either beg for help or let him take her back to his father. It was either appeal to Texas or die.

Lily opened her eyes. She felt weak, and her heart was pounding, but she got to her feet and climbed the sloping bank of the wallow to where Texas stood. The evening sent shadows over his cheekbones. The blueness of them bruised his face. He didn't move as she approached, and he didn't acknowledge her presence in any way, not with a sideways glance or a tightening of his jaw or a subtle step away. She followed his gaze to the water and saw the reflection of the growing moon there, a weak light still, rippling across with the dance of the wind, and she wondered how to start. In the end, she didn't have to. He did it for her.

"What do you want, Lily?"

Lily took a deep breath. "I want to make a deal with you," she said.

He laughed grimly. "No deals."

"Please, Texas. For the sake of what we are to each other."

"What we *were*," he corrected.

"What we were, then," she said. "I'm asking you to remember that. I'm asking you to help me."

He was quiet. She plunged ahead.

"Don't tell Hank the truth about Lampasas. Please. I'm asking you. I'm . . . begging . . . you not to tell him. He'll kill me if he finds out. You know he will."

"You should have thought of that a long time ago," he said. His voice was so quiet she had to strain to hear it.

Lily swallowed. "I was stupid then," she said. "I was desperate. Texas . . . if you do this for me now, I promise you I'll walk away. I'll leave you and Hank alone for the rest of my days. It's all I want. It's all I ever wanted. All I'm asking in return is that you give me that chance. Please. Please. Don't tell Hank the truth."

He didn't look at her. He didn't give her a single indication that he'd heard. He just stood there, gazing bleakly at the moon rising in the water, his thick hair blowing gently back from his face. She'd been wrong, she realized with a surge of desperation. There was no vulnerability in him; just a hardness, an emptiness that was nothing like compassion at all. He didn't care; he wouldn't help her.

She closed her eyes, struggling for a control that escaped her. This was her last chance, the only chance she had, and she was failing. "Please, Texas," she whispered. She grabbed his arm and felt the warmth of his flesh through his shirt. "I'm so afraid."

He jerked away, his jaw stiff, his eyes suddenly riveted to her. "Don't touch me," he said hoarsely. "And don't say another word, or so help me I'll drag you into Lampasas bound *and* gagged."

She saw something in his eyes then, a remnant of compassion, a pain that gave her hope, and she grabbed onto it so desperately she barely heard his words. "Say you'll help me," she said. "Tell me—"

He was on her so quickly she didn't have time to be surprised. He grabbed her arm, his fingers biting into her flesh, nearly jerking her shoulder from its socket as he pulled her after him. She cried out in pain, stumbling against him. "Texas—"

"Shut up." He didn't slow down. He yanked her after him toward the campfire, where Josie and Old Sam looked up in surprise.

Josie started to her feet. "Christian, whatever are you—"

"Sit down," he ordered with such violence in his tone that Josie sank immediately, silently back to her knees. He jerked Lily around to face him, his grip so hard she winced. With his free hand, he reached into his pocket, and, when she saw the bandanna he drew out, Lily tried to step away.

"No, Texas," she said. Desperation made her voice high and whiny. "You can't. Please."

He released her arm and grabbed her by the back of the head, his fingers plunging into the drawn-tight braid at the nape of her neck, curling around to hold her prisoner. With a slow, even pressure, he pulled her closer, his gaze fastened on hers, and in the darkness she felt his intensity, in the faint light of the fire she saw the set of his mouth. He bent his head, only a breath away, and Lily thought, *He's going to kiss me,* and closed her eyes and leaned into him, her blood singing with unexpected relief. A kiss, that was all. Not a gag. He was going to help her.

"Not this time, baby," he whispered against her mouth.

Then she felt it, the coarse cloth against her lips. Lily wrenched away, but his grip was too tight. The movement sent a sharp spike of burning pain into her neck. She tried to protest, and he shoved the bandanna into her mouth, between her teeth, so hard tears of pain and frustration filled her eyes. She tasted the dry, cottony fabric against her tongue, the salt of his sweat, and made a sound of protest when he drew it tight and knotted it. The fabric burned across her cheeks.

"Christian, I can't believe you're doing this." Josie's admonition was quiet, but Lily heard the strain behind it. "It's—it's inhuman. What's she done?"

"Stay out of this, Miss Jocelyn," Old Sam warned.

"I will not. I won't stand by and watch such barbaric behavior."

"Then don't watch," Texas said harshly. "And shut up." He took Lily's arm, forcing her into an awkward sit. "Lily's going to be a good little girl tonight, aren't you, baby?"

His eyes chilled her. That impenetrable gaze, that desolate emptiness. All Lily could think as he turned on his heel and walked away, leaving her alone with only the feeble warmth of the fire and the curious stares of Josie and Old Sam for comfort, was that she was truly a prisoner now.

Lampasas rose through the rosy-colored dust like a dream, hazy and melting and not quite real. Texas would almost have believed it was an illusion, except the sight of it was burned into his brain, a memory of violence and pain he couldn't run from, couldn't forget.

He stopped at the crest of a hill and looked down at the town. His lung ached, and his hip, and he felt hollowed out and too heavy to move, and all the time Lily's words kept circling through his mind, a rhythm that had not left him since she'd said them last night. *"If you do this for me now, I promise you I'll walk away. I'll leave you and Hank alone for the rest of my days. It's all I want. All I ever wanted."*

He thought of how she'd looked when she said it, the desperation, the vulnerability in her face. It had been too painful to look at, so he hadn't looked, but still it had moved him. He couldn't ever remember seeing Lily that way before, never so afraid. Even when he'd cut her down from that hanging rope, she had only looked at him with brown eyes that seemed even colder and more remote than before.

But last night she'd almost had him. Her words had been tempting. He could imagine it, an end to the constant watching, an end to his pain. Let her go, and she would run away and he would never see her again. Let her go, and give her the dream he hadn't known she wanted. The dream he'd heard for the first time last night. *"I'll walk away. It's all I want. All I ever wanted."*

He hated how those words hurt him. He hated how

strange it was to hear them coming from her and know they were true and that he'd never seen before how badly she wanted out.

Unexpectedly, he thought of the hat in his saddlebags, the cherry poke bonnet.

He swallowed and pressed his heels into the gelding's sides, and reminded himself that Lily was a liar. He told himself that her vulnerability, her fear, had been an act, emotions calculated to pull at whatever compassion he had left. And those words that wouldn't leave his mind, they were the biggest lie of all. *"I'll leave you and Hank alone for the rest of my days."* Yes, no doubt she would. After she killed them.

He told himself all that, just as he'd told himself last night, but, like last night, he couldn't make himself really believe it. He had seen something in her eyes, a humanity he recognized, a glimpse of her soul he couldn't forget, and it paralyzed him. That look scared the hell out of him.

It was why he'd gagged her. Because that humanity reminded him of the girl she'd once been, and that was someone he could not turn away from, someone he would do anything for. A day ago, he'd told himself that his Lily was gone forever and it was time to get on with his life. But last night had told him he was wrong, and it didn't matter how many times he called himself a fool or how much he tried not to believe her. The truth was that he did believe her, and he couldn't help himself, and he didn't know what to do about it. He didn't know how he would survive believing her again.

Texas clenched his jaw and forced his thoughts away from Lily, focusing on the trail. A half a mile or so from town, he turned east, heading toward the dense, twisted thickets near Cowhouse Creek. They were only an hour from the hideout, and he wanted to get there quickly now. The dread he felt over facing his father again was gone, replaced by the need to turn Lily over, to release her from his care. Let Pa decide what to do with her; Texas was tired of thinking. He was tired of everything.

The trail was sinuous and hard to follow, but he knew the route so well he could have done it blindfolded and in the dark. Without hesitation, he rode through the low-hanging branches and the brambles that pulled at his clothing. Behind him, he heard Josie and Old Sam's soft exclamations, heard them swipe at the bushes and thorns crowding the narrow pathway. When he finally led them into the clearing only a few yards from Cowhouse Creek, Josie sighed with relief.

"Are we here?" she asked hopefully.

Texas motioned for her to be quiet. He drew back his duster, rested his hand on the hilt of the Colt, and slowed his horse. The two cabins were just beyond, hidden in the edges of the brambled woods, their tiny shuttered windows affording whoever stayed there a clear view of the path. If Schofield or someone else was in the cabin, he would be watching their approach.

Texas moved carefully, but when they rounded the corner and he peered into the woods, the cabins looked abandoned. Still, he gestured for the others to wait. He dismounted and handed the reins to Old Sam, and then Texas shoved through the brambles until he reached the first cabin a few yards away.

The door was hung crookedly and wedged shut. Texas pushed against it with his shoulder, kicking at the bottom until it squeaked open and scraped against the pounded-dirt floor. It was dark inside, and musty, and it looked as if no one had been there for a long time, but Texas went to the windows and pushed at the shutters. They opened easily enough, shrunken by heat that even humidity couldn't affect. Immediately, the small room was filled with light.

He glanced around then, and in the daylight he saw the evidence that someone had been there, a recently used oil lamp and a bucket of water and the browning curls of apple peel on the table. Texas looked up at the loft, but it was quiet and empty. He went to the window on the other side of the room and pushed it open, too, looking beyond to the small cabin that belonged to him and Lily. It was dark and closed up.

His hand eased off his gun. There was no one here. He walked painfully to the door and went to the clearing again, where the others waited.

"All right," he said. "It's safe."

Josie smiled. "As if it wouldn't be," she said. "Didn't you say Schofield was watching it?"

He didn't answer her. Texas went over to Old Sam. "There's a lean-to in the back," he said. "We can put the horses there. You go ahead and take them down to the creek first, and I'll get Josie and Lily settled in."

Old Sam nodded. He glanced at Lily. "You think you can handle the both of 'em, Mister Christian?"

Texas gave a short laugh. "We'll see."

He stepped away from Old Sam and went to Lily's horse, quickly untying the thong that fastened her bound hands to the saddle horn, stepping back to help her dismount. But she only glared at him until he stepped away and let her help herself. By the time he got to Josie, she was already off her horse, pulling at the heavy saddlebags.

Just as he reached her, she gave a final tug. The saddlebags landed with a *thunk* in the dirt. He heard the clank of the silver inside.

Jocelyn frowned. "Christian—"

"We'll come back for it," he said. He waited for Lily,

took hold of her arm tightly, and started toward the cabin. "This way, Josie."

"I don't suppose you've thought of trimming this pathway," Josie grumbled as she followed them into the woods. "All these branches . . ."

"You could always talk to Pa about it," Texas said.

"Oh, I suppose there's something important about keeping it this way," Josie said. "Something like . . ." Her voice trailed off. Texas glanced around to see her standing there, staring at the cabins in dismay. "Oh, my Lord," she said. "This is awful."

He gave her a smile. "Not much like home, is it, Josie?"

She shook her head and glanced at Lily before she looked back at Texas again. "You make her live here?"

"Not here," Texas said. He nodded to the cabin beyond. "That one's ours."

Jocelyn frowned. "It doesn't look much better."

"It isn't."

"Oh, my." Her voice was faint, but she followed him and Lily inside gamely. For a moment he saw the cabin through her eyes: the packed-dirt floor and the dust covering every piece of furniture, the old, battered chairs and the scarred table and the single bed built into the wall just beyond the stove. What books there were had curled pages and split leather covers, and dusty, crackling newspapers were piled on the bed and stuffed into the cracks in the hewn-log walls. A dirty, crumpled sketch of a half-naked woman fluttered from a nail stuck into the windowsill. "It could use some . . . cleaning."

"Well, Pa and the others haven't been here for a while." He led Lily to a chair and waited while she sat. "You can do whatever you like to it."

"Whatever I like," Josie repeated softly. "What I'd like is to tear it down and start again."

He grinned. "It's not so bad, Josie. You'll get used to it. And we're never here for long."

She sighed. "Well, then. Where do we sleep?" She glanced at the bed and shuddered. "Not there, I hope."

"There's the loft." He angled his head to the ladder climbing one wall. "I think we should stay together tonight. At least until Schofield gets here and we break Pa out."

Jocelyn sobered. "Should we go check on him, do you think? What if he's not all right?"

"It's better to wait for Schofield," Texas said shortly. "If anything's changed, he'll know it."

He saw her doubt, but she nodded anyway. She went to the window and leaned on the sill, blocking the sun. "So now what?"

"Now?" Texas started toward the door. "Now I'll get the saddlebags and you can make dinner."

"We just wait? That's all?"

Texas glanced at Lily, who was staring at the table, at the rotting apple peel, her bound hands clenched in her lap. The sun glinted bronze on the braid tossed over her shoulder, played across her face. "Yeah," he said slowly. "We just wait." And then he went out the door and back to the trail to help Old Sam bring the horses home.

11

It was very late. Josie and Lily were asleep in the loft, Lily leashed safely to an old metal drying hook embedded in the wall, and Old Sam was half-sitting, half-lying on the bed in the corner downstairs, slumped against the wall, his grizzled head falling forward as he fought sleep.

Texas was wide awake.

He sat at the table nursing a cup of coffee that had long since grown cold, staring out the still-open shutters at the darkness outside. He'd turned the oil lamp down so low it barely emitted any light, but he didn't need illumination. He'd found an old, well-worn deck of cards by the stove, and he shuffled them over and over again, never playing a game, not even looking at them. His gaze was focused on the window, his ears tuned to sounds beyond Old Sam's gentle snoring and the whisk of the cards.

He had a premonition, or something that kept sleep from him, that strung him tight. It was stupid to expect Schofield, to expect anyone, to show up tonight, but Texas did. He'd hung the signal bandanna in the huge old oak to tell them a member of the gang was here, and now he waited in the darkness for the sound of hoofbeats, for the unmistakable break of branches and the brush of brambles against clothing. He watched for shadows in the night.

Then, finally, he saw it, heard it. A shift of shadow, a quiet whisper. Texas stiffened in his chair, put the cards aside, blew out the lamp. He wrapped his hand around the hilt of his gun, pulled it from its holster, and went to the window, angling his body so he could see without being seen, holding his breath as he waited.

He didn't have to wait long. The shadow evolved into two, then three. The quiet snorting of horses pricked his ears. Texas's fingers tightened on the trigger. He kicked the edge of the bed with his foot.

"Wha—" Old Sam was startled awake. Texas threw him a quick look and the old man shut up. He heard the quiet rustle of the moss-filled mattress as Old Sam got to his feet, heard the shuffle of Sam's movement. In moments, the old man was standing next to him, the old Sharps rifle in his hands.

The trees shrouded whatever moonlight there was, but Texas could still see. Three men, bent low, were leading their horses through the branches guarding the narrow path, toward the cabin. Three men, not one. Not Schofield. Texas jerked his head at Old Sam, motioning the man to the other side of the cabin, flanking the door. Sam was there in an instant, the rifle butt shoved against his shoulder.

Texas looked back outside. The men were coming closer now. They'd reached the clearing where the cabins stood. He hoped they wouldn't head around to the lean-to and find the horses already there, and stifled a sigh of relief when they didn't, when they just tethered their horses to the rotting hitching rail out front.

He flattened himself against the wall and waited. Their footsteps came closer, a muffled sound on the weed-packed dirt, the jangling clank of spurs on the porch. They weren't expecting anyone to be there, he thought, and they weren't making much of an attempt to be quiet.

He pulled back the hammer of the gun, heard Old Sam cock the rifle. The door eased open. Texas leveled the Colt and took aim in the darkness.

"Take another step," he warned, "and you'll get a bullet for your trouble."

The door halted its swing. "Shit," came the voice, an unmistakable voice. "Texas, is that you?"

Texas caught Sam's glance and eased his thumb off the hammer. "Schofield?" he asked.

"Christ almighty, it's dark as hell in here. You got a lamp?"

Texas didn't lower his gun. "Who the hell's with you?"

Schofield laughed. "It's a surprise," he said. "Now can we come in, or is that finger of yours still itchy?"

Texas jerked his head at Old Sam. The old man lowered the rifle and backed away from the door. "Yeah," Texas said. "Come on in."

"It's about time," another voice said, and, with a shock, Texas recognized it as his father's. The door scraped open and the unmistakably tall form of Hank Sharpe eased inside, followed by Schofield and another, shorter man. Bobby.

"Goddamn," Texas breathed. "You're out of jail."

"No flies on you," Schofield said. "Now light the damned lamp."

Texas shoved his gun into his holster and lit the lamp. Instantly, the room flickered into light. Carefully, he reached back and pulled the shutters closed.

Bobby walked to the table. "We were starting to wonder if somethin' happened to you."

"I wasn't gone that long," Texas said. "A week or so."

"'Time waits for no man,'" Hank quoted. He was smiling, but there was a considering look in his blue eyes. "Lollygagging around the Texas plains while your poor old pa languished in jail, huh, boy?"

"Just looking for women and playing cards," Texas joked. He limped across the floor to shake his father's hand and found himself instantly enveloped in a strong hug.

"Cards I believe," Hank said. "But looking for women?" He pulled away. The lamplight made deep shadows of his eyes, glinted off the silver in his mustache. He glanced around. "Doesn't look to me as if you found any—Sam? Is that you hiding in the corner there?"

Old Sam came out of the shadows, a broad smile splitting his dark face. "It's me, Mr. Hank," he said. He leaned the rifle against the wall and stepped forward, holding out his hand. "You boys managed to scare us pretty good."

Hank chuckled and shook the old man's hand. His gaze went again to Texas. "Dare I hope this means that Jocelyn's here, as well?"

Texas nodded. "She's sleeping in the loft."

"In the loft," Hank repeated slowly. His expression was thoughtful, uncomfortably questioning. He smoothed his mustache and licked his lips. "Just Josie?"

Texas felt the sudden strain that filled the room. Bobby sagged into a chair. Schofield stiffened. Texas saw his father's slow, assessing expression, and suddenly he was strangely reluctant to tell them he'd found Lily, that he'd brought her back here. He took a deep breath and spoke. "Lily, too," he said, and knew when he said it that he'd hesitated just a second too long. The question in his father's eyes intensified.

"In the loft? With Jocelyn?" Hank asked quietly. "You left her alone with my daughter?"

Texas thought of Lily upstairs, bound to the wall, gagged. He shrugged with deliberate casualness. "Josie's safe enough."

"Is she?" Hank's eyes narrowed.

"Goddammit, go ahead and ask him, Hank," Schofield urged. "Ask him what the hell he found out."

Hank didn't even turn. "Shut up," he said.

"You did ask her about Lampasas, didn't you, Texas?" Schofield ignored Hank's warning. "Did she tell Petry or didn't she?"

Hank's eyes went blankly cold. "You disobeying me, Schofield?"

Schofield clamped his lips together tightly and backed against the door. Texas met his father's gaze.

"Well?" Hank queried softly. "What's your answer, boy? Did she confess?"

It was a quiet question, but there was something beneath the words, a spark of rage, maybe, an intensity that seemed vaguely wrong, and the thought came into Texas's head: *He hates her.*

For just a second, it startled him. For a moment, he denied it. But then he realized he wasn't surprised, not really. He guessed he'd always known it; the truth of his father's feelings had rested beneath his consciousness, a thought too ugly to face. Now any hope Texas had of convincing his father to show mercy for her disappeared. Hank was just looking for an excuse to kill her. Lampasas would be more than reason enough.

Texas told himself it was what she deserved. He told himself she'd known the risks and taken them gladly.

She'd left them all to die in the thunder of gunfire, and she had never meant to come back. He didn't believe she'd thought about them at all.

He told himself this was his chance. His chance to reclaim his life, to end his torment completely and forever. There it was, all tied up in such a simple, easy question. *Did she confess?* All he had to do was tell the truth. Just the truth, and the temptation of Lily, the disappointment, would be gone, his life would be his.

All he had to do was answer yes. Just one simple word.

Texas looked at his father, at the intensity in his eyes, then beyond to a taut Schofield. Finally, he looked at Bobby, who slumped over the table, his fingers steepled, pressed against his forehead.

Texas thought of Lily's limp body dangling from a too-long rope. He thought of a cherry poke bonnet and words that tossed in his mind like an uneasy sleep. *"I'll leave you alone for the rest of my days. It's all I want. All I ever wanted."*

He caught his father's gaze and held it. "I couldn't get it out of her."

Schofield cursed and slapped his hand against the wall. Texas heard Bobby's chair scoot from the table. But he didn't take his eyes from his father's.

Hank rubbed his mustache. His expression was shuttered, but Texas felt that stare go clear into him, picking truths from his bones.

"Not a thing, eh?" Hank spoke softly.

From the corner of his eye, Texas saw Old Sam's knowing look, his quietly condemning gaze. He shook his head. "No."

"Ah." Hank sighed. He stroked his lip. "Did she have any explanations at all?"

"She thought we were dead," Texas said tersely.

"Well, we might have been." Hank's smile was humorless. "Would that have made her glad, I wonder?"

Texas shrugged. "You'll have to ask her yourself."

"Oh, I will. I will." Hank smiled slightly. His gaze swept Texas's face. "I imagine she was . . . ecstatic . . . to see you again. The love of her life."

The words hurt, as his father must have known they would. Texas glanced away. "Yeah. Something like that."

"Something like that," Hank repeated, "or nothing like that?"

Texas's gaze ricocheted back. "You don't believe me, Pa?"

"Love is blind, boy," Hank said slowly. His eyes narrowed. Texas felt the keen edge of his father's suspicions hovering between them, the question of loyalty that trembled unasked, unanswered. "Perhaps you're not hearing everything. Perhaps you missed something. Think hard. Did you miss something?"

Texas met his father's stare. "You accusing me of lying, Pa?" he asked slowly, coldly.

Bobby's quick inhalation seemed to fill the room. Hank didn't move. Texas tensed. It had been a calculated question, one meant to turn his father away from the too-potent, too-obvious lie, and now he wondered if he'd gone too far. But then Hank stepped back, his lips curved in a smile.

"You're overreacting, son," he said quietly. "If you say she didn't tell you, she didn't tell you."

There was a lie in the words, a suspicion Texas heard but couldn't find. He searched his father's eyes, but the question he'd seen before was gone. Texas nodded, then he looked over at Bobby and forced a smile. "Tell me about the jailbreak," he said, trying for a light tone.

"Is half of Lampasas county after us now, or did you manage to do it right without me?"

It was nearly dawn when Texas finally climbed the ladder to the loft. Bobby and Old Sam were snoring downstairs, and Schofield and Pa were yawning as they carried on a halfhearted argument about some woman in Lampasas, nodding off between words and then waking again just to mumble another point.

Texas wasn't tired at all. He'd sat there and talked and laughed and cursed with the rest of them, but inside his heart was pounding and he felt restless and distracted. All he could think about was Lily and his lie to his father. It was so loud in his mind he wondered that Pa didn't hear it.

He'd called himself a fool a hundred different ways; he'd opened his mouth to tell them the truth twenty times. But each time, he'd heard her words again, the promise she'd made him, and he hoped he'd read her right for once, hoped that those dreams of hers were real ones and not just something she'd made up to fool him. He remembered that boardinghouse in Denison and how easily she'd left those hats behind, and he hoped that was the lie. He hoped she thought about those hats all the time. Because if he was wrong, he was a dead man.

Texas sighed. He paused at the edge of the loft, looking into the darkness, wondering if she was awake.

It was quiet, and Lily and Jocelyn were lumpy shadows on the floor, barely discernible, very still. Texas watched for a moment, waiting for movement, but there was none. Lily was probably sound asleep.

Texas bent to avoid the low ceiling and crept along the edge of the loft toward the far wall, where he'd tethered

Lily earlier in the evening. Slowly, his eyes adjusted to the darkness; he made his way unerringly to the shadow of the rope that led from the drying hook in the wall. She had rolled onto her side, and the rope stretched taut across her hip. He squatted beside her. Downstairs, he heard Schofield laugh, heard his father's answering chuckle.

It was then he realized she was awake. She lay there, her body too still for sleep, her breathing shallow and rapid. She didn't move, but when he reached over and unknotted the gag, she didn't pretend he hadn't touched her. She spit out the cloth, and her voice floated to him, a soft whisper in the darkness. "Are you going to take me to him?"

Texas's heart contracted. Though there was no fear in her voice, he heard it in the words, heard her wary readiness. "No," he said.

She rolled toward him. Though he couldn't see her eyes, he felt the intensity of her gaze in the darkness, heard the single word of her question like an arrow to his gut.

"Why?" she whispered.

Because I'm an idiot and a fool, he wanted to say. Instead, he shrugged and met her gaze in the night. "You were right," he said. "Pa will kill you if he finds out the truth."

She was quiet for a moment. He could practically hear her thinking, putting it together. "You didn't tell him."

"No."

Her sigh was soft, barely audible. Her words came on the end of it, a rushed, breathy whisper. "Thank you."

Texas shook his head. "It's not over, Lily," he said. "I did the best I could. I told him I couldn't get it out of you. I'm not sure he believes it."

She struggled to sit up. "He doesn't believe you?"

"He doesn't know what to believe."

"Then untie me," she said. Her words came out fast, tumbling over each other, as if she had only a moment to convince him. "Let me go. I'll do what I promised. I'll ride away."

"Don't be stupid. Don't you think that would tell him the truth quicker than anything?" He leaned closer, so close he felt the heat of his own breath on her cheek, felt the touch of her hair. "Think a minute. I just told Pa I don't know what happened in Lampasas. Understand? You didn't tell me anything. I don't know whether you betrayed us or not. Why the hell would I untie you? It doesn't make sense."

He felt her nod. She exhaled slowly. "Yeah. I see."

"The way I see it, it's only you and me who know the truth."

"What about Petry?"

"Petry's dead. Pa killed him during the robbery." He took a deep breath. "You're a good liar, baby. Tomorrow you better be the best."

Her silence was only a pause in words; he imagined he heard the churning of her mind like the long, slow grind of machinery. Then she nodded tightly.

"All right," she said. "I'll convince him."

"Good." He reached for the rope leashing her to the wall and untied it, throwing it to the side of the loft. He started to move away, and then he felt her hands on his arm, stopping him.

"Texas," she said. "Thank you."

Her words were deep and warm and heartfelt, and they sent the blood racing in his veins, made his skin burn where she touched him. And, though he told himself not to say anything, he couldn't stop his next words, or the regret that colored them.

"Lily," he asked quietly. "What happened to us?"

He expected a derisive answer, or no answer at all, but instead her hand tightened on his arm, her short, broken nails pressed into his flesh.

"I don't know," she said slowly, in a voice almost too low to hear. "Maybe . . . it was just life."

Then she released him. It was cold where her hand had been.

Texas nodded. "Yeah," he said. "Maybe." And then he moved away. He got to his feet, bowing his head and shoulders beneath the low ceiling. When he reached the other side of the loft, he grabbed the bedroll he'd left there and spread it out. Without taking off his boots, he wrapped himself in his blankets and lay down.

He lay there a long time before he heard her sigh and lie back again. Longer still before he heard the soft, even tone of her breathing. He didn't sleep at all.

12

When she first woke, Lily thought for a moment that Texas had been a dream. Then she tested the tether that had tied her bound wrists to the wall. It was gone. Lily felt a relief so strong it made her dizzy. It was morning, and she was alive, and likely to stay that way. If she could convince Hank of her innocence, she could walk away from all this. She could be free. All she had to do was talk her way out. All she had to do was find the right words.

God knew she'd spent most of her life finding the right words, fooling most people. But Hank was not most people, and she could not rid herself of the haunting image of his chilling blue gaze or the anxiety that made her palms sweat and her stomach tight. Texas had been right last night. Today had to be the performance of her life. Anything less . . . anything less would mean her death.

Beside her, Jocelyn stirred, murmuring in her sleep, stretching her body along Lily's like a cat, pointing her toes. Her long hair swept Lily's arm. She yawned and opened her eyes, looking up blearily.

"Is it morning already?" she asked.

Lily nodded. "Yeah."

Jocelyn rose to her elbows. "I thought I heard voices last night."

"Your pa's here," Lily informed her quietly.

"Pa's here?" Josie sat up so quickly that watching her made Lily dizzy. She pushed back the blankets of her bedroll and got to her feet, her movements jerky with excitement. Nervously, she smoothed the sleep-ironed wrinkles of her dress.

"Oh, I look a fright, I'm sure." But there was no real worry in her voice, only exhilaration.

It was as if Hank were Christ himself, Lily thought derisively, and then remembered there was a time when she'd felt just that way about him. A long time ago.

She felt a nudge of sadness at the thought, sadness for her own foolishness, for the stupid naiveté of a young girl with her first lover. Josie would eventually learn the truth about her father, just as Lily had, and, for a moment, Lily felt sorry for that, too, for Josie's inevitable disillusionment, for the bitterness that seeped inside and never went away. No one was ever what you wanted them to be.

But Josie had to live her own life; there was nothing Lily could say to help her, even if she wanted to. Still, as Lily watched Josie's preparations, watched her comb her hair with her fingers and twist and turn to straighten her clothing, that sadness seemed to well up in Lily's soul. She couldn't quite banish it, even when Josie smiled at her and asked, "Aren't you coming?"

Lily shook her head and looked away. "Maybe later."

She heard Josie's pause, heard the hesitation, the sudden stillness.

"What is it, Lily?" Jocelyn asked, her excitement disappearing in sudden sobriety. "Something's wrong, isn't it?"

"Nothing's wrong." Lily met her eyes and smiled. "Go on down and say hey to your pa."

Jocelyn frowned. She was at the edge of the ladder, and now she hurried back to Lily, kneeling beside her, touching her arm. "Oh, Lily. You can talk to me, you know. You can. Tell me what's bothering you."

Such sweet words, such warmth. With horror, Lily felt a tight ache behind her eyes, the press of tears. She shut her eyes, took a deep breath, and shook her head. "You go on down."

Jocelyn didn't go. She scooted back against the wall, into the corner, and leaned her head back. In the pale dimness, she was nothing but dark and light shadows, and Lily liked it that way, liked not being able to see Josie's face.

"You know, I can't believe I'm here," Jocelyn said, her tone light and distracting. "It's like a dream come true."

"A dream come true?" Lily snorted. "A nightmare, more like."

Josie shook her head. "Oh, no. I can't tell you how many hours I spent wanting this very thing. I'd be sitting there in the barn, milking the cows, and all I could think about was Pa and Christian. I wanted so much to be one of the gang." She paused, laughing slightly. "Oh, I know you'll think this is silly, but I even used to imagine the outfit I'd wear. A divided skirt with fringe all down the sides, and a bright red bandanna."

The picture came into Lily's head, ludicrous and absurd. She glanced away, hiding a bitter smile.

"I didn't think that . . . trousers were allowed," Josie went on. "And I didn't picture"—she gestured at the loft—"this."

This. Dirt and ugliness. A house that let the rain in and the dust. Lily's throat felt tight. "Disappointed?" she asked.

"No. Oh, no." Josie let out her breath in a sigh. "I didn't expect this, it's true, but I don't care. It's worth everything just to be here."

Lily stared at her. The extent of Josie's innocence continually startled her. The fictions Hank had taught his daughter about the gang were dangerous and skewed, and the fact that Josie believed them so thoroughly, that she yearned for this life in spite of the harsh reality of the last few days, angered Lily for no reason she could say. "Don't say that," she said sharply. "You don't know how good you have it. Things are so damned easy for you."

"Not easy," Josie said. "Just boring. Sometimes a neighbor would drop by, or Pa and Christian would visit. But other than that, it was just me and Ma and Old Sam. The days were all the same."

There was something strangely pensive about Josie's words, a pain in her tone that touched a bruise inside Lily.

"There are times I wish the days were all the same," Lily murmured.

"You wouldn't like it. You're not like other people," Josie said, and again Lily heard that admiration, that hero-worship that made her feel guilty and angry and confused that she felt either one. "You and Christian, you're not like anyone I've ever met. The two of you know how to live. You reach out and grab the things you want. I don't think you've ever been afraid of anything."

How self-assured her words were. How damned naive. The words of someone who had never really felt fear, who didn't understand how just living could suck away a person's soul. Josie didn't know the pain of being orphaned or the terror that made a girl trade her virginity for her life. She didn't realize yet that death was always there, stalking like a relentless shadow, hungry and waiting for the slightest misstep.

Lily looked into the shadows of Josie's eyes. "Oh, I've been afraid," she said quietly.

"Of hanging?"

Lily shook her head.

"Oh." Josie paused. "Of dying, then."

Josie's guess stabbed clear into Lily's heart. She couldn't answer, but Josie pressed on, undeterred.

"I guess . . . I guess I'm not afraid of that," she said. "Mama taught me that death was only another kind of life."

"You mean heaven," Lily said.

"Yes."

Lily sat back. "I don't imagine I'll be seeing you there."

Josie smiled gently. "My God is a forgiving one."

"Well, my God isn't."

"You haven't been listening to Pa's reading, have you?"

Lily laughed then. A full-out, bitter laugh. "Hell, Josie. I've never heard a word of scripture pass Hank's lips."

Jocelyn frowned. She leaned forward, and in the half-light her eyes held a saintlike compassion, an understanding that made Lily want to curl into herself, to hide her face.

"He's a forgiving man," Josie said. "Whatever it is you've done, whatever it is Christian tied you up for, it doesn't matter. Pa will understand."

The declaration was so absurd Lily stared at her. "Hell, Josie."

"I know it's true," Josie said with conviction. She got to her feet, brushing off her skirt. "And I mean to talk to him anyway. What Christian's done, it's not right. Pa will make him undo it."

Lily didn't know whether to laugh or cry. Such damn innocence. It would take Hank all of ten seconds to disabuse Josie of it, and the knowledge squeezed Lily's heart. The thought of Jocelyn's disillusionment made her feel tight and hollow.

"Josie," she objected softly.

Jocelyn took her hand and squeezed it. She pulled Lily to her feet and drew her to the edge of the loft. "I'll make everything all right. You just wait and see."

Lily tried not to wince. "But you don't—"

"Oh, Lily. What are friends for?"

Friends. Lily stopped short, staring after Josie, watching as she started down. Her own anxiety faded, replaced by a twinge of regret, again that bruising touch. She thought of Hank down there, waiting for his daughter, and knew that, in less than an hour, Josie's naiveté would be shattered.

When he first saw the two of them, Texas thought he was hallucinating. Josie was coming down from the loft, and though there was nothing strange in that, what was strange was the way she waited at the bottom for Lily, the way she reached for Lily's bound hands and held them tightly.

He nearly choked on his coffee at the sight. He could barely swallow when he saw Pa look up. Texas waited in anxious watchfulness as his father looked toward the ladder. He saw Pa's eyes flash to Lily, and then Hank looked deliberately away, to Josie, and his face broke into a smile. He flattened his palms on the table, rising so quickly the legs shook.

"Josie," he said, holding out his hands. Jocelyn let go of Lily long enough to run into his arms.

Pa held her tightly, the force of his hug lifting her off the ground. "Josie, darlin'," he said. "Ah, my darlin' girl."

"Oh, Pa." Josie buried her face in his shoulder. "It's so good to see you." She took a deep breath and drew away enough to smile into his face. Her eyes were wet. "I've missed you so."

"I've missed you, too." Hank smoothed her hair back gently from her face. "I wish I could have attended to your mama's burial, darlin'," he said. "I wanted to be there."

Texas looked down into his coffee. There was something so intimate about their greeting; there was a softness to their relationship that he himself had never had with his father. And, though Texas understood that Josie was nothing like him, it still needled him whenever he saw his father and her together, a jealousy he couldn't control, an old, childish wish that his father would love him half that much.

He glanced up at Lily, hoping she would make him forget those feelings, and she didn't disappoint him. She stood at the foot of the ladder watching Josie and Pa with an intensity that made Texas as nervous as it reassured him.

She looked over at him, and the darkness of her eyes surprised him, the seriousness of her expression. For a moment, he had the startling thought that they were together in this, that she was looking to him for support, for strength. He dismissed the notion quickly, feeling like a fool. Lily didn't need his strength. She didn't need an ally. And God knew she didn't need him. She'd made that clear enough.

But, still, the feeling wouldn't leave him, and he took a deep breath and forced himself to turn back to Josie and his father. They were whispering, heads together, exchanging soft, mellow love words, remembering Annie, and Texas felt intrusive and out of place. His fingers curled around his coffee cup, clutching it even when the heat of the chipped yellowware burned his fingers. He wanted this to be over. The sooner the better. He wished his father would look up and start questioning Lily. He wished it was settled one way or another.

Then he heard Schofield's crazy, tuneless whistle on the porch, and Texas sat up, leaning back in his chair, struggling to maintain nonchalance.

The door to the cabin opened, flooding the interior with hazy morning light, and through it came Schofield, Bobby close behind, Old Sam bringing up the rear. The three of them had been down at the creek washing up, and now water dripped from Schofield's thin brown hair, darkening the shoulders of his shirt. Bobby was fresh-faced and awake-looking again, and droplets sparkled in the tight curls of Old Sam's grizzled head.

Schofield stopped just inside the door, stiffening. Texas saw him take in the intimate conversation in the center of the room, and then his eyes riveted to Lily, who looked up and smiled, the sweetest damn smile.

"Hey, Schofield," she said quietly. "Bobby."

Bobby paled. He raked his hand through his dark hair, standing the wet strands on end. "Lily," he whispered. "Jesus, it's really you."

He took a step forward, but Schofield stopped him with a raised hand. "Wait a minute," he said, and then, "Hank."

Pa looked up from Josie as if he hadn't heard them enter the room. He glanced at Schofield, irritation crossing his face, marring his too-pleasant smile. "You lost your manners, Schofield?" he asked. "It should be obvious I'm engaged in conversation with a lady."

Schofield cleared his throat. "Sorry."

Hank took Josie's arm and turned her to face them. "Darlin'," he said. "I'd like you to meet the rest of our merry band. The tall, ugly one without any manners is Schofield. The one next to him is Bobby."

Jocelyn smiled. "Pleased to meet you both."

Schofield mumbled something. Bobby moved forward and shook Josie's hand with a gentle wariness that Texas would have found gratifying at some other time. Old Sam slipped past them all, disappearing into the corner by the door, watching quietly.

Hank squeezed Josie's arm. "Now go on and sit down, why don't you, darlin'? Have some coffee. The boys and I have a little business to discuss."

Josie didn't budge. Her face was set with a determination Texas was beginning to recognize.

"I have a little business of my own to discuss with you, Pa," she said, and then she threw Texas a look of such venom he nearly fell back in his chair.

Pa lifted a brow. "Business?"

"Yes." Jocelyn crossed her arms over her chest and lifted her chin. "It's about Lily."

"Ah, yes. Lily." Hank glanced past her to where Lily stood, his expression measuring. Lily didn't look away. She met his gaze, held it, and, if Texas had sensed earlier that she needed reassurance, there was no sign of that now. She looked as self-assured and daunting as he'd ever seen her. "What about sweet Lily?"

"Look what Christian's done," Josie said. She stepped over and grabbed Lily, pulling her forward, forcing Lily's hands out flat so Hank couldn't avoid seeing them. "She's been bound up like that since they came to the farm—since before that, even. Last night he even gagged her!"

"Horrible," Hank murmured.

"It's shameful, the way he's treated her. His own wife! And for no good reason, Pa. No good reason at all. He said she's dangerous, but I don't believe it. I mean, look at her. Why, Lily couldn't hurt a fly. She's so little herself. Surely she's nothing for a grown man to be afraid of."

Texas felt Schofield staring at him, but he kept his eyes on his father.

"Is that right?" Pa asked softly.

Josie nodded vigorously. "I know you didn't raise either of us to be heathens, Pa, but Christian has acted no better than one of those dirty Comanches."

"But Josie, darlin'. Perhaps Texas knows best," Hank said.

"It's savage, Pa. I know you wouldn't condone such a thing. Why, if Mama knew, she would roll over in her grave!"

Lily didn't move. She was as still as Texas had ever seen her, her face sharp and watchful, and suddenly he understood. He saw his father's hesitation, Josie's vehemence, and realized at once what Lily had done. Somehow, she had engaged Josie's sympathies. Somehow, Lily had manipulated all this to get what she wanted.

He couldn't help the rush of admiration he felt. She was so damn smart. She'd managed to back Pa into a corner without saying a word, and it was Pa's own fault. Hank had spent the better part of Josie's life fabricating lies, convincing her he was a God-fearing, moral man, when in truth he was neither. Now, all those years of reading Bible verses and making sure his daughter admired him were ricocheting in his face.

Texas was still reeling from the pure cleverness of it when he realized he'd missed something. There was a tightness in Lily's bearing, not confidence, as he'd thought, and not self-assurance. There was a guardedness in her expression, a high-strung set to her shoulders and the way she held her head, and it seemed familiar to him in some vague way.

The memory came to him suddenly, bringing with it strains of music and a thin and wavering voice. *Rock of Ages.* Texas rubbed his jaw and looked away, his vision suddenly filled with the sight of a blindfolded twelve-year-old girl.

"Rock of Ages, cleft for me. Let me hide myself in thee."

Confused, Texas looked at her again, wondering if it was just another illusion, or if it was really vulnerability he saw. He looked at her hard, but he couldn't tell. She was too wary for him to know.

Then Hank turned to him, and Texas forced himself to concentrate on remembering his role, on not getting caught in his own lies.

"Is this true, boy?" Pa asked. "You tied Lily?"

Texas shrugged though his shoulders were stiff with tension. "I told you I didn't know what happened in Lampasas. It seemed the best thing to do."

Pa pulled away from Josie. He strode across the room until he was even with Texas. Then, with a quick thrust of his boot, he kicked the legs of the chair Texas sat in, throwing it back, forcing him to his feet.

Hank leaned close. Texas saw the anger in his father's face, but there was none in his eyes. "Your loyalty is admirable," he said, and, though his tone was stiff, Texas heard the praise hidden behind it. "But if I ever see you tying up a woman like a dog again, I'll be the one you face in hell." He jerked his head toward

Lily. The act of his anger was convincing, formidable despite the fact that it was all a lie. "Untie her."

It was time for Texas to play his part. "But Pa—"

"I said untie her." Hank stepped back, leaving room for Texas to get by. Slowly, Texas pulled his knife from his belt and approached Lily.

She didn't move. He thought she would look at him and wondered what he would see in her eyes if she did, but she kept her eyes lowered as he came near. She held out her hands, and with one quick slice he was through the bandanna. It fell to the floor, a dirty, twisted scrap of material, leaving her wrists bare and red and welted. Texas averted his gaze, stabbed his knife back into his belt.

"I hope I don't regret this," he murmured, too soft for anyone but Lily to hear.

She didn't respond.

"Wait a damned minute," Schofield cut in. "Listen, Hank, we don't know—"

Hank's glare silenced him. Pa strode back toward Josie and gave her a soft smile. "Is that what you wanted, darlin'?" he asked. "Happy now?"

Jocelyn beamed. "Much happier."

"Good. Then why don't you go on out to the creek with Old Sam for a minute? The boys and I have something to discuss."

"A wash would be nice," Josie said. "Lily, come on with—"

"Lily needs to stay," Hank said firmly.

"But—"

"There are a few things we need to get straight," Pa explained.

Josie nodded, though she still looked unconvinced. "You won't let Christian tie her up again, will you?"

"I'm not a savage, Jocelyn."

"Good," Josie said. She shot Texas a triumphant look, and then she smiled and kissed Hank on the cheek. "I knew you would do the right thing, Pa."

She started toward the door. The rest of them stood in silence until she disappeared outside, Old Sam following close behind. The door closed behind them.

Then all hell broke loose.

Bobby and Schofield talked over each other, Hank told them to shut up, and Lily just leaned against the wall, crossing her arms over her chest, facing them with that incredible, implacable strength.

She lifted her chin and smiled. "How're you all doing, boys?"

Her voice blasted through the noise like a gunshot. Schofield clamped his mouth shut. Bobby looked like he might cry. Texas pulled out his chair and sat again, the crooked legs rocking and squeaking beneath his weight. The nervousness that had riled his stomach earlier came back with a vengeance.

Hank strode toward her, the rhythm of his boot heels deliberate, ominous. He stopped just a few feet away and looked at her, his fingers stroking his mustache, his eyes narrowed.

"Well, well," he said slowly, his voice so devoid of emotion it made Texas's skin prickle. "You're back."

She met his gaze. "I couldn't stay away."

"Is that so?" Hank glanced over his shoulder at Texas. "She was dying to come home, boy, is that it?"

Texas eyed his father steadily. "She wasn't happy about being tied," he said, evading the question.

"Would you be?" Lily asked miserably. "I missed you all so much. I thought you were dead. And then here comes Texas, and the first thing he does is tie me up and accuse me of treachery."

"You thought we were dead?" Schofield asked.

"I thought I saw Hank and Texas get shot," she said. "Then Bobby took that bullet in the shoulder and I—I just panicked. I knew Petry would be after me soon enough."

She looked at Hank. Texas was startled at how real the fear and distress in her eyes looked. Whatever vulnerability he'd sensed earlier was gone. He'd told her last night she was the best liar he knew, and now he was stunned to see the evidence of it again, stunned to see the same look that had fooled him in Denison. Hell, it could fool him again now.

She swallowed. "I was afraid."

Bobby laughed nervously. "Damn. I think we were all afraid."

Hank threw him a look that shut him up instantly. Then he turned back to Lily. "So you were mourning us?" he murmured. "Singing dirges for our poor souls?"

She nodded, swallowing as if her throat held her tears. "Yeah."

Hank reached out, cupping her chin in his hand, stroking her cheek with his thumb. He laughed shortly. "But my boy didn't believe that, now did he, Lily-loo?"

Texas stiffened. For a moment, he could barely breathe. But Lily didn't flinch. "I guess not," she said.

"Now that's what makes me wonder." Hank didn't stop touching her, and though his tone was light, there was a danger beneath it, a deadliness Texas recognized. "You've always been able to talk your way out of anything. Why is it you're suddenly quiet when Texas asks you about Lampasas?"

She said nothing for a moment; it seemed like an eternity. Then she lifted her hands, and, even from where he stood, Texas could see the raw red welts at her wrists. She laid her hand on Hank's chest, near his heart. Her face was so stark with yearning and hope it was chiseled and planed. She looked at the other men, standing quietly, listening, and then back to Hank. "You're my family. All of you. The only family I have. I couldn't bear it if something happened to you. I couldn't bear it. And when Texas thought—" She choked off the words and looked down at the ground. When she continued, her voice was almost too quiet to hear. "I wanted to punish him for believing I could betray you. So . . . I wouldn't tell him the truth."

"What is the truth?" Hank asked.

She raised her eyes. "I had nothing to do with Lampasas, I swear it."

Schofield stepped forward. "You didn't tell Petry we were hitting the bank?"

"No." She shook her head. "I never talked to Petry. Not ever. Ask him if you don't believe me. He'll tell the truth fast enough when a gun's pointed at his head."

"Petry's dead," Bobby said.

It was incredible; she actually seemed to pale. "He's dead?"

Pa's smile was cold. "Mourning him, Lily-loo?"

"No . . . I . . ." She swallowed. There was a touch of fear in her eyes. "He's the only one who could have told you the truth. Him or me. If you don't believe me . . ." Her voice fell to a whisper. "You have to believe me, Hank. Please believe me."

Her face was so tight with emotion that even Texas felt himself responding to her, believing her. He glanced over at Schofield and Bobby. There was no doubt in Schofield's eyes now, and Bobby was hanging on her every word.

Damn, she was good. It was somehow painful to know that, to see the evidence of it before his eyes, to realize that she was capable of such cunning lies, even as he'd trusted that she would be. How many times had she wrapped him around her finger just this way? Crocodile tears and pretty hesitations, words that appealed to instinct and emotions she read far too well.

Texas turned his eyes back toward his father. Hank and Lily stood there in silence, her eyes filled with unshed tears as she stared at him in supplication. Hank was quiet. He smoothed the ends of his mustache over and over again, drawing his mouth down in a frown. Texas's skin felt too tight. His hand clutched his cup so hard he felt it might crack beneath his fingers.

"Bobby," Hank said. His soft voice seemed to reverberate in the room, so startling Bobby jumped at the sound.

"Yeah?"

Hank didn't take his eyes from Lily. He didn't stop his incessant stroking. "What do you think? Do we believe her or not?"

"Well, I . . ." Bobby stuttered. His face seemed very pale beneath the darkness of his hair. He looked at the floor when Lily turned her eyes to his. "I think . . . I think she's tellin' the truth."

"What about you, Schofield?"

"Goddamn." Schofield took a deep breath, shook his head. "I don't know, dammit. But I guess . . . I guess I agree with Bobby."

Hank's fingers stilled on his mustache. Texas tensed, waiting for the next name, feeling the force of it in the air before his father even asked it.

"Boy?"

The word was explosive. Texas clenched his jaw. He looked past his father at Lily and saw with surprise that she was looking straight at him, those dark eyes darker than he could remember seeing them before, the plea in their depths soft and tempting. Again he had the feeling that they were together in this, partners in deception, partners in lies, and the thought was so powerful, so hard to ignore, it sent a shiver into his bones. He shifted his glance to his father.

He shrugged, deliberately casual. "Seems enough like truth to me."

"Does it now?" Hank turned. His blue gaze was piercing. "Well then, you're in charge of her," he said. "She doesn't make a step without your knowing about it."

Texas raised his eyes to his father. "You've decided to trust her then?"

Hank smiled. "I've decided that you're Lily's husband," he said. "And so I put her into your care. She's a delicate female, as Josie said, and after so many days on her own, I expect she will turn to you for guidance. Now, if you were to guide her wrong"—his smile turned thin; the threat in his voice shuddered in the stillness—"If you guide her wrong, boy, there'll be hell to pay. I promise you that."

13

"*I promise you that.*" The words took on a power of their own in the crowded, tiny room.

Hank didn't shift his gaze from his son. He waited for something, hesitation, maybe, a slight pause, a telling discomfort. But there was nothing like that. Texas's lips tightened, but his nod was quick and instantaneous, emotionless.

"All right, Pa," he said. He got to his feet, walking lazy and slow toward the stove. He poured himself another cup of coffee, and then his gaze went to Lily. "You heard him, Kittycat."

Lily smiled; it was small but dazzling. "I heard him," she said. And then, "Thank you, Hank."

Oh, she was good. Hank would grant her that. If she was lying, as he suspected, she wasn't showing it. Her dark eyes were nearly brimming with gratitude. For a moment, he was afraid she would throw herself into his arms. And if she did, he would know for sure that she was lying. But Lily had never been a demonstrative woman, and she didn't overplay her hand now.

Hank smiled slowly back at her. "Welcome back,

Lily-loo," he said and felt a stab of satisfaction when her eyes darkened at his use of the nickname.

"You won't regret it, Hank," she said, her voice low and fervent. "I'll do whatever it takes to show you. I swear it."

Whatever it takes. The words reminded him of another time, of a look in her eyes that had said the same thing, that stoic endurance she'd worn when she first came into his bed. He had the feeling that every moment since then had been building up to now, to this woman who stood there promising a loyalty he'd long since lost belief in.

He knew she'd betrayed them. He understood human nature; it was a gift he prided himself on, a gift that had kept him alive these last thirty years despite the fact that his face was on wanted posters in three states. He sensed people's weaknesses, he sniffed out secrets. And there was a smell about Lily, the nasty stench of lies.

The problem was, he smelled the same thing on his son.

Sharper than a serpent's tooth, he thought, watching Texas wrap his hands around a cup and take a long gulp of coffee. Even that movement, simple and normal as it was, cut through Hank. There were no longer any simple things between himself and his son; there hadn't been for quite some time. But he couldn't help wishing for it, wishing his son was truly his heir in spirit as he was in body, wishing their relationship was as uncomplicated as Hank's with Josie.

But he supposed he was to blame for that. He should have listened to Annie all those years ago, should have let Texas find his own way in the world instead of bringing him into the gang. But Texas had already been too old at thirteen, and Hank had relished his son's idolization. He'd had fond visions of the two of them riding the plains together, of teaching his son all those fatherly lessons a man looked forward to handing down.

He'd wanted a son to carry on the family business, and he supposed he had him. But, somewhere along the line, Hank had lost what he wished for most: Texas's respect. His loyalty.

And Hank knew just who to blame for that.

He restrained a grim smile as he looked at Lily. She had gone over to talk to Schofield and Bobby, and even that cynical bastard Schofield was fawning over her.

Hank took a deep breath and went to the table. He sat down heavily, twisting in his chair to motion to Texas behind him. "Sit down, boy," he said in a low voice. "We should talk."

He had to give his son credit; the boy didn't even flinch. He ambled toward the table and sat down. His cup hit the table with a heavy thud. Hank said nothing, waiting for Texas to fill the silence. His son didn't disappoint him.

"I told Josie to pack light," Texas said slowly, bringing his gaze up to Hank's. "She'll be wanting to get the rest of her things. She brought the silver, but we left Annie's furniture at the house. It's going to take a couple wagons to get it all."

Hank raised his brow. "The silver? Good. We'll need it. The money's running low."

Texas winced. "She won't want to sell it."

"She'll do what I tell her to do," Hank said. He leaned back in his chair and reached into his pocket for his pipe and a pouch of tobacco. He felt his son's eyes on him as he filled the bowl and tamped it down, but he didn't look up, liking the suspense and the control it gave him. "I've been thinking. It's been a while since we took on a challenge."

"A challenge?" Texas asked carefully.

"A train."

Texas started. "A train? Christ, Pa."

"Think of it. Split-second timing. Everyone working as a team." Hank mouthed the stem of his pipe, reached for the matches. He studied his son beneath hooded lids. "A challenge, as I said."

He saw the exact moment Texas understood his meaning. His son glanced across the room to his wife; his fingers tightened on the cup before he shifted his gaze again to Hank. "You mean to include Lily in this."

Hank lit the pipe. He took a few puffs, waiting for the tobacco to catch, then breathed the smoke into his mouth, tasting it before he exhaled it again, watching the tension grow second by second in the set of Texas's shoulders, the tightness in his jaw.

For a moment, it disappointed him. It was too easy; he'd expected Texas to at least feign support for Lily. But then he realized Texas's question might be as much an act as Lily's innocence. It was the right thing to ask, a clever way to hedge his bets, to determine if Hank was telling the truth about believing her.

Hank smiled around the pipe. "She says she didn't turn us in."

Texas's eyes were sharp. His voice was low. "I wasn't sure you believed her."

"This will be a good test for her, don't you think? We'll give her a horse and a gun and see what she does." He watched his son carefully. "If she's with us, there'll be no problem. If she's not . . ." He let his words trail off. He puffed on his pipe and narrowed his eyes at Texas. "She'll be guarding your back, boy. I guess the better question is: Do *you* trust her?"

Texas didn't get a chance to answer. Just then, Josie came back inside, followed by Sam. She was bubbling and happy, and Hank turned his gaze from his son and drank her in, for the moment not caring about Texas or Lily, for the moment simply invigorated by his daughter's presence.

"I hope you're done discussing business, Pa," she said, smiling, "because I couldn't find another thing to do out there."

Hank took his pipe from his mouth and smiled at her. "We're done, darlin'," he said. He patted the chair beside him. "Come on over here and sit down next to your dear old dad."

He saw Lily turn abruptly. Her eyes followed Josie as his daughter made her way toward him, and there was an expression in her face Hank couldn't read.

"You're frowning, Pa," Josie teased as she came over.

"Am I?"

Lily's face was blank again. Hank turned away from her, taking his daughter's hand and pulling her into the chair beside him. "Well, now you're here, darlin', and there's no reason to be sad."

She flushed prettily and smiled into her hands. It reminded him of when he'd first fallen in love with her, his baby daughter. When her eyes laughed at him, and her gummy grin sent dimples into her cheeks. In his mind, she would always be that baby, even though she sat beside him now a full-grown woman. He thought of his plans for her—a good marriage to a just and moral man, a home, a place where she could bring up his grandchildren without worry—and it made him sad suddenly that he would have to give her away, that she was no longer his baby girl.

Ah, how things changed. He glanced at his son, and Hank's stomach tightened. Yes, things were always changing.

He smiled back at his daughter. "We'll be going into San Antonio soon," he told her. "Just you and me."

"Of course." She made a face. "To find a husband, I know. But not just yet, Pa, please. I'd like to spend some time with you and—and everyone."

"Oh?" He raised a brow at her. "Don't tell me you've fallen in love with our little hovel here."

"Not the hovel." She laughed. "But I've just seen you again, and I, well, to be honest, Pa, this is the most exciting thing I've ever done. Even when Texas took us into Fort Griffin."

"Josie," Texas warned.

"Fort Griffin?" Hank straightened. He jerked his gaze toward Texas. "You took her into Fort Griffin?"

"I—" Josie squeezed his arm. "Oh, Pa, I'm sorry. I didn't mean— Pa, please don't be angry. He and Lily were just doing what I asked."

The thought of Jocelyn in Fort Griffin, in the Flat—it made Hank crazy to imagine it. His Josie, stared at by all those lying, cheating dogs, those stinking buffalo hunters. He leaned forward. "I told you to protect her. You, boy. I'm talking to you."

The words were unnecessary; Texas was already looking at him. So was everyone else. Conversation had faded; Hank heard his own voice echoing in the eaves of the cabin.

"Pa," Josie said softly, urgently in his ear. "I insisted he take me. It's my fault."

Texas licked his lips and smiled slightly. His gaze was challenging. "She wanted to play a little faro, Pa," he said, "since she'd heard you talk so much about it."

For a moment, Hank wasn't sure he'd heard correctly. There was tacit criticism in his son's voice. Again that challenge, that faintly accusing stare.

It took Hank aback, and in that split second he realized there was something different about his son, something he hadn't noticed last night. There was an anger that seemed to shimmer on his skin, a dangerous carelessness in his tone and his bearing. Hank had thought earlier it was tension, but he was wrong. It wasn't tension, and suddenly he remembered he'd seen that kind of recklessness in Texas once before. Five, maybe six years ago now. Hank glanced at Lily. She and Schofield and Bobby were quiet now, watching them. Her face was still expressionless.

"Oh, please," Jocelyn said. "Pa, don't get angry with him. I asked him to take me. Really I did."

"I was there," Lily said. "She was safe enough."

"Was she?" Hank asked slowly.

Lily lifted a brow and smiled. "I glared at anyone who came near her, Hank."

He didn't like it. He didn't like it at all. Not his son's challenge nor Lily's flippancy. They were together in this some way, and he meant to find out exactly how.

Hank's palms itched at the thought of it. His anger over Fort Griffin faded. He glanced back at his son. *Slowly*, Hank reminded himself. *Take it slowly.* The best hunters stalked their prey for a long, long time.

Josie's hand still rested on his arm. He patted it reassuringly. "I suppose no harm came of it," he said deceptively lightly. "I know you don't want any harm to come to your sister, boy. I imagine you did your best to protect her."

A quick glance down, a nod. "Yeah," Texas said. "I did my best."

Ah, there it was. The weak point. And it had something to do with protecting Josie. Hank pressed further. "If I thought anyone even started to get too familiar with her—"

"No one came near her," Lily said. She sauntered

over to them, the raw, red welts bright and obvious
bracelets on her wrists. She smiled. "Texas stayed by
her side the entire time."

Hank thought he heard jeering in her voice, a soft
sarcasm that had him looking at his son. Texas's jaw
jumped, but other than that, there was no reaction to
her words.

"Is that so?" Hank asked. "Well, then, boy, I'm sorry
to have lost my temper with you." He forced himself to
grin at his daughter. "Did you enjoy yourself there, darlin'?"

"It was . . . exciting," Josie said, and Hank realized
suddenly that she was lying, too. "But I don't think I'll
want to go back."

Her lie sickened him and made him angry again, but
Hank only nodded and got to his feet, leaving his pipe
smoldering on the table while he went to the stove and
poured a cup of coffee. He took a sip. It was black and
strong, just how he liked it, and it put an edge on the
tobacco smoke in his mouth, melded it all into a taste as
bitter as the betrayal he sensed in the room.

"Well, that's good, darlin'," he said, not looking at
her, focusing on the loose chinking in the wall behind
the stove. He felt Bobby looking at him, and Schofield,
and he felt the stillness in the room, the arrested
breathing. It gave him back the control Josie's comment had taken from him, and he turned slowly and
smiled at his son and Lily, at Jocelyn. He made himself
tease. "You won't be trying to get me to teach you faro,
then."

Jocelyn laughed lightly and shook her head. "No, Pa."

"Because I don't guess your new husband would
appreciate a card-playing wife."

She blushed prettily. "Oh, Pa."

"No, no," he said thoughtfully. "I don't guess he

would. But, then again, look at your brother and Lily there. Some men don't give a damn what their wives do."

Texas went still. "Pa," he said, and Hank heard the warning in his son's voice.

"Ah, that's right." Hank smiled. He looked at Lily, who met his gaze steadily. "Forgive me, Lily-loo. I didn't mean to insult you."

She gave a short nod, but her eyes didn't soften. Hank moved slowly to the table, feeling a gratifying surge of power as all eyes turned toward him, as the tension in the room grew. They were afraid of him, all of them but Josie, who sat watching him with wide, adoring eyes, blissfully unaware. It warmed him. He smiled.

"I'd guess the two of you have quite a bit to talk about." He smiled indulgently. "There's no need to stay here with us. Not with your own cabin standing empty."

Texas smiled back, but there was an edge there, a dullness in his eyes that made Hank think he was right, that the last thing his son wanted was to be alone with Lily. Lily's expression revealed nothing, as usual. She was good, Hank had to admit. She was as good as he'd raised her to be.

But the game wasn't over, not yet. This was only the first step. There was still plenty of time for Lily to crack.

"All right, then." Texas got to his feet. "You been in the cabin lately?"

Hank shook his head. He stroked his mustache. "Not since you left."

Texas nodded shortly. "We'll see you later," he said, inclining his head toward Lily. He went awkwardly to the door, and Lily followed behind him.

Hank watched them go with a smile. They would reveal themselves in time. *Patience is a virtue.* Luckily, it was one of the only virtues he had.

Lily's heart was beating in her ears as she followed Texas to their cabin. She didn't want to be anywhere with him, and especially not this little cabin where they'd lived together the last few years. But there was nowhere else to go.

For a split second that morning, it had not been that way. She had thought she was finally free. It had been all Lily could do to keep from falling over in a dead faint when Josie's pleadings worked and Hank ordered Texas to cut the bandanna from Lily's wrists. When the dirty scrap of scarf was finally gone, falling to the floor, she had expected to feel overwhelming relief.

What she felt instead was panic.

Hank didn't believe her. In the end, it was just that simple, and she had looked into his cold blue eyes and seen the truth of his skepticism there. He thought she was lying, but he couldn't do anything about it without showing he disbelieved his son, and that Hank wouldn't do, at least not yet. He wouldn't cause friction by accusing his son of lying. No, far better to catch them in the lie, to watch and wait.

It was what she would do. Lily's jaw tightened. She would have to abandon her plans to leave. She couldn't run without proving Hank right. The moment she rode away, he'd know for sure she'd betrayed them, and he wouldn't rest until she was in her grave. All she could do was try to convince him she wasn't lying, to prove to him that the gang was still her life, that she would do anything for them.

She grimaced at the thought. Staying alive was just

an endless string of "anythings," of sacrifice and suffering and giving pieces of herself away. Lily sighed silently. Just once, she wished it could be different, but she guessed maybe that was asking too much. Maybe that was a wish that didn't come true for anyone.

They reached the cabin in only a few yards. Lily took the two steps to the sagging porch in a stride. Texas sprang the lever, but the door didn't open until he set his shoulder against it and pushed. Then it creaked and groaned, catching on the slanted floor until it finally dragged free and cracked against the wall.

The smell assaulted her; rancid grease and old wood and the dusty, fading scent of aging coffee beans. She saw immediately that Hank was right; the cabin hadn't been disturbed since Lampasas. Everything was just as she'd left it the morning of the robbery: the coffee grinder sat on the table beside a half-opened bag of coffee, the cast-iron skillet soaked in the washtub, the bed was unmade, the blankets rumpled and sour.

She felt as if she'd stepped back in time. The events of that morning came back to her so strongly it was as if she were reliving them. She had been nervous and distracted and excited, knowing that the life she dreamed of waited for her. She had ground the coffee but forgot to make it. She had burned the bacon in the skillet. She'd let Texas make love to her without protest. She'd walked out this door leaving everything undone and not caring. She had never expected to see this cabin again.

She realized suddenly that Texas was still beside her. She glanced up at him, following his gaze to the bed, seeing the memories in his eyes. Deliberately, Lily turned away. She walked to the washtub. There was still some water in it, a thin and oily surface scum studded with trapped flies and mosquitoes. The skillet was rusted where the water touched it, and the thick, greasy cinder of bacon crusted the rest.

It brought a lump to her throat. She heard Texas walk across the floor; the boards creaked beneath the heavy thud of his boots. She heard him pull out a chair and the wheeze as he sat in it. Lily glanced over her shoulder at him.

He was angled back in the chair, one booted foot on the floor, the other resting on the brace. He'd taken off his hat and put it on the table, and the indentation of the hat brim was pressed into his long, blondish hair in a strip above his ears. He looked hot and sweaty and pensive, and when she turned into his gaze, she saw the way his blue eyes shuttered.

She came right to the point. "He doesn't believe us."

"I know."

"I can't leave."

He sighed and played with the brim of his hat. "I know that, too."

"I can convince him," she said. "I know I can."

He lifted his eyes. "Can you?"

Lily went to the table across from him and leaned flat-palmed into it. "I've got no other choice, do I?"

"You could kill him," he said quietly. "Or me."

Unexpectedly, the words wounded her. Lily set her lips. "You've got no reason to believe me, I know. But this isn't about you anymore, Texas. It's about Hank. I told you I'd ride away and leave you all alone if you helped me, and I haven't forgotten that. I owe you."

He made a soft sound, a bitter laugh, and looked down at his fingers, fumbling with the soft and broken leather of his hat. "He's going to be watching us, Lily."

"Yeah," she said slowly. "I know."

He looked at her, and in his hooded blue eyes she saw an emotion she couldn't name, a wistfulness, per-

haps, a longing she didn't understand, and suddenly
Lily found herself asking the question she'd refused to
think about before. Texas had lied to protect her. He
had looked his father in the eyes and told him he didn't
know what had happened in Lampasas. Even after
she'd tried to kill him and done her best to make him
hate her.

Why? *Why?*

Her throat grew tight, and finally she couldn't stand
to look at him anymore. Lily turned away and walked
through the door. She felt the soft, cooling wind coming through the trees and heard the birds singing noisily
on the branches by the creek. But the thought didn't go
away, and the question nagged at her. It sang in the
breeze and in the rough caw of the crows. Texas had
helped her and she didn't know why.

And not knowing frightened her as much as anything
Hank could ever do to her.

14

The afternoon crept slowly. Hank kept his word and left them alone. No one came over to the cabin, not Schofield nor Bobby, not Josie. Oddly enough, Lily found herself missing them. Or perhaps it wasn't so odd, given that, without them, she was on her own with Texas, and she couldn't look at him now without feeling evil somehow.

He was no better than she was, she told herself, but it wasn't reassuring because deep inside she knew it wasn't true. How would God judge them if they ever got to the doors of Josie's heaven? If it were only about numbers, well, Texas had killed a hell of a lot more men than she had. He had joined the gang willingly, and she'd joined simply to stay alive.

But she guessed those things weren't enough, that maybe killing a man wasn't enough to keep you out of heaven. Maybe honor was more important. Maybe regret meant something, too.

She thought about Texas's nightmares. He'd had them as long as she could remember. Dreams where the men he'd killed came back to haunt him, the nighttime prickings of his conscience. Before she'd left them in Lampasas, his nightmares had happened with weekly regularity, but he hadn't had one since she'd seen him again in Denison. At least not that she knew of.

She supposed that meant something and wished she knew what it was. It seemed important to understand the change.

Lily sighed and glanced around the old ramshackle cabin. Texas was outside tending the horses, and she was by herself for the first time in days. It didn't feel as good as she wanted it to. Instead, she felt at loose ends, and the cabin seemed too big and too hollow.

Unerringly, her gaze went to a small brown jug hidden behind the stove. It was still there, just where they'd left it. Lily reached around and looped her finger through the handle, shaking it a little as she picked it up. The whiskey inside sloshed; it was about half full. She was almost embarrassingly relieved. She grabbed a cup from the shelf above the stove and walked out to the porch, where the boards moaned and sagged beneath her weight and a loose one caught at her boot. She kicked it, splitting it before she settled on the edge of the step. She had the cork out of the jug before she even sat down.

The whiskey smelled raw and warm and sweet. The fire of it pricked her nose, cleared her head. Lily poured a measure into her cup and swirled it around, breathing deeply before she took a gulp. It was cheap and harsh and it burned down her throat and set fire to her belly. Without hesitating, she poured another.

She heard the squeaking of the door at the other cabin. Lily looked up to see Jocelyn stepping outside, waving out a washtowel. It was wet and it slapped in the wind, snapping back over Josie's forearms. Josie shook back her hair, tilting her head to let the breeze blow strands from her face. Such an innocent, graceful movement. It made Lily's stomach clench to look at her.

She thought of this morning, when Josie had gone running into Hank's arms, when she had looked at him with adoration, and he had smiled in answer, and the memory brought back the discomfort Lily had been feeling since, the vague and uneasy hurt that had no place and no explanation, a lonesomeness that seared right through her.

That lonesomeness caught her by surprise, and it was so aching and vast that she found herself wishing, just a little wish, that Jocelyn might glance her way. Not because she particularly cared for Josie, but because Lily suddenly wanted badly to talk to someone. It didn't matter who. She wanted to see herself reflected in someone else's eyes, because she had the strange and uncomfortable feeling that she was disappearing somehow, that she was fading away, and she needed to feel alive again. And Josie . . . Josie was the only one around.

Almost in answer to Lily's thought, Josie caught sight of her. Jocelyn's head cocked a little to the side, and she smiled. She was halfway across the clearing before she stopped uncertainly.

"Oh," she called, a little catch in her voice. "I suppose you and Christian want to be alone?"

Lily lifted her brow and shook her head. "Not me."

Jocelyn frowned. "But Pa said to leave you be."

Pa. How simply Josie said it. What respect she accorded him. Jocelyn glanced back at the cabin as if expecting him to burst through the door and stop her at any moment, and in that second the sun gilded the darkness of her hair, and Lily had the sudden and perverse urge to live up to Hank's image of her. To be the sinner he'd made her, the devil to corrupt his angel. Not smart, Lily thought. Not smart at all, but, still, she raised her hand and motioned Josie over.

"Come here," Lily said. "Talk with me a while."

Josie smiled. It was like the sun breaking through a cloudy day. "Don't mind if I do," she said.

She hurried over, her skirt flapping against her legs. She still had the washtowel in her hands, and when she got to the porch she draped it over the edge and settled herself daintily on the step. She looked at the jug sitting beside Lily, and her pretty forehead wrinkled in curiosity. "What's that?"

"Whiskey," Lily said.

"You're drinking whiskey in the middle of the day?"

"Why not?"

"Well, I . . ." Jocelyn frowned. "Well, I guess I can't think of a reason why not. Except that drinking whiskey anytime is, well, it's not exactly . . ." Josie looked at her as if she expected Lily to know what she meant.

"Not exactly what?" Lily asked.

"You know. It's not quite respectable."

Deliberately, Lily brought the cup to her mouth. She took a long, slow sip. "I guess I've got nothing to worry about then, do I?" she asked after she swallowed. She wiped her mouth with the back of her sleeve. "Since I'm not respectable."

"No . . ." Josie's voice trailed off. She bit her lip prettily and looked at the cup in Lily's hand, and there was a pinched and transparent yearning on her face, a wistfulness in her eyes. "Do you think I— Could I try some?"

Lily knew she should say no. She wanted to say no. If Hank caught Josie drinking with her, well, trouble would be all over her, and Lily didn't need it. But then she thought again of that morning, of Josie's pure belief in her father, of Hank's tender smile, and it raised that bitterness in Lily's soul.

She thrust her cup into Josie's hand. "Take this," she said. "I'll drink from the jug."

The faintly horrified look on Josie's face made Lily feel sinfully wicked, as bad as she was rumored to be. But this time it was a pleasurable feeling; she supposed ruination always was.

Jocelyn wrapped her hands around the cup and took a deep breath. She held it out brightly. "Very well," she said. "I'm ready."

Lily grinned. "It's not poison, Josie."

"I had some in Fort Griffin, you know," Josie said. "I didn't much like the taste, I have to admit."

"Well, you won't like it much better now." Lily poured. The whiskey plopped and splashed into Jocelyn's cup.

Josie's nose wrinkled. "Oh, it smells awful."

"Don't drink it."

"No, no, I asked for it. I want to." Bravely, Josie lifted the cup. "Here's to being home."

"Such as it is." Lily toasted with the jug. Then she brought it to her mouth and tipped it back.

The second swallow was even better than the first. The warmth spread through her veins and loosened the muscles in her neck, her face. Beside her, Josie choked and sputtered. Her eyes were watering.

"Oh, good Lord," she said, bringing her hand to her mouth. "Th-that's strong."

"The best the McHaney boys have to offer," Lily said.

"The McHaney boys?"

"They live over near Belton," Lily told her. She took another sip. "They make this stuff."

"Oh my." Josie's second sip was a little bigger than the first. "Well, they do a fine job."

"They surely do."

Jocelyn drained her cup. Lily poured another generous shot into it. For a moment, the only sounds were those of sipping and swallowing. Lily closed her eyes and leaned back against the post. The wood creaked; she felt it shudder into the porch roof. The whiskey and the late afternoon sun brought a fine film of sweat to her face, and the breeze blowing from the creek was refreshing against her skin.

"They're over there playing cards," Josie said. "I'll bet they haven't even noticed I'm gone."

"Hank has," Lily said without opening her eyes.

Josie sighed. "It seems I've been waiting half my life to meet Schofield and Bobby, and now I have, and they aren't anything like I pictured."

Lily kept leaning her head against the porch and looked at Josie through slitted eyes. "Oh yeah?" she asked. "How did you picture them?"

"Oh, I don't know." Jocelyn shrugged and took a gulp of whiskey. "Like Christian, I suppose. Handsome and romantic."

Lily snorted. "No doubt you were piteously disappointed then."

Josie laughed lightly. "Well, I suppose. Bobby's sweet as pie, and he's handsome enough, I guess. But Schofield . . . My, I wonder that his mama didn't wash his mouth out with soap a hundred times a day."

"She didn't. His teeth are rotting, too."

Josie wrinkled her nose. She downed the rest of her whiskey and took the jug. She splashed more into her cup. "Mama always said he had a way with words. I thought she was being complimentary."

Lily smiled. "She was just trying to keep the truth from your delicate ears."

"I guess that's so." Josie leaned back against the

other post. The whole porch shook, but she didn't seem to notice. She drew her knees up and clasped her hands around them, the handle of her cup hooked through her fingers. "Mama was so protective, and I wish she hadn't been. There's so much of life I don't know."

"That's not such a bad thing, you know."

"That's what Pa says."

"Well, maybe he's right, too."

"You sound just like him," Josie sighed. "I don't need two fathers, Lily."

Lily was—surprisingly—chagrined. "Sorry."

"Oh, that's all right. I know you mean well." Jocelyn set her gaze so hard Lily felt battered by it. "But you know what I really need, Lily? I really just need a friend."

Lily started. It was the second time Josie had said such a thing to her, and the words surprised Lily just as much now as they had in the loft that morning. She swallowed and sat up, taking the jug into her hands. But she didn't drink any. She stared down at it, ran her finger over its glazed surface. "Maybe you don't want me as a friend," she said carefully. Then, at Josie's start of protest, Lily hurried on, "No, really, Josie. It's not seemly for a woman like you."

"You're being like Pa again," Josie said. "Don't you think I can decide what's seemly? I'm not a child, much as everyone likes to think I am."

"You don't know shit about the world."

Josie widened her eyes and chuckled. "My, my, a curse. Are you trying to shock me, Lily?"

Lily looked away. "It's the truth."

"Maybe you don't know everything either. The world's an awfully big place." Jocelyn took another gulp of whiskey. "And maybe robbing stages and being written up in newspapers isn't all there is."

Josie made Lily feel like a fool without even trying. Lily spoke softly. "Yeah, well, that's true enough."

"You see?" Jocelyn gave her a bright, wide smile. "Neither of us knows shit about the world."

Lily laughed. She held up the jug in a mock salute, and then put it to her mouth. "You say that word around your Pa and you can kiss me goodbye."

"I don't think so," Jocelyn said. "He loves you like a daughter, you know."

"Oh yeah," Lily said. "Just like a daughter." She said the words sarcastically, but the very syllables of them twisted her heart. She took another swig from the jug. "I don't want to talk about Hank," she said.

"He admires you, you know," Josie went on, blithely ignoring her. "I've heard him. He once told me you were stubborn as ten men and twice as brave. He's never said anything so nice about me."

Once again, Josie had it wrong. There was no admiration in Hank's voice when he used those words; Lily had heard them often enough to know. She remembered the first time she'd heard them. She'd been fourteen then, and they had been sitting around the fire after robbing some stage somewhere. Hank had drawn on his pipe until the saliva gurgled in his mouth and the smoke curled in the bowl, and his eyes had been angry, his voice hard. *"You're too damn stubborn, Lily. Stubborn as ten men. Next time I tell you to shoot a stage driver, goddammit, you'd better do it."*

She had nodded and swallowed back her hurt and her anger. Then she'd leaned against his knee and curled her hand around his thigh and determined to do what he said no matter how much it scared her. Through it all, she'd prayed that he still loved her.

Lily cut dead the memory. Instead, she thought of

that morning and the compassion Josie had wrung from her father. Lily drank deeply from the jug. This time, the liquor seemed to wash over her very brain, a welcome numbness. She looked at Josie. "Do me a favor and don't listen to everything your pa says."

Jocelyn laughed. She put a hand to her throat. The motion was graceful despite the calluses on her skin. "You know, I think I'm getting a little . . . drunk."

"Have some more."

Josie held out her cup. "I'm not sure I should. There's so much still to do."

"Nothing that won't wait." Lily motioned toward the house. "This one's been waiting about thirty years."

Jocelyn smiled. "I don't guess you care much about keeping house, do you?"

"No."

"You know, it seems I've spent the whole of my life being busy. Mama used to say, 'Idle hands are the devil's workshop.' This . . ." Josie made a wide, sweeping gesture. Her words were starting to slur together, her eyes were overly bright. "This feels so good. Just sitting here. Talking. Doing . . . nothing."

Lily laughed softly. "Yeah. I guess it does."

Jocelyn leaned forward. There was a sudden intensity in her eyes. It should have warned Lily, but it didn't. She was too busy thinking how much that expression on Josie's face made her look like her brother. "Lily," Josie said. "Will you tell me something?"

"If I can."

Josie took another sip of whiskey and then nodded, a short, hard nod, as if giving herself permission to speak. She looked straight at Lily. "Why did you try to shoot Christian?"

The question jarred Lily. It cut through the smooth, easy lethargy of impending drunkenness, surprising her so much she laughed nervously. "Why did I shoot him?"

"Yes. What did he do to you?"

"Not any one thing," Lily said, but the memory slammed back. Just the one memory, of the rope tightening around her throat as she watched the horizon and waited for him. Lily started to look away, but her gaze caught on Josie's legs, on the awkward, playful angles of her knees beneath her skirt. *Little-girl legs,* Lily thought, and the notion brought a lump as big as all Texas into her throat.

"Not any one thing . . ." Josie prompted.

"It's my business," Lily said tersely.

Josie stiffened. "You don't trust me."

The hurt in her voice and in her eyes was uncomfortable to see, and Lily turned away, feeling rude and coarse in spite of the fact that Josie had brought it on herself. Half the people in Texas were running from some law somewhere. It was an unspoken rule that you never asked questions about someone's past. If Josie didn't know that by now, well, it was time she learned.

But the thought didn't stop a vague, nagging prick of guilt. Josie's next words only made it worse.

"I'm not trying to push in where I don't belong," Josie said quietly. "It's just . . . I thought we were friends, and I'm trying . . . I'm trying to understand. I mean, you must have loved him once. You married him."

Lily's fingers tightened on the jug. It had never been so black and white. If love meant the emotion Texas felt for her once, then she hadn't loved him. She had admired him, and laughed with him, and found solace in his friendship. She had enjoyed his body next to hers and the touch of his hands. His kisses had stirred her. But love . . .

"I don't know."

"But you married him."

"Your pa's readying to marry you to some man in San Antonio you've never seen in your life," Lily pointed out.

Jocelyn lifted her chin. "Not unless I'm willing."

"Well, you seem pretty willing to me."

Josie flushed. "But I've got no choices, Lily," she said. "You did. You could have said no to Christian, and you didn't."

"You don't know anything about it."

Josie hesitated. She leaned back again, and her sigh was as loud as the wind; it carried as much desolation with it. "I guess that's true," she said. "I wasn't there."

"That's right."

"And I've got no cause to pry."

"That's right, too."

"It's your business."

Lily lifted the jug and poured into Josie's cup.

Josie made a little hiccuping laugh. "I am gettin' very drunk."

"If you're going to have a headache in the morning, you might as well make the night worth it."

"It's not even night yet."

"It will be," Lily said. "In a few hours."

Josie chuckled. It turned into a full-out laugh. "Pa . . . is going . . . to kill me."

"No, ma'am," Lily said, tilting the jug to her mouth and swallowing deeply. "It's me he's going to kill."

"A double funeral," Jocelyn said, still laughing in loose, jumpy hiccups of sound. "Won't that be sad. No one will be there to sing a psalm."

"Oh yeah? I thought you told me Hank was always talking the Bible."

"Talking, yes." Josie flipped back the hair falling over her shoulder. "But I don't think I've ever heard him sing. Have you?"

Lily laughed shortly. "No."

"And I don't imagine Schofield and Bobby know many hymns."

"I don't imagine so."

"Even Christian, why, I doubt he's set foot in a church."

Lily laughed again. "Only to rob the collection plate."

"That just leaves Old Sam." Josie sighed. She smiled into her cup. "I've never heard him sing either."

"He can do the eulogy," Lily said wryly. "I can just imagine all the sweet things he'd say about me."

Josie threw her a look, a flirty, slanted-eyes kind of look. "He doesn't like you much, does he?"

"He's not the only one."

"Well, *I* like you," Josie said. "So I guess it's left to me to sing you to heaven."

Lily took another swig. "It'll take more than singing, I can promise you that."

But Jocelyn only laughed and leaned her head back against the post and began to sing. It took a moment for Lily to recognize the tune, a half second before it plunged into her consciousness, bringing back memories so old and faded they seemed to belong to someone else.

"Amazing Grace, how sweet the sound, that saved a wretch like me . . . "

The memory came out of nowhere. Candles and quiet voices, a man standing at the pulpit, his robes edged in a wide purple collar. Her mother crying beside her and pews that were hard against her back, that cut into her thighs through her many petticoats. The words in the prayer book her father held blurring and shaking while he sobbed without sound.

The coffin was closed. Her brother Billy's body had been too shattered for the mortician to pretty-up.

"I once was lost, but now am found. Was blind, but now . . ."

Lily closed her eyes and joined in.

Texas straightened. He brushed his hands on his thighs and pushed back his hat so the breeze touched his forehead. He took his time doing everything: currying the horses until they gleamed, taking extra care with their feed, watering them at the creek until they'd refused to drink another drop. By the angle of the sun, he figured he'd been gone the better part of two hours, but it didn't feel long enough. The thought of going back into that cabin, facing Lily alone, made cold sweat break out on his skin.

He didn't even know what to say to her anymore, and he didn't want to go back and stare into her cold and challenging eyes. With Josie and Old Sam around, the chill that was Lily had seemed less somehow. More bearable. But now there was nothing but cold.

He sighed and looped a rope, hanging it on a nail stuck into the lean-to wall. There was nothing else to do, not a single thing to delay him longer. He stepped out of the lean-to and pulled his hat down again to shade his eyes. Then he started around the house.

He was just rounding the corner when he heard it. At first he thought it was the wind, squealing in that high-pitched way it did when it got caught up beneath the eaves. Then he realized it was singing. Quiet at first, and faltering, and then gaining strength as the singer gained confidence.

It was Josie; he knew it by the sound. He thought the song was "Oh Susannah," but he couldn't be sure, because as fine and cultured as Josie was, she couldn't carry a tune to save her soul. But then he heard the strain of melody more clearly. It wasn't "Oh Susannah" after all. It was a hymn of some kind. "Beulah Land," he thought, startled at the sweet pierce of recognition. And, though it had been just Josie singing at first, it wasn't anymore. There was a second voice, and it was quiet and so clear and sweet it made his heart ache.

He hadn't heard her sing for a long time, and he thought he'd long ago forgotten it. But he hadn't. He knew her voice the way he knew the fit of his gun in his palm. When she first joined the gang, she had never stopped singing. Hymns mostly. Haunting, lovely melodies he'd never heard in his life. She washed dishes and she sang. She went to sleep at night to the sound of her own music. She learned how to clean a gun with the clean, pure jubilation of a psalm in her voice.

He had grown used to the sound of it, had come to know the songs by name. "Rock of Ages" and "Amazing Grace" and "Beulah Land." He had never cared about the words, had thought he didn't even know them. But, as he listened to the song, to Josie's thin, faltering line and Lily's strong harmony, he found the words coming from some deep place in his heart, tripping through his mind in time to the music as if they'd never left him. *Oh Beulah land, sweet Beulah land, as on the highest mount I stand . . .*

It occurred to him that he had no other memories of her singing beyond those early days. It was as if she'd been struck dumb somehow, one day, suddenly, and he'd never even noticed, had not thought to comment on it at all.

There had been too many things to think about back then, he supposed, and the thought saddened him. He stood there, at the side of the cabin, hearing them sing and afraid to join them, afraid of what Lily singing meant. But in the end he couldn't stay away; the temptation of the old Lily was too hard to resist. He rounded the corner so quickly that Josie jumped in surprise, gulping and stuttering to a stop. Lily turned to look at him, but she didn't stop singing. She finished the last two words of the stanza and then let her voice trail off, easy and slow. And then, while he was standing there, feeling stupid, she picked up the jug and took a long, deep swallow and set it aside again.

"Hey there, Texas," she said.

He saw that Jocelyn had a mug in her hand. She looked as guilty as if he'd caught her—well, drinking in the middle of the afternoon.

Lily held out the jug. "Care to join us? We were just holding a funeral."

Texas frowned. His gaze slid to Josie. She smiled sheepishly. "Our own," she explained. "'Cause we'll both be dead when Pa sees how drunk I am."

She sure as hell sounded drunk. Her words were all slurred together, and there was a fine, nearly hysterical edge of laughter beneath them. Almost as he had the thought, she started to laugh, so hard her eyes watered and her nose ran. She buried her face in the crook of her arm, rubbing it against her sleeve until she had managed a kind of sloppy control.

"You know," she said, "I'm feeling a little dizzy."

"Hell." Texas lunged forward. He grabbed her arm, ignoring her protest as he jerked the cup from her hand and slammed it on the porch. Then he pulled her after him, stumbling and complaining. He took her around the side of the house, past the lean-to, to the narrow path cutting through the trees to the creek.

"Easy now, Texas," Lily warned lightly. "She's just drunk, she's not a criminal."

He glanced over his shoulder. She was following them, her pace slow and leisurely, the jug hooked negligently through her fingers. She smiled at him, that half-sarcastic smile he hated.

"This is your fault," he muttered.

"It surely is."

"Oh, don't blame her, Christian." Jocelyn gulped. She paled, and her hand went to her mouth. "Oh, my."

He turned away from Lily and dragged Josie to the edge of the creek just as she started throwing up. She stumbled to her knees on the edge of the bank, and he held her shoulder with one hand and pulled back her long hair with the other.

"You'll feel better when it's over, Josie," Lily said, settling herself against a tree.

Texas twisted to glare at her. His sister's shoulders were jerking beneath his hands. The sounds of her retching only fed the anger deep inside him. "What the hell were you thinking?"

"That I wanted a drink. Josie just happened by."

"And you didn't think to tell her no."

"I didn't know it was my turn to watch her."

"Please," Josie sputtered. She reached back, grabbing for his arm. "Please don't—"

He bent over her as another spasm wrenched her body. Finally, Josie quieted. She breathed deeply, unsteadily, and then she pushed him away and cupped water in her hands, splashing it over her face.

Texas got to his feet. He took the few steps to Lily and grabbed the jug from her hand. Then he pitched it, hurling it as far as he could. He heard it crack apart on the rocks in the creek.

Lily rolled her eyes. "Don't you think you're overreacting just a little?" she asked. "That's all we had."

"Oh, Christian." Josie spoke his name on a sigh. He

turned to see her rising slowly, brushing back her hair with a shaky hand, but there was a force to her voice that surprised him. "You're as bad as Pa. You'd think Lily held me down and forced me to drink it. It's not her fault."

"It's all right," Lily said. She pushed away from the tree. "I shouldn't—"

"Don't be silly," Josie said. "I'm not a child." She threw a haughty look at Texas and stumbled past him right up to Lily, so close Lily took a step back in surprise.

"Don't you dare take the blame for this," she said. And then she leaned forward and kissed Lily on the cheek. She drew away slowly, with a smile, looking at Texas over her shoulder. "I'm going back now," she said.

She went slowly and carefully through the trees, leaving Lily looking dazed and stunned and an equally surprised Texas staring after.

15

"What was that all about?"

Lily pulled her gaze away from the trees, from the path Josie had just stumbled down, and turned to Texas. He looked as uncomfortable and uncertain as she felt. The question he'd asked rang with an awkward loudness.

She shrugged, forcing nonchalance into her voice, trying to settle the strange bruise in her heart, the tenderness that lingered on her skin in the moist and gentle pressure of Josie's kiss. *You're just drunk,* she told herself. That was all it was. "Hell if I know," she said.

"I should go after her," he said. "Pa'll be—"

"Oh, leave her be," Lily said. "She can take care of herself."

He frowned. "She's drunk."

"So's Hank half the time. And she's not a child. She's a woman grown." Lily pushed a loose hair back from her face and gave him a contemptuous look. "Besides, it's not as if Hank's going to beat her or anything."

"Not her, no."

"Not me either," she said with false confidence. When she pushed away from the tree and started back down the path to the cabin, she was tense and wary. She wished like hell she had more whiskey, because the truth was that she half expected to see Hank at the cabin door, waiting with death on his face, and she didn't think she was drunk enough to brave it.

But when she got to the shanty, there was no sign of Josie or Hank, and the cabin next door was quiet.

Lily had herself worked up for a confrontation, and now that there wasn't one she just stood there, uncertain and, despite her fear, strangely disappointed. It took a moment for relief to set in, and with it came weariness. It felt suddenly as if all her strength had been sapped away. Lily walked through the door and stopped, staring at the little room, waiting for the safety of it to envelop her, waiting for its familiar welcome.

It looked just as it always had; the narrow bed built into the corner and the scarred and crooked table in the middle, the sheet-metal stove squatting just behind. Even with the battens open and the door swung wide, the cabin was dark and uninviting and close. Still, it was home. The only home she could remember. It had always reassured her before.

But not today. Today, just being in the room brought back her lonesomeness and the clawing desperation that stuck in her throat and stole her breath. Maybe it was the whiskey that made it worse, she didn't know, but when she turned around and saw Texas coming up the steps just behind her, Lily felt a relief so overwhelming she had to close her eyes from the pure dizziness of it.

When she opened her eyes again, he was staring at her, a puzzled frown between his brows. "How about a game of poker?" she asked.

He took his hat off and ran a hand through his hair. His expression was careful, his voice even more so. "Yeah," he said. "All right."

She gave a short nod and went to the shelves above the washtub, feeling around the few cups and plates there for the deck of cards they kept in the back corner. She felt a soft satisfaction when she pulled them into her hand and thumbed through them and the quiet fanning sound filled the silence.

"Here they are," she said unnecessarily. She hooked the bottom rung of a chair with her boot and pulled it out, slumping into it.

Texas set his hat on the table and sat across from her. When she glanced up, she saw him look toward the back corner of the stove, where the whiskey jug had been until a few hours ago. He was probably wishing he hadn't been so free with it, because the silence between them was hard, and at least the liquor could be counted on to take the edge off.

She gave him a small smile. "It would taste good, wouldn't it?"

He started and then smiled back sheepishly. "It was a stupid thing to do," he admitted.

"Uh-huh." She dealt the cards for seven-card stud. Then she reached into her pocket and pulled out what little change she had. She scattered it on the table between them, some silver, a little copper, coins rolling into the knife marks carved into the surface.

Texas sighed and picked up his cards, unfolding them in his hand. "She'll have a headache in the morning," he said.

She stared at him, confused. Then she remembered Josie.

Lily nodded. "Yeah." There seemed to be nothing else to say.

The word faded into silence. Texas was focused on his cards, and so Lily looked down at hers. She was too muzzy-headed to concentrate, so she settled for just rearranging them in her hand; the Two of Hearts here, next to the Six of Diamonds. The King of Spades clear to the end, a one-eyed Jack beside. The air was heavy; she thought she remembered other times in this cabin when she and Texas had sat playing cards just like this. She thought she remembered laughing, but maybe that was just a whiskey-induced memory, because right now she couldn't think of what they would have laughed about.

Those things seemed a hundred years ago now. Not quite real. Maybe she was just imagining them.

"You and Josie were singing."

Texas's voice was easy and casual, but, again, it took her a moment to understand what he was saying, a moment to straighten out her thoughts. She and Josie singing. Hymns and drunkenness.

She nodded. "Yeah. Josie's fault."

"It's been a long time since I heard you sing," he said.

She looked up. "It's been a long time since I wanted to."

"You have a nice voice."

She gave him a wry half-smile. "Thanks."

"Josie can't sing worth shit. Never has been able to."

"She does have a way with a tune."

"The only person worse is Schofield. Christ, I'd hate to hear the two of them together. They'd scare the birds clear to Georgia."

Lily laughed softly, falling into the comforting casualness of small talk. "That's true enough." She moved a card, tucked it back in. "I thought maybe she was just too drunk to be any good."

"It's got nothing to do with drunkenness."

She threw a copper coin onto the middle of the table. "Ante up," she said. Then, "I admit I was surprised. You don't expect a woman as pretty as Josie to sing so . . . "

"Bad?"

She chuckled. "I guess that's the only way to put it."

"I think Pa's already instructed her not to sing until after her wedding day."

Her wedding day. The conversation between her and Josie was there again, seeming clearer through Lily's drunkenness. She suddenly remembered every word, every hard syllable. *"Why did you shoot Christian?"*

Lily sobered. She looked down at her cards. "Is he really going to marry her off?"

"What other choice does he have?"

"I don't know." Lily shrugged. "He could wait for her to fall in love."

"With who? Schofield? Bobby?"

Lily glanced up. "I don't think she's interested in either of them."

"Who else is there?"

"Maybe we should have left her in Fort Griffin. She knew people there."

Texas gave her an odd look. "Better watch it, Lily," he said. "You're beginning to sound like you give a damn."

She met his gaze evenly. "You're imagining things."

"Of course I am. After all, Josie's only your sister-in-law. Why the hell should you care about her?"

His words hurt. She tried not to let them, but she was too drunk for them to roll off. She stared down at her cards. *Don't let them see what you're thinking.* The lesson was too hard-learned to lose in liquor. "Don't make me insult you, Texas," she said. "I'm trying to be nice."

"Nice." He put a bite on the word. "Well, you're doing a fine job."

"Look, I owe you."

"Let's forget about debts, Lily," he said. He laid his cards on the table and lurched from his chair. "Let's just be people for once. Let's just be honest with each other. Think you can do that?"

There was a challenge in his voice that made her want to do as he asked. To be honest with him. Or maybe it was just the whiskey. Whatever it was, Lily found herself nodding. She kept her voice careful and even. "I can be honest with you," she said slowly. "If you're sure that's what you want."

She had surprised him, she saw. He looked guarded suddenly. Wary. "Think I can't take it?" he asked.

"You tell me."

"I can take it." He leaned forward, palms flat on the table. "I can take it."

"All right." Slowly, she laid her cards down. She folded her hands together. "What do you want to know?"

He swallowed. There was the barest of hesitations, as if he were weighing his words. "When I found you in Denison, did you ever mean to come back?"

She'd promised him honesty, and she gave it to him now. "Nope."

His fingers flexed against the table; it was the only sign that her answer had had any effect on him. "Out there on the prairies that night, you would have shot me. You would have killed me if I'd given you the chance."

"Is that a question?"

He nodded tersely.

Lily paused. There was a tightness around his mouth, but there was no shield in his eyes. Hurting him was as easy as shooting a lame horse; it was target practice, pure and simple.

And Lily didn't want to do it. Not this time. Maybe it was just that she was drunk and maudlin. Maybe Josie's kiss had somehow addled her brain. Or maybe it was nothing more than the relief she'd felt when he'd followed her back from the creek, that momentary gratitude that she didn't have to be alone. She sighed and caught his gaze. "Don't do this to yourself, Texas," she said softly.

"Answer me."

She looked away. "It doesn't matter, does it?" she said. "I didn't get the chance."

Her answer hurt him even though she'd tried not to. She glanced at him again, and he looked as if he were sagging in front of her, just bending beneath a heavy weight. He looked down at his cards.

"No," he said. "You didn't get the chance."

Her heart felt tight. The whiskey was wearing off, and she felt the hardness of his silence again, the sharp edges of it, the chill. She waited for him to ask her another question, but it became obvious he wouldn't, and so finally she laid her cards down and got to her feet.

Her boot heels made a hard, hollow thud on the floor as she went to the stove. She squatted and reached around it, searching through the bags of cornmeal and flour and beans. "You hungry?" she asked.

"Yeah," he said. The word was harsh and broken.

She ignored it. "There's not much." She pulled out a tin can without any markings and shook it. "Corn, I'd guess."

"It's fine."

She swiveled on her heels, still squatting, and looked up at him. He looked emptied out and tired, and too damn sad to be alive, and it turned her inside out, that look. It made her want to be kind.

"Look, Texas," she said quietly. "I'll leave like I promised I would. It'll be better for both of us. You know that. But I can't go until Hank believes me, until he believes you, too. And I think"—she inhaled deeply—"I think it would be best . . . it would be easier . . . if we tried to forget the past. If we just forgot what we were to each other."

He looked at her. His expression was weary and heartsore, and so lonely it cut clear down to the bone.

"Isn't that the problem, Lily?" he whispered. "That you can forget it?"

She was just drunk, she told herself. That was all it was. Just that maudlin pain that comes with whiskey. It wasn't real pain at all.

Hank was frying bacon the next morning when Jocelyn finally came down the stairs and stumbled toward the table. He heard Schofield's low chuckle and Bobby's solicitous "Morning, Miss Josie," and he looked over his shoulder to see his daughter looking bleary-eyed and pale. The sight of her made his anger from yesterday rise again; it was as hot as it'd been when she fell into the cabin yesterday afternoon, drunk and nauseated. She had stumbled right to bed then, so he hadn't had a chance to vent his anger, and he was glad for the time because he was able, with effort, to keep it tamped now.

"Good morning, darlin'," he said. "Sleep well?"

She sagged into a chair and put her hands to her head. "Oh, Pa."

"Nothin' like a damn hangover to show you who your friends are," Schofield said.

"I've got a headache powder if you want one," Bobby offered.

She peered at him from between her fingers. "Thank you kindly."

Bobby got up to search his saddlebags, and Hank speared the bacon onto a plate and set it on the table. "How about some coffee?" he asked. He didn't wait for her to answer. He poured a cup and put it in front of her.

Josie curled her hand around it as if she could draw strength from its heat. "Oh, Pa," she said again. "I feel awful."

"Unfortunately, there's nothing for it," he said. He took a seat across from her and grabbed a plate and a fork. His arm knocked against Schofield's as they both reached for the bacon. Hank glared, and Schofield backed off. "By tomorrow, you'll be feeling better."

"Tomorrow." She groaned. "I don't think I can stand it that long."

Bobby strode back to the table, a small packet in his hand. He set it in front of her and patted her shoulder gently. "That should help some," he said. He reached for a piece of bacon and slapped it between corn bread halves, not bothering to sit as he ate, dropping crumbs all over the floor.

"I have despaired of ever teaching them manners," Hank explained.

Josie made a pathetic attempt at a smile. "I don't mind."

"Well, you should."

"I would have said grace if I'd known you were so goddamned offended," Schofield said. "How's this: Thanks, Lord, for—"

"Shut up," Hank said. "I won't have profanity in front of my daughter."

Schofield looked hurt. "I learned that prayer from my mother."

"A whore in Kansas City." Bobby grinned.

Hank stared at him until Bobby's grin died from his face.

"Sorry," Bobby mumbled.

"It's all right." Jocelyn waved her hand and took a tentative sip of coffee. She put the cup down again, so quickly it splashed on the table, and put a hand to her stomach. "Do we have anything else?" she asked. "Water, maybe?"

"Bobby'll get you some." Hank looked pointedly at Schofield. "And Schofield will help him."

Schofield gave him an exasperated glance. "Dammit, Hank, I'm still eating my breakfast."

"Eat it outside."

"Fine." Schofield got to his feet, clutching his fork in one hand and his plate in the other. "Come on, Bobby, let's go."

Hank waited until they went outside and the door slammed shut behind them, and then he finished off the last pieces of bacon and took a long, slow sip of coffee. Josie sat moaning softly into her hands, the untouched packet of headache powder at her elbow.

"You're going to yell at me, aren't you, Pa?" she asked finally, without looking up. "Just go ahead. I know I deserve it."

Her willingness to be chastised warmed him. He took another sip of coffee. "I'm not going to yell at you, darlin'," he said.

She looked up from her hands. "You're not?"

"I'm not."

Josie frowned. "I don't understand. You made Bobby and Schofield leave. I assumed it was because—"

"I wanted to talk to you alone." Hank finished his

coffee. He rose and put the cup in the washtub, along with the empty plate. He took his time, feeling his daughter's tension build, waiting until it was at its trigger point before he sat down again and smiled at her. "About Lily."

"Lily?" Jocelyn visibly relaxed. "Oh. Lily. Thank you so much for making Texas untie her, Pa. I hated how she was a prisoner. I can't tell you what a relief it was to talk to her yesterday without seeing those ropes."

"I want you to stay away from her."

Josie stared at him in surprise. "Stay away? But—but why?"

"Because I said so, that's why."

"That's not a good enough reason." Jocelyn set her mouth stubbornly. "I'm not ten years old anymore, Pa. You can't order me to do something just because you want me to."

She surprised him. He couldn't remember that she'd ever defied him before, not even a little. It was disconcerting that she was now. It was because of Lily, he told himself. She and Josie had spent too much time together. No doubt Jocelyn had learned some bad habits. Luckily, they were new enough that they should be easy to unlearn.

He gave his daughter his best stare, the one that had cowed dozens of men. She only glared mutinously back at him.

"A reason, Pa," she reminded him tartly. "You tell me why I should stay away from Lily."

"She's trouble, that's why."

"She's my best friend."

"Your best friend?" Hank laughed. "She's a liar and a killer, Josie. You could find a better friend in hell."

Josie frowned. "You don't know anything about it,

Pa," she said. "I don't mean to be disrespectful, but you couldn't possibly understand."

"Couldn't I?"

"No, you couldn't." Jocelyn sighed. "I've never had a friend before, not really, and not like Lily."

Hank stared at her. "You've had plenty of friends."

"I have not." She shook her head. "You couldn't know, Pa. You weren't around enough. But those families who used to come by now and then, well, they were Mama's friends, not mine. I never knew anyone even my own age. I was . . . I was lonely."

There was a plaintive tone in her voice that cut clean through him. Hank felt a little ache near his heart, an ache that grew when he looked at her pretty face and those eyes that were so like Annie's eyes. Not for the first time, he wondered if his infamy had affected Josie. The people of Fort Griffin had been good to him, but it was still an army town, a respectable town, and he was sure there had been women who knew of his notoriety and kept their daughters away from Josie deliberately. Still, it had never occurred to him that she might be lonely, and neither she nor Annie had ever given him a reason to think otherwise.

"I'm sorry for that," he heard himself saying. "I didn't know. But it doesn't change my mind about Lily. She's an outlaw, darlin'. She's wanted in three states. She's got a bounty on her head."

Josie's eyes widened. "Does she really?"

It wasn't the effect he wanted. Hank tried again. "You know she was hanged once."

"I know." Josie nodded eagerly, as if she were expecting a good story. "For killing a man."

He banged the table in exasperation. "Josie—"

"She's lived the most exciting life I've ever seen," Jocelyn said. "I used to read about her in the papers.

'Lily the Cat,' they called her. 'The lady outlaw with nine lives.'"

"This is not a dime novel," Hank said. "She's not the kind of woman a lady should be around."

"I'm tired of being a lady," Josie said. She rose from her seat and paced back toward the stove. "Being a lady is boring, Pa. Compared to Lily, I've just been wasting time. My life is ticking away, and when it's gone, I'll have nothing to show for it."

"You'll have your children," Hank said. "You'll have your husband. Lily won't have those things."

"She's got a husband."

Hank's temper cracked. "Goddamn it, girl, you know what I mean."

"I just want to do the things she's done," Josie pleaded. "Oh, not the killing, but I'd like to ride with the gang once. I'd like to take on those carpetbaggers."

"Absolutely not," Hank said. It seemed too loud in the little house. But Josie was undeterred. She leaned over the table, her hair trailing into her face, unwashed, unbrushed. She was turning into a heathen before his eyes. His adorable daughter, changing, casting aside the trappings of respectability without a care, all those little niceties he and Annie had worked so hard to give her.

It was unbearable. She was too damn innocent to know how important those trappings were, how they would buy her a safe and decent life. It was time he took the upper hand. She was his daughter; he didn't need to use reason. Hank narrowed his eyes and spat his words in short, hard syllables. "You will stay away from her, do you hear me, Jocelyn Marie? If you go near her, I'll—"

"You'll what, Pa?" she challenged.

"Goddamn it!" He got to his feet. "Why the hell is she so important to you? She's nothing, a cheap little liar. She's not good enough for you to even look at. You're making a mistake to care about her, Jocelyn. God knows she doesn't give a damn about you."

His words echoed; he was sorry he said them the moment he saw the hurt in Jocelyn's hazel eyes, the tight pinching of her face. He waited for her to burst into tears.

But she only nodded solemnly. "Oh, yes, she does," she said quietly. "She does. She just doesn't know it yet."

Hank waited until Josie was at the creek washing up before he went out the door. He crossed the short distance between the cabins in only a few strides. In moments, he was knocking on the door of his son's house, the door shaking beneath his fist.

It was Lily who answered, though Hank saw Texas standing at the table in the middle of the room, looking drawn and tired and anything but happy to be alone again with his bride.

"What is it?" Lily asked. She looked puzzled to see him, and Hank realized he'd never before come over this way. Whenever he'd wanted something, he'd sent one of the boys to get it. "What's wrong, Hank?"

He stared down at her, at her deceptively delicate face and her big brown eyes, and his gaze ate up the scar she hadn't yet covered with a bandanna. He was glad it was there.

"I want you to stay away from Josie," he said. "Come near her again and I'll make you sorry you were ever born." And then he turned on his heel and walked back down the steps without a backward glance.

16

Texas stared at Lily's back. She stood at the open door, watching Pa walk across the yard, but Texas heard her soft curse, the muffled, "Dammit," before she wiped her hand across her face and turned away. She saw he was watching her then, and she gave him a stiff smile.

"I wish to hell you hadn't thrown away that whiskey," she said.

Texas winced. The motion made his already pounding headache worse. He rubbed the back of his neck; it was sore from sleeping all night in the chair. "Pa'll calm down soon enough."

"Yeah, well, he should be talking to his daughter, not to me. I never asked for her to come around."

Texas smiled dryly. "Josie does what she wants, and in the end Pa will cool down and let her. If she feels like coming around, she will."

Lily stared at him. "You sound like it's all right with you if she does."

"I'm not too worried about it," he said, and it was true. He remembered their conversation last night, remembered the way she'd tried to hide her concern for Josie behind deliberate nonchalance and careful words.

He inhaled deeply and ran his hand through his hair. "I don't think you'll hurt her," he said. "At least not if you can help it."

"Why, thank you," she said sarcastically. "Your trust just gladdens my heart."

"It's pretty damn miraculous, if you ask me," he pointed out, "given that less than two weeks ago you had your gun pointed at my head."

She sighed, closed the door gently, and leaned against it, angling her head back, looking at him between lowered lids. Texas felt himself tighten, though he could not have said why, except that maybe there was a strange thoughtfulness in her face, and it wasn't a familiar expression. It made him think of last night, the way she'd made dinner in silence and eaten it as quietly. She hadn't said another word to him. She had crawled into bed and was asleep within seconds, leaving him to stare at the cards spread on the table. And, though he'd fallen asleep in the chair until the early morning hours, he'd dreamed of her, and it was the dream that came to his mind when he looked at her now. The dream, and a wish that he didn't feel anything for her, that his heart was as numb as he'd told himself it was.

But there was no numbness inside of him. Just a sore tenderness that ached at the very mention of her name. Lily was destroying him slowly, look by look, word by careless word, and he hated her for it, and hated himself more. Because, in spite of it all, he could still think of his dream last night and that old, stupid wish that they could be together forever. Running a ranch or walking down a street or . . . just together. It didn't matter how. He wanted to touch her and know what she was thinking, what she was feeling. The yearning was so strong that, for a moment, he gave in to it.

"What is it, Lily?" he asked softly. "What are you thinking?"

The look disappeared from her eyes then, as he'd known it would.

"I'm thinking nothing," she said.

Just as he'd thought. In her own way, she was as predictable as the sun rising. He stepped close to her, and then, because he wanted to, no other reason, he reached out and traced the scar on her throat, over her jaw, behind her ears. He felt the roughness of it clear into his heart, and his own throat closed up in response. She was so tight her skin seemed to vibrate beneath his touch. Her eyes followed his, dark and wary. He dropped his hand and felt her exhale with relief, a soft, barely released breath. He wrapped his fingers around the door handle.

Her voice was soft and low. "Texas . . ."

He looked away from her, hearing that protectiveness again in her voice, the tone that always came just before she was going to hurt him, and he didn't want to hear what she had to say.

"Come on," he said. "Let's go next door. Pa's planning a new job. Something about a train."

The walk to the other cabin was the longest Lily had ever taken. She stayed behind Texas, watching his slow, half-limping walk, and wished it were two days ago. Before Texas had touched her and seemed so sorry for that brand around her throat, and she'd had the notion that she didn't want to hurt him. Before Josie had taken it into her head to get drunk on Lily's front porch and Hank had come over and told her to keep the hell away.

His threat didn't frighten her. He'd already made her sorry she'd been born; that had been true for years now. If she'd been smart, she would have laughed in his face and told him to save his threats for Josie.

But the truth was, she couldn't just laugh off the words. Because, though she'd told herself that his admonition to stay away from Josie didn't bother her, Lily couldn't banish the dull bleakness that had settled in her chest.

And she couldn't banish a tiny, niggling jealousy, a pain that Hank cared about Josie enough to protect her at all costs, but he hadn't hesitated to put a gun in Lily's hand when she was thirteen years old and tell her to kill a man.

It doesn't matter, she told herself. It was already done, and there was no changing it. She did her best to remember that as she and Texas crossed the yard, but, when she saw Josie on the porch washing out rags in a big tub, Lily felt a heavy emptiness in her gut. And when Josie looked up as they approached and gave Lily a guilty, quick glance and then looked down again, scrubbing those clothes as if she could clean the color right out of them, that sadness rose right up into Lily's throat so it was hard to breathe.

She forced herself to look right at Hank when they went inside. He barely acknowledged her, which was fine. Bobby was hunched over the table, studying a ragged piece of newsprint. Schofield leaned against the wall, picking his teeth with a sliver of tree branch. Old Sam was on the bed cleaning a rifle.

"Well, well, 'something wicked this way comes.'" Hank grinned meanly. "I was just getting ready to send Bobby over after you two."

Texas crossed the room slowly, deliberately so, Lily was sure. He reached for a cup and the coffeepot and held it up to Lily with a silent question. Lily shook her head, and he shrugged and poured himself a cup.

"You said something about a train," Texas said. He leaned against the wall next to Schofield, behind his father, so that Hank had to twist to see him. The willfulness of it made Lily smile, and she ducked her head and took a seat across from Hank at the table.

"A train," Hank repeated thoughtfully. "Yes, I did."

Bobby looked up in startled surprise. "A train?"

"Jesus holy hell." Schofield whistled low through his teeth. "You thought about this, Hank? We ain't never done a train before."

"The stages are too smart now," Hank said easily. "Too many guards, too much risk. Look at what happened to Lily the last time we attempted the mails."

He gave her a nasty smile. Lily felt herself pale. The scar on her throat itched.

"But a train . . ." Bobby's brow furrowed. "Nobody's done that here. I heard the James and Younger boys did it in Kansas."

"Well, if they can do it, I guess we can," Hank said. "Or are you boys chickening out on me?"

Schofield shook his head. "Not me."

"Not me either," Bobby said uncertainly.

"Good." Hank grabbed the newsprint from Bobby's hands and took a lead pencil from his pocket. He smoothed the paper onto the table. "Now, I've been doing a little studying. The Houston and Texas Central does the Austin Freight every day from Houston to Hempstead."

"There's a lot of people between Houston and Hempstead," Texas said quietly.

Hank's jaw clenched. "That's why we're doing the mixed train to Austin," he said. "They stop to wood up and take the mail at Chapel Hill every day." He smiled.

"There's an express car on that route once a week. I've got it on good authority that the next one's on Wednesday."

"You mean next Wednesday?" Bobby asked hopefully.

"I mean this Wednesday," Hank said.

Lily felt a prickle at the back of her neck, a foreboding that lifted the hairs on her nape. She looked at Hank, forcing a nonchalance she didn't feel. "You have it on good authority that there's money in that car?"

Hank's lips thinned in a cramped grin. "Payroll, Lily-loo."

There was silence. Hank sat there smiling while the rest of them looked at each other. Even Schofield looked doubtful, and he was never anything but game. Lily met Texas's gaze. There was a seriousness on his face that only increased her nervousness, a measuring look in his eyes, and suddenly she realized what this train job was all about. It was for her. A test for her.

She looked straight at Hank. Her heart beat heavy in her chest, but she took a deep breath and leaned forward over the table. "All right, then," she said. "What's the plan?"

Hank glanced at the others. "Are we agreed then?"

Schofield nodded slowly. Bobby shrugged. And Texas . . . Texas just gave his pa a lingering look and sipped his coffee.

Hank turned back to the table. He made a quick sketch of the Chapel Hill station. "It's in the middle of nowhere," he said, "and it's manned by one agent. There are section hands about, but they're usually out on the track. We shouldn't have any trouble from them."

He showed the sketch around the table. The Chapel

Hill station was a lone, small building sitting on a platform edged by tracks and a telegraph pole. Hank's drawing showed the building split into two rooms, a telegraph office and a waiting room with a ticket desk, and a privy out back.

"Two doors," he said, as they passed it around. "One in the front facing the track, one in the back. We go in the back and take the agent just before the train is scheduled to arrive—less time for a section hand to show up that way. Texas, you dismantle the telegraph. Bobby, you put out the signal light. When the train stops, Schofield and I will take the engineer and the fireman. And Lily covers Texas until the conductor steps out. Then he's hers. Got it?"

He smiled meanly, and his gaze was cold and challenging. It sent a shiver down Lily's spine. Cover Texas. This was the test, then. She eyed him steadily. "The conductor," she repeated, nodding.

"We'll throw water on the fire to make the train useless. Bobby, you'll uncouple the express car. That way, we don't get any passengers deciding to play hero."

"Then what?" Texas asked quietly.

Hank twisted in his chair. "You, boy, will take the stationmaster to the express car. Lily, you go with them to make sure nothing goes wrong. By this time, Bobby will join you. Get the stationmaster to tell the Wells Fargo agent he's got some freight. He'll open the door. Schofield and I will be along. And then"—Hank grinned broadly—"and then we take the money and ride away. *Veni, vidi, vici.* Simplicity itself."

Simplicity itself. It did sound easy enough. But the cold foreboding didn't leave Lily, and the scar at her throat tingled. There were too many people on a train, too many for just the five of them to handle. If even one thing went wrong . . .

She swallowed and glanced at Texas. His eyes were hooded and thoughtful, but she couldn't read his expression. When she looked back at Hank, he was staring at her, his gaze avid. "Well, Lily-loo?" he asked. "Any questions?"

There was a sudden shadow in the light slanting through the open door. Hank glanced over, and Lily turned to see what he was looking at. It was Josie, standing in the doorway, wiping her hands on her skirt, her eyes bright with excitement.

"I have a question, Pa," she said breathlessly. "What's my job?"

Lily winced. Josie's anticipation was painful to see. It would take about two seconds for Hank to set her straight, Lily thought as she waited for him to speak.

"Josie, darlin'," he said. "You've got the most important job of all. You get to stay here and have dinner ready for us."

Josie's face fell.

"But, Pa," she said. "You can't mean that. I've told you—"

"This isn't a game, Josie," he said.

"I know it's not." Her face set in stubborn lines. "I want to help."

"It's not a place for a woman."

"Lily's a woman, and I don't see you excluding her."

"Lily's part of the gang."

"Well, I'm just as capable as she is," Josie said. She stepped all the way into the cabin, her expression purposeful. She went over to the table, stopping behind Lily's chair and resting her hand on the back of it. Lily saw the way Hank's eyes followed the movement. She saw a muscle jump in his jaw, and she wished Josie would stand the hell away, because she knew Josie would expect her support, and Lily couldn't give her any. Josie involved in a train robbery. Just the thought made Lily feel sick.

She glanced up, catching Texas's steady, assessing glance. He sent her a look, a warning, she thought, but she couldn't be sure, and Josie kept talking behind her.

"I can help you all, truly I can, Pa. And I want to. I want to be part of history."

"History?" Hank frowned. "What are you talking about, girl?"

Josie flushed. "History," she repeated stubbornly. "I want to help the South. I want to be a Robin Hood, like the rest of you. I hate those Yankees, too."

Schofield chuckled. Lily heard Bobby's quiet laughter beside her. She saw the way Old Sam turned his face into the wall. Even Texas cracked a smile. But Hank stared at his daughter as if she'd just sprouted horns and a tail.

"That is what you're doing, isn't it?" Josie hurried on, though her voice was wavering now, as if she'd begun to realize she'd said something wrong but wasn't sure what. "That's what Mama said. That's what the newspapers say, too. They say you're heroes to steal from those carpetbaggers. They say you're avenging the war. . . ." Her voice trailed off. The room was silent.

Lily didn't bother to twist around. "Don't believe everything you read, Josie."

Hank glared at her. "Shut up," he said. Then he looked beyond her at his daughter and his gaze softened. "This is not a game, Jocelyn," he said again. "These are real guns we're talking about. Real bullets. These railroad men aren't going to spare our skins because we're avenging the South. They're going to hate us for it. Do you understand?"

Lily felt Josie's movement, felt the chair shake when

Josie tightened her hand on it. "I can help," she said quietly. "Just tell me what to do."

"I am telling you what to do," he said. "You will stay here with Old Sam and make dinner."

"I can do this, Pa." There was the trembling of tears in Josie's voice. "You tell him, Lily. Tell him that just because I'm a woman doesn't mean I can't help."

Lily's chest tightened. She felt Josie's need, the held breath of her expectation; it seemed to take all the air in the room, and Lily knew Josie was waiting for her to speak, to take her side. *"What are friends for?"* Josie had said. And *"I really just need a friend, Lily."* And now Lily was caught. Caught because friends helped each other, and Josie had helped her, and now it was time to return the favor.

But there was Hank, staring at her, measuring her, and there was Lampasas to atone for. There was her life hanging in the balance. And there was the reality of a robbery. She thought of the Southern Overland Mail, the job that had nearly led to her death. She thought of the thunderous crack of gunfire and the bitterly hard truth of bullets spitting past. A robbery was no place for illusions. A bullet was as real as it got, and the thought of Josie out there with her naive smiles and her thirst for adventure made Lily's belly clench; she felt a shiver of cold sweat between her shoulder blades.

She couldn't help Josie this time. It was the way things had to be. Lily had no other choice. But, still, she knew Josie wouldn't understand, that she would see this as a betrayal, and Lily felt ugly and small as she spoke the words.

"You don't know shit about robbing a train, Josie," she said dully, looking at the scabbing rope burns on her wrists, feeling their sting. "It's better if you stay here."

The air felt suddenly cold. Lily felt Josie back away as though she'd been hit, heard the sharp wickedness of her indrawn breath.

"I . . . see," Josie said, her voice quavering. "And that—that's what you really think?"

Lily nodded. "That's what I think."

"Well, then. I guess I—I guess I'll be a good girl and do what everyone tells me."

"That's the way, darlin'," Hank said gravely. "Believe me, I know what's best."

"I know, Pa." Josie's voice was so tiny and thick with hurt that Lily couldn't look at her. And when she heard Josie's steps across the floor, heard the catch in Josie's breath as she hurried out the door, the hard footsteps that faded to nothing in the grass, Lily just looked at her wrists and thought of how Josie had begged Hank to release her. How he'd done just that.

"I've got to get that girl married before she's the death of all of us." Hank laughed. He reached across the table and patted Lily's hand, and she glanced up in surprise. "You did good, Lily-loo."

And, though Hank was smiling at her, Lily looked beyond him, to Texas, to the tired understanding on his face haunting his ice-blue eyes, and she felt bad. Just plain bad.

17

That hatefulness stayed with her the rest of the morning and clear into the afternoon, a dull and constant press at her temples that didn't go away, even when she and Texas left Hank's to go back to their own cabin.

Lily tried to tell herself it didn't matter. Josie was going to get married and live her safe little life in San Antonio, and, even if that didn't happen, Lily didn't plan to be sticking around long enough to see different. She didn't need friends now and she didn't want them. What she wanted was to get the hell away from here, and if today brought her even an inch closer to that goal, well, that was what was important.

But she didn't quite believe the lie as she and Texas went into their cabin, and she couldn't look at him because of what she was afraid he would see in her face.

He didn't seem to notice how she avoided him. He walked past her and reached for the leather gun case hanging on the wall, and then he sat down at the table and pulled his gun from his holster. He spun open the cartridge and spilled the bullets onto the table, and then he opened the case and took out his cleaning tools, the rod and bore brush and the oil rag. He laid them neatly on a grease-stained piece of flannel and dismantled his gun part by part.

"You'd better clean yours, too," he said without looking at her. "There aren't enough of us to pull this off well. We can't risk a jammed gun."

Lily nodded. She pulled her gun from her gun belt. It felt heavy in her hand, pulled at the tendons in her wrist. She laid it down across from his and sat carefully in the chair.

The room was silent as she began taking apart the reconditioned Army Colt, and, though Lily kept glancing up to see if Texas's eyes were on her, he never looked at her. He was concentrating on his gun, his dark blond hair falling forward into his face, his mouth set, and she knew by his very avoidance that he was thinking about what she'd done in Hank's cabin, about how she'd failed Josie.

"I had to do it," she said, clicking open the cylinder. "If she went along it would take her about two seconds to get herself killed."

He glanced up at her, picked up the brush, and jammed it down the bore of his gun. "I know you had to."

"She didn't know what she was asking."

"No, she didn't."

"I don't know why the hell she thinks I would help her."

"You're a hero to her, Lily," he said, glancing up. "Like it or not, she thinks of you as a friend. But you're right. She doesn't know what she's asking."

His words only made her feel worse, and Lily thought of how Hank had just sat there watching her, knowing she would have to betray his daughter, waiting for her to play the villain so he wouldn't have to. She couldn't keep the resentment from her tone. "Maybe

she wouldn't even have asked if Hank had told her
what this business was really like."

"He's just trying to protect her."

"Protect her, hell," Lily said. "He wants her to stay
innocent whether it's good for her or not. He likes having his own little angel, that's the only reason."

Texas stared at her, and there was something in his
eyes that made her look away, a sense Lily had that
she'd said too much, that he'd heard the anger she
couldn't keep from her voice.

"His little angel," he repeated thoughtfully, and then,
"I guess he got a devil, too."

Lily laughed shortly. She gave him a mock bow. "Say
hello to Lucifer herself." She said the words and felt the
heavy ache behind her eyes. Lily grabbed the bore
brush Texas had just abandoned and shoved it into the
chamber of her gun, scrubbing without delicacy or
grace, ramming it clumsily up and down. And when he
had been quiet for so long it was uncomfortable, she
hazarded a glance at his face.

He was watching her, and there was pity in his
expression. "I'm sorry, Lily," he whispered. "I wish . . .
things were different."

"Different how?" She wanted to sneer, but her voice
came out embarrassingly weak.

Too much. She'd shown far too much. The knowledge sank into her belly, an uncomfortable weight, a
humiliating heaviness. She forced herself to meet his
gaze, saw pity coloring his eyes deeper and harder.

She'd seen that pity before. A long time ago, when
he was just a boy and she was a new-made orphan and
he was standing in the bright sunlight of the open door
of a stagecoach. The memory was suddenly so damn
strong, stronger than it had been in all the years since.
Lily remembered her fear and shock, remembered how

she'd held her hands out to him. *"You killed her."* And his answer, as desperate as her statement. *"Not me."* No, not him. Teddy Lee had killed her mother, and her father, too. And now Teddy Lee was dead. Gone for the past ten years.

Lily swallowed. She put her gun and the brush on the table and pushed back her chair, and, when she would have got to her feet and walked away, Texas reached out and clasped her hand, keeping her in place.

"Don't go," he said in a soft, slow voice. "Lily, come on. Something's bothering you, I know it is. Why don't you tell me what it is for once? Talk to me."

Lily pulled her hand away. She made her tone tough and sharp. "About what? Saint Josie?"

"What did you expect? She's Pa's daughter."

"And I'm not."

"No, you're not," he said slowly. He hesitated as if he were searching for words, and then said, "The only other choice was to kill you, Lily. Is that what you wish we'd done?"

"There were other choices," she insisted. "You could have left me there to wait for another stage."

"You knew what we looked like."

"I would have forgotten if you told me to."

"Maybe."

"It was what you wanted to do then," she pointed out. "You wanted to leave me. But Teddy Lee—"

His head snapped up. "Don't mention Teddy Lee to me."

"Why not?"

"Just don't."

Lily pressed on, unable to resist. "Because you killed him?"

His gaze lowered. He took a deep breath. "Lily—"

"You know, I've always wondered," she said, leaning

forward, taking refuge in his reluctance, feeling the sudden urge to punish him for his pity, to hurt him because he'd seen her vulnerability. "Why did you shoot him? I remember you said it was an argument, but I never knew why."

"It doesn't matter."

She raised a brow. "I guess it probably mattered to Teddy Lee."

"Lily—"

"Come on," she needled. "Just fill in the sentence. 'I killed Teddy Lee because . . .'"

He looked right at her, and his expression was so stark that Lily sat back in her chair. He was going to tell her, she knew, and also knew that she wouldn't like the answer, that it would tell her something she didn't want to know.

"Never mind," she said quickly. "I—"

"I shot him because he brought you home that day," he said without hesitation. "I shot him because he should have left you there to wait for the next stage."

The words were there, laid flat on the table, a bridge between them. Lily stared at him, stunned and speechless. She had believed that Texas never thought twice about what they'd done to her, but there it was, his regret, his guilt, trembling in the words.

He looked down at the table, at his now-folded hands. "I knew what Pa would do to you. I knew it and I didn't stop it." He paused. It seemed like a long time. And then he looked up again, into her eyes.

Lily trailed her finger over the grooves of her gun, following the lines, feeling the cold and lifeless metal warming beneath her touch. Something inside her seemed to give just a little, a crumbling, a painful tearing, and the question that had burned since she'd first met Josie rose in her throat, a question she suddenly realized she needed to ask.

She took a deep breath. "Yesterday," she began quietly. "Yesterday, when Josie said she was going to ask Hank to untie me, I thought she was crazy. I mean, I couldn't make him do something like that, so I figured there was no way she could. But when she was talking to him, I was watching his face, and I, well, I knew it was going to work. I knew he was going to untie me just because Josie asked him to do it and he didn't want to look bad in front of her."

Texas said nothing. He just sat there, watching her.

"Just tell me something, Texas," she said, and the pain from yesterday came back, the bitterness she'd felt whenever she looked at Josie and Hank together, only now she understood it. Now she could put words to it. "Tell me why. Why did Hank decide to make me an outlaw? What did he see in me? I was just a little girl. He had the choice, didn't he? He could have made me into Josie. Why—why did he make me *this* instead?"

She heard her own bitterness. It was heavy and pathetic, and she wanted to swallow it again when she saw how Texas leaned back in his chair as if he were trying to put distance between them.

"That's what you wonder about, Lily?" he asked. "What Pa saw in you? What I saw?"

"Yeah," she said simply. "That's what I wonder about."

He hesitated, and when he spoke there was a tension in his voice, a too-stiff sound that echoed in that hollow space inside her, that made her feel awkward and sick to her stomach. "There was nothing, Lily," he said. "It was just—just Pa's way. It was like you said. You were just a little girl. Just a normal little girl."

But his voice said something different, and his eyes did, too. He was lying, Lily knew. What she didn't know was why.

He stared at her and saw her eyes shutter when he finished speaking. He saw the way she looked quickly down at her gun and busied herself with rubbing the oil rag over it, buffing the metal, scrubbing until it shone.

He thought of all the games they'd played over the years. Robbing stages and banks, and now trains, had been a game. Killing had been a game, too. *"I can pick off that stage driver from forty feet." "I can do it from thirty."* He and Lily and the others, they'd all done it. It was easier to think of men as game pieces. Easier than seeing how red the blood was when it spilled, how unforgivable death was. Those weren't real men dying. They were just obstacles in one giant chess game. Pawn takes king. Checkmate.

So many games. So many unforgivable things.

But the most unforgivable thing was what they'd done to Lily.

She had been a game piece back then, too. She was just a child, a little girl with a brave chin and a voice that seemed to cut straight to the heart. Her father had been a Union man, and it was war, so his death was justifiable. Her mother had been a fool, and so her death was all right, too. And, because of those things, Lily had seemed like a gift. A doll they could dress up and play with. A pet they could teach to do tricks. And the fact was that, in the beginning, none of them loved her. Even Texas had felt sorry for her more than anything. She was no one's daughter. She was not quite real.

What he'd said to her was the truth. They hadn't seen anything in her eyes, nothing that said to them: "Make her into an outlaw." She had been a normal little girl, and it had been a challenge to see what they could make her do. Once Pa made the decision to keep her, they had no choice but to make her family, to make her as guilty as they were.

It was only later that the game had turned really ugly, when she became the only thing linking Texas and his father. It was his fault and Texas knew it. If he hadn't fallen in love with her, none of the rest would have happened. But, as it was, he'd fallen in love and decided he wanted to make a life with her away from the gang. A real life. He dreamed of the two of them striding down the street together, her dress rustling and whispering against her ankles, the feathers in her hat bobbing as she smiled up at him. He'd thought they might have a ranch. Certainly children.

His biggest mistake was that he'd told his father his dreams. He'd been just sixteen. Lily had been thirteen.

And Pa had taken her as his whore just to show Texas he could do it.

Looking back on it now, Texas realized he should have left then. Should have taken her and ridden into the sunset and said to hell with his father. But he waited too long and, when he finally managed the courage, Lily had fallen in love with Pa the way every young girl does with her first good fuck, and Texas had been left pining for her so hard he couldn't ride away without her.

And, though her affair with Pa had only lasted a few months, his father had used Lily to control him every day since, and Texas knew it and let it happen. Just as he was letting it happen now.

He thought, *This is over, let her go,* and wished he could do it. Wished he could kiss her goodbye and watch her walk out of his life and know he could go on without her. But somewhere inside him something was holding him back. His father, maybe, or the past, or maybe it was just that he couldn't get the taste and the feel of her out of his mind, and he wasn't sure he could go on breathing if it wasn't the same air she breathed.

Those illusions again, he thought, but he knew it wasn't true. He no longer looked at her and saw the young innocent he'd befriended, the girl who sang hymns for every passing hour. Those illusions had been shattered for good outside Denison, and now there was nothing left of them, and he was glad.

No, it was something else. Something that had come to him when he saw her and Josie sitting around the fire, when he'd heard Jocelyn's too-fast voice and Lily's low and laconic reply. When he'd heard Lily's care for Josie yesterday. When he'd come around the corner and heard the sweetness in a hymn, a sweetness that seemed to come straight from a God he'd long ago abandoned.

There was something left in Lily yet, something he and his father hadn't got to, and he wanted to know what it was. What part of Lily hadn't they touched? He thought he'd known her inside and out, but she had surprised him since Denison, or since Lampasas, actually, and now he found himself wondering about a Lily he'd never seen.

She had never talked about what she wanted for herself, about her dreams. Was it because she had none? Or was it because they were buried deep inside her, hidden from everyone, poured into a cherry poke bonnet and left in an empty boardinghouse room in a faraway town?

He didn't know, and he wanted to find out. He wanted to reassure himself that there had been a reason for his illusions, something his instincts had found in her. He didn't want to believe he'd been completely a fool.

"Tell me something, Lily," he whispered.

She glanced up at him. Her expression was strained and wary. "What?"

"You have dreams, don't you?"

"Dreams?"

"Yeah. Dreams. Like everybody else."

"Sure. I have dreams. Once I dreamt I was riding that old paint mare of yours through a river filled with water moccasins."

He smiled and looked down at the wicked blue gleam of his gun. He spoke slowly, careful to keep any emotion from his voice. "You know, there was a time when I thought you and I could leave all this, maybe start a ranch."

"Start a ranch?" She laughed shortly. "What do you know about cattle, Texas? Except how to rustle them?"

"I don't know." He shrugged. "I was just a kid. I guess I thought, maybe, one good robbery, a couple hundred dollars, I could hire a foreman." He glanced away before she could answer, spoke before she could make some flip and hurtful response. "What about you, Lily?" he asked. "What happens when you leave here? Do you just keep going on? Do you plan on being an outlaw forever?"

"Don't you?"

He forced his gaze to her. He watched her put her gun back together, her clean and efficient movements, and the age-old vision came into his head again, the thought of Lily and him together running a ranch. It raised a sour taste in his mouth, a faint and unpleasant bitterness. "I suppose I'm afraid maybe I will be."

She jerked her gaze up to his, and the surprise he saw there would have been gratifying if he cared about surprising her. But just now he didn't. Just now, all he cared about was knowing what her dreams were, knowing if they included him.

"What do you think dreams are, Lily?" he asked. "Just things you want that you don't expect will ever happen? What about wanting something different someday? Something better? What about— What about Denison?"

She frowned. "What about Denison?"

"When I found you there you were all decked out in petticoats and corsets. You had hats."

"What was I supposed to do, walk around in trousers with a gun on my hip?" She glared at him defensively. "Nothing like advertising yourself to the law."

He leaned forward. "I think it was more than that," he said. "You told me you were going to make a try at being respectable."

She said nothing, but she didn't look away.

"Seems to me," he said, "that being respectable might be something you dream about."

He expected her to laugh that short, sarcastic laugh and tell him to go to hell. He expected her to lie to him.

But, instead, she was still for a long, long moment. Then she put her gun down and gave him a frank look. "Why is it so important for you to know, Texas?"

"It just is."

"Why?"

He said nothing, not knowing what to say. What could he say? That he wanted to believe in himself and her dreams would help him do that? That he'd invested too much of his life in hers and he couldn't bear to know he'd been wrong? He wasn't ready to tell her those things, and there was no other answer to give her.

Lily sighed. She looked at the table, ran her fingers over the barrel of her gun. "I thought once that maybe I could be . . . respectable. Maybe I could have the life I was supposed to have."

"The life you were supposed to have," he repeated slowly. "You mean before we—"

"Yeah. Before that."

"But you don't think that now?"

She looked up at him then, and he was struck by the sheer power of the yearning in her eyes, the wistfulness that seemed to emanate from every part of her. Her hand went to her throat, her fingers caressing that red and angry scar, an intimacy that made him flinch, that nagged at that guilt inside him. He was relieved when she let her hand fall and shrugged. "I don't know what I think anymore," she said.

Texas felt a rising hope, a pain too sharp to acknowledge. "But if you could have it, Lily," he said. "If someone came up to you and said you could have that life, would you take it?"

She met his gaze steadily. "You want to know the truth, Texas?"

He nodded.

She took a deep breath. "Then, yeah," she said. "If I thought . . . if someone told me I could ride away from here and start my life over again, if I thought no one would hunt me down . . . hell, I'd sell my soul. I'd do whatever I had to."

There was something in her words, something some part of his brain heard. "*I'd ride away from here,*" she'd said, and he knew without asking what that really meant, what she was really saying. "*I'd ride away from you.*"

She was quiet for a long time, long enough for her dream to rip through him, and then she gave him a hard and brittle smile. "Stupid dreams," she said. "Thank God we're so good at being outlaws."

"Yeah," he said. The admission rang hollowly in the little room. "Thank God."

18

Lily woke with a start. Hank's words of yesterday came rushing back. *"Cover Texas."* She jerked up to find that Texas was already awake, setting their saddlebags at the door. He turned at her movement.

"Let's get going," he said tersely.

Lily nodded and got to her feet. She dressed quickly, not bothering to wash her face or brush her hair before she tugged on her boots and drank her coffee. She shoved her hat on her head and grabbed her holster, then drained her cup of coffee. "All right," she said. "I'm ready."

The others were waiting outside, the horses gathered in the yard, whickering and snorting quietly. There was a chill in the air that came off the creek, and the early morning sun hadn't managed to warm it yet. Lily shivered as she threw her saddlebags over the roan and tied the rifle over her bedroll. She glanced to where Hank stood talking animatedly to Jocelyn and Old Sam. All three of them were mounted up. Sam looked thoughtful, but Josie was nodding her head and trying to look serious and quivering like a leaf on a windy day.

Lily looked at Texas in surprise. "She's coming?"

He nodded stiffly. "Schofield was over this morning. Pa changed his mind. It's too dangerous to leave her here."

Lily looked over at her. Josie fairly hummed with excitement. She was trouble waiting to happen, Lily thought, and her foreboding grew so strong she could taste it. She looked over at Texas and saw that he was watching his sister, too.

"We shouldn't take her," Lily said in a low voice.

He glanced at her. "We can't leave her behind."

"Maybe we should leave her in Belton," Lily suggested. "The McHaneys—"

"The McHaneys?" Texas snorted. "There isn't a woman within fifty yards safe with those boys."

"No, I guess not."

"She'll be fine," he said, but Lily saw that his jaw was tight, and his eyes strayed to Josie as if the sight of her could reassure him. "Pa wouldn't take her if he thought otherwise."

That was true enough. But the thought didn't comfort Lily. Hank might think of his daughter as a little angel, but there was some of the devil in her, too, enough so that Lily wished Josie a hundred miles from Chapel Hill.

"We'd better get the hell on the road," Schofield said. "We've got a lot of miles to cover today."

Bobby came from the creek, canteens swinging over his shoulders. "Schofield's right," he said, handing one to each of them. "Let's go."

It was a fast and silent ride out of Bell County. There were too many people who knew of them in these parts, and there were still men in Lampasas who hadn't given up on finding them again. Even Josie must have sensed the tension, because she was quiet, her eyes wide and wary. It wasn't until they stopped to water the horses at Little River that anyone spoke.

"I thought we'd stay at Yegua Creek tonight," Hank said. "We'll leave Josie and Old Sam there, pick them up again after the job."

Josie looked up from splashing her face. "Unless you change your mind and let me ride along," she said.

Hank frowned and walked away, leaving the rest of them gathered at the river's edge.

Old Sam shook his head. "You'd best keep quiet about that, Miss Josie," he said in a low voice. "We won't be robbing no train."

Josie looked over her shoulder at Lily. "I guess not," she said. "Since Lily talked Pa out of it."

Lily didn't miss the anger in Josie's voice, nor the disappointment. It hurt, but Lily kept care out of her voice. "He wasn't going to let you go, Josie," she said.

"She's right about that," Texas said.

Josie's eyes glittered. "Why, Christian, that's the first time I've heard you take her side about anything."

"It's no place for a lady, Josie."

"I can't tell you how tired I am of that word," Josie said bitterly. She glared at Lily. "I thought you were my friend."

Lily met her gaze evenly. "Did you?"

Josie got to her feet and walked stiffly past Lily to where Bobby was watering his horse. He looked about as uncomfortable as a man could be when she started chattering to him.

Lily glanced at Texas. "Well, I guess she hasn't forgiven me yet."

He shook his head. "Josie can hold a grudge better than most people."

"She takes after her pa, then."

"Let's go!" Hank called.

They rode away from the river and into the sparsely wooded countryside, and everyone was quiet. There was none of the usual anticipation that came before a robbery, none of the familiar nervous laughter or the silly talk about spending money. *"I think I'll get me a couple bottles of whiskey and a good steak dinner."* *"Throw in a whore and I'm with you."*

Lily sighed. It was just as well. She couldn't have enjoyed it anyway. There was too much at stake. This robbery meant everything. It meant freedom if she could prove herself to Hank, and that was what she meant to do no matter what.

Her tension only increased when they reached Lexington. It was a little one-street town. The few buildings rose out of the burnt grass like a mirage. But the dust was real, and so was the smell of cattle and horses. There was a general store and a saloon with rooms above to let and one or two withered whores dispensing their favors for pesos.

The sun was beginning to set, and they'd been riding fast and for a long, long time. Lily was hot and tired and sweaty. The others didn't look much better. Bobby's dark hair was nearly brown with dust, and Schofield had licked his lips until they were chapped and red. Old Sam was sagging in his saddle, and Josie . . . Josie looked as if she couldn't go another step. She hadn't said a word for miles, and her face was dry and windburned in spite of the sunbonnet shading her skin. Her shoulders hunched forward, and her hands clutched the saddle horn as if it were the only thing keeping her in her seat. Lily saw how badly Josie wanted to stay here, to rest.

Hank didn't seem to notice, or, if he did, he didn't care. "We'll go on to the Yegua," he said. He motioned to Texas. "Boy, you and Lily get yourselves down to that store and get some food. We'll meet you at the creek."

Texas nodded wearily. "All right."

He and Lily held back as the others rode off.

It was near suppertime, so there were few people out on the narrow street; a drunk reeling out of the saloon, a rough and weathered man on a wagon, another picking his teeth in front of a blacksmith's shop.

It was a quiet town, and, for the first time since they'd left Cowhouse Creek, the heaviness in Lily's chest lightened. Maybe it was just that Hank was gone, and Josie with him, and trouble felt far away for once. But Lily suddenly felt easier than she had in days.

The others had disappeared over the next rise when Texas turned to her. "Let's do it," he said. "I'm damned tired."

Lily nodded and followed him down the street. They hitched their horses to the rail in front of the general store and went inside.

It was a tiny place, too hot even in the cool of evening, and it smelled, like everything else in this town, of dust and sun and manure. Only here the manure was perfumed with the scents of sorghum and coffee and goat, and the little man who looked up when they came in smelled of sweat.

He squinted at them. "Hey, there."

"Hey yourself," Texas said. He pushed back the brim of his hat and leveled his piercing, blue-eyed stare at the man. "You got food in this place?"

The man eyed them for a moment and then shrugged and turned his back, dismissing them. "There's an old squaw selling goat down the street."

Lily shuddered. "No goat."

Texas looked at the clerk. "I guess we're not that interested in goat."

The clerk pried the lid off a barrel of crackers. "Sorry about that," he said, not sounding the least bit sorry.

"You got money to spend, I suggest you go on over to the saloon. They're used to dealing with cowboys."

Lily stared at him incredulously.

"Excuse me?" Texas said. Lily recognized the tone, the silky danger in it.

Apparently, the clerk didn't. "You heard me," he said without turning around.

"You telling me you won't sell to us?"

The man sighed heavily. He turned around, squinting. "You hard of hearing, mister?" he asked. He inclined his head toward Lily. "Boy, you explain to your friend here that we're a respectable store."

"Mister," Lily said slowly, "you'd best watch who you're talking to." She reached up and took off her hat, and the heavy braid she kept coiled there fell between her shoulders. "My husband isn't used to being treated rudely. No telling what he'll do."

The clerk's mouth dropped open.

Texas strolled to the counter. He leaned over it, smiling his sun-breaking smile, but there was danger in his face, a ruthlessness lighting his eyes. "No telling," he repeated softly. "Now, then, why don't you wrap up some beef and tortillas?"

The clerk snapped his mouth shut. He reddened and nodded toward Lily. "We don't serve your kind in here," he said stubbornly. "Not her kind either."

Texas lifted a brow. "Her kind?"

"She's no lady."

It surprised her that the same old words still hurt. Lily turned to walk out. Texas's voice stopped her before she took a single step.

"She's my wife," he said smoothly, "and you will treat her politely, or—"

"Listen, mister. We simply don't—"

Texas made a lightning-quick move, and suddenly

the Frontier Colt was leveled right between the clerk's eyes, the hammer pulled back. It surprised Lily almost as much as the clerk.

"Don't be stupid," Texas said, still smiling.

The clerk swallowed. "N-no, sir."

"Apologize to my wife."

The man shifted his gaze toward Lily. "F-forgive me, m-ma'am."

It was insincere, but, still, it felt good. Not because he was apologizing, but because Texas had demanded it. Because he was defending her honor and he was smiling that charming, dangerous smile, and it was so much like the old days, those days when they had ridden together and laughed together and all of life was a game.

He was watching her now. "Well, baby?" he asked. "Is that good enough for you, or should I shoot him?"

It wasn't an idle question. He would shoot the clerk if she asked him to, and she smiled at the knowledge and hesitated as if she were considering it.

"He wasn't very sincere," she said.

The man blanched. "P-please," he said. "Please. I-I'm sorry. Please, take anything. I'm happy to serve you."

Texas looked at her questioningly.

Lily smiled prettily. "Maybe if you were on your knees . . ."

Texas looked back at the man. "You heard the lady."

The clerk fell to his knees, disappearing behind the counter. Texas looked over it. "He's groveling pretty well," he said casually.

"Please, ma'am." The clerk's voice was high and muffled. "Please."

"Lower your head a little more," Texas instructed. "Yeah, that's it." He glanced back at Lily. "I think he's got it now."

"Oh, all right," she said, feeling strangely light-hearted. "He's forgiven."

The clerk appeared again, looking red and flustered. Texas eased off the hammer of his gun, but he didn't put it away. He gestured with it to a barrel behind a counter. "Now, then," he said easily. "If you could just wrap those things up."

The clerk nodded. His tight little face creased with worry, his hands trembled as he hastily grabbed a pile of tortillas and wrapped them clumsily in paper. "Beef," he repeated. "And tortillas. Anything else, sir? Or"—he threw a glance at Lily—"anything for you?"

Lily smiled at him. "Thank you kindly," she said in her best feminine voice, still wanting to punish him for his rudeness and his words, hating him for calling a spade a spade. "There's the matter of some bullets."

The clerk went white. He turned to the shelves behind him, his hands trembling. "G-got all kinds," he stammered. "You just tell me what you want."

Texas leaned on the counter, still wearing his smile. "Give me a box of .45s," he said.

Lily sauntered up to the counter. She pushed back the flap of her duster and checked her gun belt, lingering at the task, letting the gun and the bullets glint in the lamplight before she let the flap fall again. "You better get some for me."

The clerk ducked his head and pushed a box of shells across the counter along with the wrapped packages of tortillas and beef. His whole body seemed to be vibrating, and he couldn't look her straight in the eye. "Anything else?" he squeaked.

"That's it." Texas reached into the pocket of his duster, and the man visibly jumped. Texas's smile grew broader. "How much do I owe you?"

The clerk mumbled something.

Texas leaned forward. "I don't think I heard you right."

"Nothing," the clerk said.

Texas's grin widened. "But I insist."

"A d-dollar and—and t-two cents."

Texas pulled out his money pouch. He dug around in it until he had the money and slapped it onto the counter. The clerk cupped the money in his hand and squirreled it away in seconds. Lily smiled and turned to go.

"Oh, just one other thing," Texas said.

Lily looked back at him. He was leaning over on the counter, and the clerk was sweating again.

"Y-yes, sir?"

"How much is that horehound candy?"

The man grabbed a handful from a small box on the counter. He threw it down so hard the candy skittered across the wood. "Take it," he said in a low voice. "Just take it. It-it's a gift."

"A gift," Texas repeated. He gathered up the pieces with a slow, easy smile. "Well, thank you kindly. I'll be sure and tell all my friends what a nice place"—he looked around, frowning—"What's the name of this place?"

"Arneson's," the little man whispered.

"Arneson's." Texas tucked the candy into his pocket. "I'll be sure and tell them all to stop by if they're ever in Lexington."

"Thank you," the clerk said, though it was clear he'd rather be boiled alive than have any of their friends stop by.

Texas tipped his hat. "You have a good day, now," he said, and then he spun on his heel and took Lily's arm, his hold loose and gentle, his walk slow as he led her back to the door and outside into the darkening street.

"Let's get the hell out of here," Texas said, and Lily laughed as he released her arm and they raced to their horses. They rode out of Lexington so fast there was nothing but dust following them, and Lily felt alive and exhilarated, all her weariness gone. They rode fast and hard until they were only a few miles from the Yegua, and then they slowed to a walk. Texas rode up close and held out his hand.

"Candy?" he asked.

Lily laughed and took the horehound from his palm. "Nothing like laying low."

"You started it."

"I did not."

"Sure you did." He smiled and raised his voice in imitation of hers. "'My husband isn't used to such rudeness.'"

"I couldn't help it." Lily unwrapped the candy. "He was a mean little man."

"Well, he'll be the first one to point to us when they hear about the train," Texas said. "But by then I guess we'll be long gone."

"Yeah," Lily said. "I guess so." She put the candy in her mouth. It was darkly sweet, like sassafras and mint. Such a simple pleasure. It was funny how warm it made her feel, how alive. Or maybe it was the incident in the store that had done it, the way Texas had demanded an apology. The way he'd defended her.

She looked at Texas and smiled. "Thanks for the horehound," she said. "It's my favorite."

He gave her a small smile back. "I know."

And there it was again. A careful kindness, like washing the dust off her face and bringing her water. Like lying to his father. Only a piece of candy, but Lily felt a subtle, discomforting surprise that he could remember what her favorite candy was when she could not even have told him whether he preferred whiskey or tequila.

She was oddly moved. She looked away. "Well, thank you. For the candy, and for . . . standing up for me."

"You can thank me by covering me tomorrow," he said, and when Lily looked back at him, he was staring into the distance, a sharp, thoughtful expression on his face. "I'd like to be able to count on you."

She deserved his words, but, still, they hurt. Even more when she realized that, through his distrust, he'd still been kind.

He had plenty of reasons for distrusting her, she knew. And there was no reason for her to trust him either. But she owed him now, for lying to Hank about her if nothing else, and Lily thought of that, and not of why his distrust stung so damned much.

"Texas," she said slowly. "I owe you."

His face was stiff. He looked carefully at the darkening prairie. "So you've said."

"I know you don't believe me, but that means something to me. I'll cover you. I promise I will." Simple words, but they were so loaded Lily sagged beneath the weight of them. She licked her lips, and then she found herself riding close, leaning over to touch his arm. "Look, you've got no reason to believe me, so all I can say is that I-I'll do the best I can tomorrow. I mean that."

Maybe it was the touch that finally did it, she didn't know. But he twisted in the saddle to look at her, and he studied her as if he thought he could see clear into her brain, as if he could sniff out a lie. Lily kept her expression as open as she could and met his gaze. Finally, he gave a short nod and turned away.

"That's good," he said. "Because I've got a feeling about tomorrow."

"So do I," Lily said quietly.

That was all, but it brought the tension back again, and their camaraderie faded in the few miles to the creek. By the time they made it to the camp where the others waited, the chill was between them again, the strain from that morning, the careful avoidance.

But, later, after they'd eaten the dried beef wrapped in tortillas and played a few hours of poker, after everyone had crawled into their bedrolls and the fire had died to glowing embers, Lily lay back and watched Texas hesitate before he put his blankets next to hers. And, though she turned her back to him when he crawled in beside her and they didn't touch, when she woke again in the dead of night, it was to find herself spooned into his body, with his arms holding her tight and his lips against her hair. She felt the rise and fall of his chest and the moist heat of his breath against her temple, smelled the faint scent of horehound candy, and she closed her eyes and fell back into a deep, dreamless sleep.

19

She woke the next morning to the sound of nervous laughter. Lily cracked her eyes open. Texas was pulling on his boots, laughing at some joke Schofield had just made, and the three of them, Texas and Bobby and Schofield, were joking and talking like long-lost brothers.

Finally. The anticipation that should have been there yesterday was here now. The challenge of a robbery, the risk, shivered in the air. In spite of her foreboding, Lily felt it, too. She couldn't resist a smile as she pushed back the covers.

"'Morning, boys," she said. "Sleep well?"

"Like a baby," Bobby said smiling.

Schofield threw her a rolled tortilla. "Better grab some breakfast while you can," he said. "Before Hank marches us all out of here."

"Where is he?"

Schofield shrugged. "Walking around somewhere. Taking a piss."

Lily choked down the tortilla. She was just pulling on her boots when Hank came walking back.

"There's an old cabin over there," Hank said, pulling a pocket watch from his vest. "Josie and Sam can wait it out there. It looks abandoned."

"It seems an awful waste of time to me," Josie said quietly. "I mean, you'll just have to come back for us, and—"

Hank's sharp look cut her off. Jocelyn swallowed and looked down at her feet, then glanced at Lily. The accusation in her eyes sent guilt through Lily's growing excitement, and Lily felt the foreboding again.

She looked away, hardening her heart and everything else against Josie's hurt. There wasn't time for it now. Distraction was the worst possible thing on a job like this, and she couldn't afford to be feeling bad about Josie or anyone else.

Including Texas. Lily looked over at him. He was checking his gun, but his eyes were distant, his motions purely automatic. There was something disturbing about him, but she couldn't put her finger on what it was. He hadn't spoken to her since she'd awakened, which she guessed wouldn't have been so odd if not for yesterday. And last night.

The image came to her again, the feel of his arms and the soft, steady rhythm of his breathing. Lily tamped it down ruthlessly. She would wonder about it later, after this job, after she was fixing to ride out. No distractions.

She was still telling herself that as she buckled her gun belt around her waist, patted her derringer into place beneath her vest and grabbed her saddlebags. The horses were stomping impatiently in the edgy chill of the autumn morning, whickering softly. Hank motioned Josie and Old Sam over and handed Sam a spare rifle.

"If nothing goes wrong, we'll be back this way sometime in the next few days. Sooner if we can. We may have to ride around a bit to lead any lawmen off." Hank reached into his saddlebags and drew out what was left of the tortillas and beef.

"Stick to the water, Pa," Josie offered helpfully, suspiciously so. "I hear the dogs can't find your scent there."

Hank gave her a fond look. "We'll do what we can," he said. "You stay here with Old Sam, darlin', you hear me? I don't want to have to be worrying about you."

"Well, I wouldn't want that." Josie flashed him a smile, and Lily was struck with an apprehension so strong it took her breath away.

"This is dangerous, Josie," she said in a low voice.

Jocelyn flashed her a smoldering, angry look that only thickened Lily's dread. "I told Pa that he doesn't have to worry about me. That goes double for you."

Texas looked over his shoulder. Josie's words seemed to have broken through whatever he was thinking, because he frowned. "Pay attention to Sam, Josie."

Jocelyn exhaled a harsh breath. "Thank you for your concern, Christian, but it's not necessary." She turned to Hank and kissed him lightly on the cheek. "Good luck, Pa. Give those Yankees hell."

"All right, then." Hank nodded and Lily saw the hesitation on his face and knew he was feeling the same thing she was, that vague notion that something wasn't quite right. But he only smiled at Jocelyn and gave a curt nod to Old Sam. Then he dug his heels into the flanks of his mare and they were off, riding south for Chapel Hill and the train.

Every now and then, they passed farms that dotted the prairie landscape, looking rustic and serene beneath groves of pecan and bois d'arc. Lily didn't do more than glance at them as they rode by. Looking at those farms only raised that yearning again in her chest, and she couldn't afford it. Maybe she would look tomorrow, when they were riding back to Lampasas, their saddle-bags filled with gold or silver or whatever the hell it was the express car on the Houston and Texas Central carried.

Right now, she felt plucked taut. The excitement was gone, replaced by tense anticipation. Her mouth was dry, and there was a shivering between her shoulder blades that made her clench her hands on the reins and focus on the reassuring weight of her gun against her hip.

It grew quieter as they neared Chapel Hill, and anticipation sharpened. When the station house appeared in the distance, Lily slowed her horse and checked her gun, clicking open the cylinder and shutting it again, then sliding it loosely into her holster. She grabbed her rifle from the back of the saddle and cocked it open to make sure it was loaded. The others were doing the same. Then, with quick nods and hasty looks, they rode in.

The station house sat in the middle of nowhere, a lone building beside the track, with a platform out front for passengers to step onto. Just now it was still. They rode to the back. The door was there, just as Hank had said. Lily pulled the bandanna from her throat loose, tying it over her nose and mouth while the others did the same. She and Texas and Bobby went to the back door. It was hard to breathe through the heavy, stale bandanna. Hank and Schofield crept around to the front.

Texas's hand was on his gun. He half turned, and she and Bobby gave him a nod. He opened the door and stepped inside. They were right behind him.

The stationmaster didn't even look up. He was leaning in his chair reading a newspaper, his back to them, his feet propped up on his desk.

"I just got a message there's some loose track about ten miles down," he called out. "Why don't you head on out there now and we'll have some lunch when you get—"

Texas cocked his gun and pressed it against the man's temple. "I got a better idea. Why don't you hand me that gun you're wearing?"

The newspaper dropped. On cue, Lily and Bobby cocked their weapons.

"My God," the man whispered. "Sweet God."

"I don't think your prayers will help you now," Texas said. "The gun."

The man reached for his gun with a trembling hand. He was shaking so bad when he handed it to Texas, Lily thought he was going to pass out. Texas shoved the gun in his belt.

"Now, real slow, take your feet down."

The front door opened. Hank and Schofield stepped inside, guns drawn. Hank smiled. "Well, well," he said. "The train on time this morning?"

The stationmaster looked up at Texas. "Please," he said. "Please don't kill me. I've got a wife. A baby girl—"

"Shut up." Texas shoved his gun harder against the man's temple.

Hank's grin broadened. "The train?"

"It-it's on time," the stationmaster said.

"Good." Hank jerked his head at Bobby, who crossed the floor and went out the front door to put out the signal light. Hank stepped closer, caressing the trigger of his gun as if he couldn't wait to pull it. "We'll wait out of sight." He jerked his head at Lily. "Stay here and help until the train pulls up." He aimed his gun at the stationmaster, who seemed to melt beneath his gaze. "Now then, about you . . ."

"Please," the man whispered. "Please—"

Hank pulled the trigger. At the last second, he jerked his hand to the right, and the bullet whizzed past, drilling into the wall next to the ticket desk. The stationmaster swooned. A large, dark stain wet his lap. Hank laughed. He was still laughing when he and Schofield went out the front door.

"Dammit," Texas cursed. He slapped the man's face lightly until he started to stir and whimper again.

"Oh, my God." The man's voice was weak and pathetic, the voice of a man who knew he was about to die. "Our father, who art—"

"Shut the hell up," Texas said. "You want to come out of this alive you'll do what I say."

The man slanted a glance at Lily. "I'll do anything. Please, tell your friend not to hurt me. I'll do anything."

Lily steadied her gun. There was an invigorated tingling in her blood, the pure hot rush of energy. It was so familiar. So damned easy. She gave the stationmaster a one-sided smile. "I can't control him, mister. You'd best listen to him. He has a mean temper."

Texas leaned close. "Very mean," he agreed in a voice that was quiet and deadly through his smile. He caressed the man's temple with the mouth of his gun, slowly, until the man was shaking visibly and rivulets of sweat ran down his face. "Now, where's the telegraph?"

The man swallowed. He glanced toward the other desk. "Over there."

Texas looked over his shoulder. "Over where?"

"On the desk."

Slowly, Texas straightened, drawing back his gun. He threw a glance at Lily. "Cover him," he ordered tersely and took a step toward the telegraph.

The man eased toward a desk drawer.

Lily fired. The bullet slammed into the wall a few

inches from the man's head. He recoiled. Texas spun around.

"No funny business, mister," Lily warned. "The only reason you're alive is because I can't aim worth shit."

Texas lifted his brow at her and smiled. "That's what makes her so dangerous," he said, coming back to stand beside the stationmaster. He eased back the hammer on his revolver. "You never know whether she's going to shoot your head off, or your balls. Which would you rather have?"

"I'm sorry." The stationmaster was crying now. "I'm sorry."

"Look, mister." Texas squatted down and whispered into the man's ear. "You done playing the hero? Or do I let her have you?"

The man glanced back at Lily. She fingered the hammer of her gun, tightened her hold, and gave him her best cold smile.

"She's a woman," he whispered. "She's a woman, ain't she? My God, you're the Sharpe gang."

Texas laughed shortly and brought his gun up. He looked over at Lily. "What do you think, partner? Should I kill him or not?"

The two of them together worked like clockwork. She knew his moves as well as her own, knew every step in this familiar game. Lily shrugged as if she didn't care one way or another. "Let him live," she said. "For now."

"Whatever you say." Texas backed off, still holding the gun inches from the man's temple. "Get up. Slow and easy. That's the way. Now, you and I are going to walk over there, real slow, and you're going to dismantle that telegraph. You decide to play the hero again and I let my partner take another try at you. Got it?"

"All right." The man held his palms out and nodded with alacrity. "All right."

The Army Colt was starting to pull at her wrists, and Lily tightened her hands on it and kept it aimed at the stationmaster, not budging as he and Texas inched slowly over to the telegraph. She shot a glance out the window of the station; there was no sign of the others. They were at the side of the building, out of sight, as they'd promised. It was all going as planned. Smooth and easy. Her earlier foreboding was weak and faraway, and this moment was what was real, the heaviness of her gun and Texas's smile and the way they played this stationmaster. It was just like it had always been.

From down the line, she heard the sound of a train whistle.

"Here it comes," she whispered.

Texas ignored her. He was watching as the stationmaster bent over the telegraph. The man's hands were shaking as he lifted something off and set it aside. Texas grabbed it up and shoved it into the pocket of his duster. "Sit down," he said.

The man collapsed into the chair.

The train whistle sounded again. Closer now.

Texas jerked his head at Lily. "Get out there," he said. "The conductor's yours. Get out there."

"But you—"

"I'm fine. Go on."

Lily nodded. She ran across the small room, out the door. The signal light was shining red, and down the track she could see the train, belching smoke and steam. Quickly, she jumped off the platform and went around the side of the building, where the others waited, kneeling in the hard dirt beside Bobby, her heart pounding.

"You ready?" he asked.

She nodded and tried to answer him, but her words were lost in the sudden, roaring clang of the train, the long, steady squeal of brakes. The sound of it made her heart race; it pounded in her ears in a sudden roar of exhilaration. They were going to succeed, dammit. It was going to be the most famous job the Sharpe gang ever pulled.

The train stopped. Hank and Schofield rushed past her, jumping onto the platform, approaching the train. She heard Hank's voice.

"Send the fireman down!" he called. "And the engineer!"

Lily peeked around the corner. Hank and Schofield were standing there waving their guns. Bobby scuttled out from beside her and ran to the express car.

"Go to hell!" The fireman threw a chunk of coal out the window. It thunked just to the left of Hank's foot and rolled.

Schofield fired into the cab, and he and Hank rushed the engine. She heard shouting and another gunshot, and then the engineer and the fireman were being ushered out and there was steam coming from the windows.

Just then, she saw the conductor stepping down, a puzzled frown on his face. "What's going on here?"

Lily stepped away from the building and onto the platform, leveling her gun at him, stopping him in his tracks. "Why, mister conductor," she said sweetly, "this is a holdup."

His jaw dropped open and he raised his hands in the air.

"The car's free!" Bobby called from the coupling.

Lily smiled. She gestured with the gun. "This way," she said, motioning toward the station house. "We've got a nice comfortable chair just waiting for you."

The conductor frowned. "There's nothing but freight on this—"

She cocked the Colt and aimed for his heart. "Shut the hell up," she said. "And move."

He did. He marched across the platform just as Schofield and Hank brought the fireman and the engineer to the station house. Texas met them at the door. She saw the stationmaster inside, sitting in a chair beyond at the telegraph desk, his hands bound behind him.

Just then, she heard gunfire in the distance. Lily jerked around, her hand on the hammer ready to shoot. The conductor broke away and ran for the engine. She fired at him and missed, and a gun went off beside her—Hank's gun. The bullet caught the conductor in the back. He fell facedown on the platform. The engineer sagged against the wall, cowering behind the fireman. Texas came running, his gun drawn.

"What the hell's going on?" he yelled.

"Holy shit," Schofield said. "What the hell is she doing here?"

It took Lily a moment to see the *she* they were talking about. When she did, her mouth fell open in disbelief. The gunfire was coming from a lone horseman who was approaching quickly, waving a gun and shooting it off in the air like a heroine in a dime novel, her dark auburn hair trailing behind.

Josie.

"Jesus Christ," Texas spat. He jerked around to Lily, his eyes blazing. "Did you know about this?"

"No." She shook her head.

"Come on!" Bobby yelled from the train. "Let's get going!"

Hank's face stiffened. He spun on his heel, jabbing his gun in the fireman's stomach. "Get the hell inside," he said. "Now."

The fireman nodded and turned into the doorway.

He no sooner had his back turned when Hank fired. With an aborted scream, the fireman slumped to the ground, blood spreading over the torn, blackened hole in his shirt. Beside him, the engineer fell to his knees.

"Please," he begged, clasping his hands together in prayer. "Please—"

"Pa!" Josie yelled, pulling up at the edge of the platform.

Hank scowled and pulled the trigger. The engineer fell back, mouth working, a hole between his eyes.

Texas stepped back. "Christ, Pa," he said in disgust. "You—"

"Pa!" Josie was off her horse and running across the platform, her voice high and hysterical. "You shot them! I can't believe—"

Hank whipped around. He grabbed Josie's arm and yanked her against his side so hard her head snapped back. Then he pushed her toward the door of the station house. "Get the hell in there," he ordered. "Now."

"But—"

"Get in there."

Josie didn't argue. She hurried through the door, two high points of color in her cheeks.

Hank turned back to Lily. "Get to the express car," he said. "Take Bobby if you have to."

Lily stared at him in surprise. "Me?"

Texas shot her a concerned look. He glanced quickly at his father. "But Pa, the stationmaster—"

"Get going," Hank said. He glared at her, his hand shaking with anger.

Lily nodded tightly. She couldn't breathe, could barely swallow, but she went across that platform and met Bobby at the edge of the stairs to the express car. By now, there were people leaning out the windows of the passenger car calling to each other. *"What's hap-*

pening?" "A robbery, I think." "Oh, my. Good Lord."
Somewhere, a woman screamed.

Lily licked her lips. They should just ride the hell away from here. Cut their losses and get the hell away. She looked up at Bobby. His face was white beneath his dark hair, and what she could see of his eyes between his hat and the bandanna were wide with worry.

"Is he crazy?" he whispered.

"Crazy enough," Lily said. She nodded at him, and Bobby pounded on the express car door.

"Open up!" he called. "We've got some freight!"

"I heard gunfire," came the uncertain response.

"Just a few prairie dogs on the track," Bobby said. "Target practice."

"Oh." The voice behind the closed door was hesitant. "I don't know—"

Bobby pounded again. "Open up!"

Lily heard the other train before she saw it. It was still a far pace down the track, but there wasn't supposed to be another. Not now. She shot a look at Bobby, and then she saw the others run from the station house, making for their horses.

"Lily!" Texas shouted from the door. "Bobby! Get the hell out of there!"

"Shit." Bobby jerked to face her. The other train was barreling closer. Close enough that she saw rifles protruding from the windows. Gunmen. The other train had been warned.

"Shit!" Bobby said again. He leaped down the stairs. "I thought Texas dismantled the telegraph."

"He did." Fear rose so sharp in Lily's throat she could barely speak. "Let's get the hell out of here."

The two of them ran across the platform just as the other engine squealed to a stop. She heard the ping of gunfire behind her. At the back of the house, Texas was waiting. Josie was on her horse, halfway across the yard after Hank and Schofield.

"What happened?" Lily yelled as she mounted.

Texas gave a quick shake of his head. "The telegraph," he got out, and then shut up as a volley of bullets creased the air above their heads.

Lily dug her heels into her horse and bent low over the saddle.

The stationmaster burst from the door, a rifle in his hand. The first bullet whizzed past her. Lily pulled her gun and shot back. Missed. She glanced over her shoulder, saw him look up, and aim past her. Past her to Josie.

"Josie!" she screamed.

Incredibly, Josie stopped. She stopped and turned around, a puzzled look on her face.

Lily kicked her horse into a run, moving right between the stationmaster and Josie. She turned in the saddle and aimed for him.

"Lily! No!" Josie yelled.

Lily fired. The stationmaster fell to his knees. She twisted back again, seeing the relief on Josie's face. Relief that turned to panic in one split second. "Lily!" she screamed.

Too late. Lily heard the crack of the rifle behind her at the same moment the force of the bullet slammed into her. The pain took her breath. She heard Texas's "No!", heard his answering shot, and that was all.

20

He heard Josie scream.

After that, everything happened at once. Texas saw the stationmaster fall to the ground. Lily jerked forward, and then she was still. *Shot. Oh Jesus, shot.* Texas's heart stopped, he couldn't breathe for the cold numbness in his chest.

"Goddammit, no! No!" He twisted in the saddle and rode hell-bent for her. He reached her horse just as Josie did.

"Oh, my Lord, my Lord." Josie was wailing, reaching for Lily. "It's my fault. It's my fault she's dead."

Lily slumped over her mare's neck, unnaturally still. Blood spread in a dark red stain over her shoulder. Desperately, Texas pushed Josie back. He hauled Lily roughly toward him. Her eyes fluttered and she moaned. Relief made him almost dizzy.

"She's not dead," he said quickly. He glanced over his shoulder and saw men swarming over the platform, rifles in hand. "Stay low, goddammit, Josie. Stay low and get the hell out of here."

"But—"

"Just ride!" He cracked her horse on the rump, and the animal took off so fast that Josie nearly fell from the saddle. Texas grabbed Lily and dumped her unceremoniously in front of him. Then he took her horse's reins and nudged his own to a gallop.

He heard the singing of a bullet close to his ear and leaned low over Lily's body, so close he felt the wetness of her blood spreading onto his shirt.

"It's okay, baby," he said, as much for himself as for her. He urged the paint to a faster pace. "It's okay."

Then he didn't think anymore; he just rode. He rode until the gunfire of the men behind him faded to nothing, until the wheeze of the train disappeared in the sound of his horse's thunder. The others were ahead, and he followed them blindly, not even sure when the shooting stopped or where they were until they crossed the Yegua and Pa led them into the grove of elm shielding the little cabin where they'd planned to meet Josie and Sam.

When they rode up, Old Sam came out to greet them, his dark face gray and pinched. He searched the group until he saw Josie, and then he closed his eyes, and his lips moved in what Texas supposed was a prayer.

Josie nearly fell off her horse. She stumbled over to Texas. "Is she all right?" Josie's face was wet with tears, streaked with dirt. "Please, tell me she's all right."

Before Texas could answer, Pa was dismounted and jerking on his daughter's arm. His face was red and mottled with rage.

"I told you to stay here," he said, shaking her so her hair fell into her face. "What the hell did you think you were doing?"

"P-Pa, I-I wanted to help."

Hank slapped her. Josie stumbled back, falling to her

knees, her shoulders shaking in harsh, silent sobs. Pa reached down to grab her again, but Old Sam was at his side suddenly, catching his arm, giving him a quick, silent look.

Texas climbed down, pulling Lily's limp body into his arms. The blood was dripping down her arm now, staining her fingers, and, though she was unconscious, she groaned when he slumped her over his shoulder. Her weight made his chest ache. He tried to take a step and his hip gave out beneath him.

"Christ." Schofield was at his side in an instant, taking Lily into his arms. "She still alive?"

Texas nodded. He gave the same assurance to Bobby when he came striding up, and then the three of them left Josie and Hank and Sam and took Lily into the cabin.

There was a bed built into the wall, but the stand had collapsed on one side, and the whole thing tilted into the floor. Leaves and dirt and spiders littered it, and the mattress had long since deteriorated into dust and bits of fabric. Bobby shrugged off his duster and laid it on the floor, and that's where Schofield put her. Texas knelt beside her, turning her so he could see the bullet wound. The movement sent fresh blood oozing, and he tore the bandanna from his face and sopped at it until he saw where she'd been hit. In her back, just to the left of her spine near the shoulder blade.

He glanced up at Bobby. "We need a doctor."

"Where the hell are we going to get that?" Schofield asked. "We don't know anyone down in these parts. How much do you want to bet there're lawmen waiting for us in Lexington? We can't take the chance."

Schofield was right. Texas clenched his jaw and eased Lily's arm from her duster, ripping her shirt until he saw the wound clearly, a gaping, bloody hole against her pale skin. She moaned a little. The sound made his throat so tight he could barely breathe.

Bobby got to his feet. "We can't stay here long either," he said, wiping his hands nervously on his thighs. "We've got to get her home."

"Either of you got any whiskey?" Texas asked.

Schofield drew a small flask from his pocket and shook it mournfully. "Not much."

Texas met his gaze. "Enough to get a bullet out?"

"Oh, man." Bobby shook his head and stepped back. "Oh, man, you ain't gonna try this yourself?"

"What other choice is there?" Texas grabbed Schofield's flask and unscrewed the top. Not much at all. Probably not enough to clean and certainly not enough to give her if she decided to come to in the midst of his digging around.

She moaned again, and Texas reached into his boot for his knife and hoped like hell she wouldn't wake up for the next fifteen minutes. He remembered the doctor in Lampasas, remembered the man's words as he bent over Texas with a sadistic gleam in his eyes and a shining scalpel. *"Got to get the bullets out, d'you hear me, man? There's infection to worry about."*

Texas took a deep breath. Carefully, he ran his knife under Lily's clothing, cutting her shirt cleanly away from her back, peeling back the leather of her vest to reveal her smooth skin. His hands were trembling and he licked his lips, wishing he could spare a sip of that whiskey to calm himself down. He couldn't, so he set his jaw and picked up the flask and poured it over the wound.

She jerked a little and mumbled. The whiskey mixed with the blood and ran pink over her shoulder, pooling in a dark stain on Bobby's duster beneath her. Texas held his knife out, and Schofield had a match ready.

Texas ran the blade over the tiny flame, blackening the edge. He heard Schofield's breathing, Bobby's nervous shuffling. Texas pushed back his hat and bent over her. He touched the knife to the wound, started to cut. Lily stiffened and then went lax. He nearly fainted himself when the blade sliced into her skin and the blood ran freely.

He wiped his forehead with the back of his arm. Schofield leaned in, sopping up blood with a bandanna, his tobacco-scented breath moist and hot on Texas's cheek.

"I hope to hell you know what you're doing," he murmured.

"So do I." Texas angled the blade, edging the point into the bullet wound, digging for the ball.

"Oh, Christ." Schofield's hands shook.

There was a sudden commotion at the door.

"How is she? Is she all right?"

It was Josie. She rushed in, kneeling on the floor beside him, her hair falling into her face, tears still wet on her skin. The bright slap mark on her cheek had faded to pink. She grabbed his arm and Texas stopped, holding steady. "Is she all right? Tell me she's not dead."

"Let go of me, Josie," he said evenly. "Sit down."

"He's trying to find the goddamn bullet," Schofield said. "She's all right, so far."

"Oh, thank God." Josie released him with a sigh and sat back on her heels.

Texas bent back to Lily. Sweat was wet on his forehead; he felt it sliding down his temples. He wiped his face against his shoulder and leaned closer. "Hold her down," he directed Josie. "I don't want her jerking around if she wakes up."

"Oh, God," Bobby said.

Texas went back to his work. It made his stomach turn, but he kept digging, wincing as the blade scraped against bone, as the blood poured out, wetting his fingers so they slipped on the hilt and he had to wipe them on his pants and wait for Schofield to sop up more so he could see. His hair was falling into his face, and when he licked his lips, he tasted the salt of nervous sweat. He poured more whiskey on the wound, but Lily was mercifully quiet. It was only her harsh and ragged breathing that told him she was alive.

It seemed to take forever, but he found it. Lodged against her shoulder blade, the bullet clicked against the knife blade. Texas reached in with his fingers until he drew out the ball. It was flattened and bloody. He flung it to the floor. "That's it," he said, putting the knife aside. He grabbed the bandanna from Schofield and pressed it against her wound, holding hard, trying to stanch the bleeding.

Josie sat back, taking a deep breath, and Schofield mopped his forehead with the back of his sleeve. "Jesus holy—"

"What the hell's going on here?"

Pa's voice made them all jump. Josie flushed and looked down at her hands. Schofield got ponderously to his feet. Texas didn't even look around. The sound of Pa's voice suddenly filled him with a heavy, bitter rage. He didn't trust himself to look at his father, so he kept his eyes focused on his hand, on the bloody bandanna he kept pressed against Lily's wound.

"L-Lily," Bobby got out.

"Is she dead?" Pa asked. There was a crudeness to his question, a lack of feeling that made Texas clench his jaw.

"No," Schofield said. "Texas just took the bullet out. It's a shoulder wou—"

"Then let's get the hell out of here. There'll be lawmen all over these parts before nightfall."

"We aren't going anywhere," Texas snapped.

There was silence. Texas felt his father's gaze burning the back of his head, heard Schofield's quick breath.

"Boy?" Pa asked. "I don't think I heard you right. I could have sworn you contradicted me. Now, then, that can't be so, can it? Not from my obedient son?"

"You heard me fine," Texas said. He pressed harder on Lily's wound.

"Did I now? Since when are you the leader of this merry band?"

Texas's jaw was stiff. "I'm not moving her. Not now."

"You'd put us all in danger, then?"

Texas looked over his shoulder at his father and faced the thunderous look in Pa's eyes with a harsh and uncaring anger of his own. "You can go if you want, or you can stay. But I'm not leaving her."

Pa's eyes narrowed. "You're that devoted to her? She's just a—"

"Don't say it, Pa," Texas warned. Slowly, he turned back to Lily. "Just don't."

"What happened to the telegraph, boy?"

The question came out of nowhere. It was like a knife in his back, a swift, malicious stab. Texas stared down at Lily's wound, at his hand, smeared and red with her blood, at the stained bandanna. He glanced at Schofield, who hastily averted his glance. *What happened to the telegraph?*

Texas squeezed his eyes shut. He heard again the train bearing down on them, saw the smirk on the stationmaster's face and the vibrating telegraph. In his mind, his hand curled around the sounder in his pocket.

Just the sounder. He had never dismantled the relay. He'd been too distracted. Too damn busy watching Lily go out to the platform and thinking about yesterday, Lily's smile and the candy swelling the side of her cheek and her promise to cover him. Too worried about her to think straight.

He had messed it up. He'd left the telegraph working and turned his back long enough for the stationmaster to get out a call for help. Because of him, there was no money, and Lily had got shot.

"Well?" Pa needled.

"I don't know what happened," Texas lied quietly. "I don't know."

"But if you had to guess," Pa urged.

"That's enough, Pa," Josie said, and the calm control in her voice surprised even Texas. She rose, her skirt brushing gently across her boots, and her face was set and uncompromising even through the redness of her eyes and the dirty tracks of tears staining her face. "The only thing that matters now is for Lily to get better. I'm staying here, too."

Pa frowned. "Don't defy me, daughter. You'll do whatever the hell I say."

"No, I won't," she said, lifting her chin. "Not until Lily's all right. It was my fault she got shot, and I won't have her death on my conscience, too."

She sounded stronger than Texas had ever heard her, but still he stiffened, waiting for Pa to unleash his temper, to slap her around again the way he had out in the clearing.

He didn't do either of those things. He stepped back and stroked his mustache thoughtfully before he spoke again.

"I don't give a damn how she is in the morning," Pa answered her. "We're leaving then."

Hank turned and walked out. Texas heard his low and muttered voice to Sam outside. Josie sank again to her knees beside Lily. Her hands were trembling; all that cold defiance had faded from her eyes. It was hard for him to remember how it had even looked.

Schofield sighed and got to his feet, wiping his bloodied hands on his trousers. He slapped Bobby on the shoulder. "I need a goddamn smoke."

They left the cabin. Texas heard them walking around on the other side of the wall. He closed his eyes, feeling the rise and fall of Lily's strained breathing beneath his hand, feeling the heat of the wound against his skin.

"It was my fault," Josie said again, and the words were all caught up in sobs. "It was all my fault."

He looked up at her. "No, it wasn't," he said slowly.

"But if I hadn't—"

"You were just one more thing," he said, and suddenly a memory came into his head, the memory of a woman sprawled on a carriage seat, her pale pink bodice stained with blood, her mouth open while her daughter cried beside her. "You were just one more thing."

"Maybe." Josie looked down at her hands, and then she glanced up again, her hazel eyes wide and questioning, filled with an intensity that demanded attention. "Why did it happen, Christian? Why did God let Pa just shoot those men? Why did He let Lily get shot?"

He could have answered her easily. Could have said the truth as he knew it, which was that God was paying them all back, that it didn't matter how far a man ran, his transgressions caught up with him. God kept score of evil. Of cruelty. There was no point in confession. And there was no savior in the world who could take those sins away. One day, Texas knew he would die by a bullet or a rope, and there was nothing he could do about it. Not even if he quit the gang and lived the rest of his life martyring himself for others. In the end, God made everyone pay.

But there were some things he didn't want to take from Josie. There were beliefs he wanted her to hold on to, because she was a woman and she would need them.

So all he said to her was, "I don't know, Josie."

"Pa's a . . . he's a bad man, isn't he?"

"He's an outlaw. We all are."

"But he's not like you."

"He's exactly like me," Texas said bitterly. He looked up at his sister and saw lingering hero-worship in her eyes, and it made him so angry he couldn't keep the rage from his words. "We're not your fucking heroes, Josie. We're just men. And we kill other men because we want their money. There's nothing good or just about it. There's nothing . . ." He trailed off when he saw the shock on her face, the stark sadness.

Texas jerked to his feet and stepped away from Lily. "Hell," he muttered, wanting to hit something, wishing something that simple would take away the anger and hopelessness in his soul. "Christ, Josie."

Josie gasped. Texas spun around. Lily was moving, her limbs twitching, her lips forming unspoken words. He was on his knees beside her in a moment, pushing past Jocelyn to lean close to Lily's mouth.

"It hurts," she whimpered, a sound so quiet he barely heard it.

He smiled at her and stroked her cheek, smoothing back tendrils of hair sticking to her sweaty skin. "I know, baby," he whispered back. "It hurts like hell."

"Sorry," she said. "So . . . sorry." And then she was gone again, limp and quiet, and Texas felt his heart go with her.

"She's going to be all right." It was Schofield, standing in the doorway, a cigarillo dangling from his lips.

"I hope so."

"She will," Schofield assured him. "We won't let her die, man. She's one of us."

Texas thought of the station house. Of the way she'd held that gun. Of the look on her face. And Schofield's words sank inside him, a curse that swung him back through his nightmares again, an accusation that brought the sadness so strong within him he could barely breathe.

He nodded slowly. "Yeah, she is," he said and wished he could believe she would get better. But he knew the truth. This could be his payback now, God's punishment for his sins. If it was, no amount of worrying would change it, not a single sleepless night of watching and bathing her and feeling her shake beneath his unsteady hands. She could die. She could die without ever opening her eyes again. He thought of the last time he'd seen Lily this way. Cold and lifeless, with the bright red of a bleeding rope burn around her neck.

Texas closed his eyes. He heard her breathing, short and labored. His own lungs ached with it. He took her hand in his. Her fingers were cold, and he squeezed them and tried to warm them with his palms. And he promised himself that, if Lily lived through this, he would let her go, the way he should have done long before. He would take her back to Denison if that's what she wanted. He would buy her respectable clothes and set her up as best as he could and then he would leave her to her dream.

He would give her the life he'd taken away.

"Please, God," he whispered, "let her live."

He prayed all through the night.

21

She heard the yelling, but she couldn't understand the words. At first it was a relief; the sounds eased the burning, unbearable pain, the shivering and the heat. They kept the swirling, strange images at bay. But then she stopped wanting to listen. Sleep was beckoning, and she wanted to give in to it, because it was too cold where she was, too hot, too painful.

The voices were louder.

"You got a death wish, boy? Lawmen are crawling all over Lexington!"

"Go without me, then."

"You think they give a damn that there's a sick woman here? They'll shoot you both where you stand, and then they'll hang you for good measure."

"I'm not leaving her."

"Me neither, Pa."

"Jocelyn, goddammit!"

Lily tried to fight them, but in the end sleep eased away, and she was left with just the pain and the yelling. She felt sick and hot. Her mouth was so dry that when she opened her eyes and tried to ask for water, no sound came out.

They wouldn't have heard her anyway. Hank stood at the door, his eyes hard and angry, and Jocelyn's hands were curled into fists at her sides. Texas was yelling something, and Bobby and Schofield were standing back, Bobby looking down at the floor and Schofield fingering his gun. It took her a minute to concentrate on what Texas was saying, a longer minute to realize he was talking about her.

"Hasn't she proven herself? What the hell else does she have to do?"

"She saved my life, Pa," Josie put in. "I would've been dead."

"Don't remind me," Hank said angrily. "You shouldn't have been out there to begin with."

"Would you leave me the same way, Pa?" Texas asked. "Or doesn't being a member of this gang mean shit?"

Lily was so thirsty. She struggled to sit up. Pain washed over her in such a dizzying wave she fell back again with a cry.

"Lily!" Josie was at her side in a second, kneeling beside her, the smell of roses on her skin so strong Lily wondered if she carried perfume in her saddlebags.

Lily heard the quick thud of boot steps and looked up, beyond Josie, into Texas's face. "Lily," he whispered.

Lily closed her eyes. "Water," she managed.

"Here." Bobby's voice. She heard the pass of a canteen, the slosh of water. It drew up her mouth so tight she had to work to open it when Texas held the canteen to her lips and tipped it. Water ran over her tongue, down her throat. It splashed on her chin and her shirt, and she gulped it greedily. When they took it away, she lay back again, jerking when her shoulder met the ground, crying out as the pain radiated through her.

"Oh, Lily," Josie whispered.

"This is idiocy." Hank's voice was coarse and faraway. "Let's ride."

The words played games in her mind. *"Let's ride, let's ride, let's ride to Beulah Land."* She closed her eyes and they wound around her dreams, coming out of Hank's mouth and then Texas's, and then a cave so deep and dark that there seemed to be no bottom to it, and she went inside and washed herself in a cool pool of water. Cool against her forehead and her arms and against that burning pain in her shoulder. She wanted it to go on forever, those easy hands on her skin, soft first and then just gentle, and that blessed coolness. But it was gone so quickly, and she was burning up again, and the words came to the tune of "Amazing Grace." *"Let's ride away . . ."*

"Lily." A soft, whispered voice. She thought it was part of the song at first, and then she felt the touch on her cheek and opened her eyes. It was dark. She couldn't see a face. She felt the breathing, heard the breathing, felt the brush of long hair on her face and knew without seeing it that it was blond. Texas.

His hand was on her forehead then, brushing her hair away, and she heard his sigh like music. She was on her side, and his hand moved over her shoulder, pressing lightly against her wound, checking the dressing. She gasped a little; the pain was excruciating even with his gentle touch. He withdrew instantly, leaned over her, and whispered, "Lily," again, and, in the darkness, in the quiet reverence of his voice, she felt treasured and safe, as fragile as the pretty porcelain dolls her mother had once kept adorning a bedside table. *"Don't touch those, Lily, dear. They're so very old."*

Texas's earlier words came back to her then. *"I'm not leaving her."* Lily squeezed her eyes shut.

"Hank's right," she whispered. "Let's go. Let's ride in the morning."

He pressed his finger gently against her lips. "I'm going to change the bandage now," he said. "That okay with you?"

She nodded. She felt him move away, and then she heard the sloshing of the canteen and the rip of fabric. It was so dark she couldn't even see his shadow, and she wondered briefly why he was doing this now, but then she felt his hands on her skin, felt the moist heat of his breath as he leaned closer and worked.

He was gentle, but still she couldn't help wincing at the pull of the bandage, and the tepid water burned. She jumped when he dabbed at the wound, and he whispered, "Shhh," and held her shoulder still and kept dabbing.

When he was finally done, she was sweating. He wiped the wet rag over her face and wrapped the bandage again. He put the canteen aside. She felt him back away, felt the start of his withdrawal, and suddenly the night seemed too big and dark, and the dreams began to breach the edges. Lily reached out and grabbed his hand.

It surprised him, she knew. He froze, but she wove her fingers through his and held on as tight as she could, even though the movement hurt.

"Don't go," she said hoarsely.

"All right," he said, settling back again. She heard his bewilderment, but she didn't explain. Her shoulder was throbbing again, and she didn't want to talk. She just wanted him beside her, because she was afraid she was going to die and the night seemed so empty without him. The warmth of his touch eased through her, a comforting beacon in the dark, a reassuring presence, and Lily closed her eyes again, no longer afraid. Because when he was beside her, she was safe again, she was alive. And she could find her way back through those swirling, bloody dreams, led by the anchor of his touch.

Lily was roused from sleep early. It wasn't even sunrise, but the night was lightening, those last few hours before dawn. She heard the harsh whispers, felt the urgency in the air. She was half awake when Texas picked her up, angling her body to keep from jostling her shoulder.

She was freezing, and shaking so hard with chills she couldn't keep a blanket on. The room seemed wavery and not quite real, and people kept popping in and out, Schofield and Josie and Bobby. When Texas—was it Texas?—took her outside, the trees grew strange before her very eyes. She didn't know how she got there, but suddenly she was sitting on a horse in front of Texas, and the throbbing in her shoulder seemed to vibrate through her whole body.

The moon was at a crescent, falling off the horizon, and the warm southwestern breeze only made her shake harder. She passed out only minutes into the ride, and, when she woke again, it was afternoon, and the pain had spread up her neck and into her head, and she was so damn hot—where was that breeze now?

It was almost as if the weather read her mind, because the breeze came just then, a puff of wind that brought with it the smell of burning hay. Lily raised her face into it, but then it turned cold suddenly, and she was shaking again and clenching her teeth and closing her eyes against the swirling world. She felt Texas's arms tighten around her, his hands clenched on the reins.

"Pa!" he called. "Feels like the wind's picking up."

Almost as he said it, there was another blast of

chilled air. Lily looked up and saw the grass blowing, stiff, burnt-off strands bobbling. In the distance, at the northern horizon, a thin line of clouds raced in a wind that was increasing moment by moment.

"It's a blue norther," Texas whispered, pushing her duster into her lap.

The wind came up hard then, and it was cold, like a blue norther always was. Lily struggled with her duster, but her shoulder hurt too bad to do much, and the wind blew so much dust into her face she was nearly blind. Texas grabbed the coat from her. The leather flapped unwieldy and stiff in the wind, but he cursed under his breath and wrapped it around her, fastening it at her throat so she was huddled in it like a caterpillar in a cocoon. The paint struggled against the wind, bowing its head and pushing into it.

"We've got to find a place!" Bobby yelled. His voice sounded faraway and strange, like in a dream. "See anything ahead?"

"Just a bunch of goddamned grass!" Schofield called back.

"Keep going," Hank directed. "We'll stop at the next farm."

Lily had never been so cold. It cut through her duster. Her hands turned red and then white and then blue. The wind and dust stung her face and her eyes, even when she bent low over the horse's neck and tipped her hat forward. The only part of her that was warm was her back, and that was just because Texas was there. His hold tightened and he leaned forward.

"Am I hurting you?" he shouted in her ear.

She shook her head. They had slowed, and the paint mare was straining. Clouds raced across the sky. They looked heavy and gray, full of rain, but the wind was pushing them so fast there wasn't time for it to fall.

Lily closed her eyes and dug her chin into her collar just as a furious blast hit. Texas bent forward over her, and this time it did hurt. It hurt so damn bad. But she clenched her teeth and bore it, because the wind was colder than anything she'd felt in a long time, and it was then she felt the first drops, the iciness of sleet, the sting of hail.

The paint jerked and shied a little. Texas cursed under his breath and held her steady, but she pranced and mouthed the bit. The mare hated hail, Lily remembered, and then cried out herself as it began pouring from the sky like someone had turned a barrel upside down. Texas angled his body over hers, protecting her shoulder, but still the hail was hard and angry. She heard yelling behind them—she thought it was Schofield—and Hank calling back. She heard Josie's voice, high and spinning away in the wind.

"There's a grove of trees!" Texas yelled in her ear. "I'm making for it!"

She didn't answer. She felt him strain to rein in the mare and start her in the right direction, felt his thighs tighten to urge the horse to a faster pace. The wind was too hard. It was slow going. They were halfway there when the hail eased up and it started to rain.

It didn't just rain. It poured. It soaked her duster within minutes. Rain fell off the brim of her hat like a waterfall, ran in gulleys onto her shoulders and down her face. It was so cold it seemed to seep through her skin. Lily stopped feeling her face. Her fingers had lost all sensation a while back. The pain in her shoulder was terrible, more so now because Texas was almost lying on top of her, trying to protect her with his body. His hair was soaking wet and dripping against her cheek, into her collar. But in spite of his protection, Lily was so racked with chills she couldn't even tell him he was hurting her.

The others were riding close as they approached the trees. They dodged into the grove, brushing past branches that cut the wind but sent huge splashing drops of water plopping onto them. The world tilted before Lily, a wave of sickness so intense she swooned. Texas's arms tightened on either side of her. "Hold on, Lily," he said. And then, in a low and whispered voice, he said, "Thank God. A cabin."

It was the last thing she heard for a long time.

When she woke again, she was sore and tired and she didn't know where she was. She was on a bed and she was warm; those were the only things she knew. A cabin; she thought she remembered Texas saying that. It was all she remembered.

She heard voices and turned her head. The boys were sitting around a table in the middle of the room, talking and smoking cigarillos while Hank puffed on his pipe. Josie bent over the fire, stirring a pot. Beyond her, spotting the untanned deerhide floor, were crockery bowls sitting in strategic places, collecting rainwater that dripped from holes in the roof. Lily felt a cold draft by her head and noticed the broad cracks in the logs that had been only partially covered with split boards. The cabin was open to the rafters, with a stone chimney at one end. The bed she was in was a big canopy that took up nearly a quarter of the room.

It was a poor excuse for a cabin, but it was homey enough for now. The lamplight and the fire cast a golden glow throughout the room. She smelled tobacco smoke and cornmeal, and the low and easy talk had Lily closing her eyes just to listen, glad for something besides her strange and disturbing dreams.

She felt someone beside her. Lily opened her eyes to

see Josie standing there, a cloth in her hands. She nearly dropped it when Lily looked at her.

"Oh, my," she said, and then a smile burst over her face. "Oh, Lily, you're awake."

Lily nodded. "Yeah," she said slowly, "I guess I am."

"Are you thirsty? Can I get you something?"

"Some water would be good."

Josie hurried away. She was back in seconds, holding a dripping cup. She knelt beside the bed and angled her arm under Lily, bringing her carefully up so she could drink. Lily's shoulder throbbed, but she ignored it and gulped the water. It was cool and sweet.

Lily drained the cup and closed her eyes. Josie eased her back to the bed.

"How are you feeling?"

"Tired," Lily answered. "Sore."

"You've been feverish for four days," Josie said. Then, when Lily opened her eyes in surprise, Josie nodded. "You were. Texas wouldn't leave you until this morning, when your fever broke."

Lily frowned. "Where is he?"

Josie jerked her head to the corner. "He's sleeping," she said. Lily followed her gaze. Texas was curled by the fire, as sound asleep as she had ever seen him, his blankets crumpled around his chest, leaving his booted feet bare.

"I made him lie down," Josie went on. "I've never seen a man so tired and worried." She looked down at her hands, and Lily saw how she clenched her skirt convulsively, saw the sudden sagging of her shoulders.

Lily frowned. "What is it, Josie?"

Jocelyn looked up. Her eyes looked red-rimmed in the dim light, her gaze hopelessly sad. "Oh, I shouldn't. You're still sick."

"Tell me."

Josie hesitated. Her hands tangled in her skirt. Then, in a soft, whispering voice, she said, "I'm sorry. I'm sorry you were wounded. It-it was my fault."

Lily didn't try to gild it. "Yeah, it was."

"I should have listened to Pa."

"That's true enough."

"I thought"—Josie choked back a sound—"I thought it would be so . . . romantic."

There was so much disillusionment in her voice. So much disappointment. It hurt Lily's heart. "It's not the grand adventure you wanted it to be."

"No." Josie met her gaze. Her voice broke. "I saw Pa shoot those men, Lily. They were just standing there. They weren't doing anything. And he just . . . he just shot them."

Lily looked down at her hand, at her dirty, broken nails, remembering the first time she'd seen Hank kill a man, trying to remember how she'd felt. It seemed far away now, too hazy to recall, and she wondered when it was she'd forgotten it. When had she stopped noticing how many men Hank had killed?

"And then you . . . It didn't—it didn't even seem to affect you. You just pulled the trigger, and that man died. He just . . . died."

Lily glanced up again. "He was aiming for you."

"I know, I know. I'm not saying you shouldn't have shot him. It's just that—" Josie's brow furrowed as if she were trying to find the right words. "Have you even thought about him since then? Have you thought— I mean, he might have had a family."

The stationmaster's words came back to Lily then. "*Please. Please don't hurt me. I have a wife. A baby girl.*" She thought of how easily she'd killed him, how she'd pulled that gun and shot without hesitation. She swallowed and blocked the vision from her mind. "I suppose he might have," she said quietly.

"He'll never see them again."

"What about your heaven, Josie?" Lily asked. "Won't he see them there?"

"It's not the same. His children will grow up without him. And his poor wife—"

"Maybe he was single."

"Then his parents," Josie said. "And those men Pa killed. What about their families? They didn't deserve to die."

"Maybe they did," Lily said softly. "You don't know. Maybe we all deserve it somehow."

Josie's gaze caught hers then, and it was so full of pity and sorrow that Lily felt flayed by it.

"What about you, Lily?" she asked softly. "Did you deserve it when they put that rope around your neck?"

Lily's throat went tight. She looked away. "I don't know. I suppose."

"I remember reading about it, you know," Josie said. "It was the Southern Overland Mail. You all robbed it, and you were captured." She laughed a little bitterly. "I thought it was an honorable thing. I thought you were all stealing from them because they were taking over the South and you hated them just like the rest of us. I thought"—Josie licked her lips—"I thought you were a saint. But it wasn't like that at all, was it?"

"No." Lily shook her head. "It wasn't like that." She closed her eyes, thinking back to that day, how there were a few clouds racing across the sky and the wind was hot and full of dust while they waited for the stage. She smelled the air again, smoke from some faraway fire, sage and dry earth. "We'd robbed it before, you know. We had an informant who marked the stages with chalk if they carried gold. All we had to do was wait. Bobby saw the marked stage at the last stage-house, so we waited, and when they were close enough, we just spread across the road. Easy." Lily snorted softly; the motion hurt her shoulder. "But they were ready for us. I guess they caught Frank marking the stage and he squealed like a trapped pig."

"They were inside the coach, then. Waiting for you," Josie said quietly.

"They came out guns blazing," Lily said. She squeezed her eyes tighter shut, fighting the memory, the dust and the smoke and the confusion. "There was so much . . . noise. It was like a whole damn army."

"They caught you."

"Shot my horse out from under me," Lily said. She opened her eyes and stared bleakly up at Josie. "I was in that jailhouse so fast I didn't even know what happened. They scheduled the trial for the judge's next visit, about two weeks later. I got a note from Texas smuggled into a Bible telling me they were going to break me out. All I had to do was bear that hellhole for three days." Lily sighed and turned her face to the wall, staring at the rough gray wood and seeing the gray adobe walls of the jail. "But we had a reputation already for escaping from jails, and we picked the wrong damn town, the wrong stage."

Army payroll. An army town. She remembered how she'd felt the anger in the air building every day, the men and women who gathered outside the jail, shouting and swearing at her. The mood had been so ugly she couldn't breathe for its heaviness. But mostly she remembered her terror when those people broke into the jail, lamps swinging in the darkness, their frenzied eyes glowing yellow in the light. She wondered if she would ever forget it.

"We should have known," she whispered, closing her eyes again. "Texas . . . should have known." She swallowed. The scar on her throat tightened until she felt the pure physicality of the rope again, the splintery hemp against her skin. "There was a lynch mob. They broke in the second night. I thought . . . I was dead."

"But you weren't," Josie said.

"No." Lily looked up at her. "They didn't know what they were doing. Texas and the others came riding up just as they kicked the horse from underneath me. I guess"—she took a deep breath—"I don't remember after that."

"So Christian saved you."

Lily shook her head and laughed bitterly. "Don't make this into one of your romances, Josie. There's only one reason I'm still alive, and it's because the rope was too long."

"But he tried," Josie insisted. "Doesn't that count for something?"

"Dead is dead," Lily said. "All the trying in the world can't change that."

"But you're not dead," Josie whispered. "You're alive, and he loves you, you know. I heard it in his voice. There's still a chance for you. For the two of you. You could change. You could do something . . . different."

"You don't know shit, Josie," Lily said. "It's not that easy."

Josie flinched. "That's what I don't understand," she said. "You're just going to keep on this way. You'll just keep killing. It won't ever end, will it?" She got to her feet and sighed. "I don't know how you can go on living with it. I don't know how any of you can."

She smoothed her skirt and went back to the fire.

22

Hank lit his pipe and waited. He was in the lean-to that passed for a barn, watching the horses chomp up the ears of dry corn in the crib, husks and all. It was cold and damp, and he cupped his hands around the bowl of his pipe for its meager warmth. But right now he needed the privacy of the barn, so he stood in the tiny space, heated by the horses, and listened for footsteps.

He heard them quickly, as he knew he would. Hank puffed on his pipe and looked toward the entrance, waiting for his son to come inside, feeling the old wound—anger and disappointment and resentment. It saddened him that he felt this way after so many years, that, after all this time, his son was not the man he wanted him to be. That he couldn't trust him.

Hank looked up to see Texas yank at the door and come inside, ducking through the doorway, his hat dripping rain and his duster dark and spattered from the short walk from the cabin. He glanced up, nodding shortly at Hank before he jerked on the sticking door to shut it again. Then he turned and leaned back against it, crossing his arms over his chest, his eyes as cold and icy as Hank knew his own were.

"Waiting for me, Pa?" he asked.

Hank said nothing.

"You've been watching me since we left Chapel Hill," Texas went on. "Why?"

"Don't you know?"

"I have a guess," Texas said evenly. "You're wondering about the telegraph."

Deliberately, Hank took a drag on his pipe. He blew the smoke out again so it formed a cloud between them, obscuring his son's face. "Well then, now that Lily's better, why don't you tell me what happened?"

Texas laughed shortly. "I'm not sure what happened."

"Take a stab at it."

Texas reached into his pocket. He took out something and held it between his fingers. The sounder for the telegraph. He flicked it away, his gaze following as it spun over the dirt and rattled to a stop in a dark, damp corner. "Just the sounder," he said bitterly. "I forgot to dismantle the relay. I turned my back on him for a minute when you were arguing with the engineer. He got out a call for help."

"I see." Hank studied his son's face, seeing the regret, the touch of shame. "That's where the other engine came from then."

"Probably they got the message down the line," Texas said.

"I imagine," Hank said dryly and thought that if it had been anyone but Texas's mistake, that person would be dead right now. Hank hadn't stayed alive this long by tolerating mistakes. His hand went to his gun. He fingered the hilt and looked at the boy—the man—standing before him. There was something about Texas's stance that reminded Hank of his first wife, of Texas's mother, Mary. The admission of failure. The acceptance of blame. It irritated the hell out of him. Hank wanted the fight; he wanted confrontation and anger. He wanted his son to say what he would have said to his own father: *"Go to hell, Pa. So we missed this one. We'll try again in a few weeks."*

But Texas wasn't that way. He was more like his mother, had always been. Charming and pretty and compassionate. The only thing Hank had given his son was his temper, but there was no evidence of that now.

Hank bit down on the stem of his pipe and eyed his son. "So tell me, boy, what the hell were you thinking to not dismantle the relay?"

Texas looked up at him. "I was . . . distracted."

"Distracted?"

"Yeah."

"About what?"

"Nothing." Texas shook his head. "Nothing."

But Hank knew what *nothing* was. *Nothing* was that lying whore sleeping only a few feet away. *Nothing* was the wife with a bullet hole in her back that Hank wished had been only a few inches to the right. When they'd arrived back at that ramshackle cabin and he'd seen her slumped over Texas's saddle like a sack of grain, Hank had thought she was dead, and he'd felt relief and joy so intense he couldn't control his anger or his bitterness when he heard Texas tell Josie that Lily was still alive.

Because of it, Hank had lashed out at his daughter, and he would regret that forever. He would regret the horror on Josie's face and the red mark that stained her cheek for hours after. He'd been angry at Jocelyn, yes, but he would have been able to keep it tamped if not for Lily. He would never, ever have hit her.

Lily was to blame for all of this—for Texas's distraction and Josie's attempt to play Robin Hood. It was her fault his family had fallen apart before his very eyes.

Hank looked at his son. "I want her dead," he said quietly. "I don't care how. Either you take care of it or I will."

Texas's startled gaze met his.

"She betrayed us in Lampasas," Hank continued, "and I think you know it. But I was willing to forgive you for lying to me, boy. I was willing to overlook it. But now . . ." Hank shook his head sadly. "This job didn't get us caught, but there'll be a time when you're thinking about her and we'll all pay for it. She's too damn dangerous."

"The train was my fault," Texas said evenly. "Lily had nothing to do with it."

"Like hell," Hank said. "You trying to tell me, boy, that she didn't cause you to miss that relay? Or that she didn't influence Jocelyn to come riding up like some dime-novel heroine?"

Texas's face tightened. "I'm telling you that Lily's trying damn hard—"

"I want her dead." Hank spat the words, tired of arguing. "Who does it? You? Or me?"

"I'm not touching her," Texas said, and Hank heard the danger in his son's voice, that smooth, threatening edge he'd taught him. "And if you hurt her, you'll have to kill me, too, because I'll come gunning after you with everything I have."

The words didn't startle Hank; in a way, he'd expected them. But the venom behind them did, as did the purpose he heard in them, the hard, steady threat that told him exactly how much his son cared for Lily.

It was more than he'd imagined. A hell of a lot more. Hank gripped the bowl of his pipe and studied his son. Texas was staring at him, and for a moment it was as if Hank were looking into a mirror. Those hard, cold blue eyes were his, and the stiff jaw, the tightness that chiseled every feature into a cold, ruthless mask. For an instant, Hank understood what his victims must have felt like before they died, what they must have seen in that last merciless moment before the trigger was pulled. He felt the ice rush through his veins, the desperate horror. But the feeling was gone quickly, leaving in its place a sickness in his gut, a dull pain. Because, in spite of everything, he loved his son. Too much, maybe. Enough so that he'd wanted Texas in the gang, had yearned for him to carry on the Sharpe heritage, to be just like his father. And now he had it. That heritage was staring him in the face, unfamiliar and sickening, and Hank didn't like it at all.

He puffed on his pipe. The fire was gone. He got nothing but a cool and bitter gulp of air. Hank drew it out of his mouth. He struck the bowl on the heel of his boot and shook out the ashes, striving for nonchalance, wondering what to say to the man who was, in this moment, both the son he'd always wanted and not his son at all.

The tension grew. The horses stamped and blew into the crib; that and the rain were the only sounds. When Hank straightened again, he saw that Texas hadn't moved. He was still watching, and his face was still tight and dangerous.

"What then," Hank said slowly, "should we do about her?"

Texas frowned. "You won't hurt her?"

"You just told me not to."

Texas's laugh was short and sarcastic. "Yeah? So what?"

"I won't hurt her," Hank said.

Texas paused only a moment, then said quietly, "Lily wants out. Let her go."

"She's too dangerous."

"She doesn't have anything to gain by turning us in. There's a bounty on her head, too."

"She can make a deal. She's done it before."

Texas shook his head. "She won't do it now."

"I can't take the chance."

"You have my word," Texas said harshly. "My word, Pa. I promise you she'll keep her mouth shut."

Hank looked at his son. *"You have my word,"* he'd said. Hank couldn't remember the last time Texas had said that to him, the last time he'd offered his honor. It moved Hank now. He studied his son and suddenly had no questions about Texas's loyalty.

Slowly, Hank stroked his mustache. "You trust her that much, boy?" he asked.

Texas didn't look away. "Yeah," he said softly. "I do."

The wind picked up. It whistled through the cracks in the lean-to, bringing rain with it. Texas's paint mare pranced a little and nickered, and Hank put his hand on her flank to calm her down and turned to his son with a nod.

"All right, then," he said slowly. "The minute she's well enough to ride, tell her to get the hell out of here. But if you're wrong—"

"I'm not," Texas said. And then, "Thank you, Pa." He turned to go. The lean-to door creaked and protested when he opened it and pushed it closed again, leaving Hank alone with the horses and the rain.

"Thank you, Pa." Hank snorted softly to himself. Something about Texas's words made Hank think of a week ago, when he'd told Josie to stay away from Lily. He thought of how he'd told her that Lily didn't care

about her, and Josie's response. *"Oh yes, she does. She just doesn't know it yet."*

He wondered what it was his children saw in her. And why he couldn't see it at all.

Josie came racing in as if demons were after her, breathless and white-faced, her hair tangled about her shoulders and flying into her face. Rain whooshed in behind her along with the freezing wind, and she pushed on the door to try to close it. It stuck, wedged open. Bobby stepped away from his card game with Schofield and Old Sam and lent his weight to it. The door slid slowly closed. Josie didn't even offer a thank-you, which was odd, Lily thought sleepily. Instead, Jocelyn hurried over to the bed. She sat on the edge; the shift of weight nudged at Lily's shoulder. She groaned.

Josie leaned over immediately, her face lined with concern. She smoothed the hair back from Lily's forehead. It was a soft, soothing touch. The touch of a mother. Lily closed her eyes. She was so damn tired, and her whole body ached, her shoulder burned. She wanted to sleep forever.

"Lily." Josie's voice was low and urgent, intruding into Lily's drowsiness. Lily turned her head away and tried to ignore it. But Jocelyn was insistent. "Lily," she said again.

Lily licked her lips. They were dry and hot. She peered at Josie through lowered lids. "Hmmmm?"

Josie's gaze shifted toward the others as if she was about to tell a secret. Her mouth tightened, and she looked back at Lily again. "I just went out to get some ribbons from my saddlebags," she said, her voice hushed, strangely stiff. "I thought you might like to tie up your hair."

Ribbons. Lily closed her eyes again. "Uh-huh."

"Pa and Christian were out there. I heard them in the barn. They were talking. About you."

Lily nodded wearily. "They probably stopped when they saw you."

"They didn't see me. I-I didn't go in. Oh, I know it was wrong, but I couldn't help myself. I just"—she leaned so close Lily felt her breath against her temple— "I just stood there and listened."

It was too much effort to open her eyes again. "Bad . . . girl."

"Oh, Lily." Josie's voice broke on a sob.

Lily did look then. She opened her eyes and glanced up at Jocelyn, whose face was drawn and sad. Josie looked old just then, like one of those women who had spent all their pretty years on the dried-up prairie, wasting away, bending into the wind. Lily had seen that kind of disappointment too many times not to recognize it now. And the fact that it was on Josie's face, well, it sent a sharp pang into Lily's heart.

"What is it, Josie?" she asked slowly. "What did you hear?"

"It was . . . Pa," Josie got out. She was wringing her hands in her skirt. "He said— Oh, I don't know if I can say it."

Lily frowned. She touched Josie's hand, stilling it. It was freezing cold. "Just tell me."

Jocelyn squeezed her eyes shut. She took a deep breath. "He was— He blamed Christian for the train. He said th-the telegraph wasn't taken apart."

Lily nodded. Her skin felt suddenly as cold as Josie's. "And?"

"And he blamed it on you." Josie said the words in a rush. She opened her eyes and clutched Lily's hand in her own, and her big hazel eyes were dark with sympathy and pain. "He said it was all your fault. Christian and . . . and me . . . and he . . . Oh, Lily, I can't believe he said it. I just can't believe it. My own pa."

"Said what?" Lily prompted gently, though her throat felt too tight to speak and she wanted to shake Jocelyn and shout out the words. "What did he say?"

The tears in Josie's eyes overflowed. They streamed down her cheeks, glittering in the lamplight. "He said . . . he said he wanted you dead."

Lily's gut clenched. The cold fear spread over her, numbing her hands and her arms until she could no longer feel the warmth of Josie's hands. The scar on her throat tightened until she felt strangled by the memory of splintery rope and sudden, jerking pain. She had tried so damn hard. She'd lied as well as she could lie. But the robbery had failed and Hank was blaming her, and there was nothing she could do about it. Nothing except . . .

Run.

Lily jerked her hands from Josie's. The wound on her shoulder tore. She felt the fresh, hot seep of blood, the too-tight burn. She ignored it and pushed at the covers.

Josie frowned. "What are you doing?"

"What does it look like? I'm getting the hell out of here."

"But—"

Lily pulled her feet loose from the blankets. The motion brought a wave of dizziness so strong she fell back. "Shit."

"You can't go anywhere," Josie protested. "Look at you, Lily. You're too weak."

Lily leaned her head back against the wall, waiting for the nausea to pass. She slanted her gaze toward the others, bent over their cards and talking loud and fast over each other. They weren't paying any attention to her and Josie, thank God. Lily's hands clenched on the covers. "Look," she said in a low voice, "you want me dead, Josie? Because that's what you're going to get if I hang around."

"No. No, you don't understand."

"What's to understand? Hank blames me for the robbery. He wants me dead. You just said it."

"I didn't tell you everything," Josie said. "You didn't hear it all."

"No?"

"No."

Lily stilled. "Why don't you tell me, then?"

"Christian—" Josie paused. She wiped at her tears. They smeared across her cheek, dirty and wet. "Christian said that Pa would have to kill him, too."

Lily stared at her in disbelief. For a moment, she wasn't sure she'd heard correctly. "He said what?"

"That if Pa wanted you dead, he would have to go through Christian first." Josie swallowed. She looked down at her hands. "And h-he made Pa promise to let you leave if you wanted to. H-he promised you would keep quiet about the gang."

Lily couldn't speak. Josie's words rang in her head, too loud, too unreal. Hank had wanted her killed, and Texas had stood up for her. Texas had put his own life, and his honor, on the line. For her. Again.

The thought brought the blood rushing hot and heavy into her head. In that moment, the things she'd blamed Texas for—her near-lynching, his tardiness—faded in importance, and she felt dirty and ugly, unworthy of Texas's honor or his compassion. Just as she felt unworthy when she looked—really looked—at Josie's face and saw the tears and the harsh, gray misery and understood how hard this must have been for Josie. How those words must have hurt coming from the father she idolized.

How did those two come from a man like Hank? How did such a selfish, pitiless man manage to raise children with so much honor? Lily swallowed and looked down at her hands, at the rope burns on her wrists. She was the kind of child Hank should have had. She was as selfish as he was, as ruthless. She had none of his blood, but she might as well have had, because it seemed as if that coldness ran through her veins. For the last ten minutes she had watched Josie cry and not done a thing about it. She had seen Texas's pain over and over again these last years, and she had only dug the knife deeper.

She thought about how easy all this was for her. How easily she'd raised her gun and shot that stationmaster, even knowing he had a wife and a child at home. How easily she'd threatened that poor clerk in Lexington, how she'd played with him until he was sweating and incoherent.

How easy it had been to aim her gun at Texas.

Lily closed her eyes and swallowed, and the bullet wound in her back felt big and wide and set her whole body to aching. Hank was right about one thing, anyway. She sure as hell deserved to die.

She laid her hand on Josie's. "Look," she said in a hoarse voice. "I'm sorry. Your pa, he's just—"

"I know what he is," Josie said bitterly. "He's a murderer. He robs banks. He takes money. You were telling me that all the time and I just wouldn't listen."

"He still loves you," Lily murmured. It was the one true thing about Hank. "That won't change."

Josie looked up at her. "Maybe I don't want him to love me. Maybe he doesn't deserve to."

"Maybe. But you've loved him all your life. You must've seen something there."

"If there was, I can't remember it." Josie squeezed

Lily's fingers hard. "I think it's best if I just . . . go on.
Maybe to San Antonio, like Pa planned. He was right,
you know. I don't understand this life. I don't . . . want
it. I don't know why any of you do." She paused and
looked straight into Lily's eyes, and her gaze was bright
and wistful. "You can't make me believe you still want
to live this way. I don't believe you don't wish for something different."

Lily laughed shortly, bitterly. She swept the room
with her gaze. "Now why the hell would I want to give
this up?"

"Oh." Josie's voice was small. "I see."

Lily sighed. "Josie. You're a lady."

Jocelyn's head jerked up. "You always say that like
you could never be one. How hard is it, really? So you
wear the right dresses and learn how to dance."

"I think it's a little more than that."

"Oh, Lily, you could do it. It would be so easy."

"You remember those women in the Flat, Josie?"

Jocelyn frowned. "What women?"

"The ones in the cribs. The ones leaning in door-
ways. The faro dealers."

"I remember the dealer, of course," Josie said. "But I
hardly recall seeing any other women at all."

Lily plucked at the blanket and measured her words
carefully. "You didn't see them because for you they're
not there," she said slowly. "They turn their eyes away
when they see you coming, and you look right through
them." She cut off Josie's protest with a wave of her
hand. "It's not right or wrong, Josie. It's just the way
things are. You learned it all without even knowing you
were learning it. You're respectable. And that means a
hell of a lot more than pretty clothes and learning how
to dance."

Josie looked away. The absence of her gaze was like

a brush of cold air on Lily's skin. "You think I would look right through you if I saw you coming?"

Lily shrugged. The motion made her wince. "Yeah. Probably."

"I don't think I would."

"It doesn't matter, Josie. You can't change what you are. Nobody can."

"It seems so unfair, doesn't it?" Josie asked quietly. "To think that you could never change. Is that really what you believe?"

"I don't know," Lily said. "I suppose."

"So there's nothing for it. I'll spend my life setting out silver for company and making sure the damask napkins are put just so, and you'll spend yours robbing trains, and that's just the way God meant for it to be."

Lily said nothing. She leaned back against the pillows again and closed her eyes and thought of Josie's words. Of damask napkins shot with gold thread and silver polished to such a sheen it glimmered in the dying sunlight. She thought of bending over a table and setting a napkin just so, of waiting for the sound of a wagon and the hearty hellos of couples who had nothing more threatening in mind than coffee and conversation.

And then she thought of the stationmaster quivering in his chair, his eyes red and filled with tears as she and Texas played their cat and mouse game.

"Yeah," she forced herself to say to Josie. "I guess maybe so."

"I don't want to believe that, Lily." Josie's voice was soft and low, but there was a seductive urgency to it. "There are so many other choices. I just don't think you've really thought about it. I mean, what about opening a store, or . . . or maybe starting a ranch?" Her color heightened and Josie smiled eagerly. "Why yes, that's it. We could start a ranch. You and me and Christian."

A ranch. Texas had said the same thing the other night. Lily remembered the wistfulness in his voice, the longing he'd tried to hide beneath blank words. "*Stupid dreams*," he'd said, and she had agreed.

Except there was something about the way Josie said it. Something that didn't seem stupid at all. Something that dangled before Lily, a shining lure, a *maybe*.

She looked away from Josie. "A ranch," she repeated.

"We could get away from this," Josie said. "Away from Pa. We could be on our own. Think about it, Lily. Think about it."

Lily closed her eyes. She didn't mean to think about it. She didn't want to. But there it was, forming before her eyes. A little house with a stone fireplace and chinaberry trees in the front yard. Cattle lowing in the night and, in the morning, the soothing lullabies of the cowboys singing the steers to sleep. Suddenly Texas's dream didn't seem so absurd after all.

She felt Josie move on the bed; Lily opened her eyes to see Josie leaning forward, her eyes bright. "We could have a house. A little one at first. And a place for the cowhands. And every Saturday night we could have a dance. Oh, picture it, Lily. You and me, why, we could bake applesauce cakes and Christian could open barrels of cider. We'd have bunting and paper streamers all around. You know, I hear that in Mexico they fill eggshells with bits of colored paper, and they try to break them over each other's heads. We could do that, don't you think? And after dancing we could sit under the stars and tell stories."

The dream faded away, smothered by the weight of Josie's embellishments, nothing but an impossibility after all. Lily closed her eyes again and sighed. "You're such a dreamer, Josie."

Jocelyn fell silent. Then, in a voice so soft Lily barely heard it, she said, "What's wrong with dreaming?"

She was gone then. Lily felt her weight ease from the bed, heard the soft swish of skirts. But Josie's words lingered, a soft, haunting whisper. *"What's wrong with dreaming?"*

Nothing was wrong with it. Nothing. Except that a long time ago, when she was twelve years old, dreams had been taken from her. They'd been shoved aside by the realities of surviving. Because when other young women were dreaming of white knights and true love and first kisses, Lily had already killed a man. She already had a lover. She was already too old.

And now she looked at Josie and understood how absurd the respectability she'd wanted had been. As fanciful as Josie's ideas about outlaw life. It was not real. It was more than wearing dresses and buying hats and putting on airs. Respectability wrapped itself around a person's very bones. The little things Josie understood, the gentle morality, were beyond Lily. They would always be beyond her, she knew that now.

How fragile hopes were. One touch, and they were broken, irreparable. Respectability fell out of reach, and Lily let it go, let it slide through her fingers and fade away, and felt the pure, hollow emptiness of nothing. There were no other hopes to take its place. She'd never thought beyond escaping. She'd never wanted anything else.

She shut her eyes tighter, against the sadness that flooded her. It was so fierce she was afraid she would cry. She clenched her fist, welcoming the pain the motion sent into her shoulder because it told her she was alive. The sling flexed against her chest, and she focused on it because it was something she could touch. Texas had fashioned it from his own bandages. He had unwrapped them from his chest and washed them and hung them to dry before the fire. They were still damp, but they were warmed by her body now, and they smelled of him.

She turned her face against it, breathing deeply, and suddenly she felt real again. The vision of him came into her head then, one she'd forgotten until now: the way he'd come riding up into the middle of that lynch mob shooting off his gun and shouting. And then of later, when he'd cradled her head in his lap and his tears had fallen on her lips, warm and salty, and she heard his whispered words like a breeze in the night. *"Lily, Lily, I love you. I love you. I'm sorry."*

She had never dreamed of white knights. She had never dreamed of true love or romance or first kisses under starlit skies. She had never thought to even want those things. But if she had . . .

If she had, she would have dreamed of Texas.

23

He put off telling her she could go. After he left Pa, Texas walked outside and stood in the harsh, freezing rain of the blue norther. He huddled against the wall of the cabin and let the rain slash him. He watched Pa leave the barn and go into the house, and still Texas stood there until he was soaked through and cold to the bone and the sky was darkening not with clouds, but with evening.

Lily would be happy, he knew. He tried to think about that, about her lit-up eyes and her smile. He tried to think about the dream he was giving her instead of the fact that his own dream was dying before him. He tried to think about his own victory; this was the only time he could remember talking his father out of anything. But, still, he felt hollow and empty, as if the light inside him had gone out. And, though he told himself that light had died the day she told him she had betrayed them in Lampasas, Texas knew it was a lie.

He didn't want to love her, but he did. He always had, illusions or no, and he had made a promise to himself and to God. If she lived, he would let her go. Well, she was alive. It was time to live up to his vow.

Texas bent his head. Water cascaded off his hat, puddling on the muddy ground. He shoved his hands into his pockets, rounded the corner of the house, and pushed open the sticking door. It gave, and he eased in and pushed it closed again.

The little cabin was warmer than outside, but that wasn't saying much. Someone had lit a fire, and, though it was burning away, most of the heat was being sucked out through the cracks in the walls. He smelled the remnants of dinner and the rich, warm scent of coffee. Old Sam was pouring it into the cups Schofield and Bobby and Pa held out while Josie turned her stockings out before the fire. Beyond them, Lily lay on the bed, staring listlessly at the wall, her long braid trailing over the blanket.

"Come on over, Texas," Bobby said. "We need a fourth."

"Get Old Sam," Texas said shortly. He shrugged out of his duster, shaking it so water droplets scattered on the deerhide floor. He hung it beside the door, letting the rain stream off it in small rivulets. Then he took off his hat and ran his hand through his hair.

"Coffee, Mister Christian?" Old Sam asked.

He shook his head. "Not right now," he said. He stood at the door for a moment, suddenly uncertain, but just then Lily turned her head and caught his gaze and he knew he couldn't hold off telling her any longer.

Texas swallowed and went over to her. He squatted beside the bed. She looked a little pale, but that could be a trick of the light. Her eyes were sharp as ever.

"You feeling all right?" he asked softly.

She nodded. "Yeah. Yeah, I'm fine."

"Good." He took a deep breath, suddenly feeling

nervous and ill-at-ease. "I, uh, I had a little talk with Pa."

She looked right at him then. "I know," she said slowly. "Josie told me."

"Josie?" He frowned. "What d'you mean?"

"She overheard the two of you," she said. She looked down at her hand, at the dirty gray sling he'd fashioned. Her voice lowered. "I know Hank wanted to kill me. You told him . . . no. Thank you."

"Christ." Texas winced. "She heard everything?"

"I guess so." Lily gave him a small smile. "You've got to watch out for her every minute."

"I can't believe she—"

"She's okay, Texas," Lily reassured him. "She— It's time she knew about Hank anyway."

He glanced at his sister. "She's stronger than I thought," he said.

"Yeah, she is," Lily said thoughtfully. "She's a handful. But I don't think you'll have to worry about her getting involved in any jobs from now on."

His gaze shot back to Lily. "That's what she said?"

"In so many words."

"What about her and Pa?"

"I guess she'll have to make her own peace with Hank," Lily said.

Texas sat back on his heels. "It won't be easy."

"Yeah, well, nothing ever is." Lily sighed. Her free hand clutched the bedcovers. He watched as she picked off a piece of lint, and then another, and, without thinking, he reached out and stilled her hand with his. She looked up at him in surprise.

"Pa agreed to let you go," he said softly. "If you feel like it, you can ride out of here tomorrow. Go back to Denison, or . . . or anyplace. You can have that life you always wanted."

She snorted softly. "The life I always wanted," she repeated. " You think so?"

"Why not?"

She looked at him and smiled. "No reason, I guess," she said. And then, "What about you, Texas? What about your ranch?"

His gut clenched. His heart felt sore. "I guess that'll have to wait for another life."

"You could still do it, you know. You could do it without me."

"Yeah," he said, though the words were meaningless, a platitude and nothing more. "I could."

"All it would take is rustling a few cattle. Hell, Schofield would probably help you. He likes that kind of thing."

"Well, maybe I'll ask him."

"You should," she said, nodding. "You should."

He didn't answer her. He let the quiet come between them, heard the boys in the background, their laughter and their talk.

"I'll raise you two bits," Bobby said.

"You're bluffing," Schofield said. "Show me those damn cards before I lay down another nickel."

"Now, boys . . . "

Texas looked down at the floor and smiled at the familiarity of it. This little cabin was cold and ill-made and about as bleak as anything he'd known, but it felt like home, or, at least, like the only kind of home he'd ever had. He wondered how it would feel when she was gone, and the thought made him so sad he didn't know how he could bear it.

"Texas," she whispered.

He looked up at her. She was smiling, and her eyes were warmer than he could remember seeing them in a long, long time.

"You look cold," she said.

"Yeah," he said.

She patted the bed. "Come on," she said. "Come here beside me."

For a moment, he wasn't sure he'd heard her right. But then, carefully, wincing, she scooted over and lifted the blankets for him. He saw her long, naked legs and the shirt that came down to her thighs and scrunched up into her lap, and a lump rose into his chest and then in his throat.

He shook his head. He could barely speak. "I'm wet," he managed.

"I know," she said. "Come on."

He wasn't strong enough to resist her, he knew that from the start. He rose and sat on the edge of the bed, and then he pried his boots off. It took what seemed like a long time. She didn't say anything; she just waited with the blankets open, and, when he had his shoes off, he twisted around and lay beside her, pushing his feet into the warmth of the blankets, feeling the heat on the mattress where she'd been. It was so warm, and he was so cold that he shivered when she covered him up, and then, with the ease of old habit, he let his arm fall back on the pillow and she eased into his side and laid her head on his chest. Like a wife. Like a lover.

"Thank you," she whispered into his jaw. "Thank you."

And then he knew. He understood why he was here in this bed beside her, and why she was curled into him as if she cared. It was her way of repaying his favor. His heart sank at the realization, and the dull and steady ache of disappointment filled his chest. And though he knew he should leave her, should walk away and refuse her, he was too weak to do it. He loved her too much;

enough to take whatever she was willing to give him.
For whatever reason.

He closed his eyes, and the pain welled up inside him
as he kissed her forehead, felt the fineness of her hair
against his lips. She relaxed against him, and he felt the
steady rise and fall of her breathing, the moist heat of
her breath.

They lay there that way for a long time, not speaking,
listening to the card game and the low murmur of
Josie's voice as she talked with Old Sam, listening to
the hiss of the fire and the brisk rush of the rain. When
the night grew darker around them, so the little lamp
barely held the shadows at bay, Texas stared into the
darkness and waited. She was awake beside him, still
except for her soft breathing and the gentle flex of her
fingers on his chest. One by one, the others went to
sleep, crawling into their damp bedrolls, their soft
snores chasing the night.

Then, slowly, he touched her. Her cheek at first,
then he traced her jaw and her lips, trailed his finger
down her throat. She breathed into his hand and
pressed closer, and Texas closed his eyes against the
heady joy of touching her again and wished he could
say the words he wanted to say. *"I love you, Lily. I want
you."* But he didn't speak. He reached down and lifted
her chin, and then he kissed her. Softly at first, a test.
She opened her mouth beneath his, and then he was
kissing her with the stored-up passion of years, sucking
her inside of him, committing the feel and taste of her
to memory, wanting a night to last him a lifetime.

He ran his hands down her sides, cupped her
curves, formed his palms to the lines of her body. He
gripped her shirt and pulled it up over her hips, her
waist, slid his fingers beneath it so he could touch her
breasts. He was exquisitely careful, but still he heard

the sharp intake of her breath, the flinching whoosh of pain.

He kissed his apology, and felt her fingers at his shirt. He helped her undo the buttons. Then she was touching him, and Texas closed his eyes against the sweetness of it, breathed in the dust and rain smell of her hair and skin, kissed her harder.

The bed rocked beneath them, the corn-husk mattress rustled and poked, but when Texas was finally inside her, he didn't care about that. He made love to her to the music of snoring and the wild crash of the rain, breathing in her breath and hearing the beat of her heart next to his. He wanted it to never end.

And it didn't. Not until the night did. Morning came too soon, and the interlude was over, leaving nothing but her taste and the feel of her still in his arms, her heart beating hard against his. The grayness of dawn crept into the cabin. It was still raining, still so damn cold, biting his nose and his face. He heard someone stirring on the floor below.

He looked into her face, and Lily kissed him. Then she leaned back and closed her eyes, pulling him close. "That ranch of yours," she whispered. "Josie said we should do it. The three of us." She smiled sleepily. "Silly, isn't it?"

He knew she was waiting for him to laugh back, to say, "It's the stupidest thing I ever heard," the way he'd done before. But he didn't laugh. He didn't say anything. He leaned his cheek against her hair and held her in his arms, and he felt her sag, felt the soft and even tenor of her breathing. And then he closed his eyes and let the dream carry him to a house in the middle of the prairie, where cowhands sang the herd to sleep, and where in the morning he would wake to find her in his arms.

24

When she woke again, she was alone in the bed. Texas was gone, and she didn't see him anywhere in the cabin. Hank was gone, too. Bobby and Schofield were talking in low, intense voices, and Old Sam just sat there taking everything in the way he always did. Josie was at the fire, stirring something—cornmeal mush probably—in a big pot. The whole cabin smelled like coffee and tobacco and rain.

Lily pushed herself up. Her shoulder was stiff, her whole body sore, as much from lovemaking as from the bullet. The bed was cold where he'd been, and she found herself wishing he were still there, not just because he warmed the bed, but because she wanted to see him.

It was an odd feeling; she couldn't remember having it before, and it was disconcerting. When he had come into the cabin yesterday, he had looked as lost as she felt, and she had made love to him because he'd asked his father for her freedom and she understood the sacrifice. She had wanted to thank him. But it was more than that. It was, well, Josie's talk and her own memories had shaken her, and she had looked at him and felt sad for everything that had gone wrong, everything they would never have. There had been a chance once, or maybe there had never been. She didn't know.

But it was too late now. Just as the life he'd promised her was too late. She'd wasted so much time wishing for escape, and now Texas had given it to her. He couldn't know that she didn't know what to do with the chance. He couldn't know how alone freedom suddenly felt, or how much she'd needed his reassuring arms and the soft comfort of his touch.

She looked over at Josie, standing by the fire, and felt alone again. The emptiness was back so strong she couldn't bear it.

"Josie," she said.

Josie turned and her eyes lit up in a way that made Lily feel warm. "You're awake!" she said, hurrying over. "How do you feel this morning?"

"Right as rain," Lily said wryly.

"You look better." Josie sat on the edge of the bed and leaned forward, pushing a hair back from Lily's face. Josie's hands were warm from the fire. Her touch was soft and tender.

Lily swallowed. "I feel good," she said. "Good enough to ride."

Josie sat back. Her eyes shuttered, her mouth tightened. "You're still planning to leave, then?"

As if she had a choice. As if there were anything else to do. All her dreams had come true. Lily nearly laughed at the irony of it. She nodded. "When the rain lets up, I guess."

"There's nothing I can say. . . . "

Lily looked at her. She saw the concern in Jocelyn's eyes, the caring, and it made her feel weak and a little giddy. She heard Josie's words again. "*We could start a ranch. . . . "* She heard herself saying them to Texas last night, heard his silent reply. A fairy tale, she told herself. Still, in her mind, chinaberry trees bent in the wind. Smoke threaded from a chimney.

"Josie," she said. "Tell me about that ranch again."

"The ranch?" Josie smiled and shook back her hair. "Well, it wouldn't be much at first. Just a few head probably, maybe a section of land. But then we could have a real house, you know, like the ones they have in Houston. Real boards, with a fine brick chimney and a front porch."

"A front porch?"

"Or maybe pillars. I haven't decided." Josie looked off into space as if she could see it before her eyes. "We'll have a rose garden at the back of the house, and every summer you and I will make rose water and sachets."

Lily smiled. "I've never made a sachet."

"I'll teach you how. It's easy," Josie said. "Christian will come in from the stock after a long day, and we'll all dress for dinner. We'll have company. Maybe even the governor. He and Christian will smoke cigars and drink whiskey after dinner, and you and I will embroider until they come into the parlor. We could hold musical entertainments like they did in the old days. I'll learn to play the piano, and you can learn the harp."

"The harp?" Lily laughed.

"Well, why not?" Josie said. "I think you'd look like an angel. You'd be the finest lady around these parts. People would say: 'Lily Sharpe, why she's the kind of woman you'd be proud to know.' And then, of course, there would be the children. . . . "

The kind of woman you'd be proud to know. Lily tried to picture it. She tried to picture herself surrounded by guests and fine things. She tried to imagine being the kind of woman someone might be proud to know.

But the dream was hazy and faraway, and it eluded her when she tried to capture it. She wasn't kind. She wasn't good. She had killed men without thinking twice about it. The only living she made was stolen from men who had earned it. *"Survive,"* Mama had said, and Lily had done that. But now she wondered if that was really what her mother had meant. If maybe Mama had expected something different, if maybe she'd believed Lily's principles would survive as well.

Lily looked down at her hands, at the one resting against her chest, supported by a sling, and the one gripping the bedside. She saw the healing rope burns circling them, the bright-red marks like the scar on her throat. She thought of how she had earned them. *The kind of woman you'd be proud to know.*

Josie's dream melted away. It was a fantasy, just like all of Lily's other fantasies. Damask napkins and silver and people who smiled and tipped their hats and were happy to see you when you came. Those things were so beyond her knowledge she felt herself folding beneath the weight of them, suffocating at the sheer impossibility. It was not her life. It would never be her life. She'd been a fool to ever think anything different.

"We'd have servants, of course," Josie was saying dreamily. "And there would be—"

"It's a pretty dream," Lily said abruptly. She sat up, wincing at the sharp pain in her shoulder. She pushed the covers aside and tried to get out of bed. Her shirt fell around her thighs.

"Wait," Josie said, grabbing her hand. "What are you doing?"

"Getting dressed." Lily grabbed her trousers and slid her feet into them, trying to pull them up one-handed.

She got them halfway past her knees and then tried in vain to shimmy them up over her hips. She couldn't use her bad arm; just this effort made sweat break out on her forehead.

"Damn," she cursed quietly. She sat back on the bed again and motioned toward the pants hanging limply around her knees. "If you could help me with this—"

"You should stay in bed," Josie said. "You aren't well."

"I'm well enough to ride," Lily said. "And the storm's let up. There's no reason to stay around here any longer."

Josie looked as if Lily had just slapped her. "You can't mean it," she said. "You can't mean to go today."

Ruthlessly, Lily fought the tightness in her chest. "Why not today?" she asked.

"Why, because . . . because . . ."

Lily looked back at her. "Josie," she said softly. "I can't stay. You know that."

"But there are other things to do. The ranch."

"The ranch is just a stupid dream." Lily was deliberately cruel. Even so, it hurt when she saw the way Josie flinched, when Josie turned away.

"I guess you're right," she said softly. "And you don't have stupid dreams, do you, Lily?"

Lily didn't answer. She sat there on the bed, her trousers sagging around her knees, and wished like hell that her arm was good enough to dress by herself and get the hell out. She took a deep breath and said, "I need to talk to Hank, Josie."

"Of course." Josie's voice was cold. She got briskly to her feet and helped Lily pull the trousers up, fastening them so they hung loosely on Lily's hips. "Your boots?"

"Please."

The boots were hard to get on. Lily'd had them for a long time, and they were weather-shrunk and formfitting. But Josie worked diligently until she'd tugged them on. They were both breathing hard when Josie finally pulled away and sat on the bed. She didn't look Lily in the eye a single time.

"Where's your pa?" Lily asked.

"Outside," Josie said mulishly. "He and Christian went hunting."

"Well." Lily got to her feet. "Guess I better go find him then."

Josie didn't say anything, but Lily felt her hard, sharp gaze as Lily grabbed her duster from the foot of the bed and wrapped it around her as best she could. Jocelyn didn't try to help, and she didn't follow when Lily made her way slowly to the door. She couldn't open it by herself, but Schofield helped her. Lily gave him a thankful smile and then stepped outside.

It was raining still, but it was easing up, and it wasn't as cold as it had been when they first rode to the cabin. The norther had blown on, and Lily knew the rain would end soon, too. There was blue sky just beyond the thin line of clouds. It would be a good day to ride. Lily tilted her head back, letting the raindrops pelt her face, washing away Josie's dreams and Texas's kisses and the warmth of his arms.

But the rain couldn't wash away the loneliness she felt when those things were gone. And it couldn't wash away the memories playing in her head, the darkness in Texas's eyes and the gentleness of his kiss. The way he'd cradled her so as not to hurt her arm. The way he loved her.

Lily sighed. *You're leaving,* she told herself. She was going, well, somewhere. Someplace where she could start her life over again. But the thought left a

lump in her gut, and her words felt empty and meaningless. She thought of Josie inside that cabin, of the
pity Lily had seen in Josie's eyes. *"I don't know how
you can go on living with it."* Well, people just kept
on living. You shot someone and you went on. You
took some man's life and you just forgot about it and
kept going. That was all you had. Some people could
take the life that God gave them and make something
of it. Lily wondered if she would ever be one of those
people.

Probably not. But she would try, she supposed. If
she could just figure out what she was meant to do.

She heard a branch crack and looked up to see Hank
and Texas coming through the woods toward her. Hank
held a dead partridge and Texas had a rabbit, and when
he glanced up and caught sight of her, he stopped in his
tracks.

"Lily," he murmured.

Not many people knew how to breathe that much
emotion into a word. Texas did. It made her think of
last night, of the things he'd said with his body, the *I
love you*'s she'd heard that he hadn't spoken. He
showed too much. He always had.

Despite herself, Lily smiled. "Hi there," she said.
"You look wet."

"Yeah. Well . . ." He broke off, smiling back at her.

Hank stepped forward. "Lily-loo," he said coldly.
"Feeling better, are you?"

"I want to talk to you."

Texas's smile died. "Go on inside, Lily," he said.
"Your shoulder—"

"You go on," she said, inclining her head. She softened her words with a quiet smile. "Let me talk to your
pa a minute."

He looked uncertain.

"Go on, boy," Hank said, handing him the bird. "Take these to Josie."

Texas's jaw stiffened. He looked like he was biting back words, but he nodded tersely, gave her an uncertain look, and left them. Lily waited until she heard the door of the cabin scrape open and close again and then looked straight at Hank through the falling rain.

"So, Lily-loo," he said with a cold smile. "I understand you're leaving us."

She nodded.

"Where're you off to?"

"I don't know."

Hank eyed her thoughtfully. "Texas says I can trust you to keep your mouth shut," he said. "Can I?"

"I've got no reason to say anything," she said.

"Not yet," he agreed. "But maybe they'll catch you one day, Lily-loo. Maybe they'll threaten you with a noose."

Lily swallowed, but she didn't take her eyes from Hank's face. "Maybe."

"What if they make you an offer?"

Lily heard his allusion. He wasn't talking about some future time, she knew. He was talking about Lampasas. She gave him a small smile. "I won't say shit."

Hank smiled back meanly. "Is that so, Lily-loo? Is that what happened in Lampasas? You didn't say shit?"

"It's old news, Hank."

"Maybe." He stroked his mustache. "But suppose you tell me about it anyway."

She met his gaze evenly. "Suppose I don't."

He laughed. "Christ, you never give an inch, do you?"

"I learned from the best." Lily kept her expression blank. "Texas says you're going to let me ride away from here. Is that true? Or are you going to hunt me down?"

"I don't know." He kept smiling "I haven't decided yet."

His words made her stomach clench. Lily worked to hold his gaze without flinching. "Well, Hank, I guess I see it this way. It's either me or you. You let me ride away from here, and I give you my word I'll keep my mouth shut. If you don't"—she shrugged—"I'll just have to kill you before you kill me."

"You threatening me, girl?"

"What do you think?"

Hank just looked at her. She knew this trick of his, how he let silence fill the space, how he used it to create fear. She stared at him and steeled herself against the quiet, listening to the rain and the shiver of the trees around them.

"I think," he said finally, in a too-quiet, too-soft voice, "that you don't love me anymore, Lily-loo."

That voice. They had only been lovers a few months, but in that time she'd heard that voice a hundred times. She'd heard it deep in the night and in the soft light of morning. She'd heard it in her daydreams and in her nightmares. When he used that voice, it all came back to her, the memories she'd tried hard to forget, the feel of his hands and his mouth, the way he'd bent her to his will with cold kisses and smooth, practiced sex.

She thought of all the times she'd lain beneath him and tried to draw him into her, wanting to see the look he only wore when he spoke of Annie, the warmth he saved just for his wife.

Lily felt a surge of such vicious hatred it was all she could do to keep from killing him where he stood. "Let me go, Hank," she said coldly. "If you let me ride away, I can put all this behind me. If you don't . . . if you don't I swear to God it will be my gun that sends you straight to hell."

His eyes changed. They grew small and mean and hard.

"It's not a threat," she said evenly. "It's a promise."

"A promise," he repeated, and then he laughed. It was long and rattling, and it seemed to gain strength in the rain, filling the air around her. "Sweet Christ," he said. "You've got a lot of nerve for such a little girl."

"I'm not a little girl," Lily reminded him. "I'm an outlaw, Hank. And I've got you to thank for that."

He sobered and stared at her, and, for the first time, Lily saw a flicker of uncertainty in Hank's icy blue eyes, just a flicker, soon gone, but there nonetheless.

"I'll make you a promise, too, Lily-loo," he said quietly. "Make no mistake, if it were up to me, I'd kill you straight out. But I promised my son that I'd let you go, and I'm a man of my word. But if I ever find out you've betrayed us, all bets are off. I'll make sure you see that rope you should have got six months ago, and I'll make it last a long, long time."

Lily's chest tightened. She nodded tersely. "You got a deal."

"Then get the hell out of here," he said, turning away. "I don't want to see your face again."

The rain had stopped, and Texas leaned against the wall of the cabin, watching Lily pack. She worked clumsily because of the sling, shoving what little she had into her saddlebags: a worn, gray shirt, the vest he'd slit to get to the bullet, a pair of long underwear. She didn't have much; none of them did. He wondered where she was going to go, what she would do when she got there. He wanted to ask her, but he knew she wouldn't tell him, just as he'd known their lovemaking was her way of saying thank you and goodbye.

There was a knot in his stomach that wouldn't go away, a sadness lodged so deeply against his heart he wondered if anything would ever reach it. She would still be here if he hadn't gone to his father. If he hadn't lobbied for her freedom. She would still be here, and she would still be his, or, at least, as much his as she ever was.

But he also knew it was time for Lily to leave.

He wanted to take comfort from the thought, but he couldn't. He kept thinking of her in some other town, wearing corsets and petticoats and bonnets. Smiling up at some other man. Making a life without him. It struck such a blow to his own dream that Texas wondered if he would ever be able to think of it again, and knew he wouldn't. The day Lily rode away, his own fleeting hopes would fall away from him, and he would truly be just the outlaw he had always been afraid he would become. He would live his life riding the prairies he loved, and one day he would look into a gun and his life would be over.

What were dreams anyway? Just things you thought about that you never expected to come true. Just that.

Josie came up beside him, so close her skirts brushed his legs, and he smelled the faint scents of rose water and firesmoke on her skin. Her eyes were wide and troubled, her mouth tightened into a frown.

"I can't believe she's really going," she said.

"Well, she is."

"You could stop her if you wanted, Christian," she said, looking up at him with pleading eyes. "Maybe . . . maybe we could go to San Antonio. We could get a house. We could be a family."

He smiled slightly and shook his head. "I don't think so, Josie."

"Why not?" Her voice rose. He heard the faint edge

of hysteria beneath it. "Maybe you could, well, I suppose you could be a cowboy. Or maybe a clerk in a store."

"A clerk?" he asked. "In a store?"

She flushed. "Well, you *could*, you know, if you wanted."

He didn't say anything.

Josie glanced down at the floor. "Don't let her go, Christian," she whispered. "Make her stay here, where we love her."

Where we love her. Texas swallowed. "She doesn't want to stay, Josie."

And that was it. Josie fell quiet beside him, and they watched Lily and listened to Schofield and Bobby arguing over coffee and smelled the round, rich scent of Pa's pipe tobacco.

Finally, Lily buckled her saddlebags and stepped away. She took a deep breath and looked over to them.

"Well," she said. "I'm ready."

Schofield and Bobby stopped talking. Bobby cleared his throat. He stepped over to her and put his hand on her good shoulder, looking like he would have hugged her if not for the sling keeping her arm pressed into her chest.

"Well, then," he said uncomfortably. "Good luck, Lily."

She gave him a smile. "You too, Bobby."

Schofield rubbed his lips and shifted from one foot to the other. "You gonna be all right?" he asked. "You need anything?"

"No," she said. "I'm okay."

He nodded and swallowed, his Adam's apple bobbing.

She looked over at Hank, who just sat there, watching, saying nothing, and then she turned to Texas and Josie.

Texas felt her gaze like a warm burst of sunlight. It seemed to rush through his blood, making his heart race and his whole body feel tight and unsettled. He stayed leaning against the wall while Josie ran over to Lily and gave her a big hug.

Josie stepped back, wiping her face. "Oh," she said. "I'm sorry. The sling—"

"It's all right," Lily said.

Josie smiled weakly. "Please, Lily," she said. "Please don't go."

Lily smiled back. "You'll be fine. You go on to San Antonio. Marry your rich man. I'm sure you'll be happy."

"If . . . if that happens, will you come to the wedding?"

Lily nodded. "Sure," she said. "Sure." But it was a lie, and they all knew it, even Josie, who made a little half laugh, half sob.

"You have a good life, Lily," she said. "Don't forget that I love you."

Lily looked startled for a moment, as surprised as she'd looked that day by the creek when Josie had got drunk and kissed her on the cheek. And when Josie stepped over now and kissed her again, Lily flushed. Texas tried to remember the last time he'd seen that and couldn't.

"Goodbye, Josie," Lily said. She stepped away, and her gaze rested on Texas. Her eyes were clear and warm, and he thought of how she'd felt in his arms, how her hair felt against his hands, and missed her already. It was a sharp pain inside him.

He stepped over, past her, and grabbed her saddlebags from the bed. "Come on," he said. "Sam's got your horse waiting outside."

She took her rifle and followed him without a word. Sam was standing at her mare's head and nodded at them. "'Bye now," he said and stepped away, back into the cabin.

Lily smiled. "He doesn't like me much."

Texas shrugged. "Annie—"

"Oh, I know," she said. "I know."

She stood awkwardly beside her horse. He threw her saddlebags over, grabbed the Winchester from her hand and tied it on over her bedroll. His fingers were stiff and clumsy as he fastened her things down. When he was finished, he turned to find her staring up at him, a strange look on her face, a look he couldn't read.

"What?" he asked. "What is it?"

She looked startled for a moment, and then she shook her head and smiled. "Nothing."

"Well." He took a deep, uncertain breath.

"Thanks, Texas," she said. "Thanks for everything."

Her eyes were sincere. He'd never seen them look quite that way. It took his breath from him, and into his head came that dream where she was looking up at him just this way, and he thought of that hat again, the one in his saddlebags, the cherry poke bonnet.

"Just a minute," he said. "Stay here."

He left her standing there and rushed into the cabin. His saddlebags were slumped on the floor, and he searched through them, fumbling past his clothes and his gunpouch until he found it. Still where he'd put it all that time ago, in the corner, stuffed with a shirt to keep its shape. He pulled it out and hurried outside again. She was waiting for him, a puzzled look on her face.

He held out the hat to her. It was slightly misshapen, and he plumped it a bit and gave it to her. "Here," he said. "You might need this."

"This—" she glanced up at him. "This is my hat."

"Yeah," he said.

"You've had it all this time? From Denison?"

He nodded. "I thought . . . maybe someday . . ." He stopped. "It doesn't matter."

She looked at the hat, and then she looked at him, and then she said, "Well." She hesitated for so long he thought something was wrong. The she tucked it under her arm and unbuckled her saddlebag. He took the hat from her and, when the bag was open, he put the bonnet inside and fastened it closed again. Lily stood back. When he was finished, he turned to her and held out his hand to help her onto the saddle. She stepped toward him, and he couldn't help himself, he dragged her against him, feeling her body against his, her heat and her bones.

"I'll miss you, baby," he said so softly he didn't think she heard, and that was all right. It was better if she didn't hear, because he'd poured his whole heart into the words, and she was leaving, and none of it mattered.

He let her go and helped her into the saddle. Once she was there, he stepped away. "You going to be all right?" he asked.

She smiled at him, but it was a strained smile. It didn't quite reach her eyes. "Yeah," she said thickly. "I'm going to be just fine."

"All right, then," he said. "All right."

"Goodbye, Texas," she said. Just goodbye, and nothing else.

Then Lily rode away.

25

"Another drink, señorita?"

The bartender's voice seemed to come from far away. Lily looked at the nearly empty glass in front of her. She took a final puff on her cigarillo and stubbed it out, and then pushed the glass toward him.

"Yeah, Manuel," she said. "Another."

He sloshed the liquid—*aguardiente*—into the glass. It was some of the worst she'd had, but it was liquor, and that was all that mattered. He pushed her glass back and went on down the dirty, dusty bar, catering to the few men who sat there. It was the middle of the afternoon, and the sun was shining in through the cracks in the door, but the streets seemed quiet today, and the tavern seemed emptier than usual, or at least emptier than it had been in the days she'd been here. But, then again, maybe she was just mixing it all up in her head. One day was like any other. Every bar in every little backwater town was just the same. She'd gotten so she couldn't tell them apart anymore.

Lily curled her hand around the glass and brought it

to her mouth, downing the *aguardiente* in one gulp, choking a little as it burned her throat and her tongue. She pushed the glass away and the bartender was there again with the bottle. She tossed a coin onto the rough, splintery plank, and he glanced up with a smile.

"Gracias, señorita," he said. *"Feliz Navidad."*

Feliz Navidad. Lily looked at him in surprise. "Is it Christmas already?"

"Sí." He gave her a puzzled look and motioned behind him, toward a battered wax nativity on a shelf. "Could you not see it?"

For the first time, Lily noticed the decoration. It hadn't been there yesterday, or the day before, but, then again, she wasn't sure she would have noticed it anyway. The nativity was old, the wax grayed from dust. Joseph had a broken arm and the three kings were faded and half-melted from the sun. But the baby Jesus looked brand-new, and Mary's smile was like all mothers' smiles.

A wave of sadness swept her, and Lily hardened her heart against it and glanced back at Manuel. "Yeah. Well, *Feliz Navidad.*" She motioned to the bottle in his hand. "Why don't you just leave that with me? It'll be my Christmas present to myself."

He sighed and set the bottle down. He leaned over the bar, breathing his onion-scented breath in her face. "It is a special day, eh? Not a day to spend in this stinking place. Why do you not go home, *señorita*? To your family."

"No family," Lily said shortly. She poured another drink and gave him her best stare until he sighed again and eased away down the bar. She picked up the bottle and raised it in salute. "Glory to the newborn king," she mocked. The blasphemy didn't feel as good as she wanted it to; when it was over, she only felt old and tired and alone.

Lily sighed. It was Christmas day. She tried to remember how she'd celebrated it last year and couldn't. Probably it had been no different from any other day. Maybe a game of cards and a jug of whiskey. Maybe she and Texas had made love.

It made her sad that she couldn't remember, but she supposed it was better that way. Better to forget that life and go on. After all, it was what she'd spent the last week trying to do. She'd ridden to this tiny little stinkhole town and lost herself in a moth-eaten hotel room and this gray and ugly saloon. She'd played cards and drunk enough *aguardiente* to kill every last bit of sentiment. She'd left her old life behind her for good. Finally, she was safe. Safe from hanging ropes and men who were too late to save her from them.

"He tried. Doesn't that count for something? You're alive, and he loves you."

Lily reached blindly for the *aguardiente*. If she drank it fast enough, she might be able to escape Christmas altogether, or at least be too drunk to care.

Lily gulped the liquor and closed her eyes against the burn. It was all behind her now. Damned if she would let some holiday she'd never celebrated change that. It was just another day.

But when the door to the saloon opened, bringing wind and dust with it, and a tall man huddled in a duster and a low-brimmed hat shoved his way inside, Lily's heart skipped a beat. Because, just for a moment, for a split second, she had thought it was him, following her the way he'd followed her to Denison. Coming to take her back.

"There's still a chance for you. For the two of you." The bottle slipped from her fingers, splashing on the counter. Lily pressed her fingers over her eyes. She was drunk and alone at Christmas, that was all it was.

Tomorrow she'd be fine. Tomorrow, she'd get back on her horse and ride out of Nuevo Laredo and go . . .

Where?

The single word jeered at her. Where? Some respectable town? She'd already been in those places; she knew what they were like. She knew the ladies who walked down the street, their ostrich feathers bobbing over their ears and their hat ribbons tied in crisp bows beneath their chins. They would look right through her, just like they always did, just as she'd told Josie they would. There wasn't a cherry poke bonnet in the world that could change that.

And she didn't even think she wanted it to. Not anymore. She remembered the way Texas had handed that hat to her when she'd left, how rough and dirty his fingers had looked against it, how tenderly he'd primped it before he put it in her hands. As if that bonnet was the key to everything she wanted. As if she could put it on and suddenly be the woman she'd thought she wanted to be. How long ago that seemed now. It felt as if she'd lived a hundred years since then.

No, respectability wasn't for her. There was nothing for her anymore. Nothing she wanted.

As if to make her a liar, she heard his voice whispering in her mind. *"I'll miss you, baby."*

Lily forced it away. Texas wasn't what she wanted either. Deliberately, she remembered the rope around her throat and the madness of the lynch mob. She remembered her fear and the way he hadn't been there. The memories came, just as she knew they would.

But they felt faded and unreal; their power was gone. And other memories beckoned with their bright shadows and clean colors. Memories shiny as new-minted gold: Texas teaching her how to shoot a gun, his arms around her as he steadied it in her hands. *"Breathe in, that's the way, baby. Hold it steady . . . Now, fire."* And his smile when she'd hit the target, that lightning-fast grin that made his whole face shine and his eyes look so impossibly blue. Texas sitting with her and the boys around a fire at night, laughing while she tried her first cigarillo. Texas holding her at the river's edge while she cried because she loved Hank and he didn't love her back. His soft, tender words while he stroked her hair. *"Ah, Lily, you shouldn't show so much. You shouldn't care so much."*

Lily stared at the bottle of *aguardiente* before her and remembered her boardinghouse room in Denison. How the river smell filled the air in the early morning and the dead of night. How she'd lain awake there and thought about Petry's men filling Texas with bullets.

She'd told herself then that she didn't care. She'd believed it. She had wanted them all dead. But she'd awakened sometimes in the middle of the night, shivering in the cool air and reaching for someone who wasn't there.

And now, suddenly, Lily understood why the respectability she craved hadn't come to her in Denison, why the dream felt oddly empty once she had achieved it. It wasn't because of the things Josie had said. It wasn't because of some deep-to-the-bone gentility. It wasn't because she had lost the ability to understand integrity or refinement. That dream of hers felt so empty because it wasn't respectability she craved.

It was safety.

She had not let herself forgive Texas for being late that night, and yet it couldn't have been any other way. He couldn't have known about the lynch mob. He couldn't have foreseen it. She thought of Josie's words again. *"He tried. Doesn't that count for something? You're alive."*

She was alive, and he had been there. In the end, he had been there, just as he had always been, and the safety she longed for was there, too, in his blue, blue eyes and those arms that always opened so readily to hold her.

She thought of how he could look at her and say everything in her name. *"Lily." "I love you, Lily."* No one had ever loved her like that. Texas had given her his whole heart and soul, even when he got nothing in return. He had protected her and loved her and kept her as safe as he could, as safe as she had ever been, even when she had not trusted him to do it. Even when she had not believed he would.

Lily heard Josie's words again in her mind. *"Lily Sharpe, why, she's a woman you'd be proud to know,"* and she thought about the things that made people proud. Things like trust and love and honesty. Things like the vulnerability she'd lost a long time ago. She wondered if she could ever get those things back again. If she would ever be able to look in Texas's face and say, "I love you," and mean it.

Josie thought she could. Josie saw something inside her that Lily had thought was long gone. And, suddenly, Lily knew that, if she didn't try now, if she didn't try this one time, those things *would* be gone forever. If she didn't make the attempt today, right now, Hank would win. Because she would be just like him. She would be the outlaw he made her. There was nothing else out there for her. Nothing but lonely towns and emptiness and strangers. Nothing but a hanging rope or a drawn gun. There would not be another chance for her.

A woman you'd be proud to know.

And, suddenly, another memory came to her. The memory of a Christmas spent on the prairies beneath the stars, the dark press of night and the feel of Texas in her arms, the hush of his whispered *"Merry Christmas, baby,"* and the touch of his hands.

Christmas last year. She had celebrated it after all.

Lily pushed her drink aside and got to her feet. From down the bar, the bartender looked up.

"You leaving, *señorita*?"

Lily nodded. "Yeah," she said. *"Adiós*, Manuel. I'm going home."

He knew nothing else, so he stayed. They were his family, his only blood, so he had no place else to go. Josie needed him, so he let her need him. But it felt as if his soul had left him. He'd known it would be that way when Lily rode away, and it was. He felt as if he just disappeared as he watched her riding into the thin line of gold at the horizon.

He supposed it didn't matter. He was twenty-eight years old, and he was a criminal. He was wanted in three states. One day, he would ride into the right town, and the right man would shoot him. All he was doing now was waiting.

Sometimes, he imagined that he just rode away. He thought about how it would be, how he would wander over the prairie and wonder where she was and think that one day he might run into her again. He might see her in some town, smiling up at some man and pushing back the feathers bobbing near her ear. He would stand back and watch her and think, *Good for you, Kittycat,* and then he would ride on without speaking to her. Without touching her.

It was funny how his hopes could spiral down to just that, to seeing her again, knowing she had what she wanted, knowing she was happy. How little he needed, after all.

"Christian." Josie came up beside him where he sat on the porch, his boot balanced on the rail, his chair angled back. Her arms were full of washing.

Texas pushed back his hat and squinted up at her. "Yeah?"

"Do you—? Maybe we could play some cards later?"

He looked back down at his feet. "Ask Bobby. He's around here someplace."

She dropped the basket with a thump and a sigh. "You can't keep doing this, you know," she said quietly, kneeling beside him. "She wouldn't want you to be this way."

"Wouldn't she?" he asked bitterly. "Seems to me she'd like this just fine."

"She wouldn't," Josie said fervently. "She would hate it."

"Josie—"

"It's not like she's gone forever, anyway," she said. "She'll come back."

Texas laughed shortly. "Oh yeah? You been visiting gypsy fortune-tellers again?"

"I know she will," Josie said stubbornly. "She wouldn't leave us this way."

Her confidence exhausted him. Texas closed his eyes. "Leave me alone, Josie," he said quietly.

She touched his arm. He was so cold, the heat of her touch nearly burned him. "Christian."

"I'll be fine," he said. He opened his eyes and looked into her gentle face. "Just give me some time, Josie," he whispered. "I just need a little time."

She nodded and squeezed his arm, and then got to her feet. "I'll go find Bobby, then," she said. "And we can—" She frowned and went still, looking past him. "Who's that?"

Almost at the same moment she asked, he saw the

rider. Coming through the trees, shielded by branches. His heart raced, his fingers tingled. He should have gone for his gun and yet he didn't, because he recognized her from the start. Something deep inside him knew her even when he couldn't see her face.

She broke through the trees and stopped at the edge of the clearing. Beside him, Josie gasped. "Lily!" she called out. "Lily, you've come back!"

Lily smiled and called back, "Hey there, Josie." Then her gaze slid toward Texas. He felt it lingering on his face like sunlight, so warm and bright he felt blinded by it.

He sat there not knowing what else to do until Josie said in a low voice, "She's come back for us, Christian, I know she has."

"Don't get your hopes up, Josie," he whispered, and the words were for himself as well. "She might disappoint you."

Josie shook her head. Her eyes were luminous. "She won't," she said.

But he wasn't so sure. He was afraid to hope; he'd been disappointed so many times before. But he steeled himself and left Josie standing there and went to Lily. Her eyes didn't leave his face, but when he got there she looked down at the reins in her hand.

"Hey, Texas," she said.

"Hey, Lily."

"You know, I was thinking," she said. "About that ranch you and Josie were talking about."

His heart beat so hard in his chest he could barely breathe. "Yeah?"

"And I thought"—she took a deep, uneven breath—"I thought maybe it wouldn't be so hard to rustle a few cattle."

"No," he said. "I guess it wouldn't."

"I hear that's how the Bar X got their whole herd."

"I heard the same."

She swallowed and tried to smile, and it was little and clumsy and so damned heart-wrenching he reached out his hand and helped her dismount. She didn't pull away. She went into his arms. He held her loosely, gingerly, careful of her wound.

"I'm tired of being afraid," she said.

"Lily—"

She held up her hand to quiet him. "I don't want to live this life. And I'm not sure I'm cut out to be a lady either. But there is one thing I do know." She looked up at him, and her eyes were more honest than he'd ever seen them, and there was something else there, too, something he didn't dare believe. "I don't want to leave you, Texas," she said. "I don't ever want to leave you."

He stared at her, holding his breath, afraid to hope. "You don't want to leave me," he said slowly. "Are you saying—"

"Just tell me you love me," she said. "And I'll do whatever it takes to love you back. We can try that ranch, if you want to. Or we can just ride from town to town. Whatever—whatever you want. Just don't leave me, and I swear I'll never leave you."

He closed his eyes, and it felt as if the world was opening up inside him, with all its possibilities, all the things he'd ever wanted and never had the courage to ask for. He thought of how it would be, him and Lily and Josie starting over.

Starting over.

Her voice was small and quiet. "I know . . . I know it's hard to forgive me—"

He opened his eyes to see her uncertainty, the vulnerability he hadn't seen for years, the vulnerability he'd taught her to hide. To see it again, God, it made him so damn glad.

"I love you, Lily," he said softly. "There's nothing to forgive."

She smiled a little, ironic smile. "Oh, yes, there is."

"No," he said, kissing her. "There isn't."

And that was all. But it was everything.

AUTHOR'S NOTE

After the Civil War, outlawry was prevalent in the South, a response both to losing the war and to the carpetbaggers who came from the northern states looking for ways to make money in a war-ravaged land. During the Reconstruction and into the 1870s, banks, railroads, and express companies (due to their northern owners and affiliations) were popularly regarded by southerners as enemies of the people, and the outlaws who robbed them, like the James-Younger gang in Kansas and New Mexico's Billy the Kid, were considered by many to be heroes.

In 1874, the James-Younger gang robbed a train in Kansas. Four years later, on February 22, 1878, Sam Bass and his followers held up a train north of Dallas, at Allen Station. This was the first train robbery in Texas.

Readers will note that the train robbery in *Fall from Grace* takes place two years earlier, in 1876. For the purposes of this story, I felt it necessary to take liberties with the timing. In all other respects, the taking of the Chapel Hill train is very much like the Allen Station robbery.

Let HarperMonogram
Sweep You Away

HEAVEN IN WEST TEXAS by Susan Kay Law
Golden Heart Award-winning Author

Joshua West is sent back from heaven to protect Abigail Grier, the Texas beauty who once refused his love. As the passion between them ignites, Joshua and Abigail get a second chance to find their own piece of paradise.

THE PERFECT BODY by Amanda Matetsky

Annie March has no idea how a dead body ended up in the trunk of her car, no less a perfect body! When someone tries to pin the murder on her, sexy police detective Eddie Lincoln may be Annie's ticket to justice—and romance.

"Smart and sassy...a charming combination of mystery, romance, and fun." —Faye Kellerman

CANDLE IN THE WINDOW by Christina Dodd
A HarperMonogram Classic

Lady Saura of Roget is summoned to the castle of a magnificent knight whose world has exploded into agonizing darkness. Saura becomes the light of Sir William of Miraval's life, until a deadly enemy threatens their newfound love.

Winner of the Golden Heart and RITA awards